"What see you, soothsayer?" boomed the voice from above.

"Two have come to Grixis, master," she replied, falling into a strange, vaguely disturbing cadence. "World-walkers, mana-drinkers. Vital still, they stand amid the rising dead."

"Two?" The cavern resounded with shifting scales from above. "Two . . . Tell me."

"Mind-breaker, thought-taker, eye-blinder, dream-raker. He walks the intentions of others as easily as he walks between worlds, but knows not his own.

"Death-bringer, corpse-talker, spirit-rider. She teeters on the edge of death, and fears to fall in after those she has sent before her. A blossoming of truth that rots around a seed of endless lies."

"Ah," came the voice from above. "Them."

MAGIC
The Gathering®

Ignite your spark.

Discover the planeswalkers in their travels across
the endless planes of the Multiverse…

THE PURIFYING FIRE
BY LAURA RESNICK
The young and impulsive Chandra Nalaar—planeswalker, pyromancer—
begins her crash course in the art of boom. When her volatile nature
draws the attention of megalomaniacal forces, she will have to learn to
control her power before they can control her.

CURSE OF THE CHAIN VEIL
BY JOHN VORNHOLT
(February 2010)
The mercurial necromancer Liliana Vess and psychic sorcerer Jace Beleren
are back and ready to challenge the netherworld forces that threaten to
tip the delicate balance between life and death. Can Jace help Liliana
learn to control her new-found power, or will it control her?

ZENDIKAR: IN THE TEETH OF AKOUM
BY ROBERT B. WINTERMUTE
(April 2010)
Deep in the heart of Zendikar lies a threat deadlier than any of the myriad
pitfalls that await the fortune seekers who comb its ruins.
Nissa Revane, a planeswalker and native of Zendikar, thought she'd
seen it all. But if she has any hope of seeing more,
she will need to stop this burgeoning evil.

And revisit these classic planeswalker tales,
repackaged in two volumes

ARTIFACTS CYCLE I
THE THRAN
by J. Robert King

THE BROTHERS' WAR
by Jeff Grub

ARTIFACTS CYCLE II
PLANESWALKER
by Lynn Abbey

BLOODLINES
by Loren L. Coleman

TIME STREAMS
by J. Robert King

MAGIC
The Gathering®

A PLANESWALKER™ NOVEL

AGENTS OF ARTIFICE

ari marmell

Agents of Artifice

©2009 Wizards of the Coast LLC

Published by Wizards of the Coast LLC

Magic: the Gathering, Wizards of the Coast, and their respective logos, Planeswalker, are trademarks of Wizards of the Coast LLC in the U.S.A. and other countries.

Printed in the U.S.A.

Cover art by Aleksi Briclot

Hardcover First Printing: February 2009
This Edition First Printing: November 2009

9 8 7 6 5 4 3 2 1

ISBN: 978-0-7869-5240-3
620-24202000-001-EN

The Library of Congress has catalogued the hardcover edition as follows:
    Marmell, Ari.
      Agents of artifice / Ari Marmell.
        p. cm.
      "Magic: the Gathering."
      "A Planeswalker Novel."
      ISBN 978-0-7869-5134-5
      I. Title.
      PS3613.A7666A7 2009
      813'.6--dc22
                                                        2008044672

U.S., CANADA,	EUROPEAN HEADQUARTERS
ASIA, PACIFIC, & LATIN AMERICA	Hasbro UK Ltd
Wizards of the Coast LLC	Caswell Way
P.O. Box 707	Newport, Gwent NP9 0YH
Renton, WA 98057-0707	GREAT BRITAIN
+1-800-324-6496	Save this address for your records.

Visit our web site at www.wizards.com

To George, for trying to keep me sane—
but even more so for going nuts with me
when that didn't work

Author's thanks for...
Means: Fleetwood and Courtney
Motive: Mom, Dad, Naomi, and George (again)
And opportunity: Phil

ΦROLOGUE

Through a place that wasn't, where time held no meaning, the figure walked.

Winds blew, and they were not winds. Without source, without direction, they tossed the outsider's hair one way, clothes another. They were the hot gusts of an arid desert, the frigid breath of the whirling blizzard. They bore the perfume of growing things, the rancid tang of death, and scents unknown to any sane world.

The ground rolled, and it was not ground. Shifting grays and black—not a color so much as a lack of color—formed a surface scarcely less treacherous than quicksand. Through it, deep beneath it, high above it in what could hardly be called a sky, snaked rivers of fire, of lightning, of liquid earth and jagged water, of raw mana. Colors unseen by human eyes flew overhead, refusing to congeal, soaring on wings of forgotten truths, borne aloft by stray gusts. Mountains of once and future worlds wept tears of sorrow for realities that never were, unchosen futures that no other would ever mourn.

Chaos. Impossibility. Insanity.

The Blind Eternities.

Far behind, and falling ever farther, a curtain of viscous light separated the maddening expanse of raw creation from one of the many worlds of the near-infinite Multiverse that existed within. There was nothing special about this world, at least not when viewed from without, save that this was whence the figure had come, and where it must soon return.

The figure. Here, in this realm beyond worlds, that was all it was. Was she male? Was he female? Short or tall? Human or elf or goblin, angel or demon or djinn? All and none, perhaps, and none of it of any import. Any normal mortal would already have been lost, body and mind and soul torn apart and absorbed into the twisting maelstrom of what was, is, and could be.

Not this one. Anchored by a spark of the Blind Eternities itself that burned within the figure's soul, a planeswalker strode through the tide, and the maddened chaos between worlds was just another obstacle on a road that few would ever walk.

Danger and distaste aside, the figure persevered, continuing ever onward for who knew how long. Finally, when perhaps a whole heartbeat and perhaps a mere century had passed, another curtain of light loomed from the roiling instability. The traveler passed through and was born into a new reality, standing once more on the solid ground of a real world.

It had no name, this world, for it had long since died. No winds blew, the stale and nigh-poisonous air sitting heavy on the earth. No trees or mountains broke the featureless contours, and nothing but a fine dust coated the world's skin. Long dead, lifeless, desolate . . .

Private.

And there the planeswalker stood, and waited, and paced, and waited longer still, until the Other finally appeared.

The figure's first thought was not relief that the wait was over. That would come shortly. No, that first thought was, instead, Next time, I choose the meeting place!

ARI MARMELL

That would not, of course, be the most political thing to say. So the figure bowed, deeply enough to show respect, shallow enough to say I do not fear you. "Have you decided?"

The Other gazed unblinking for long moments. "I have. Perhaps a better question would be, 'Are you still certain?'"

The walker shrugged, a strangely mundane gesture in so peculiar a discussion. "I've put too much time into this, and I've too much riding on it to back out now. You know that."

"This is a complex scheme you bring me. Convoluted; labyrinthine, even. A great many things must go precisely right if you're to deliver me what's mine.

Another shrug. "My bargain comes due before too much longer. It's not as though I've much left to lose."

"There is that, yes," the Other conceded.

"And this way, I'm protected. If I were to go after it myself, and I were discovered—"

"Yes, yes. So you've explained.

The walker lapsed into silence, a silence that stretched horribly across the entire world.

Then, "You know what must happen now?" the Other asked. "To ensure the mind-speaker cannot just pull the truth from you?"

One deep breath, a second, and a third, to calm a suddenly racing heart. "I do."

"Then do not move."

And then there was only the scream, breathless, endless, a scream that would have drowned even the roaring of the Blind Eternities . . . as the Other stretched forth inhuman fingers, reached into the planeswalker's mind and soul, and began, oh so carefully, to fold.

CHAPTER ONE

As it turned out, the district of Avaric wasn't any more appealing when one was drunk than when one was sober. The fog of irrimberry wine didn't make the filthy cobblestones, the half-decayed roofs, or the sludge coating the roadways any more attractive; and the sweet aroma of that libation didn't remain in the nose long enough to muffle the stagnant rot and the eye-watering miasma that passed for air. The rows of squat houses and shops leaned over the road like tottering old men, and the wide spaces between them resembled gaps left by missing teeth. Perhaps the only redeeming quality of the entire evening was the surprising lack of mosquitoes. Normally the rains brought plague-like swarms up from the swamps and sewers that were Avaric's unsteady foundation, but apparently even they were taking the night off for the Thralldom's End celebration.

Kallist Rhoka, who had spent a considerable amount of coin on the journey to his current state of moderate inebriation, glared bitterly at his surroundings and felt that the world's refusal to reshape itself into a passingly tolerable form was the height of discourtesy.

Then again, the Avaric District wasn't alone in its refusal to change its nature to suit Kallist's desires or his drunken perceptions—and between the stubbornness of a whole neighborhood, and that of a certain raven-haired mage, he was pretty certain that the district would break first.

At the thought of the woman he'd left at the Bitter End Tavern and Restaurant, Kallist's stomach knotted so painfully it doubled him over. For long moments he crouched, waiting as the knot worked its way up to become a lump in his throat. With shaking hands—a shake that he attributed to the multiple glasses of wine, and not to any deeper emotions—he wiped the pained expression from his face.

Not for the first time, Kallist spat curses at the man who'd driven him to such a sorry state. Less than a year gone by, he'd dwelt in the shadows of Ravnica's highest spires. And now? Now the structures around him were barely high enough to cast shadows at all. Now he'd have had to actually live down in the sewers or the under-cities of the larger districts to sink any lower.

It was enough to make even a forgiving man as bitter as fresh wormwood, and Kallist had never been all that forgiving.

Still, it would all have been worth it, if she'd just said yes. . .

Kallist, his wine-besotted mind swiftly running out of curses, stared down at his feet. He couldn't even see the normal color of his basilisk-skin boots, one of the few luxuries he still owned, so coated were they in the swamp sludge that always oozed up from between the cobblestones after the rain. The boots kept swimming in and out of focus, too. He wondered if he might vomit, and was angered that he might waste the expensive irrimberry wine he'd drunk. The notion of falling to hands and knees on the roadway was enough to steady him, however. He could still hear, ever so faintly, the singing and dancing of the Thralldom's End festival, back in the direction of the Bitter End, and he'd be damned thrice over if he'd let anyone from the tavern find him pasting a dinner collage all over the road. With a rigid, yet swaying gait that made him appear sober to nobody but himself, he resumed his trek.

Avaric wasn't really that large a place; none of the local neighborhoods were. It was a backwater district, surrounded by other backwater districts save for those few spots where the underground swamps pooled to the surface, ugly and malodorous cysts on Ravnica's aging face. Those who dwelt here did so only because anyplace else they could afford to move was even worse, and a few small fungus gardens were more than enough to feed the lot of them. Thus, even though the Bitter End was at the far end of Avaric from the house Kallist shared with the woman on whom he currently blamed his inebriated state, it should normally have taken only about twenty minutes to walk from one to the other.

"Normally," of course, allowed neither for Kallist's current shuffling gate nor the fact that he'd already taken the same wrong turn twice. It had now been well over half an hour, he could still hear the faint strains of singing off in the distance; his eyes were beginning to water and to sting . . .

And he really, really had to find somewhere private to release some of that wine back into the wild. Kallist looked down at his feet, looked over at the nearest alley—filled almost ankle deep with a juicy mixture of swamp-water and refuse—muttered a brief "Hell with it," and strode off the avenue.

He shuddered at the soft squishing beneath his boots, but tonight, the urging of a bladder growing fuller by the moment outweighed Kallist's concerns for his footwear. Had he been either a little more sober, or a little more drunk, he might've worried about encountering sewer goblins, or even Golgari fungus-creatures leftover from the struggles that ended guild rule, but as he wasn't, he didn't.

With a deep sigh, Kallist relieved himself against the stained wall that was also the back wall of somebody's house, and staggered back to the road just in time to all but run into a fellow striding the other way.

"Gariel," he greeted the newcomer, trying to straighten himself into a semblance of sobriety.

"Who . . . Kallist? What're you doing in the alleys this late at night? You're not worried about gobbers?"

Kallist spun, expecting in his drunken haze to see a gang of the foul creatures behind him. When none appeared, he sank slowly to the muddy road, waiting for yet another surge of nausea to pass.

Irritably, he looked at his friend, who failed to suppress a smirk. Physically, Gariel was everything Kallist wasn't: dark-skinned to Kallist's natural pallor; heavily muscled where Kallist was wiry; exceptionally tall where Kallist could have been the standard by which average was measured; and with earthen-colored eyes to contrast with Kallist's own oceanic blue. Gariel even wore a well trimmed beard, not out of any desire to follow current trends—the styles of Ravnica's affluent meant little here in the backwaters—but simply because the man had an intense dislike of shaving. "Any knife comes near my face," he'd told Kallist once, "it damn well better have a sausage on the end of it." Had their hair not been similar shades of wooden brown, they might as well have been of different species entirely.

Something must have flashed across his face, something Gariel saw even in the feeble moonlight and the glow of the emberstone he held in his left fist. He dropped his hand and lowered himself to the grimy roadway beside his friend.

"This doesn't look like a celebratory drunk," he observed, leaning back against the nearest building.

Kallist looked up at him, all but trembling with the effort of keeping his face a stony, emotionless mask. He glared at Gariel as though daring him to say something.

Silence for a few moments, broken only by the call of a spire bat flying low over the few pools of exposed swamp between the wide roadways and cheap row houses.

"She said no, didn't she?" said Gariel at last.

Kallist's shoulders slumped. "She said she'd 'think about it.'"

Gariel forced a grin, though he felt the blood pounding in his ears, furious on his friend's behalf. "Well, at least that's not a 'no,' right?"

"Oh, come on, Gariel!" The smaller fellow punched the mud. "When was the last time you knew Liliana to take her time to think about anything? Everything she does, she does in the moment." He sighed, and tried to swallow the lump that had climbed once again into his throat and appeared bound and determined to stay there. "You know as well as I do that 'I'll think about it' means 'I don't want to hurt you by refusing.'"

Gariel wanted to argue the point, but the words clung to the roof of his mouth like a paste. "Well. . . Look, Kallist. You've been together—what? A few months?"

"Yeah. Ever since . . ." He didn't finish the sentence. In all the time Gariel had known him, Kallist had never finished that sentence.

"All right, a few months. Give it some more time. I mean, she's obviously not ending it, or she wouldn't have bothered to spare you the 'no,' right? Maybe in another year or three . . ."

Kallist couldn't help but laugh, though the sound was poisonous as hemlock. "Right. Because the one thing Liliana does more often than anything else is to change her mind once it's made up."

In fact, in the time Kallist had known her, Liliana had done so precisely once.

And again, Gariel knew them both too well to argue. All that emerged from his mouth, escaping like a fleeing convict before he could think better of it and snap his teeth shut, was, "So maybe you're better off this way.

"I'm sorry," he added immediately. "That didn't come out right."

"Nothing tonight has." Kallist rose and set his bleary eyes toward the southeast. "I'm going home."

"Wait." Gariel rose, too, and placed a hand on his friend's shoulder. "Where is she, anyway?"

"Where else would she be during Thralldom's End?"

Gariel actually saw red. "What?" He'd doubtless have awakened half the street with that squawk, if they hadn't all been out celebrating. "You mean even after your talk . . ."

Kallist shrugged, and couldn't help but smile a bit. "She said there was no reason to ruin a perfectly good dance. Even asked me to stay, but—Gariel? Where are you going?"

The larger man was already several yards down the road. "I'm going," he answered, barely turning his head, "to give your woman a piece of my mind for treating you this way."

"Gariel, don't . . ." But he was already gone around the nearest bend. Were Kallist less exhausted, less depressed, and certainly less drunk, he might have caught Gariel, or at least tried. As Kallist was, he could only drop his chin to his chest and shuffle home, hoping he remembered to get even drunker before he fell asleep.

He did, however, spare a brief thought to hoping that there was still a Bitter End Tavern standing, come tomorrow morning.

⁂ ⁂ ⁂ ⁂ ⁂

Though the guilds were gone, much of Ravnica still celebrated the Festival of the Guildpact, as if remembering the years of prosperity and order might keep them from fading away in these modern, more tumultuous times. Much of Ravnica—but not all. Some of the plane's districts had suffered rather more than others beneath the guilds, and not a few were just as happy to see them gone.

Some such as Avaric, whose families had long labored in all but serfdom to the usurious patriarchs of the Orzhov. So when the so-called Guild of Deals had fallen, it was the best news the citizens here had received in several thousand years.

The walls, the floor, the tables, and the chairs of the Bitter End shook as though in the midst of an earthquake, as the good folk of Avaric celebrated Thralldom's End. In one corner, a gaggle of performers pounded on drums, plucked the strings on a variety of instruments, blew through various horns, in a veritable frenzy of activity that should have produced nothing but anarchic noise, yet somehow managed to shape itself into actual music. Around the perimeter of the common room, the people not currently caught up in the dance clapped or stomped to the highly charged beat, and the footsteps of the dancers themselves kicked up clouds of sawdust from the floor and brought showers of dust sifting from the rafters. Before the start of business tomorrow, a handful of floorboards, a couple of chairs, and a legion of mugs and plates would need replacing—but the Bitter End was the largest establishment in Avaric to hold a Thralldom's End gala, and if a bit of ruined furniture and broken crockery was the price for such a huge influx of custom, it was a cost Ishri, barkeep and the tavern's owner, cheerfully paid.

Liliana Vess was a whirlwind sweeping through the assembled dancers, leaving footprints not merely in the sawdust, but on the hearts of a score of hopeful men. Her midnight-black hair moved about her head like a dark cloud, or perhaps a tainted halo. Her cream-hued gown, which was cut distractingly low, rose and whirled and fell, promising constantly to reveal more than it should, but, like a teasing courtesan, always managing to renege.

She breathed heavily from the exertion of the rapid dance, spinning and twisting through the arms of a dozen of her fellow celebrants. Her smile lit up her features—high and somewhat sharp, forming a face that few would envision when imagining a classic beauty, yet which all would agree was beautiful once they saw it—but that smile failed to reach her eyes. For all that she tried to lose herself in the festivities, in the adoration of those who watched her, who reached out in hopes of a simple fleeting touch, she could not.

Damn him anyway! Guilt was not an emotion with which Liliana was well acquainted, and she found swiftly that it was not at all to her liking.

The bizarre accumulation of notes and beats and rhythms successfully masquerading as a song came to an end, and so did the last of Liliana's ability to fake any remaining enthusiasm for the celebration. The musicians, bowing to much applause and acclaim, left the stage for a well-earned break, leaving an instrument with enchanted strings to play a slow and lonesome ditty until they returned. Several couples remained in the room's center, swaying to the somber notes, but most returned to their tables to await a more energetic piece.

Liliana watched them go, marveling at these people among whom she'd made her temporary home. They were all clad in their best and fanciest—which here in Avaric meant tunics with long sleeves instead of short, trousers without obvious patches, and vests that actually boasted some faint color, rather than their normal browns and grays. Nobody here could afford the rich dyes or the fancy buttons and clasps of the rich, yet they wore their "finery" with pride; splurged on lean steaks when they normally subsisted on fungi and the occasional fish or reptile hauled from the swampy pools. And they lived it up as though such ridiculous luxuries actually meant something.

Liliana didn't understand any of it. She approved of it, even respected it, but she didn't understand it.

Even as she floated back to her table, hand reaching for a glass of rough beer to quench her thirst, Liliana spotted a figure moving toward her through the crowd. A gruff face, split into what the owner probably thought was a charming smile, leered at her through a thick growth of beard. Two sausage-like thumbs hooked themselves through the pockets of a heavy black vest, perhaps trying to draw attention to the fine garment. The drunkard had been watching her all night, since well before Kallist had ruined the evening and stormed off in a huff. Every night there was always at least one, and she'd wondered how long it would take him to drink enough nerve to approach.

"I couldn't help but notice," he slurred in a voice heavy with beer, "that you finally sent your scrawny friend packing. That mean you interested in spending some time with a real man?"

In a better mood, Liliana might've engaged in some light flirting before telling the drunk to find his own personal hell and stay there. Not tonight.

Liliana lifted her dinner knife, still stained with remnants of her overcooked steak, from the table. "If you don't walk away right now," she said sweetly, "you won't be a 'real man' for very long."

It took a moment, the battle between common sense and belligerent pride that raged across the fellow's face—but finally, aided perhaps by the unnatural gleam in Liliana's eyes, common sense won the field. Grumbling, he turned and shuffled back to his table, where he would tell his friends all about how he'd turned down the woman's advances.

Liliana sighed once as she lowered herself into her chair, and found herself uncharacteristically wishing that Kallist had been here to see that exchange. Damn it, she thought once more, reaching again for her mug. If it's not one thing.

"Hey! Bitch!"

It's another.

Half the tavern turned toward the large, dark-skinned fellow who'd just come stalking through the front door, his boots leaving a trail of castoff mud, but Liliana already knew precisely for whom his call was intended. She rose gracefully and offered her most stunning smile.

"And a joyous Thralldom's End to you, too, Gariel."

"Don't 'joyous Thralldom's End' me, gods damn it!" he growled, pushing his way through a few of the slow-dancing couples to stand before her table. "I want to know what the hell you think you're—"

They were skilled, Liliana thought later, when she actually had a moment to think; you had to give them that. She hadn't noticed them at all, until a blade sped toward her from over Gariel's shoulder.

There was no time even to shout a warning. Liliana brought a knee up sharply into Gariel's gut—she had just enough respect for him as Kallist's friend not to hit him any lower—and caught his shoulders as he doubled over, using his own weight to topple them both backwards over her chair. It wasn't pretty, it wasn't graceful, but it took them out of a sword's sudden arc with half a heartbeat to spare.

The sounds of the chair clattering over, and the pair of them hitting the floor, were just loud enough to penetrate the din. First a couple of faces, and then a handful more, turned away from dinner or dancers to stare at them; a ripple in a still pond, awareness that something was very much not right spread through the Bitter End.

Liliana gasped as the wooden edge of the seat dug painfully into her side, but she didn't let that stop her from rolling. Their bodies tilted across the chair like a fulcrum, her head striking the hardwood floor, but that, too, she ignored as best she could. Twisting her grip on Gariel as they fell, she kept him from landing squarely atop her. She left him gasping on the floor as she scrabbled swiftly to her feet, trying to keep the table between herself and her attacker.

No. Attackers, plural. Damn.

They were strangers here, certainly. Avaric was small, yes, but not quite tiny enough for everyone to know everyone else by sight. From a distance, then, these two blended perfectly, both of roughly average height, both clad as workers gone out to hoist a few after a long day's work, before going home to hoist a few more. But up close, their cold, emotionless eyes marked them as something else entirely.

Well, that and the heavy, cleaver-like blades.

They advanced unhurriedly, even casually, one passing to each side of the table. Clearly, despite the speed of Liliana's evasion, they didn't expect much in the way of resistance.

And in terms of anyone coming to Liliana's aid, they were correct. The folk nearest her had only just begun to run, to scream, or to freeze in shock, as best befit their individual temperaments. From behind the bar, Ishri emerged with a heavy cudgel in hand, but hampered as she was by the bulk of the crowd retreating from the coming bloodshed, there was no way she'd reach the table before it was all over. To his credit, the suitor whom Liliana had just rebuffed was also making his way back across the tavern, fists raised, but he was already so drunk that even if he managed to reach the fray, it was unlikely he could meaningfully contribute.

But then, Liliana didn't require anyone's help.

Crouching slightly, she shifted the dinner knife— hardly an intimidating weapon, but all she had—into an underhand grip. Beneath her breath, her lips barely moving, she began to utter a low, sonorous chant. Across her neck rose an abstract pattern of tattoos that

ARI MARMELL

suggested even more elaborate designs farther down her back, as though burned across her skin from the inside out.

Had they been able to hear it over the ambient noise of a panicking tavern, that sound alone might have given her attackers pause. The tone was surreal, sepulchral, far deeper than Liliana's voice should ever have produced. The syllables formed no words of any known language, yet they carried a terrible meaning that bypassed the mind entirely, to sink directly into the listener's soul.

But they could not hear it, those deluded fools who thought themselves predator rather than prey. And even if they had, it would have been far too late to matter.

As though biting the end off a leather thong, Liliana spat a word of power into the æther, gestured with her blade. Something moved unseen beneath the table, just one more shadow in the flickering lanterns of the Bitter End, summoned from abyssal gulfs beyond the realms of the dead themselves. With impossibly long fingers it stretched out, farther, farther, and brushed the edges of two of the table's legs. Rotting away as though aged a hundred years, in single instant, they folded in on themselves, putrefying into soft mulch. The rest of the heavy wood surface toppled to the side, slamming hard into one of the bandit's calves. He cried out in pain, stumbling and limping away from the unexpected assault, a handful of dishes and a half-eaten loaf of pumpernickel bread clattering around his feet.

At that cry, the second man's attention flickered away from Liliana for less than a heartbeat—but that was enough. Ducking in low, she drew the edge of her knife across his extended arm. Cloth and flesh tore beneath the serrated steel, and the bandit barely muffled a curse of pain behind clenched teeth.

Blood welled up, beading along his wrist in a narrow bracelet. It was a shallow wound, stinging but harmless, and his grimace of pain turned into a savage grin as he realized just how ineffective his target's attack had proved.

But then, Liliana's attack wasn't intended to cause him harm. It was meant only to draw blood—and the attention of the unseen shadowy thing sliding impossibly across the floor. Invisible to all, darkness against darkness, black on black, it stretched forth its talons once more and dipped them into the welling blood. A foul corruption leeched into the seeping wound, intertwined itself around the muscles and vessels of the man's arm.

He screamed, then, an inhuman cry of agony, as gangrenous rot shot through his flesh. The blade fell from limp fingers, lodging itself in the wood by his feet, as the skin turned sickly blue, the blood black and viscous. Flesh grew stiff and cracked, splitting to unleash gouts of yellowed pus. Falling to his knees, the sellsword clutched his dying arm to his chest and bawled like an infant.

Liliana spared him not so much as another glance. His suffering would end soon enough—when the spreading necrotic rot reached his heart.

Growing ever more unnerved, the second bandit had nonetheless recovered from the impact of the table against his leg, swiftly closing to within striking range. Snarling, he raised his chopping blade high and brought it down in a vicious stroke that no parry with the fragile dinner knife could have halted.

Liliana didn't even try to lift her feeble weapon in response. No, lips still moving though she must long since have run out of breath, she raised her left hand and caught the blade as it descended.

The cleaver should have torn through her upraised limb like parchment. Should have, and would have, had it not begun to turn black at the apex of its swing, suddenly cloaked and tugged by wisps of shadow. By the time it should have reached the flesh of Liliana's hand, it was simply gone, drawn away into the nether between the worlds of the living and the dead. The swordsman was left standing, staring at his empty fist.

With a shrug, Liliana bent two fingers into talons and drove them into his staring eyes. Hardly fatal, but more than enough to take him, screaming, out of the fight.

And just like that, the tavern grew calm once more. The eldritch symbols across Liliana's back faded as swiftly as they appeared, leaving her skin pristine. Ignoring the slack faces that gaped silently at her from those partygoers who hadn't already run screaming from the Bitter End, Liliana moved away from the fallen bandit, dismissing the spectral shadow with the merest thought. Only she, of all those present, heard its woeful cry as it spiraled back into the endless dark.

She placed one foot atop the fallen chair and leaned on her knee to gaze meaningfully down at Gariel—who was, himself, staring up at her as though she'd sprouted feathers.

"What . . . What did . . . What?"

"All good questions," Liliana told him. "Are you all right?"

"I—I'll live."

"Let's not jump to conclusions just yet." She reached down to offer the flustered fellow a hand up—then yanked it away as he began leaning on her, allowing him to fall flat on his face once more. The floorboards shook with the impact. "There's still the little matter," she said with a predatory smile, "of you stalking through that door, yelling at me, calling me all sorts of ugly names."

"I—you. . ." Gariel wiped a hand across his face, smearing rather than removing the blood that now dribbled from his nose. "People are watching, Liliana."

"That didn't bother you when you were shouting obscenities at me."

Gariel could only gape once more, at the gathered audience and at the injured bandits, and wonder exactly how crazy his friend's girl actually was. He'd actually opened his mouth to ask such a question—only to choke on a spray of splinters as a bolt that appeared roughly as thick as a tree trunk slammed into the floor mere inches from his head.

Liliana heard the whir-and-click of a mechanized crossbow even as she jerked away from the sudden impact, glaring at the figures standing in the doorway.

There were three more, all strongly resembling the pair who had attacked her moments ago. Only these three, Liliana realized as she stared at a trio of self-loading identical weapons, were far better equipped.

"The next one," the man in the middle told her gruffly, "goes through his head." His gaze flickered to the two figures on the floor, one breathing his last, one blinded, and his face hardened. "I don't think you're fast enough to stop all three of us, witch."

She scowled in turn. "So shoot him. He means nothing to me, and even with those fancy crossbows, I promise you'll not have time to reload."

"Ah," the man said, voice oily, "but he means something to someone, don't he?"

Liliana's scowl grew deeper still—but her shoulders slumped, and she knew that they saw it. "What do you want?"

"What I want is to put a few shafts through you for what you did to my boys," the bandit told her. "But what's going to happen is this . . ."

A R I   M A R M E L L

CHAPTER TWO

A light rain was falling by the time Kallist opened his eyes. It was a slow, soaking drizzle, good for the swamp fungus and sewer slime and not much else, the sort of precipitation that managed to soak everything without forming into actual drops. It ran from the sloped roof, flowing around the broken and missing shingles, to pour in sporadic rivulets past the windows. The mosquitoes, Kallist thought, are going to be murder tomorrow, holiday or no holiday.

That was his first thought. His second was, Why am I stuck to the table?

He winced in pain, and more than a little embarrassment, as he peeled his unshaven face from the wood, recognizing the gluey sensation of his own drool. At least, he realized, glancing around at the familiar surroundings, he had made it home before passing out completely.

He stood up, his back protesting at the slumped position he'd apparently held for quite a few hours. Bleary-eyed, but without the pounding headache he'd expected, Kallist staggered across the room. It was a small dwelling: two interior rooms, one of which included the kitchen, and a separate bathhouse for cleaning and other necessary relief. It was tiny compared to what he'd known elsewhere in Ravnica, but by the standards of Avaric, it was almost palatial.

Rather than trudge out to the bathhouse where their well was located, which would have required getting soaked to the skin, Kallist simply cut out the middleman, threw open the shutters, and caught some of the ambient rain in his hands. The first palm-full went to quench his burning thirst, the second to scrub the sticky residue from the side of his face.

And only then, as he truly began to wake up and as the expected pounding slowly seeped into his skull, like faint hoofbeats from a distance, did Kallist wonder what had awakened him.

He froze, hands still held out the window, and tried to remember how to think. It couldn't have been thunder, but this was a gentle shower, not a storm. Someone's door slamming? Possibly. But someone would've had to give their door a blow sufficient to fell a tree for it to have awakened Kallist from his drunken slumber. It didn't seem likely.

Yet he was certain, in retrospect, that some sort of crash had roused him, a crash that could have been inside the house.

Kallist's mind finally shrugged off enough lassitude to start working at something approaching normal capacity, at roughly the same time he heard the faintest whisper of cloth against wood in the kitchen doorway.

At the best of times, Kallist wasn't a fraction of the mage Liliana was; he'd had training, yes, but his skills had always leaned more toward the sword than the spell. And now, with more than a little alcohol still flowing through his blood, anything approaching a complex incantation was beyond him. Nevertheless, spurred on by a sudden burst of fear, a swift whisper allowed Kallist to cloak himself in the thinnest, flimsiest of illusions. It wasn't much—but it made him appear as though he still held both hands outside, cupped to catch the rain, when in fact one had dropped to the hilt of the dagger he wore strapped to his right thigh. It felt awfully light in his hand, and he had a moment to wish that he'd chosen the window nearer the bed, where his broadsword rested in easy reach.

And then he felt the hot breath of the intruder on the back of his neck, and the time for wishes and regrets had passed.

Kallist spun, bringing the heavy pommel of the dirk up into the chin of the man lurking behind him. He caught a brief glimpse of unshaven cheeks and weak, watery eyes before the fellow staggered back, clutching his broken jaw. Blood dribbled from the corners of his mouth, flowing from the teeth marks he'd left in his own tongue. The intruder's weapon, a heavy wooden cudgel, landed between them with a thump.

Unsure if his attacker was alone, Kallist dropped into a knife-fighter's stance, blade held underhand and down at his side, left hand outstretched to grab or parry. It was an expert posture, yet somehow it felt wrong; off, just a bit. As though his mind knew what it needed to do, but his muscles weren't sure how to follow.

I really, thought Kallist, have to get in more practice. Or maybe just less drinking.

Keeping a sliver of attention on the man who'd collapsed to the floor, just in case he might catch his second wind, Kallist maneuvered through the room in a careful series of cross-steps that kept him on balance, ready to spring any which way. He tried for a moment to cast out with his senses, emulating a spell he'd learned to see around corners, but his faculty with such magic was iffy at the best of times. He succeeded only in blurring his vision and causing his head to pound that much harder.

By the time his sight cleared, and he realized that part of that pounding was not in his head at all, but was in fact someone who had clambered through the open window and was charging across the floor, there was no time left to react. Kallist thought he saw the edge of a face, and then his head hurt a lot more than it had.

Then everything went black, and nothing hurt at all.

❊ ❊ ❊ ❊ ❊

When Kallist finally awoke once more, he succumbed to the urge he'd been fighting since staggering away from the Bitter End, and emptied the contents of his stomach across the floor.

Well, he aimed for the floor, anyway. He discovered in the midst of his second convulsion that he was firmly tied to a chair, so a revolting amount of what had once been leathery steak, fried tubers, and irrimberry wine instead ended up in his lap.

"You know something, Rhoka? That's really disgusting."

Kallist forced his head up to glare at the man across the chamber. "Semner."

"You know me. I'm flattered."

"I've heard a lot about you, usually from people trying to explain why they felt the need to take half a dozen baths in a row. What brings you to the ass end of Ravnica?"

The other man smiled an ugly, yellow-toothed grin. "Just following the crap, of course. Today, that'd be you."

Semner was, in every imaginable way, ugly. His features were squat and broad, his straw-yellow hair thin and greasy, his clothes rumpled and stained with old beer and older blood. He stank of sweat and an utter disregard for dental hygiene.

Yet his exterior belied a still uglier core. Semner was a thug, a leg-breaker, and a murderer-for-hire so vile he gave mercenaries a bad name. In the days when the League of Wojek still enforced the laws across Ravnica, he and his ilk were nothing. Now they were still nothing, but there were a lot more of them.

Kallist nodded. It was practically the only motion he could make, so tightly bound. "So who wants me dead this time?"

"I've got an idea." Semner moved to crouch in front of the chair. "How about you shut up and let me ask the questions?"

Despite the heavy ropes, Kallist couldn't help but smile. "If you were a mage, you could make me."

Semner's face turned apple red, and Kallist's smile grew wider still. They'd never worked together, but Kallist knew people who had fought or killed alongside the mercenary. Semner, he'd been told, was in awe of the magics many of his partners wielded, and had made more than one failed attempt at learning such things for himself.

"How about," Semner growled, "I knock your teeth through the back of your throat, and make you shut up that way? Would that work for you?"

Kallist shut up. His mind, however, was racing like a tempest drake with its tail on fire. Semner was a lot of things, but subtle had never been one of them. Semner's idea of "stealth" was to kill anyone who noticed him. If Kallist was still alive, it meant that Semner wanted something from him—or whoever had hired Semner did. Kallist wasn't sure which notion was more frightening.

"Yeah, that's what I thought," Semner said, once Kallist had remained silent for a full minute. The thug pulled up a second chair and slumped down, pointing a blade at Kallist's face. He held the melodramatic pose for a moment, then leaned forward and lashed out. Kallist couldn't help but gasp as the dagger severed a splinter of wood from the chair beside his face. "If you're thinking of trying to toss any more of your little phantasms, you'd do well to forget it right now. Or I'll bleed you so badly you can't say the word 'spell,' let alone cast one."

"This is all very intimidating," Kallist told him. "But I'd really like the chance to wash these pants before the stain sets. So if you could just get to the point . . . ?"

"Fine." Semner leaned in farther still and jabbed the point of the dagger into the seat of the chair, mere inches from Kallist's crotch. "Simple question, then, Rhoka. Answer it right, maybe you actually walk away from this.

"Where do I find Jace Beleren?"

Kallist felt the breath catch in his chest, his fingers clench into fists. Anger washed over him in a wave, and he felt an almost insurmountable temptation to just give Semner exactly what he asked for. Would serve the bastard right . . .

But he wasn't certain Liliana would understand.

So instead he said, "Last time I talked to Beleren, I told him pretty clearly to pick a hell of his choice, and go. So maybe if you start there—"

Anything else he might have added was lost in the impact of Semner's fist against his face. Kallist choked back a cry as his lips split and one of his teeth turned loose in its socket. The chair teetered a moment before tumbling over backward, sending a second surge of pain through him as his aching skull bounced off the floor. For several long breaths, Kallist could only stare at the ceiling, trying hard to gather his wits.

Semner rose, placed one foot on the crossbar between the legs of the chair, and shoved downward. The entire room tilted yet again as Kallist found himself flung upright once more—to find Semner's fist waiting to meet his face this time, rather than the other way around. Blood poured from his nose to mesh with that beading up from his lip.

"What I heard," Semner said, wiping the blood off his hand on Kallist's shirt, "was you and Beleren aren't exactly friends anymore." He began to pace, spinning the blade between his fingers. "So why not save yourself a whole lot of pain and point me in the right direction?"

Kallist probed the loosened tooth with his tongue, spat a mouthful of blood to the floor, and said nothing.

"Much as I'd love to spend an evening pounding you into jerky," Semner grumbled, "I'm on a schedule. So we'll do this the easy way. Boys!"

The front door slammed open, and Kallist practically pulled a muscle twisting around so he might see. Two men and a woman, looking about as disreputable as their leader, pushed through the open doorway, manhandling someone between them. Several more thugs—Kallist couldn't get an accurate count—leered from the rainy night beyond. The bag they'd placed over the captive's head did nothing to prevent Kallist from recognizing her; when they pulled it off, revealing Liliana's face, it was almost anticlimactic.

"You bastards!" he hissed at them. How had a nobody like Semner even managed to take her, anyway?

She didn't appear wounded, at least. Her hair was plastered to her forehead, her dress to her body. Under other circumstances, it would've been alluring.

"I'm sorry, Kallist." And damn if she didn't sound like she meant it.

Semner gestured, and the bravos holding Liliana released her—only so they could make a point of leveling their crossbows at her unprotected back.

"Now," Semner said, turning back toward his beaten prisoner, "we'll do this exactly one more time.

"Where is Jace Beleren?"

CHAPTER THREE

Favarial." Kallist was denied even the feeble comfort of glaring at his interrogator, for his attention was fixed on the crossbows aimed at Liliana's back. "I couldn't begin to tell you where in the district, and I can't even promise he's still there, but last we talked, he lived in Favarial."

Semner nodded slowly and turned to the men in the doorway. "She can go. Kill him."

Liliana's eyes widened; her lip quivered as though she had something to say, something she couldn't quite voice. Three evil grins formed around and behind her, and three evil bolts shifted their aim to Kallist's chest.

Kallist felt his heart race and his palms grow clammy. And then, as though doused with a bucket of snow, he cooled. He felt calm, collected. He'd faced worse situations; hell, he'd subjected people to worse situations.

"Bad, bad idea, Semner," he said, his voice level. "I didn't think even you were that stupid."

Curiosity warred with anger on the ugliest face in the room, and curiosity beat the stuffing out of it. Semner raised a hand, halting his men even as their fingers began to tighten on their triggers.

"Meaning what, exactly?"

"Favarial's an awfully long way away," Kallist told him. "That's several days before you know for certain if I'm lying or not."

Semner ground his teeth. "Are you?"

"No." A smile. "As far as you know."

"Damn it, Rhoka . . ."

"And what if he's left?" Kallist plunged on. "Obviously, you found me more easily than you could find him, or we wouldn't be having this lovely heart-to-heart. He could be anywhere." He might not even be on Ravnica anymore. Of course, Semner wouldn't understand that. "We may not talk anymore, but I still know the man a lot better than you do. If I'm lying, or if he's moved on, how do you plan to find him without me?"

The grinding in Semner's jaw grew to almost tectonic levels. But Kallist had him, and he knew it.

"All right." The mercenary finally relented. "You get to keep breathing." He gestured toward the chair he himself had occupied a few moments before. "Tie her up. Make sure she's secure."

"What?" Kallist scowled. "You just told your men to let her go."

"That was before you pointed out that I was being stupid," Semner smirked. One of the thugs departed to locate more rope; Semner turned toward those remaining. "Errit, you and Rin stay here. Sleep in shifts; I want someone watching them at all times.

"I may not be a mage," he allowed, with a bitter glance at Kallist, "but I can hire people who are. Once we've reached Favarial, I'll find a messenger who can send you word, let you know if he told us the truth.

"And if he didn't," Semner added darkly, "your job will be to scar the woman up good."

Kallist snarled in frustration. He was not, however, the only one present to take issue with that plan.

"Um, boss?" the one named Errit interjected, his voice uncertain. "You really want us to watch these two? For days? Just two of us?"

"They'll be tied up."

"But, uh. . . Didn't you tell me they were witches? What if they put a hex on Rin, or turn me into a gobber, or something?"

"Then you'll have a better chance of attracting women!" Semner growled, though his expression had grown uncertain.

"You'll have to take us with you, Semner," Liliana taunted. "All it takes is the right word, even the right look. There's no way your goons can keep the both of us confined for days."

"The hell they can't," he snarled back, grinning suddenly. Liliana winked at Kallist, who had to struggle not to laugh out loud.

"Gag them," Semner ordered his men, "and find something to blindfold them. That should keep them from casting or aiming much of anything. And if not. . ."

Slowly he turned to Liliana, looking her lasciviously up and down. She shuddered, her skin crawling as though he'd actually run his hands across her body. Kallist wished desperately for a knife, or even a piece of broken glass.

"One of them makes even the slightest suspicious move," Semner told Errit. "Cut something personal and irreplaceable off the other one. That should keep 'em in line."

The door swung open and the other returned, a coil of rope slung over one shoulder. He dripped profusely as he crossed the floor, and the sounds through the open doorway suggested that the steady drizzle had become an honest downpour.

"Food?" Errit asked Semner as the man with the rope moved to the chair and began uncoiling his burden. "Water?"

"Eh. We'll only be three or four days. Won't kill them to go without food. Water . . . Just soak the gags every few hours, let them suck the water out of 'em."

"And if they have to relieve themselves?" Clearly he was still nervous about the notion of having an unrestrained mage in the room.

Semner just grinned. "It'll cover the scent of Rhoka's vomit."

Shoulders straight and head held high, Liliana strode across the room and sat in the chair herself, rather than allowing herself to be manhandled into it. Even as Errit and the woman—Rin, presumably—began wrapping the ropes around her, her eyes locked on Kallist's own. Slowly, deliberately, they drifted down to indicate the ropes, and back up. Ever so slightly, he nodded in turn.

Without the slightest hint of sound, Liliana's lips began to move.

In a matter of moments, she was tied as thoroughly as Kallist himself, Semner had offered them another handful of snide and threatening comments, and the house had slowly emptied out. All that remained, now, were two bound prisoners, two nervous captors, and the sound of the ever-increasing rain.

A little knowledge, or so the saying goes, is a dangerous thing. And that's what Semner, undisciplined and unstudied as he was in the ways of magic, possessed: a little knowledge. If he'd known just a bit more, paid slightly better attention to the mages with whom he'd worked or the few lessons he'd received, he might've known just how quickly simple magics could be worked; might've realized how thoroughly he was being played when Liliana intimated that binding and gagging would prove anything more than an inconvenience.

The necromancer had rotted the ropes away to sludge before Semner had even departed the house—a fact concealed by Kallist's own spell, a minimal phantasmagoria that made the bindings appear as solid as ever, even shifting and rustling with the captives' movements. And then they waited, the prisoners fidgeting, Errit nervously pacing the room, Rin digging around in the linens for viable gags and blindfolds. She finally settled on a few strips of bed sheet and the sleeves torn off an old tunic.

Kallist winced as the cloth was shoved in his mouth and draped over his head. Yet even as the room vanished behind off-white linen, he allowed his body to go limp, his mind and his focus to sharpen, as he drew upon the mana of the wells and cisterns beneath the district's roads. Earlier, hungover and all but drowning in adrenaline, he couldn't make the spell work. But now, now he cast his sight out from his head; it felt, if anything, even easier than he'd anticipated. The ragged sheet seemed to draw near and then vanish as he surveyed the room from a spot several inches in front of his face. From there he watched and waited for Liliana to make the first move.

The sound of the downpour faded, resuming the gentle background rustle of the night before. The shutters over the windows glowed faintly with the first stirrings of a bashful dawn.

Errit actually uttered a startled squeak when Liliana stood up from her chair, doffed her bonds and removed the makeshift hood and gag with contemptuous ease, offering him her most dazzling, seductive smile.

And that was more than enough distraction for Kallist to stand up and smash the thug over the back of the head with his chair.

The sound didn't wake Rin, who had gone to sleep away Errit's first shift. Thanks to the shadowy form that had lurked beneath the bed since the start of Liliana's chant, run its hideous limbs across the sleeping woman, and vanished once more into the æther, nothing would wake Rin ever again.

ARI MARMELL

"You certainly took your time," Kallist said as he stepped across the bleeding, supine form, dropping his gag on the fellow's face, a cheap and contemptuous shroud. "We've been free for over an hour."

"I had to be sure Semner wasn't coming back, didn't I?"

"Ah. Smart thinking."

"And don't forget it."

Kallist couldn't help but smile. He stepped beside the woman he loved—even if he'd also felt, over the past evening, that he could learn to hate her—and reached out to embrace her. His heart fell to his toes when she retreated before him, until he remembered the state of his clothes.

"New pants, I think," he suggested with a rueful grin.

"I'd surely appreciate it."

Kallist moved to the bed, stopping long enough to stick a hand through the shutters, collecting a handful of rainwater with which he removed the worst of the blood from his face. "Are you all right?" he asked as he knelt, wincing, to dig through the lower half of the wardrobe. "They didn't hurt you, did they?"

"Only what you saw, Kallist."

"I'm glad." He staggered and hopped his way around the room, trying to yank a clean pair of trousers over his legs even as he went about collecting certain vital items. "Who do you think hired Semner? Boricov? The Consortium itself? Or maybe that Kamigawa shaman's also a walker . . ."

"Does it matter?" Liliana bent down, wrapping the few remaining strands of solid rope around the splayed limbs of the unconscious thug. "If we sat here listing everyone who might want Jace dead, he'd die of old age before we finished, and save them the trouble."

"It matters," Kallist said, teetering into the center of the room with an armload of traveling supplies, his scabbarded broadsword protruding from the heap. "It's going to impact how we run."

"Run?"

"If it's just the ratfolk looking for a bit of payback, there's no reason to think you and I are in any further danger. But if the Infinite Consortium's hunting us again, we've got to put at least a few hundred leagues between us and our next home. One of the larger districts, do you think? Glahia, maybe? Not Favarial, for obvious reasons. Or maybe we could—"

"Kallist," Liliana said softly, laying a gentle hand across his arm, though he had no memory of her crossing the room, "hush."

He hushed.

"We can't run," she told him seriously.

"I've got a pack of supplies and two fairly sturdy feet that say we can, actually. Why—"

"We have to warn Jace."

Kallist's armload fell to the floor, the hilt of the sword landing hard enough on his foot that, had he not already put his boots back on, he might well have broken something.

"Semner must have hit me harder than I thought," he told her.

"Oh?"

"I'm hallucinating. I actually imagined I heard you say we should go warn Jace."

"Well, that's a mighty convenient hallucination, then, since I *did* say we should go warn Jace. But at least I won't have to repeat myself."

"You're insane. There's no way—"

"Someone's got to, Kallist."

"Liliana, Jace doesn't want to see us."

"And we don't want to see him," she agreed.

"Precisely. Why ruin such a mutually satisfying arrangement?"

"Kallist . . ."

"He's never forgiven you, Liliana. And he's *certainly* never going to forgive *me*."

"And that, of course, is as good a reason as any to sentence the man to death."

"He ruined my life!"

"Because he was trying to save it."

A long pause, as Kallist glared at her—and then his shoulders drooped, the breath hissing through his teeth as it escaped. "Damn it."

"Yeah."

Kallist slid down the wall to sit, arms on knees, beside the window. Liliana crouched next to him, two fingers running idly through his hair.

"When did we start worrying about the 'right thing?' " he asked hopelessly.

"I think about the time it started to involve someone who saved your life half a dozen times."

A final deep sigh deflated Kallist from the waist on up, but finally he nodded. "All right," he said. And again, "All right. Semner's got over an hour's head start. But it's pretty easy to get turned around in the streets and tunnels between here and Favarial. Even if not, if I hurry, I may still get there soon enough to find Jace before he does, assuming the bastard's even still in the district."

"By which, of course, you mean 'we,' " Liliana corrected, just the slightest coating of frost on her voice.

"Ah . . ." Kallist hedged, realizing just how deep was the mire he was about to step in, "no, that's not exactly what I meant."

"Yes it is. You just haven't had that fact explained to you yet."

"Liliana," he said, pulling his head from beneath her hand and standing straight once more, "You shouldn't come."

She rose, smoothly, swiftly, until her feet were inches from the floor, her body surrounded by a flickering aura of black mist, the arcane symbols once more inked across her back and neck. She hovered, higher, until she had to look down to meet Kallist's gaze.

Even knowing that she wasn't about to hurt him, he couldn't help but shiver at the blood-chilling, vampiric cold emanating from the necromancer. From within the midnight-tinted aura, he swore he heard the whispers and moans of a score of souls.

Yet her tone, when she spoke, was calm, collected. She was, Kallist realized with something akin to awe, simply making a point, not trying to intimidate him.

"Do you really think," she asked him, "that waiting here in Avaric, to find out if you've succeeded, is the best use of my abilities? Do you really think you can convince me that it's a trip you can make, but that it's somehow too dangerous for me?"

It had, of course, nothing whatsoever to do with danger. Kallist just wasn't remotely certain he could stand spending three or four straight days with Liliana, so soon after the crushing conversation of the previous evening.

Kallist, not being a complete idiot, knew better than to say so. "Yes. I think it's too dangerous to risk both of us."

Liliana laughed and sank until her feet once more touched the wooden planks, allowing the necromantic aura to fade. "So it's safer for one of us than both? I thought I was supposed to be the illogical one."

"Liliana—"

"Besides," she said lightly, flicking the tip of his nose with a finger, "you'd be bored without me."

Kallist knew when he was beat. It seemed to be happening a lot lately.

"Fine," he grumbled with ill grace. "Start packing up what you need. I've got one last thing to take care of."

The humor instantly fell from Liliana's face. "Would you rather I do it?" she asked gently.

"Not even a little bit."

Kallist hefted his broadsword from the pile, allowing the scabbard to slide from the blade. Mechanically, he turned and strode across the room to stand above Errit.

The bound thug, who'd regained consciousness at some point during their discussion, began to thrash. "Wait! Wait a minute!"

"Why?" Kallist's voice was as mechanical as his movements.

"I—there's no reason! Look, I'm no threat to you! I could even help you! I—"

"Should have asked Semner exactly who it was you were dealing with." Kallist brought the heavy blade down with a crash. Then, without a word, he turned away to wash the weapon clean, leaving the body to drain itself dry into the crevice he'd cleaved through the floorboards beneath it.

CHAPTER FOUR

Kallist glowered about as though hoping to cow the rain into submission. The rain petulantly refused to be intimidated, however, and he had to settle for running his fingers over his face, flinging another handful of water to the sodden earth.

"At least it keeps the worst of the stench and the mosquitoes out of the air," Liliana told him, her voice cheerful enough that it made Kallist very seriously consider hitting her over the head with the first loose brick he could find.

He glared at her instead. "Maybe if you'd take one of these packs for me, I'd be a tad less miserable."

"I have what I need. It's not my fault you pack like a girl."

"And I suppose that means you pack like a man, then?"

"I, my love," she said, with a seductive twinkle in her eye and just a faint touch of her tongue on her lips, "do not do *anything* like a man."

Kallist, still not emotionally steady enough to broach certain subjects, kept walking.

The both of them were clad in heavy cloaks, designed not only to keep the elements off but to hide the fact that their clothes were clearly of poor, peasant stock. Though the only routes out of Avaric took them through alleys, sewers, and under-streets that made even that poor district seem classy, they would soon enough be wending their way through neighborhoods of far greater affluence. They could acquire new outfits easily enough, but until then, it wouldn't do to stand out as yokels.

Kallist had topped his outfit with a broad-brimmed hat, Liliana with a deep hood, and neither had done much in the way of keeping the pair dry. Their shoes were all but unsalvageable, the rain-soaked mud of Avaric having been replaced by the much purer garbage and excess sewage of Ravnica's most foul under-streets.

A few more moments of silence, a few hundred more yards. The rains increased marginally, but enough to soak through what few spots of Kallist's outfit were still dry, and he could only shake his head.

"This is not an auspicious start to our journey," he muttered.

"Why, Kallist. You're not superstitious, are you?"

The expression he turned on Liliana was utterly bland. "I'm accompanying a sorcerer who was born on another world, on our way to warn a third that he's about to be assassinated, possibly at the behest of either an inter-planar criminal organization or a spirit-binding rat. As far as I'm concerned, what you call 'superstition,' I call 'paying attention.'"

"Fair enough. You should try that, then."

Kallist squinted, not entirely certain if he was imagining the insult there or not, but Liliana's smile suggested that she hadn't seriously meant it anyway. At least, he assumed that's what it meant.

Another few moments of silence, save the persistent rain and the squelching of boots.

"Liliana," he began hesitantly, "about our talk last night . . ."

"No."

"Fine." Kallist couldn't keep the anger or a touch of petulance out of his voice. He began to pull ahead, but a soft hand on his shoulder stopped him.

He turned, and the wide eyes into which he gazed glimmered with more than the rain.

"Kallist," Liliana said gently, "not now. After we're done with this—when we've found Jace and we're done with whatever we're doing in Favarial—if things have changed, ask me then. But not now. There's too much to deal with."

He could only nod, unable to form anything resembling a coherent word, and resumed his pace.

Struggling to keep his voice steady, he asked, "Assuming we can find him, do you think Jace'll be willing even to see us?"

"I doubt it," Liliana told him seriously. "But I wasn't planning on asking. You said it yourself, Kallist: He's never forgiven either of us. We're going to have to save him despite himself.

"And who knows?" she added, voice far more hopeful than it was certain. "Maybe saving his life one more time will help balance out the books where he's concerned."

Kallist smiled a grim, sad smile. "And when you're through with that delusion, I've got a pristine castle with a mountain view on Dominaria that I can sell you, cheap."

Again they walked in silence. As their footsteps drew them inexorably farther from Avaric, their surroundings grew ever filthier, ever more gloomy. At least the huts and shops in Avaric had no pretensions; these, however, stretched as high as those aspiring to the glory of other, far wealthier neighborhoods. Narrow windows and tall arched doorways provided ingress through walls of stone; but that stone was cracked and encrusted with dirt and droppings, those windows boarded over, those doors rotted away. Cobwebs grew thicker than curtains, and the sounds of what few inhabitants remained within were furtive and scurrying. The cobbles were colored in all manner of molds and mildews that rarely saw the sun, feeding off the runoff and waste.

His attention locked on that nightmare of abandoned, dying buildings, half-blinded by the precipitation that hung in the air like a mist, Kallist all but leaped from his skin as Liliana's fist clenched on his shoulder.

"Holy hell, Liliana! What are—"

"Shush!" The rasped whisper shut him up faster than any shout. "Listen!"

Indeed, he heard it now, cursed himself for missing it. Drums in the sewer tunnels, a dozen or more.

"Sewer goblins," he hissed at Liliana, hand dropping to the hilt of his broadsword.

"I don't understand," she admitted, even as she stepped away, clearing him room to draw. "I thought they didn't come out during the day?"

"They don't." But Kallist's voice was distant, for something else had begun to disturb him, something that tickled at the back of his mind. Something about the drums themselves, about the tale Jace once told him of the Kamigawa ratmen . . .

"Liliana," he rasped, throat suddenly dry, "I think we have bigger things than goblins to worry about . . ."

Did the goblin shamans, or the demoniac night-creeps who sometimes ruled them, call it forth from the toxic mire in which they dwelt, shaping mind and body and soul from fungal growths and human wastes and rotting, caustic refuse? Or had their primitive call been heard farther away, worlds away, summoning a vile soul to manifest through what foul materials they had to hand?

Ultimately, it made no difference. The beat of the drums rose, growing ever louder, ever more frenetic, and the worst of the sewers rose with them.

The fetid waft of methane was its herald, vicious gouts of sludge and slurry its outriders. Taller than the house Kallist and Liliana had left behind, it oozed up and through the storm drain, jaws agape in a silent bellow. Thick mud and foul slimes sluiced from its body, and always there remained another layer of corruption beneath, bubbling up to take its place. Its arms were broken boards, its claws bits of stone and rusted nails, the fangs within its cavernous maw ancient and filthy shards of glass. It was the worst of Ravnica's filth, the feces and flotsam and decay, given a terrible, primeval life. And hate.

And hunger.

The sounds within the surrounding structures turned to sudden screams, to pounding feet and slamming doors, as the destitute took what shelter they could from a menace they could not comprehend. In older times, more ordered times, such an abomination would have been met swiftly by the Legion of Wojek, or at least the forces of one of the other great guilds. But today, only those districts that could afford their own defenders, or the exorbitant fees demanded by the Legion's successors, had any such protection. Here, in the dwellings of the poor, the filthy, and the forgotten, no one cared.

Kallist, his waking mind reduced briefly to gibbering horror, reacted without conscious thought. Through instinct alone, he summoned up a shroud of magic even as he charged the abomination, blade held high. Poor a mage as he might be, his desperate illusion should have rendered him briefly invisible. He should have reached the shambling form unseen, gained precious seconds to hack away at it while it remained unaware of his location.

But Kallist was not thinking clearly, and Kallist had never faced a beast such as this. Without eyes within its face, without brain within its skull, the creature possessed no purchase on which his illusions could take hold. Even as he neared, the shambler lashed out with a fist of muck and refuse. Agony flashed across Kallist's

A R I   M A R M E L L

body as a dozen jagged edges traced a dozen lines of deep red through his flesh. He barely had time to note the alleyway dropping away beneath his feet before he slammed hard against a wall across the way. Bright lights flashed before him and the breath rushed from his lungs, leaving him gasping as he slid to the base of the house. Only sheer luck prevented his spinning body from landing across the blade of his own brutal weapon.

Nor was the beast through with him. Even as Kallist settled to earth, propped upright only by the wall, the shambler's maw split apart. First like a snake with jaw unhinged, and then farther still, it gaped wider, impossibly, bonelessly wide. And from that portal to some squalid hell, the creature vomited up a putrescent mass of sewage, a deluge that slammed into Kallist as brutally as the fist itself. It clung to him, choked his lungs, hardened about his joints and glued him to the ground.

Liliana, who had far greater experience dealing with such violations of nature, still found herself stunned. Frantically her gaze flitted from the shambling mass to her fallen companion and back again, conflicting needs tearing at her soul.

The horror started toward her, not even bothering to turn its sightless head in her direction, and the time for indecision was past. Mouthing a funereal chant, lower, more somber, more soul-churning even than that she had voiced in the Bitter End, she raised both hands and circled right, forcing the creature to move ever farther from Kallist if it meant to reach her. The runic swirls tattooed across her back began to glow, a sickly bruise-purple, pulsing in time with her heart.

With agonizing sluggishness, light returned to Kallist's eyes, feeling to his limbs. He saw only smatterings of the wall that rose above him, or the cloud-laden skies beyond, for he could scarcely turn his head. His legs and back began to itch, then burn, as the caustic fluids of the sewage seeped through his clothes. The hardened muck held him fast, and he feared he would simply lay there, helpless, until something awful appeared to claim him, or until he suffocated in the waste's poisonous effluvia.

When he felt the muck begin to break away, first from about his wrists and arms, then from around his neck—when he saw the tips of pale and slender fingers—he nearly sobbed in relief.

"Liliana!" he gasped, sucking in great lungfuls of air, "how did you—"

And then Kallist saw precisely what had rescued him. The blood drained from his face until even his lips were fishbelly-pale, and he could not help but wonder what cost Liliana had paid to cast such a summons.

The common folk of a hundred worlds believed angels were the servants of gods, beings of light who dwelt on high, graceful and beautiful, pure and righteous. The common folk here on Ravnica knew angels as their neighbors, dwellers in the same cities where lived humans and vedalken and viashino.

Nowhere on Ravnica, or on any others of those worlds, had anyone imagined an angel such as this.

She straightened the moment Kallist was free enough to extricate himself, revealed in all her nightmarish glory, this angel that certainly came from nowhere near "on high." Wings of midnight feathers, dull and grim as the blackest crow, blotted out what little sunlight had forced its way to the alley's floor. Corpse-pale skin was girded in leather armors harvested from the hides of demonic and mortal foes alike, and a deceptively dainty fist clutched a jagged, rusted shaft, less a spear than a lightning bolt of forged steel. Where she stood, even the stone-coating mildew died, overcome by the angel's essence of desolation. Beetles, rats, and other crawling things emerged from the sewer grates and the cracks between the cobblestones, desperate to flee her deathly presence, only to wither away at her feet.

Eyes, empty of anything but a need for destruction beyond Kallist's imagining, turned away to gaze with naked lust upon the conflict raging down the street. Sitting upright, digging frantically for his blade, Kallist himself did the same.

Liliana was clearly paying for her decision to send her summoned servant to rescue Kallist. She hovered several feet above the roadway, hands crossed before her at the wrists, surrounded once more in an aura of black and shifting mists. Above her the shambling thing rained down blow after blow, only to recoil each time as its murky "flesh" made contact with the life-sapping energies that cocooned the necromancer. But the thing of the sewers was not alive in the truest sense of the word, and with each strike, its denticulate limbs passed farther through those mists before it was forced to draw back. It could be only a matter of seconds before Liliana's protections failed her utterly.

"What are you waiting for?" Kallist demanded of the power that stood before him, motionless as any statue. Only later would he truly think on the fact that he had shouted at and berated an angel of the darkest depths, and then his hands would shake. For now, he saw only the imminent death of the woman he loved. "She called you here! Help her!"

It turned to him, offered him a smile of terrifying, soul-bruising beauty. Kallist's breath lodged again in his chest, as that seductively murderous face sent blood rushing to his loins even while it turned his stomach, caused his limbs to grow palsied and his head to pound. Only then, spurred on not by Kallist's feeble demands but by a silent call from Liliana, did the angel take to the air, a song of battle and blood and death flowing with heart-rending beauty from her throat. Her wings spread wide, wider, impossibly wide, until they spanned the breadth of the alley, until even the blind shambler, one fist raised over its head to strike, could not help but feel the chill of her shadow. And briefly it shuddered, in whatever primeval ember passed for its soul.

Her voice never wavered, her song never faltered, as the angel dropped upon the animate sewer, spear sinking deep into waste and mud and slime. Where it struck, what was green decayed to brown, brown and grey rotted to black. Bubbles rose to the shambler's surface, popped open with the foulest stench, leaving great, gaping abscesses in its viscous hide.

But the elemental spirit called up by the goblin shamans would not fall so easily. With another silent roar, it turned from the exhausted mage and slashed viciously at its raven-winged tormentor. She rose ten feet higher with a single vicious flap, as swiftly as if yanked by invisible strings. Just as swiftly she dropped once more, plunging her spear into the shambler's head.

It rippled, twisting and shifting, the mud and sludge rearranging themselves. From the front of its head, the glass-toothed maw slid upward to split open at the scalp. It snapped shut with a ferocious clack, locking hard onto the rusty blade. The angel yanked back, attempting to free the weapon, but even her great strength and the mighty flap of her wings could not wrench it loose. And in that moment of distraction, the foul heap reached upward and wrapped the angel in an unbreakable embrace of garbage and nails.

The angel's battle song faltered but did not end. In a grotesque dance, an echo of the spinning celebrants at the Bitter End, they twisted across the roadway, scattering cobblestones before them. Skin split and bruised, sludge flowed and rotted away.

Liliana dropped to the earth with a gasp, the aura of darkness disappearing as her feet touched down. Sweat mingled with the rain that covered her brow and plastered her hair to the sides of her face, but she kept her focus locked on the grappling angel, her lips moving in unheard mantras.

Seeing that she was in no immediate danger, Kallist dived into his pack. Leaving his broadsword momentarily untouched, lying half-covered by the hardened sewage, he pulled from the satchel one of the mechanized crossbows they'd taken from their rather ineffective captors.

Clutching the weapon in his left hand, Kallist slipped a bolt from the small quiver. Even as he placed it in the groove, his thumb traced a rune in the air above the projectile's steel head. The shape took on a substance of its own, hovering in the air above the bolt for two full heartbeats before it faded away into the rain.

For long seconds Kallist aimed, literally holding his breath. If he missed, he wasn't sure he had the energy to repeat the spell. Worse, should his bolt pass through the shambler and hit the angel . . .

The beast turned its back, and Kallist squeezed the trigger, exhaling slowly. The crossbow bucked with a *twang*, hummed as its enchanted gears ratcheted the cord back to receive another bolt. And the projectile itself flashed through the air to sink, without the slightest visible effect, into the living muck.

Again Kallist held his breath. A better mage could have targeted the spell directly, without the need for the bolt to carry it, but Kallist had barely managed the magic at all. Had he somehow bollixed it up? Had the bolt passed straight through, without striking anything solid? Would it even work on a creature without organs or muscles, bone or blood?

So determined was his stare, his reluctance even to blink that his vision blurred with strain and rainwater. Thus, when his enchantment did begin to take hold, he almost missed it. So gradually that it could easily have been his imagination or a trick of the rain-bent light, the shambler's movements slowed. Each step grew more ponderous than the last, and the beast began to teeter on the verge of collapse as its feet struggled to keep up with its forward momentum. Though its strength had diminished not at all, it could not keep pace with the angel's thrashing, and with a burst of black feathers she erupted from its grasp. Her skin was mottled with gangrenous, festering wounds, her left arm hung limp where the bones had cracked. But her voice rose with power to shame the thunder, and in her one good hand she held her spear aloft, as though to sunder the clouds from the sky.

And as her foe reeled backward, trying desperately to keep its balance, she dived.

Slowed to a dull plodding by Kallist's spell, the shambler might as well have tried to outrun the lightning as to dodge the plummeting angel. So terrible was her stroke, the creature's glutinous hide literally opened up before her. Not merely her spear, but the angel herself plowed through the beast, bursting from its back in a spray of rancid mud and filth.

Perhaps pain finally gave the lumbering construct a voice, or perhaps it was simply the rush of air between its sagging maw and the gaping fissure in its torso, but the shambler howled, a terrible sound of sucking mud and raging winds. Fungi and the bones of rats burst through its skin of muck, thrashing wildly, the legs of some horrible, dying vermin. Still, though it collapsed heavily to the roadside, supporting itself on one of its slimy arms, it stubbornly refused to die.

Liliana, also crouched in the roadway, could only hope that it was near enough to death, for she could maintain her summons no longer. With a gasp she released the energies pent up within, allowed herself to relax her almost inhuman concentration. A death-pale face, now painted in sewage, turned questioningly in her direction for just an instant before the angel disappeared, drawn back to whatever lower realm had spawned her.

Kallist didn't know if the cesspit creature was capable of recovering from such a devastating assault, but he wasn't about to wait and find out. Dropping the crossbow, he hefted his great broadsword and charged back down the alley, fully prepared to hack the thing into so many bite-sized morsels to keep it from rising once more.

But Liliana was faster, or at least a great deal nearer. Though her vision blurred and her footsteps faltered, she stepped toward the thrashing monstrosity. It would be some time before she'd dare attempt so potent a summons, yes, but even at her weakest, Liliana Vess held plenty of spells at her beck and call.

Foul fumes of diseased purple flowed from her hands, roiling against the wind. Where they passed, what few molds and random weeds had survived the struggle fell flat. At its strongest, the shambler's animating spirit could have easily withstood the arcane poisons Liliana now pumped into the soaking air, but now, its innards open to the outside, it lacked all such resilience.

Kallist skidded to a halt, sword still upraised, as the creature spasmed. It bellowed once, its final call, and crumbled into mulch, already washing back into the sewers beneath the slow but steady rain.

The tension finally left his body in a sigh of relief as heavy as the buildings looming over him. His shoulders drooped, the tip of his sword screeched against the cobblestones. Kallist opened his mouth to call to Liliana—

And something heavy, flailing, and gnashing its teeth slammed into him from behind.

Kallist toppled, long and powerful fingers on the back of his neck forcing his face down against the bruising roadway. His hand scrabbled for his sword, but even had he found the hilt, he couldn't possibly have delivered an effective stroke. Bright lights flashed once more before his eyes; his lungs and nostrils burned. Blood pounded in his ears, deafening him to the hissing and snarling of the beast on his back.

It deafened him, also, to the sudden twang of the crossbow he'd dropped. The bolt flew wide, but near enough to make its point. The weight vanished from Kallist's back as abruptly as it had appeared, and he raised his aching head in time to see a small shape scurrying back into open drain.

"What . . ." he gasped, trying to catch his breath for the fourth time in minutes, "What was . . ."

"Sewer goblin," Liliana told him, even as she sagged onto the stoop of a nearby home, crossbow dangling from limp fingers. "I don't think they took kindly to us surviving."

Kallist scowled, lowering his head between his knees as he struggled for breath. "What were they doing, anyway? They don't come out in the day, and they certainly don't summon elementals to waylay travelers!"

"Unless they're bribed to," Liliana commented. "Greedy little bastards."

"Semner?"

"Who else? Probably decided to make sure we couldn't follow him, if we managed to get away from his thugs. Even *he's* not stupid enough to assume we're no threat to him, and it wouldn't have been hard to figure out where we'd pass. It's not like we had a lot of routes to choose from."

Kallist opened his mouth to ask another question, snapped his teeth together when he lifted his head and finally got a good look at the woman beside him. Her flesh was pale and clammy, her entire body drenched. Even sitting slumped over as she was, her hands shook with exhaustion.

"You don't look well," Kallist said brilliantly.

"I need to rest," she admitted, and Kallist knew she didn't just mean physically. A summoning such as the one she'd invoked . . . Her essence must be dry as parchment. The swampy earth beneath Avaric was reasonably mana-rich and particularly suited to Liliana's style of magic—it was one of the reasons they'd moved there after falling out with Jace—but they were traveling, slowly but surely, away from it as they headed toward Favarial. Her recovery would take time.

Time that the sudden burst of frenetic drumming from deep within the echoing sewers told them they did not have.

Leaning on one another, each gasping for air and struggling for strength, they rose. One step forward, a second . . .

"Damn it!" Kallist clenched his fists in helpless frustration and failed to notice Liliana's hiss of pain as he squeezed her smaller hand in his. "The little bastards stole the pack!"

Every supply he had brought, every morsel of food, every comfort, had been in the backpack that he left behind after the angel pried him from the clinging sewage. And of that pack, there was no sign at all.

"We could try to get it back," Liliana suggested. "They're just sewer goblins."

It was an empty offer, and they both knew it. Kallist merely shook his head, and the weary couple shuffled their way along the urban chasm, struggling to leave behind the pounding drums, and the foul things that woke to their call.

CHAPTER FIVE

It was hardly one of Ravnica's richest districts. It lacked the impossibly wide avenues, lit by permanent lanterns of mystic lights. It had none of the towers that reached so high the clouds themselves struggled to climb them, nor the sweeping arches and delicate bridges that formed layer upon layer of city, stacked one atop the next until the ground was invisible from the top.

But compared to cities on most other worlds, and certainly compared to the poorer districts such as Avaric, Favarial was lavish to the point of extravagance.

Just as it had done with the hills, the mountains, and the swamps, Ravnica had annexed and absorbed the world's lakes without so much as a hiccup. Favarial was built above the surface of a deep body of fresh water the size of a small sea. The avenues and plazas stood supported by pylons that dug deep into the lake's murky floor, the buildings on great spans supported by those avenues and plazas. Unless one stood at the side of a roadway and deliberately looked over the edge, one might never notice the lake at all. Great bridges connected it to the mainland, allowing travelers and commerce to come and go at will.

Indeed, it was the lake itself that provided most of the region's commerce. The surrounding municipalities purchased much of their fresh water from Favarial, whose River Guild—not one of the true guilds of the past, by any stretch, but powerful enough in its home territory—charged an arm and a leg to keep the rivers flowing. Let a neighbor fail to make a payment and the dams slammed shut.

As this made Favarial an economic powerhouse, it was a popular destination for merchants, shoppers, and travelers alike. Thus, as the weary mages drew nearer their destination, as the skies finally cleared and the sun dried the sodden cobblestones, they found themselves joined by travelers from other communities. First a trickle, and then a veritable deluge as road after road joined the main avenue; travelers on foot, in wagons, on horses or great lizards, even the occasional domesticated wolf. Most were human, in this part of Ravnica, though some few were elves or viashino lizard-men, and none gave Kallist or Liliana a second glance as they took their place at the back of the line.

For two and a half days, the fatigued couple had lived on rainwater and what food was available in the grimy bazaars of the poor neighborhoods through which they'd passed. The gamey taste of ivysnake still clung to Kallist's mouth, possibly because he still had a thin strand of the stuff stuck between two back teeth. The first night they'd been forced to camp in an alley, huddled together against the rain and the garbage, though they'd thankfully reached an area affluent enough to offer an inn on the second night. Between Liliana's lingering exhaustion and the fact that they had precisely two crossbow bolts to their names (the others having been in the stolen pack), Kallist could only give thanks they'd suffered no further attacks in their travels.

And now that they'd finally arrived, as the zeniths of the highest buildings soared into view, Kallist remembered just how woefully unimpressive the district actually was. Yes, the people of the backwaters like Avaric found it imposing, but for a man born to the towering spires of richer neighborhoods, Favarial inspired only a resounding "Eh."

The district's defenses, such as they were, consisted of heavy iron gates at the end of every bridge, and a low wall providing some measure of security from the lake itself. Guards stood post at those gates, jagged halberds and twin-pronged spears ready to repulse an attack that would never come, and otherwise did nothing worthwhile. None bothered to check on or question passing travelers, for what was there to check for?

Shuffle. Step. Wait. Step. Wait. Shuffle. The line inched forward, and Kallist cursed every wasted minute, every pause. When Liliana leaned close and said, "It might be tough, but I could try to call something up to eat our way to the front of the line," he could conjure only a wan smile.

As they neared, the temperature rose, the sun reflecting harshly from the still waters and lingering in an air that showed no interest at all in providing a breeze. It was still preferable to days spent soaking in the mosquito-spawning rain—but not by much. And only as they approached the gate did the din of the inner streets wash over them. Again, not as deafening or oppressive as Kallist had felt in other, larger districts, but after so long in Avaric, it was disconcerting enough.

Hot, loud, bright, and smelly. So self-pityingly miserable was Kallist as he finally passed through the gate, he failed to notice one of the guards staring with abnormal intensity at him and his companion, before the press of the crowd blocked the armored woman from view.

All that said . . . It looked like home to him, at least more so than Avaric ever had. Ornate carvings adorned the columns and high arches of the monolithic buildings—many of which were sculpted from a strange, aquatic-blue stone that gleamed like the lake below—and pennants hung limply from minarets of stone or crystal. The people here were dressed in a variety of bright, jovial colors, commonly seen among the middle classes who wanted to show that they could afford such frivolities as rich and cheerful dyes.

And there were so very, very many of those people, probably at least half as many on this street alone as dwelt in Avaric entire.

Kallist turned to Liliana, his mouth open to make some disparaging comment that she would doubtless find less pithy than he did, and felt a thrill of panic run through him. His hand lashed out, viper-quick, dragging her to a halt. Before she could so much as squawk a protest, he was walking, casually but quickly, off toward one side of the avenue.

"What?" she hissed at him, mouth just beside his ear so that he might hear over the noise of the crowd.

"Probably nothing," he breathed back at her, though he slackened neither his hold nor his pace. "But one of the things I learned in my years with the Consortium was that when a whole gaggle of armed guards starts moving in your direction, you want to make a quick trip elsewhere."

"Is that so?" Liliana tossed her head, as though clearing her hair from her face, and casually glanced back. "So, um . . . What do you do when they start pointing at you and yelling, then?"

"That would be *run*."

They ran, shoving and elbowing their way through the crowds, crowds that seemed determined to meander as leisurely as possible, to cluster in every intersection, to gather thickly in the fugitives' path and to part like a curtain before the pursuing lawmen.

Kallist and Liliana swiftly grew lost in the unfamiliar byways of Favarial. They knew neither where they were going nor how to return to where they'd been. And the guards, who knew every twist and turn, every nook and cranny, gained ground.

They doubled back around blind turns, and the soldiers traced their route. Kallist cloaked them in images of native passersby while sending their own illusory doppelgangers fleeing down distant byways, yet somehow the guards always knew.

So long had it been since Kallist had faced any real danger—Semner and his thugs aside—that his instincts had grown rusty indeed. Otherwise, he might have seen a handful of Semner's people, scattered across lower rooftops and balconies or hiding within the milling crowd, watching for any sign of deception and signaling to the hunting guards.

A time or two, a thug raised a crossbow, tempted by a perfect shot, only to be dissuaded from pulling the trigger by a companion. As long as the spotters remained unseen, the guards shouldered all the risk. Should the shot go wide or draw the attention of whichever of the twosome was not the target, the results could be unpleasant indeed. And so they kept low and silent, serving only as eyes and ears, rather than hands and blades.

Panting hard, sweating like a demon in church, the mages skidded around still another corner and found themselves staring down the length of an avenue. It was much like any other street, covered in cobblestones, lined by shops that stood far taller than they needed to, in pursuit of status and respectability. It also extended abominably, almost impossibly far before any other street or alleyway offered a viable crossroad. Before them, ambling from one establishment to the next, the crowds formed a living wall. Kallist and Liliana exchanged grim glances, and each knew the other's thoughts as clearly as if they'd spoken.

There was no way they could cover the distance before their pursuers caught up with them.

"If you've been waiting to surprise me with a flying spell," Liliana said grimly, "this would be an excellent time."

ARI MARMELL

Kallist frowned bitterly. "Jace, maybe, could do it. I don't have the first clue. What about your—"

She shook her head. "I can hover, but it's not exactly a quick means of escape." She grimaced and turned to face the nearing pursuit. "We can take them, Kallist."

"No. Killing city guards is never worth the repercussions. Trust me, I know."

And then the time for talk was past. The citizens dispersed, blowing leaves scattering before a wind of armor and blades; Kallist and Liliana found themselves surrounded by a hedge of sword and spear.

"Afternoon, officers," Kallist said, a sickly grin plastered to his face. "Is there a problem?"

The man who pushed his way to the front was tall and slender, with an autumn-red mustache drooping over his mouth, and a chin sharp enough to serve as a backup weapon. Human, but perhaps with the faintest trace of elven blood in his ancestry, he wore a sulfur-yellow tabard above a shirt of chain, and a badge of red metal on his left breast in the general shape of a dragon. A mark of rank, probably, but damned if Kallist knew what it meant. Ever since the dissolution of the Legion, every district or aristocrat-employed security force on Ravnica seemed to go whole hog with their own signs and symbols.

"You shouldn't have run," he barked, his breath heavy with arrogance and a few lingering traces of breakfast eggs. "My men and I don't enjoy chasing folk. You've just made things harder for yourselves."

"But we didn't do anything!" Liliana protested, wearing her best wide-eyed, lips-parted, beautifully innocent face. "You frightened us. Of course we ran; we don't even know why you were chasing us!"

She was good, no doubt; many of the guards found themselves lowering their weapons without conscious thought. But their commander, who had seen it all before and laughed at it then, reacted only to laugh at it once more.

"How about that, boys? They didn't do anything. Guess we have to let them go."

The youngest soldier on the squad turned toward his commander with puzzled expression. "Really?"

The older guard rolled his eyes heavenward and cuffed the younger hard across the side of his head.

"We have solid reports," he told the prisoners, "of the two of you causing all manner of ruckus, disturbing the peace, and even assaulting citizens over the course of the last couple of days. You're both under arrest."

"We just passed through the bridge gates no more than an hour ago," Kallist protested. "Check with your own damned guards!"

The commander only shrugged. "They watch hundreds of folk pass in and out every day. Can't be expected to trust their recollections of any specific two, can we?

"But don't worry. If you're telling the truth, we'll get it all sorted out. Won't take more than, oh, I'd say three or four days. Maybe a week on the outside."

Everything clicked into place in Kallist's mind, and he cursed himself for an idiot. The timing on this could be no coincidence. It could only be Semner's work.

But that meant, just maybe, that the guards could point them toward the ugly bastard himself.

"Go along for now!" he hissed under his breath to Liliana, even as he saw her lips begin to twitch.

She peered at him as though he'd gone mad, but allowed herself to relax.

Two of the guards stepped forward to take the broadsword and crossbow. Grumbling, one of them patted down Kallist, searching for other weapons. The other, with a licentious grin, did the same to Liliana. Kallist recognized the brutal gleam in her eyes, and knew that the guard had better make every effort not to run into her again. Then, hands manacled together, surrounded by the entire squad, they found themselves marched down the streets of Favarial.

✳ ✳ ✳ ✳ ✳

"As far as prisons go," Kallist told Liliana some hours later, "I've certainly been in worse."

She glared at him. "If this is supposed to comfort me, may I suggest that you try some other approach? Perhaps try punching me in the jaw. That would probably work better."

"I've also escaped from far worse," he protested.

"That's almost impressive."

"Well, almost thank you."

Their current abode was a drab cell, stone-walled on three sides, with a barred gate on the fourth. One of several identical chambers in the watch-house of Favarial, all of which smelled of lingering sweat, fear, and humanoid wastes, it was probably intended to hold no fewer than a dozen prisoners.

That they were alone in the cell only confirmed that the official reason for their arrest was a sham.

Kallist and Liliana sat on stone cots that were bolted thoroughly to the floor, and the cell's "chamber pot" was nothing more than a tiny hole, far too small for even the thinnest and most desperate prisoner to squeeze through. At the hall's far end, well beyond reach of anyone within the cells, the only exit was guarded by the biggest viashino Kallist had ever seen. Her scales were a dull tan with a snake-like pattern of red and green rings. She wore a custom-formed breastplate of steel, and leaned on . . . Kallist wasn't even sure what to call the ugly weapon: perhaps a morningstar with anger management issues. It was a heavy steel bar as long as a man's leg, one end wrapped in leather, the rest of its span covered in a chaotic forest of spikes and spines and blades. She watched every one of the cells, constant, unblinking.

The prison was, by all normal measures, perfectly designed to provide neither any means of escape nor even the most crude of improvised weaponry.

"Normal measures," of course, had no meaning to its present occupants. Oh, it had wards and sigils to prevent wizards from escaping—but the prison's builders had never thought to contend with mages, with walkers, of Liliana's power.

Obviously, Semner's people hadn't told the squad commander much about whom he was dealing with. If they had, he might have taken more precautions.

If they had, the fact that the mages hadn't escaped already would have warned him that something was very, very wrong.

Kallist and Liliana sat, continuing on occasion to bicker and silently wondering how long they would have to wait. Finally, as night slowly crept up behind the loitering daylight, cudgel in hand, they heard the heavy oaken door to the prison hallway screech open. They moved as one toward the bars so they could see. The officer who had arrested them stepped past the reptilian guard, grinned broadly at both of them, and strode toward the door of their cell.

"I'm Lieutenant Albin," he introduced himself. "And you are . . . ?"

"Not," Kallist answered gruffly.

"Enjoying the accommodations?" the lieutenant asked, refusing to be put off.

"Enjoying the bribe Semner paid you?" Liliana retorted.

Albin's grin didn't falter, but his voice turned hard. "I have no idea what you're talking about," he told them, presumably more for the viashino's benefit than their own. Still, he moved nearer to the cell, so that anything else they might say wouldn't be so easy to overhear.

"Our 'mutual friend,'" the lieutenant began, "seems to think that you might know something that would help him locate his target. Cooperate and I can make your stay here a lot more comfortable; might even get you out of here faster. If not . . ."

A R I   M A R M E L L

"What are you offering?" Kallist asked. Albin smiled once more and stepped closer still so he could whisper, stopping just outside the bars.

It was precisely what they'd been waiting for. Concealed in his fist, Kallist clutched one of the iron bolts that had held the cot to the floor, a bolt that was supposed to be impossible to remove. Kallist had never mastered more than the most rudimentary spells of telekinesis—even Jace hadn't been an expert there—but chipping away at a bit of mortar? That, even he could manage. With a wolfish grin, he dropped into a crouch, stuck his hand through the bars, and shoved the rusty length of metal into Albin's inner thigh.

He and the guard fell back from one another even as Albin's scream echoed through the cells. The bolt vanished up Kallist's sleeve, hidden not merely by cloth but a thin layer of illusion. The lieutenant fell writhing to the floor, hands clasped around the jagged, bleeding wound.

The viashino leaped toward them, weapon raised high, but Kallist and Liliana had already retreated to the back of the cell, beyond her reach. Several long seconds passed as the reptile glared, her tongue flickering in and out, before she knelt and lifted the wounded man as easily as she would a newborn babe.

For a moment more she hesitated, discomfited at the notion of leaving her post. But she would be only a few moments, and the growing pool of blood suggested rather firmly that time was of the essence. She cast one more furious gaze at the prisoners and then vanished through the hall's only door, slamming and barring it behind her.

"Is this enough?" Kallist asked, producing the blood-soaked bolt.

Liliana barely glanced at it. "More than."

"Good. Then let's get out of here before some guard shows up to take her place and we have to kill someone who doesn't deserve it."

By the time anyone else entered the hall, the mages were simply gone, with no evidence they'd ever been present save a few scattered iron bars, and tiny bits of dust that had once mortared those bars in place.

CHAPTER SIX

Lieutenant Albin staggered and limped across the office to slump into his chair. For long moments he simply sat, cursing with every breath as he searched for a position that didn't pull at the bandages on his thigh, didn't send embers flashing through the constant, abominable ache. He cursed the prisoners who'd stabbed him, cursed Semner for getting him involved, cursed the city for not paying him his due and forcing him to accept outside bribes to live the lifestyle he deserved.

He cursed the paperwork on his desk, the forms and requisitions. Hell with 'em; let them wait.

And he cursed the cold draft that wafted beneath the closed door of the office, a draft he felt even through his uniform.

Where in the name of all gods and demons was the draft coming from? His office stood in the heart of the watch-house, far from any exterior exit. Even if every door in the building stood open, no such draft could have wended its way down the passages. And unless some mad deity had reached out and flipped the seasons with the flick of a divine switch, any breeze from outside should've been warm, not this icy breath of winter.

He rose on shaky legs, chair creaking, in time to see the air between him and the door turn black. A swirl of inky fog rose from the stones of the floor, obscuring all vision, all light. The air in the chamber grew colder still, until Albin's terrified gasps steamed in the frigid air, and his teeth chattered like the sound of falling marbles.

Two pinpricks of light, and then two more, formed in the whirling shadows. They glowed sickly yellow, emanating the heat of swift decomposition, as they formed themselves into pairs of eyes that gazed unblinking from opposite ends of the office. Beneath and behind them, the shadows ceased to writhe but instead hung limp, forming the faintest suggestion of long-taloned hands, bulging wings folded close, legs that trailed away into the ethereal birthplace of night.

They drifted forward, impossibly still; Albin could not shake the horrid impression that they hadn't moved at all, that he and the world itself had somehow shifted nearer to them. Fingers that were naught but wisps of deepest darkness reached out, and the corrupt guardsman found himself drawing breath to scream.

"Do not cry out . . ." A gleaming, jagged chasm of a mouth had opened beneath one pair of eyes, but Albin heard no speech in his ears. He felt it in his gut, remembered it from long-forgotten dreams. Though a low whisper, it was nigh deafening, for it was the voice of a thousand restless dead. "Do not cry out, or we shall raze the house of flesh from around your soul, and leave your five disembodied senses to linger, forever helpless, unknown, and unseen in this wretched room."

Albin bit down on the scream welling up in his throat, and all but choked on the blood he drew from his tongue.

From each side, he felt the fingers of the abyss wrap tight about his upper arms. His flesh burned as with the prolonged touch of ice, his vision blurred, his chest and head pounded as though he suffocated.

And then he was moving! Locked in a grip as unbreakable as death, he felt himself sliding backward through the wall itself. A moment of hideous nausea, as the world turned inside out and he felt the rough texture of the stone passing through his flesh, and they were on the other side. The ground dropped away beneath his feet, as he was borne aloft in the bone-crushing and soul-numbing grasp of the shadow things.

His arms were numb, but the icy burn had spread below to his fingers, upward through his chest and shoulders, until he could scarcely draw breath. Higher and higher the spirits carried him, until a wide swath of Ravnica was nothing but a map of intercrossing bridges and roadways below, until wisps of cloud mingled with the wisps of darkness that carried him.

The thing on his left tilted its head, and Albin could swear he heard an obscene chuckle even as it spoke.

"Now, if you wish, you may scream."

But he no longer had the breath.

As swiftly as they'd risen into the cold night air, they dropped again, plummeting into a neighborhood halfway across the district from the watch-house. With a bruising jolt, they stopped at the precise height of an old warehouse down near the lakeside docks, where the buildings were lower and the rooftops flatter. There they waited, hovering several feet from the roof.

And Albin, who had thought he could never again be surprised by anything, gawked at the pair who awaited them. Kallist stood at the very edge, a watch-issue long sword dangling from his fist. Behind him sat Liliana, legs and arms crossed. Her lips moved constantly in a sonorous mantra, and from beneath her closed eyelids leaked faint traces of the same sickly yellow luminescence that defined the features of the shadow-men.

"How was your trip, Lieutenant?" Kallist asked gruffly.

"I—I . . ." The words refused to come to him.

"Yes, I thought so. Let's make this is as simple as we can, Albin. We have questions for you. You're going to answer them, quickly and honestly, or things will get very unpleasant."

The guardsman felt a surge of hope, warm enough to melt through the icy lump in his throat. "If I do, will you let me go? Will you let me live?"

Kallist smiled a sad little smile. "I don't think you understand, Albin. The specters *already killed you*." Slowly, inexorably, he raised the sword, waved it through Albin's arms, his legs, his torso.

The blade touched nothing, nothing at all.

Finally, Albin found the strength to scream. Kallist, tapping the flat of the blade against his leg, waited patiently for him to finish.

"Your body," he said, and his voice was actually gentle, even sympathetic, "is lying on the floor of your office. I imagine it'll be morning before anyone finds it.

"No, Albin, your choice is not whether to help us and live, or refuse us and die. Your choice is to help us and be allowed to pass on—or to refuse, and find your soul given over to the specters for their own amusement."

Twin hisses of lustful pleasure sounded in the dead man's mind, yet they weren't enough to drown out the sound of the necromancer's chant.

And Albin, weeping phantom tears, began to talk.

※ ※ ※ ※ ※

"You sure you're up to this?" Kallist asked in a concerned whisper, for the third time since they'd reached the alley and at least the eighth since they'd set out that morning.

"Kallist?"

"Yes?"

"It would really be a shame if you made me kill you before Semner's men got a fair crack at it."

Yep, Kallist decided. She's up to it.

Summoning two specters from the depths of the void was not, in itself, a difficult feat for her—but sending them to locate Albin and binding his ghost to the physical world for long enough to obtain their answers, that should have been considerably more grueling. Her use of the lieutenant's blood as an anchor and a focus had made all the difference.

Still, she'd spent many of the following hours in rest and meditation. The waters of the lake and nearby shores overflowed with mana, but it was a mana rich with life, ill-suited for her own necromantic magic. She drew what she could from the marshy patches scattered here and there about the shoreline, and even from the fungal patches in Favarial's sewage pipes, and then cast her concentration further still, drawing from Avaric, from other domains much farther distant. She swore it had been enough, but Kallist thought she looked tired even now, though several days had come and gone.

Kallist had pretended to make full use of the time. He'd acquired them new clothes, so they might blend more effectively with the middle-class population.

And then, with that chore done, he'd fretted until Liliana recovered. But however difficult it had been, it had proved absolutely worthwhile.

Semner was indeed using Albin's corrupt guards for more than impeding his rivals; he was using them to conduct his own search. With the aid of Albin's despairing, wailing ghost, Liliana and Kallist had identified most of the lieutenant's crooked operatives, tracking them down at their favorite taverns and gambling halls and brothels. Between their knowledge of the guards' dishonest activities and threats of mystical retribution, they'd convinced the lot of them to continue the hunt, but to report their findings to them, rather than to Semner.

Those findings, delivered by a nervous guard who wasted far too much time begging them not to turn him into something viscous, had finally drawn them to this cramped and malodorous alleyway, across the street from an old tenement building in the district's poorest quarter. The aquamarine walls were cobwebbed with cracks, the arched and peaked windows covered with moldy shutters, the doors bulging from within doorways that had long since shifted several degrees off plumb. For several minutes, now, the pair had watched from the concealing shadows, and had seen nobody—Jace or otherwise—enter or leave the decrepit structure.

"If this isn't just another false sighting," Liliana muttered, "then Jace's standards of living have taken a substantial downturn in the past six months."

Kallist merely shrugged. "Hard to stay unnoticed if you're living it up like a king with no heir."

"Kallist," she asked seriously, "are we even on the right trail? I mean, would Jace even look like himself anymore?"

"I think he would." Kallist furrowed his brow in thought. "Jace is about a hundred times the illusionist I am; he could probably make a mother leonin mistake him for one of her own cubs. But even he can't make himself look like someone else every day, all day. He might use a false image on occasion, if he feels he's in danger, but otherwise—"

A horrible shriek shattered the relative stillness of the evening. From behind the shutters of a top floor window shone a sudden burst of a brilliant and ugly firelight. And then it, and the scream, faded just as swiftly, and the alleyway plunged once more into darkened silence.

"Like now, perhaps." Liliana and Kallist exchanged brief, shocked glances, and then both were charging across the road.

Kallist had just long enough to regret the loss of his broadsword. He missed its solid, comforting weight; the guard-issued longsword with which he'd absconded during their escape just didn't have the same heft. Then there was no time for thinking at all as his shoulder collided with the tenement's outer door. The flimsy planks disintegrated before him, and he found himself pounding up multiple flights of shaky, mold-ridden stairs.

The first story disappeared beneath him, then the second, then more; even the tenements in this damned place were taller than they'd any right to be! The thundering of his footsteps echoed in the stairwell, as though an entire host of trolls followed him up. Doors slammed shut, and he heard the sounds of bolts sliding home, as the people who dwelt within decided it would be wiser to hide from whatever was happening than to step out and investigate it.

As he neared the upper floor, he saw a woman he recognized as one of Semner's thugs. Precisely what had happened to her, Kallist couldn't say, but she lay sprawled across the topmost steps and was only now rousing herself from unconsciousness. Kallist wondered briefly how Semner had tracked Jace here without the aid of the corrupt watchmen, but wasn't about to take the time to inquire. Without so much as breaking stride, he ran his blade through the back of the woman's head as he passed. There would be others to question at a more appropriate time.

At the top of the stairs, Kallist took a heartbeat to orient himself, to determine which of the various doors should lead to the chamber from which he saw the flash of balefire. Then, as with the portal below, Kallist set his shoulder to that door, and the door went away.

And Kallist froze. No matter the urgency, he could not tear his gaze from the room around him. Jace hadn't abandoned his standard of living; he'd simply hidden it.

The chamber beyond occupied a majority of the top floor, someone having knocked out the interior walls that separated one apartment from the next. The remaining walls were pristine, polished to a gleaming oceanic blue; there was no trace inside of the cracks that ran through the old stone without. The carpets were thick, the furniture comfortable and well maintained. A small dining table lay on its side, the tablecloth and dishware scattered about the floor. Even amid the signs of struggle, the scent of incense hung in the air, overpowering the odors of the city.

At the sound of a dull thump, possibly that of a body hitting the floor, Kallist finally shook off his amazement. Striding toward the room from which he had heard that familiar sound, he covered perhaps half the distance when the door was thrown open from within.

For the first time in half a year, Kallist stood face to face with Jace Beleren, the man who had once been his best friend.

They could have been brothers, and in fact had passed as such on one or two occasions during their service with the Infinite Consortium. Less than two inches separated them in height, less than twenty pounds in weight. Perhaps Jace was more clean shaven, Kallist's hair half a shade lighter; not identical, certainly, but very much alike.

Jace, clad in a heavy blue cloak he'd thrown over his bedclothes when first attacked, froze in the doorway, his own eyes as wide as the saucers that had spilled from atop the table.

"You!" Never before had Kallist heard so mundane a word loaded so heavily with bile. "It wasn't enough to steal her from me? Now you want me dead, too?"

Kallist, a small part of whom had briefly been glad to see his old friend, found himself scowling with rekindled rage. "Damn it, Jace, you know better than that! We came to warn you! Not," he added, with a quick glance at the trio of fallen bodies visible through the bedroom doorway, "that you seem to have needed it."

"After all this time, I'm supposed to believe that?" Jace demanded.

"Yes." Kallist squeezed the hilt of his sword until he felt the leather wrappings start to fold. "Now, if you—"

He couldn't breathe; couldn't talk; couldn't think. Kallist froze as though struck by a basilisk's gaze. He felt a fist around his mind, keeping him from moving, from reacting, holding him firmly in place while Jace took the extra few moments he needed. Kallist felt the faintest touch, the legs of skittering spiders across the surface of his dreams.

Kallist gasped in shock and found himself slumped to the floor.

"Damn it, Jace!" Kallist couldn't decide if he wanted to kill or to cry, and settled for an enraged shout. "You swore never to read—"

"We both of us made promises back then, didn't we?" Jace snapped in turn. But the lines of his face had softened. As though forcing himself through rising water, he stepped slowly across the room and extended a hand to help Kallist off the floor.

"I'm sorry." The words were little more than a mutter, and Jace's mouth twisted as though they'd turned sour on his tongue. But still, he said it. "And I believe you," he added, as Kallist hauled himself to his feet on Jace's arm. "But I had to be sure."

"Fine. Whatever. So what happened here?"

Jace shrugged and stepped away, as though even proximity to the man who'd betrayed his trust was painful. "Some men came through my door and window, and tried to kill me."

"And?"

"I didn't let them."

"Was one of them Semner?"

Jace's jaw clenched. "Semner's here?"

"These are his people." Kallist frowned. "If he's not here, there's another attack coming."

"The Consortium send him?"

"I'd imagine so, but I can't be sure. You know Semner's reputation. He'd hire himself out to a warthog if the money was right. We need to get out of here, find someplace a little more secure to figure out our next step."

"And Liliana?" Jace asked softly.

Kallist cried out, cursing himself for ten kinds of idiot. She'd been only a few steps behind him when they left the alleyway. But so distracted had he been by his encounter with Jace, he'd not taken a moment to wonder why she hadn't followed him through the door.

Perfectly on cue, a sudden scream, terrified and clearly feminine, echoed through the stairway.

Months of anger and recrimination vanished. Kallist and Jace stood side by side, the one raising his sword in expert grip, the other focusing his will to deceive the sight or burn the mind of any who would bar his path. Neither could imagine what might draw such a reaction from Liliana, but whatever it was, Kallist intended to visit it thrice over on Semner's beaten corpse.

Kallist reached the open doorway first—and simply folded, falling back into the main room of the apartment, sword tumbling from his fingers. He hadn't seen what hit him, but whatever it was struck hard. His jaw ached, his head pounded, and he could scarcely even see, let alone consider rising to his feet. He spotted a small streak of blood staining the carpet and realized it was his own.

Footsteps behind him, but he could not turn. He saw two pairs of worn and dirty boots, doubtless belonging to more of Semner's thugs, but he couldn't even raise his head. Across the room, he saw Jace retreat several steps, ready to cast any of a score of devastating spells. From the hall beyond the doorway, he heard Liliana's voice cry out his name and then begin to intone another of her dark chants. He gave thanks that she still lived, but still he could not turn.

The pounding in his head grew heavier; the blood rushed in his ears, the lights of the room blinked and flickered. Everything was unfocused, spastic, moving in slow-motion fits and starts.

Semner's men stepped forward, naked blades extended, closing in on Jace.

The first man fell, screaming until his throat bled at the nightmares the mage's spell seared into his conscious mind.

The second was within reach before Jace lashed out. From his outstretched hand, a sky-blue eel wiggled and writhed its way through the air to wrap about the torso and neck of his attacker. Serrated fins sliced into flesh while the beast's jagged maw clamped hard upon the bandit's face, shredding skin and bone, blood and ocular fluids, into a slippery stew that flowed smoothly down its winding throat.

For just a moment, as his vision continued to fade in and out, Kallist dared to hope it might be over.

Jace's eyes grew wide at the sight of some fresh danger in the hall beyond Kallist's fallen form. Kallist saw the mage's mouth moving; saw, as well, a new hesitation, even fear, in his face. Jace took a step back, retreating from whatever was approaching.

The shutters over the window behind him exploded inward at the impact of Semner's boots. Dropping from the roof, the gorillalike mercenary wasn't slowed by the thin planks. He slammed hard into Jace's back, drawing a pained gasp even as the mage fell sprawling.

Kallist struggled to crawl forward, fingers digging into the carpet, but he couldn't make himself move. He heard feet on the floor beside him, recognized Liliana's ankles and her sharp intake of breath.

Jace rolled, coming back to his feet as Semner's dagger cleared its sheath. The first slash barely penetrated Jace's robe. Only the very tip of the blade connected, etching a line of blood across his chest; he gasped and went pale, but his stance never faltered.

Yet in the chaos, Jace allowed the pain of the wound to distract him. Catching Jace off-guard, Semner spun, hauling back his arm as though preparing for another strike, while a second dagger dropped into his left hand from his sleeve. It came up in a short, brutal thrust that his victim never saw coming. Flesh and bone parted, and beneath the merciless edge, a man's heart burst.

For what seemed an infinite instant, silence reigned. Then the room burst with a blinding flash, a blue so blazing it was nearly white. It hovered in the air between the fallen Kallist and the dying Jace, and despite its intensity, it cast no shadow from either.

Kallist screamed; no mere cry of grief or rage, but a terrible, primal yell that drew stunned looks from Semner and Liliana both. Long after his voice should have given out, or his lungs exhausted themselves of breath, he screamed.

He no longer saw the chamber at all. Images, feelings, notions, and dreams that were not his own flooded his mind until it came nigh to bursting, until he could see nothing at all of the world around him. Like an animal driven by pure instinct, he rose from the floor and fled through the gaping doorway, all prior weaknesses and wounds forgotten in a torrent of madness.

How he kept his balance on the unsteady stairs, how many corners he turned, how many passersby he shoved from his path to leave cursing in the streets behind him, he could never have recounted. He ran until the sounds of Favarial subsided, until the walls of another alleyway pinned him from taking one more step.

Still the memories swirled in his head, but finally they began to order themselves, to settle into their proper places, and he could see, and feel, and think—and remember.

Jace Beleren, who had long ago stolen the mind of a man he called friend, who had lived for half a year as Kallist Rhoka, fell to his knees in the refuse of the alley and wept.

CHAPTER SEVEN

For the span of several deep breaths, the enmity between them seemed forgotten as Semner and Liliana both stared through the open doorway, long after the running fellow was well beyond seeing or hearing. And then Semner raised an eyebrow as the necromancer turned to face him, a black blaze of flickering shadows dancing behind her eyes.

"I wouldn't recommend it," he told her, idly flipping the bloody dagger between his fingers. "Not a lot you can do for him now. And me, contract's done. Got no reason to kill you unless you make me." As before, his gaze slid like glistening slugs across her body. "And it'd be such a waste."

Liliana merely glared back at him, any revulsion she felt subsumed by a growing eruption of fury.

Despite himself, Semner began to grow nervous. "I suppose," he continued with a bit less confidence, "I probably ought to cut you down for what you did to my boys. But fact is," and he paused here, long enough to glance around, to be certain that all his men were either dead or at least unconscious, "it just means fewer ways I have to split my fee. I—"

"You idiot!" Liliana finally exploded, jabbing her finger at the thug and murderer as though lecturing a child. "You utter halfwit! What in all the worlds is wrong with you?"

"I—um, what?"

"'She can go, but kill him'?" Liliana parroted back his order from days ago. "What were you thinking?"

"Um, what?" Semner said again, apparently believing it a point worth repeating.

"You were expressly ordered to let both of us live!" She took a single step toward him, and Semner found himself recoiling. "You could have ruined everything!"

"Look, bitch, I know Rhoka's rep! The man's an assassin! I wasn't about to leave him alive to come after . . ." Slowly, comprehension dawned across his brutish face as his brain finally caught up to his ears, panting and wheezing from the unaccustomed exertion.

"How the burning, steaming hell do you know what my instructions were?"

Liliana could only roll her eyes heavenward, as though beseeching the patience of a higher power. "Wow, you really *are* that stupid."

"Listen here, Vess . . ."

"No, I mean it. It would take two of you to be any dumber."

Any reluctance Semner had to killing her outside the bounds of his contract was evaporating like morning dew. "You've just got a smart comment for everything, don't you? If I walk over there and shove this dagger through your skull, you think you'll have a clever answer for that?"

"In this scenario, I'd pretty much be dead, wouldn't I? So unless there's a necromancer hiding in your pocket, that's a really stupid question."

And that, finally, was that. Semner ceased spinning the dagger, allowing it to come to rest pointing directly at Liliana's face. "What I said about killing you being a waste? Nah. I'm going to cut the best parts off of you and take them with me. You think you can summon something up before I start cutting?"

"Now why would I need to summon anything," she asked with a sudden, vicious grin, "when I've got so many friends right here?"

Behind him, the dead bodies of both his victim and one of his own men had dragged themselves forward on bloodless hands. Brittle fingernails snapped against the weight of the corpses; twin trails of blood, already dried and blackened by the touch of Liliana's animating magic, matted and stiffened the shag of what had recently been a clean carpet.

And as Semner finally got wise enough to realize that he should probably be afraid, each of the corpses reached out a hand and clamped a deathless clutch on his calves.

Beneath the implacable strength of the risen dead, cloth and skin parted. Semner screamed, a high-pitched shriek of agony such as he had never known. So tightly did those fingers squeeze, so hard did they press, flesh peeled back from bone, muscle tore from clinging ligaments. For the dead, who feel no pain, it mattered little; to Semner, it mattered a great deal.

His body convulsed, he screamed until his lungs burned for breath. Within the meat of his legs, bony fingers clenched around the muscles of his calves and yanked them away.

The room shook as Semner toppled to the floor. Even had the fall not knocked the breath from his lungs, his scream would still have faded. Already too much blood had pumped from the gaping holes in his legs; his skin had paled, his vision begun to fade.

Mercifully, perhaps more mercifully than Semner deserved, he lost consciousness before the dead men hauled their way along his body and began to tear away pieces far more vital than his calves.

For long moments Liliana watched the carnage without expression, neither turning away when bits of Semner's body were exposed to light for the very first time, nor flinching at the terrible wet sound of ripping flesh. Only when Semner was well and truly dead did she drop her concentration, allowing the bodies to fall motionless once more, to return to the eternal rest they had earned.

She stepped across the blood-drenched carpet, her boots squelching with every stride. Gently she knelt beside the body of Kallist—the real Kallist, not the man with whom she'd spent so many months, complicit in his efforts to deceive himself—and squeezed his shoulder.

"I'm sorry it had to happen this way. You didn't deserve this." It was a whisper, and barely that. But it was all she felt entitled to offer.

For several minutes she remained, her head hanging, hair hovering mere inches above the slowly drying blood. She wanted, if only briefly, to abandon the whole endeavor. To fly from the room and down the stairs. To find Jace, to ensure she hadn't harmed him with the soul-numbing magic that had knocked him flat in the doorway, to comfort and to hold him during what could only be a terrifying, *horribly* painful time.

But she did none of these things. Instead, she rose to her feet and turned to face the darkest corner of the room, the magic already flowing through her. Perhaps when all this was over—assuming they were victorious, assuming Jace survived—she might find a way to make it up to him. But not now.

"Find him," she ordered. "He can't have gone far. But stay out of sight. Let me know if it looks like he's not going to recover; otherwise, just ensure nothing happens to him until he returns."

The darkness seemed to nod once, to blink with faintly glowing eyes, and was gone, leaving Liliana alone with the dead.

CHAPTER EIGHT

He remembered.

He remembered his childhood, before the dreams and visions came. He remembered discovering that the voices in his head were not his own, but belonged to the people around him. He remembered Kallist and Tezzeret, Baltrice and Gemreth, and of course Liliana.

He remembered pain. He remembered the rape of Kallist's mind and the loss of his own.

He remembered the day it began, three years ago and more.

✳ ✳ ✳ ✳ ✳

This was Ravnica, Ravnica as she was meant to be.

The district of Dravhoc flowed down the shallow mountainside like an avalanche trapped in amber, bewitching beneath the brilliant sun. Like the peak itself, it stretched down to the banks of the wide and rushing river, even occupying a few of the smaller isles and outcroppings that rose amid the breakwaters.

Great buildings of gleaming marble lined the wide byways, their roofs sharply sloped, their eaves adorned by figures both abstract and concrete, angelic and diabolical. Some were only a handful of stories tall, but many more towered impossibly, monolithically into the infinite sky, artificial mountains protruding from the real, or jutting from the deep waters below, casting endless shadows. From broad cupolas and needle-thin spires, a network of bridges spanned the district, a web-work of roadways that never deigned to touch the earth. Towering statues of forgotten gods and heroes stood amid broad plazas or supported heavy walkways on their pseudo-divine shoulders. Some few of the highest towers had no earthly roots at all, but were held aloft by mighty spans of stone, connecting them to other structures with more mundane foundations.

Far below ran roads cobbled in stone that never lost its sheen, from the narrowest twisting side streets to avenues so broad that a crossbow shot from one curb could not kill a man standing on the other. One of those grand avenues ran straight down the side of the mountain, terrace to terrace, level to level, providing those at the top a clear and astonishing view all the way down to the river. Along it strode an array of sentience unheard of on other worlds: Humans and elves, goblins and viashino, loxodons and centaurs, even angels and the occasional ghost rubbed shoulders or scurried from one another's paths. So many words, so many scents, combined into a voice and an ambiance greater than the sum of its parts, an atmosphere that was, among all the cities of the Multiverse, absolutely unique.

This was Ravnica at her richest—but even here she was slowly dying, just a tiny bit more every day since the guilds fell. She was beautiful still, but beneath her expert makeup she was an aged courtesan, growing ever more sickly and infirm. And whether the city would recover from the travails of the past generation to rise once more into something greater, or whether she would collapse under her own weight, even the farthest-sighted oracles would not say.

Near the uppermost levels, in the midst of that broad and sloping avenue, Jace Beleren sat beneath a parasol at an open air café called Heavenly Ambrosias and sipped a glass of cold mint tea. Though his hair was perhaps a few inches longer than the current fashion, and he eschewed a full beard in favor of a clean-shaven jaw, he looked every inch the Ravnican aristocrat. His garb was of the finest cloths and leathers, dyed not in the bright and garish hues of the middle classes, so desperate to show off, but in the somber but much richer colors of the truly affluent. His fine tunic and pants of supple suede were both midnight blue, his vest a black so deep one could almost have fallen into it. But most magnificent was his cloak, a flowing liquid hue that could have been a sliver of the darkest oceanic depths. The buttons and clasps of vest and cloak—and there were many of them, as befit the current styles—were all of burnished silver and boasted an array of symbols that looked arcane and mysterious to the uninitiated but were in fact utterly meaningless. Jace just thought they looked nice.

Across from him, drinking something Jace couldn't pronounce but that certainly packed more of a punch than his own mint tea, was—well, not a friend, exactly, but close enough. Rulan was clad much like Jace himself, though he preferred deep reds and purples to Jace's unrelenting blue and black. And unlike Jace, Rulan boasted a full, tidily trimmed beard.

A beard that, at the moment, had captured a bit of the foam from Rulan's alcoholic whatever-it-was. Jace didn't point it out.

". . . half of what's left," Rulan said, continuing the thought he'd begun before taking a heavy swig. Casually, he passed a small coin purse across the table. Jace lifted it, scowled at its weight—or, more accurately, the lack thereof.

"Half?" he asked doubtfully. "Really?"

"Half," Rulan confirmed. "And that's all the accounts, under all your names, put together."

The scowl grew, if anything, darker than the outfit beneath it. Jace took a moment to look out over the wall of the terrace to the glistening waters far, far below.

"Maybe you ought to be charging me less of a commission, then," he offered.

Rulan snickered and took another deep gulp of his drink—a drink that Jace, reluctantly, was paying for. "You find another banker willing to keep accounts in four different districts, under four different names, and see what sort of deal he'll offer you." He belched once, covering his mouth with the back of a well manicured hand, and then frowned. "Berrim," he said more seriously—for that was the name by which he knew his young client, the name under which Jace did all his business in Dravhoc—"you know I'm giving you a damned good deal already."

"Yeah, I know."

"Then I suggest," Rulan said, rising to his feet, "that you consider either a somewhat less extravagant lifestyle or a somewhat more extravagant income." He bowed once, with an almost ludicrous flourish, and left his bemused companion to pay the tab.

Swirling a mouthful of tea around his tongue, Jace lifted the coin purse, let it sit in the palm of his hand. Half? He was going to have to find another "patron," and none too swiftly. He'd always been careful about how much he demanded, how heavily he wielded the secrets that he found so easy to acquire, but he wondered now if perhaps he hadn't been too conservative with his latest mark. Grumbling to himself in a very un-aristocratic manner, he turned his gaze once more to the river below. He always found it calming, but today it offered minimal comfort. Perhaps . . .

A surge of fear from the other customers of the café, a tide of emotion Jace could sense without effort, was his only warning. Instincts born partly of experience, and partly ingrained in his mind and soul as his birthright, had him toppling sideways in his chair and ducking under the heavy table before his conscious mind even identified the threat. A blast of searing fire roared from the heavens and sprayed across the stone under which he huddled. His lungs felt seared by the heated air, and he smelled the tips of his hair burning away.

Still, the table was broad, and the air obscured with smoke. If his attacker hadn't seen him duck underneath, he might do well simply to wait, to remain hidden and allow the authorities to deal with whatever was going on. Dravhoc was, after all, wealthy enough to employ patrols of the Cloud-Winged Guard. An organization made up of a few surviving remnants of what had once been the Legion of Wojek, former keepers of Ravnica's law and order, they boasted a reputation for dealing with lawbreakers swiftly, efficiently, and permanently. Let them risk life and limb confronting whatever had hurled fire at him.

Between the crackling of nearby potted plants that had ignited in the conflagration, and the pounding feet and panicked screams of the fleeing bystanders, Jace heard something new, the sound of claws clacking across the tabletop above him. *Something had ridden the fire to earth.*

Muttering a handful of curses, he tensed. The Cloud-Winged Guard's numbers were few, and the districts they patrolled quite large. If something was hunting him in the plaza, waiting for their unpredictable response was no longer an option.

Glancing over his shoulder, he measured the distance to the nearest exit, wanting desperately to run. He might make it but without knowing what was clawing its way across the table, or how far it might chase him, he certainly wouldn't have bet what little money he had left on his chances.

A quartet of Jaces lunged from beneath the table, each sprinting in a different direction to take cover beneath or behind some other flame-resistant obstruction, this one a pillar, that one another table. The thing that had skittered across the stone watched all four. Its ears lay back in confusion, and it stretched its mouth wide to utter an angry hiss that was the crackle of a dozen bonfires.

It might have been a cat, this thing, had it not been roughly the size of a hunting dog—and had it not been made entirely of a living, semi-solid flame.

Moving in concert, all four images of Jace leaned out from cover. From their outstretched hands, a thick spray of freezing water arced across the open-air café to drench the fiery predator. A geyser of steam shot into the air, and the hiss of water-on-fire almost drowned out the terrified shriek of the elemental.

Then the images, the water, even the steam were gone. The feline creature stood, utterly confused, its animalistic mind unable to grasp the concept of illusion.

And Jace—the real Jace, who had been none of the four phantoms but wrapped tight in an illusion of invisibility—rose up before the distracted, disoriented beast, hauled back a fist and struck.

No mere punch, this, but a devastating blow of mystical force. Telekinesis had never been among Jace's stronger skills—the lifting of a simple fork or the opening of a distant window took everything he had—but manipulation of himself? That came far more easily. More than easily enough, with a few seconds of preparation and a surge of mana, to augment the strength of his own harms, to reach out and violently flip the table.

The flaming beast flew from the tabletop to sail dozens of feet through the air—clear over the protective wall that marked the edge of the terrace, plummeting from sight. Jace didn't know how many levels of Dravhoc it might have dropped, or whether the fall would be sufficient to kill it, but he knew he intended to be well gone before it could return.

Φ

For an instant, Jace cast his senses outward, peering behind walls, around corners, over ledges. But his cursory examination failed to locate the wizard who had summoned the beast, and he wasn't about to hang around for a prolonged search. The singed hem of his cloak swirling dramatically, Jace moved at a brisk walk toward the café's exit, trying hard to peer around him in every direction at once, and wondered just who he'd managed to piss off this time.

※ ※ ※ ※ ※

Two levels above, near the very peak of the mountain, a man stood within the high, arched confines of a tower window. He stared down, not with the naked eye, but through a peculiar crystalline device, globes within globes. Within its confines, he watched the events of the café unfold, lowering the sphere only when Jace Beleren swept from the open patio and into the bustling avenues.

And still he waited, until he was joined several moments later by a woman, taller than he, broader of shoulder, with a shock of ash-gray hair that made her appear far older than her years.

"Not a bad performance," he said to her without preamble. "He survived your firecat easily enough, my dear."

"Bah." She shrugged, leaning against the side of the massive window frame. "I'm not impressed. Decent reaction time, and I won't deny he's got power. But we've rejected recruits who performed a lot better."

"We have. But then, we're not after Jace Beleren for his reaction time or even his illusions, are we?

"We'll see how he performs for Gemreth. And then we'll decide if we can make Jace Beleren who, and what, we need him to be."

※ ※ ※ ※ ※

To Jace's paranoid and worry-addled mind, every insect flitting in the darkness was the eye of an enemy;

every echo the footsteps of an unseen stalker creeping across the cobblestones; every stranger an assassin set to grab him from behind; every overhanging banner a noose that hungered for his neck. He trod the roads, the alleys, and the broad steps of the descending avenues as swiftly as he dared, jumping at every sound, peering suspiciously at every shadow, until he finally reached his destination.

What Jace called home was a modest three-room flat, located in one of Dravhoc's lowest tiers, where the scents of the river filled the humid air with a vaguely fishy aroma and the cost of living was only moderately outrageous. It was cheaper than anywhere else in the extravagant quarter, yes, but its proximity to the shore and the tiny islands beyond filled Jace with a sense of security. Jace had never understood, and none of his teachers had satisfactorily explained, why the magics of the mind were best and most efficiently empowered by the mana that drifted and flowed within the waters of the many worlds; he knew only that it was so.

With a sigh of profound relief, Jace slammed his door behind him, leaning briefly against it and trying to calm himself. That he'd made many enemies throughout the past few years was no surprise at all, considering how he'd supported his preferred lifestyle. That any of them could have found him so exposed, however, was worrisome in the extreme. He turned, locking the door's four deadbolts. Without lighting a lantern, he tossed his cloak haphazardly over an old coat rack, stepped into the next room, and collapsed into bed without bothering to get undressed. He'd deal with the rumples and wrinkles in the morning; right now he just needed time to relax, to meditate on the mana flowing through the currents beyond the shore.

Despite his nervous energy, he was asleep within minutes, wrapped in peculiar and disturbing dreams wherein he tried to bribe a giant cat not to spit fire at him, only to find he couldn't afford the beast's asking price. He ran from the predator, calling for help, as embers rained from the sky.

And then he was awake, screaming at the terrible pain that throbbed in his chest.

Craning his head until his neck ached, Jace stared at the horrid shape squatting atop his torso. Only scarcely visible in the dark of the chamber, it stood on four legs that jutted obscenely from its sides like those of an insect. Two more appendages emerged from its shoulders to clutch at his collar. Its head was that of a jolly, almost cherubic old man, which stood in stark contrast to the wicked stinger at its tail, dripping with Jace's own blood.

"What—" Jace froze in mid-question, his jaw clenching tight as his body spasmed with a new surge of pain. "What do—?" He couldn't seem to force out the question.

"You tell me, mind-reader," the demon hissed in a voice that quivered with palsy.

"I—I can't!" He could barely concentrate enough to speak, let alone read its mind.

"You will! Tell me why I am here, Jace Beleren, and what I wish from you, and I will provide respite from this pain. Fail and the poison shall run its course!"

Jace scarcely even reacted to the use of his name, though he'd never done business in Dravhoc as anyone but Berrim, and never revealed the name "Jace" to anyone since he'd arrived on the sprawling, urban world of Ravnica. He struggled to rise, to throw the terrible thing away from him, but the last of his strength was drowning swiftly beneath the toxin's spreading burn.

He wanted to cry out, to scream, to rail against the unfairness of it all, but he did none of these. Squeezing shut his eyes, clenching his jaw until his teeth ached, he forced himself to calm.

Long moments passed and the pain grew steadily worse, but Jace remained focused and stared down at the creature once more. Scarcely visible even in the darkened room, his eyes began to glow.

"Your master, your summoner, is a mage called Gemreth," he told the demon through trembling lips. "You were told that *his* master, called Tezzeret, wants to meet me. The First Vineyard, an hour after dusk tomorrow." Even through the pain, Jace felt his anger growing, burning away the worst of his weakness. "This was a test!" he accused his vile attacker.

"A test indeed, Jace Beleren. And you have passed." The horrific vermin skittered off him and made for the window.

"Antidote . . ." he croaked, his throat dry with agony.

Somehow, the inhuman creature shrugged. "Poison's not lethal," it cackled at him as it scurried over the sill. "You'll be fine in an hour or two."

Jace watched it go, the rage and humiliation burning within him as fiercely as the poison itself. He fell back on his mattress, struggled to find his center, to focus on the rushing, mana-rich waters. And then, through his pain, through his confusion, through his lingering fear, he began to cast a spell far simpler than mind reading.

❋ ❋ ❋ ❋ ❋

He waited nearby, this mage called Gemreth, sitting beside a fruit-vendor's stand and crunching contentedly on a honey-apple. His salt-and-pepper beard was thick and bushy, rather than neatly trimmed, but otherwise he appeared every inch the rich and stylish citizen of Dravhoc, draped in multiple layers of tunics and coats of rich crimson and black. And he smiled, taking a last bite of the candied fruit, as his pet came scurrying around the corner, clinging to the walls and windowsills.

For a few moments they conversed, the minuscule demon hanging just above the wizard's shoulder. Only then, with an upraised hand, did Gemreth dismiss the abomination back whence it came. Picking a bit of peel from between his teeth, he strode away, merging with the nighttime traffic.

Above him, all but invisible in the darkened sky, its dragonfly wings fluttering in unnatural silence, a tiny insect-winged cloud sprite followed in his wake.

* * * * *

Not all the wealthy neighborhoods of Ravnica were quite so dramatic as Dravhoc, of course. That particular district might cling to a mountainside like a tired explorer, but much of Ravnica was covered not in great peaks, shining lakes, or thick swamps, but gently rolling plains. In the center of one of the largest was the district Ovitzia—and in the center of Ovitzia stood a number of manors, among the largest that Ravnica had to offer. And it was to one of these, up the gleaming steps from the curb, across the broad marble porch to the front door, that Jace's steps carried him early the next day.

The woman who opened the door in response to his tug upon the bell was clearly no servant. She wore a gown of the finest white gossamer over a snug slip of woven gold, a perfect match for the waist-length hair swept back behind her pointed ears. Her reed-slender figure could most generously be described as "boyish," but her features were soft and elegant, and she moved with what Jace could only think a purely feminine grace.

"Berrim!" She greeted him warmly, with an affectionate if shallow embrace, a purely chaste kiss upon his right cheek.

"Hello, Emmara," Jace smiled broadly in turn. "I hope you don't mind me dropping by unannounced like this."

"Oh, don't be stupid," she told him. "You know I don't. What brings you to Ovitzia?"

"Nothing in particular," Jace hedged. "Just fluttering around the city, and realized I wasn't accomplishing anything, so I figured I'd visit a friend."

"Well, of course you weren't. Isn't it you humans who always say 'Fluttery will get you nowhere'?"

Jace blinked, replaying the sentence to be sure he heard what he thought he had. "Funny," he finally deadpanned. "How long have you been saving that one?"

"Oh, years at least," Emmara replied cheerfully. "Elves have that kind of time, you know."

Both broke into large grins then, and she stepped back, allowing her visitor to pass through the doorway and into her home.

"Home" indeed. "Private indoor villa" was more accurate.

Emmara Tandris was the first mage Jace had met in Ravnica, and still one of the most confusing. Rumor had it she was once a member in good standing of the Selesnya Conclave, but if so, her own fortunes clearly hadn't faded with the influence of the guilds. In public, she made little if any show of her powers. But in private, just about everything with her was magic, even when it would have been just as simple, or even more so, by mundane efforts.

No living servants occupied her vast manor. Instead, various constructs—some of white marble, some of stuffing and woven fabric in the form of various humanoids and woodland animals—fetched and cleaned and gathered at her need. Most were tiny, barely able to carry a platter full of food, though a few were as large as the elf herself. Animating these "dolls" was only one of her many hobbies, and in fact Emmara had been known to take commissions for these mindless servants as a means of bolstering her income.

Even stranger, the manor boasted no internal walls, no doors, no stairs. A vast array of marble columns, carved to resemble the bark of trees, stood at intervals throughout the domicile. They supported the weight of the floors above but did little to separate one chamber from another; in fact, "chambers" pretty much began and ended where Emmara said they did. If one required privacy, one simply adjourned to a different story—and that, too, involved the many pillars. For while each seemed solid enough, if one chose, one could physically step inside (a feeling that Jace could only liken to walking through a wall of the fatty accumulation scraped from the top of a pot of heavy stew), and emerge from any of the other pillars, anywhere in the manor.

It was, all things considered, a bizarre way to live, and far more space than any one human could ever have needed. But Jace had long since given up trying to understand the mindset of elves in general—and Emmara was stranger than most.

For an hour or so, they sat at her dining table and talked about the current state of affairs: which districts were struggling to survive since the guilds disintegrated, which were thriving, which were ripped by political or criminal warfare. The little constructs scuttled about, appearing from various pillars with carafes of juices, nectars, and fruit teas, and plates of elven pastries that liquefied in the mouth, requiring no chewing at all.

Finally, when the glasses stood mostly empty, the plate of sweets far lighter than it had been, Emmara's eyes turned serious and flickered first to the vague singeing on Jace's face, which he had thought was light enough to go unnoticed, and then to the stinging scab on his chest, which should have been hidden by his tunic and vest.

"I can take care of those, if you'd like," she offered.

Jace smiled but shook his head. "They're really pretty minor. Don't hurt much at all, anymore."

"So are you going to tell me why you're really here, Berrim? I adore your company, and you know you're always welcome, but it's a pretty long walk to take by accident."

Jace lifted the last of his drink, sloshed it around in his glass and replaced it untouched. "What do you know about a man called 'Tezzeret'?" he asked finally.

The elf raised an eyebrow. "I know that if you got those wounds tussling with him or his people, you haven't run nearly far enough."

"Well . . . Yes and no." Then, "Tezzeret?" he prompted again.

Emmara shook her head. "Have you heard of an organization called the Infinite Consortium?"

"I think I've heard the name."

"Before the guilds fell, it was just another mercantile organization, but now? Now I wouldn't be surprised, some day, to see it become a political body.

"The Consortium, in brief, is one of those 'We'll find anything and sell it to anybody for the right price' operations. I'm sure they deal in contraband at least as often as legal goods, but nobody could prove it before, and there's nobody left to prove it now."

"I see," Jace muttered, leaning back and wondering what they wanted with him.

"The thing is," Emmara cautioned, "they really do seem able to get *anything*, or at least so I've heard in some of the more esoteric circles I frequent. Including objects and creatures of pretty potent mystical power, and things that don't seem to come from anywhere I've ever heard of."

Jace straightened, his brow furrowed. He'd never quite figured out if Emmara knew of the existence of other worlds, of planeswalkers and the Blind Eternities. Most folk, even most wizards, did not.

Regardless, reading between the lines, Jace had a whole new understanding why they called themselves the "Infinite Consortium."

"And Tezzeret?" he pressed. "He's their leader?"

She nodded. "Not their first, as I understand it. But certainly he's in charge now.

"He's a mage, Berrim, a potent one. And word is he's not the only one in the group, either. I've never heard of them hurting people without cause, but they'd definitely make unpleasant enemies. What's your interest in them, exactly?"

Jace offered a smile that was meant to be reassuring, but instead implied that something wasn't sitting still in his stomach. "They want to meet with me. And their invitation was, um, fairly insistent. Not to mention impolite."

Emmara frowned, and she leaned forward intently, placing one slender hand atop Jace's own. "Do you want me to come with you?"

Jace had to swallow a lump in his throat, truly moved by the elf's offer. Smiling a genuine smile now, he took her hand in his. "Thank you," he said, and meant those words more than he had in a very long time. "But no, I won't ask you to put yourself in that sort of danger. Besides, if they wanted me dead, they had plenty of opportunity when they delivered their 'invitation.'"

It was all very chivalric, quite noble, and utterly full of crap. If Jace thought for one moment that Emmara's presence would mean the difference between life and death, he'd have accepted without thinking twice. But Tezzeret's emissary had said nothing about inviting a third party, and Jace felt—given the sort of violence they were capable of just as a test—that offending them by bringing backup was probably the more dangerous option.

He spent another hour in the elven wizard's company, learning a bit more about the Infinite Consortium, and then, as the conversation meandered in that way that even the most serious conversations do, about the nature of those elven pastries, the difficulty in getting certain fruits, and just how badly the unseasonably hot summer had damaged the crop.

The sun slowly dropped below the district's tallest buildings, sending fingers of shadow reaching out to take the entire neighborhood in their grasp, and Jace knew he'd better be moving on. Thanking Emmara once more, he took a moment to steady his nerves, and stepped out onto the street.

His instincts still screamed at him to run, to avoid this meeting like a plague-rat, but Jace wasn't quite prepared to give up life in Dravhoc. And if he was going to stay, he couldn't afford to make Tezzeret an enemy. Besides, he really wanted to know how they knew who he was, what he could do, when nobody else on Ravnica did.

But that didn't mean he had to play the game they'd dealt him, not when he could take a peek at their hand. Jace concentrated briefly as he wandered down the streets of Ovitzia and waited for his summoned faerie spy to respond.

CHAPTER NINE

The First Vineyard was so called because it had stood in the same spot since before Ravnica grew up around it. (Or at least, so the tavern-keeper claimed. None of the nature-oriented guilds had ever confirmed his claim, but then, they'd never denied it either.) It was a crowded establishment, quite popular with wine connoisseurs and simple drunkards alike. It appeared, from the outside, to be little more than a long hall, its walls made up of logs and tree trunks of species no longer to be found within a thousand leagues. Most of the crowd bustling in and out of the shop was interested simply in buying bottles, jugs, barrels, or other containers of refreshment to take home with them. In the back of the building, however, near the stairs to the cellar, a smattering of tables stood to allow a few customers to sit and enjoy their drinks without delay.

At the table farthest to the back, two figures waited for a third who, it seemed, wasn't going to show. Goblets sat before them, largely untouched despite the fine bouquet of the wine within. On the left was a woman larger than most laborers. Even seated, she was clearly over six feet in height and broad-shouldered as a small ogre. Her features were flat, her eyes some dull hue that appeared gray in the dim lighting of the shop, but her ashen hair marked her as the woman who had ruined Jace's afternoon at the café.

Her companion was almost as tall as she, but far more slender, with the chiseled musculature of a smith. His hair was a dull blond, hanging just below his shoulders. Something that straddled the line between stubble and a thin beard, depending on the lighting and how generous an observer chose to be, covered his cheeks and jaw. Of greatest note, however, was the hand in which he held his goblet, for it was not flesh and bone at all, but constructed of some murky, non-reflective metal. It was the only overt sign that Tezzeret, master of the Infinite Consortium, was far, far more than he appeared.

Both were clad in dark leathers—hers smooth and supple, his covered with a vast array of buckles and pockets—and neither looked particularly pleased, despite the fine vintage that sat before them. The man grumbled something unpleasant into his goblet.

"I told you, boss," she said to him simply.

"Bah. It makes no sense, Baltrice." Tezzeret's voice was low, gravelly; it carried despite the din of the surrounding patrons. "He passed Gemreth's test. He knew when and where."

Baltrice shrugged, an impressive gesture given her prodigious shoulders. "So he's a coward. He's too afraid to take the opportunity you've offered. He's weak."

"So it seems," he replied, shaking his head. "He could have done so much for us."

"Maybe." She didn't sound convinced. "We going to let him live?"

"Hmm. Probably—he doesn't know enough to hurt us—but let me think it over." He sighed. "Be a dear and deal with the tab, would you? I believe I'd like to get out of here, give Paldor the bad news, discuss who else he might want in his cell."

The odd pair departed the First Vineyard and, despite the late hour, began the long journey home through the endless winding streets.

✣ ✣ ✣ ✣ ✣

A sprawling complex of half a dozen buildings, linked by aboveground bridges and belowground tunnels, the headquarters of the Consortium's Ravnica cell stood at the eastern edge of the Rubblefield. The neighborhood's name dated back to the day, many years gone, when it had been utterly laid waste by a summoned siege wurm; but the district, so long ignored, had finally begun to recover in recent years. Valuable property, good location, and cheap prices attracted a veritable flood of investors once the restrictions on new construction had fallen along with the guilds. Rubblefield, despite its name, was on the verge of a renaissance and the Consortium was one of its greatest investors.

The travelers were perhaps half a block from the first of the Consortium buildings when a cloaked and hooded figure stepped from a tiny alley to block their path. At first, it could simply have been coincidence; Rubblefield, though not yet thriving, was certainly not as depopulated as once it had been, and this man could be just another passerby. But when he stepped to one side, blocking them as they tried to move around him, he became far more.

"If you're here to rob us," the woman Baltrice said with a nasty grin on her face, "thank you. I could use the entertainment."

"I'm not here to rob you," the figure said, lowering his hood to reveal a young, clean-shaven face. "I'm here to meet with you. I just wanted to make it very clear that you're not the only ones who can play games."

Baltrice scowled, but her companion, after a brief widening of the eyes, suddenly laughed aloud. "Don't you see, my dear?" he said in reply to her puzzled stare. "This is Jace Beleren."

ARI MARMELL

Even though he already knew that they knew, Jace flinched at the sound of his real name. "And that would make you Tezzeret?"

"It would." He raised his artificial hand in something between a wave and a salute. Jace narrowed his eyes, unable to identify the strange, oddly dull metal.

"I don't like it, boss," Baltrice growled, unconcerned that Jace could hear her clearly. "How'd he find the complex?"

"My dear, that's what he does." His smile faded, grew thoughtful. "Very well, Beleren. You've quite made your point. Shall we find somewhere to talk? The taverns around here aren't remotely the equal of the Vineyard, but they should do."

"You mean you're not going to invite me in?" Jace asked mockingly.

"Not yet, Beleren. Not yet . . ."

※ ※ ※ ※ ※

Jace wasn't even sure what the tavern was called since he'd been too busy trying to keep one eye on each of his newfound companions. He did note that, as Tezzeret had promised, it was clearly no First Vineyard. The customers, clad in an even mix of the garish hues of the middle classes and the monotones of the lower, were scattered across an array of tables of a dozen different styles and shapes. Built as it was so near the edge of the Rubblefield, Jace guessed that much of the tavern had been salvaged from that expanse of ruin. Tezzeret and Baltrice ordered nothing more than small mugs of a light but flavorful beer. Jace, who'd eaten nothing today but Emmara's pastries, added a small bowl of cheese-and-sausage dumplings to his order.

"All right," Jace began, once they'd ordered. "What—"

Tezzeret interrupted with a raised hand, which clutched a peculiar device in its metallic palm. A pyramid of strange metal, neither the odd substance of the false hand nor any of the more mundane alloys with which Jace was familiar, it boasted a number of tiny holes, and shuddered faintly with the clicking and turning of miniature gears within.

Taking the object with his left hand—a hand of normal flesh, that one—he held it out toward Jace. "Speak into the device, please," he asked.

Puzzled, Jace furrowed his brow. "What should I say?"

Tezzeret smiled. "That'll do nicely." He placed the device in the center of the table, and seemed content to wait.

The clicking and thumping of the device grew louder, faster, until the entire table vibrated. And then the mechanism reached some predetermined threshold, and the sounds faded entirely, except for a faint background hum.

All the sounds faded—not merely those of the device, but the hubbub of the tavern, and the noises of the city beyond as Ravnica's nocturnal citizens went about their business in the darkened streets. Jace gawked at Tezzeret, unbelieving.

"It matches sounds," the other explained, "and nullifies them. That's why it needed a sample of your voice. We've already provided ours. Noises from without, unless they're really loud, cannot reach us—and our own voices, assuming you don't feel the need to start screaming at the top of your lungs, cannot be heard by any beyond the table."

"Handy," Jace said, attempting to cloak his amazement in sarcasm and failing miserably.

"It is." Tezzeret gestured melodramatically, placing his artificial hand to his chest. "Before we go any further," he continued, "I must apologize for the manner in which you were invited to meet us here. I realize that it must have been both disorienting and perhaps a tad uncomfortable."

"To say the least," Jace muttered.

"It was also, however, quite necessary. The Consortium employs only the best, and we succeed at what we do because we admit only the best. We had to be sure that you fit the bill."

"And?"

"And we're here, are we not?"

"What if I hadn't passed?"

Tezzeret said nothing. Baltrice grinned and shrugged. "Probably best none of us know." She extended a hand across the table. "No hard feelings, hey?"

Jace watched the hand as though it were a viper, then raised his gaze to meet her own and allowed just a taste of his own power to gleam in his eyes. "I'll let you know," he intoned deeply, "after I decide if I like what I hear tonight well enough."

Yeah, that's right! You bastards aren't the only ones who can be all dramatic and sanctimonious!

Baltrice snarled and dropped her hand, but Jace was gratified to see her tense. Tezzeret merely chuckled.

"I must assume," the blond mage continued a moment later, "that you've taken the time to learn a bit about us?"

Jace nodded slowly. "Tezzeret, mage and artificer of no small skill, and leader of an organization of no small reach." Tezzeret bowed his head in acknowledgment. "You," Jace said, turning to Baltrice briefly and then looking away as though dismissing her outright, "I haven't heard of."

He pretended to ignore both the snarl across the table and the gurgle in his stomach. Maybe baiting her wasn't the best idea . . .

"As far as I can tell," Jace said, choosing his words carefully, "the Infinite Consortium, at its heart, is a mercantile guild. You acquire or buy items here and sell them there, where they're a lot more valuable."

Time to put the head in the dragon's maw. "And frequently, I'm guessing, 'here' and 'there' aren't on the same world at all. You're a walker, Tezzeret, or have one working for you."

Tezzeret smiled, and actually applauded briefly. "Bravo. See, Baltrice, I told you he'd figure it out. Anything else, Beleren?"

Jace looked down at the table, fiddling with the wood, idly drawing a finger over and over across an old scrape. He chewed his lip, as though trying to build up the nerve to say something. For a moment, Tezzeret waited patiently, but slowly his lips began to curl downward, his own fingers to drum on the tabletop.

But that was fine. They'd given Jace the time to gather his concentration, to focus his mind. And using those gathered energies, Jace Beleren—who was never happy with, and unaccustomed to having, only part of the answers—*pushed*. Tezzeret rocked back in his seat as he felt the younger man peering through the windows of his mind, on the surface at first, but threatening to dive ever deeper.

"I know you weren't the Consortium's first master," Jace continued, voice puzzled. "What I don't understand is how one steals an entire organization. And from . . ."

The entire table jumped, threatening to split down the middle beneath the impact of Tezzeret's metal hand. He leaned across the wood, ignoring the spilled beer, and Jace quailed beneath his gaze as though it were a physical weight. Baltrice stood, and fire—not mere "anger," but literal flames—burned in her pupils and across the palms of her hands. She leaned forward, murder evident in her scowl, but a swift gesture from Tezzeret held her back.

Through it all, the customers at the other tables continued to drink, unaware of the volcano ready to erupt in their midst.

"I know that it's been some time since you had any formal training," Tezzeret growled, "so let me offer you a brief lesson. You may be accustomed to wading through men's thoughts without consequence, Beleren, and you may be confident in your knowledge that few mages share your gift for reading minds. But any mage with the slightest knowledge of mind magics can sense your intrusion, even if we cannot duplicate it. And we *do not care for it.*"

Slowly Tezzeret leaned back; Baltrice sat, albeit far more reluctantly. "You get this one free, Beleren, as you didn't understand the rules. But make no mistake. Try that again on me, or any of mine, and I'll kill you, no matter how useful you might be."

Jace, though he wished he'd heeded his first instincts to run, kept his face impassive as he nodded.

"To answer your prior question," Tezzeret continued, voice as calm as though nothing untoward had occurred, "I do, indeed, possess the Spark, as does Baltrice. The Infinite Consortium boasts more planeswalkers than any other organization I'm aware of, on any world."

"And how many would that be?" Jace asked, trying to sound casual.

"If you accept my offer," Tezzeret said seriously, "you'll make five. Plus three more I can hire for certain jobs but who aren't true members of the Consortium."

Ah. And now we come to it, at last.

Jace didn't bother to ask why they might want him. He knew well the value of his magics, in particular the rarity of his telepathic proficiency. Nor did he wonder, any longer, how Tezzeret knew of him; a man with his resources, spanning multiple worlds, wouldn't need to read minds to learn just about anything he could ever want to know.

What he asked, then, was, "Why would I want to join you? I'm pretty comfortable as I am."

"Are you really?" Tezzeret asked, and there was no masking the disdain in his voice. "Blackmailing the rich and foolish by threatening to spread their deepest secrets? What was the last one, Beleren? Lord Delvekkian and his Deriab-root addiction? And for keeping that little secret, he paid, what, a few hundred-weight of gold?"

Jace didn't even start this time, just shook his head at the extent of Tezzeret's sources.

"And when your funds run out, then what? Another rich fool? Living secret to secret and threat to threat, until finally you push one of them farther than he's willing to go? A bad way to live, Beleren. A shameful one. And frankly, one unworthy of your skills."

"I make do," Jace muttered defensively, but he could feel his cheeks flush, the truth behind the words stinging worse than Gemreth's demon.

"You make do," the artificer parroted. "But nothing more. You obtain nothing. Accomplish nothing. And you, Jace Beleren, have far too much potential to live a life that comes to nothing.

"You ask why you should join with me. Perhaps because you want the opportunity to make a living—a real living—that allows you to live comfortably without hopping from one depraved miser to another. Because you want to earn the respect of others, men and women who would hold you in awe based on who you are and what you've done, rather than because of what you hold over them.

"And because a part of you knows, even if you haven't admitted it, that your skills are stagnating here. You have power, Beleren, including an instinctive grasp of magics that few others can master, but you're letting it wither. Working for the Infinite Consortium, I guarantee you the opportunity to exercise those abilities, to stretch them far beyond your current boundaries, to learn from others."

Jace glanced up, his pulse quickening. "There are those among you who can teach me?" He hadn't had a true mentor in years, not since . . .

A R I   M A R M E L L

"Not thought-reading, no. But other magics of the mind, such as your illusions, your clairvoyance? Absolutely. I myself know a bit about such things, though they're not my primary area of study. I could teach you myself, when time allows. And if I cannot instruct you in reading minds, at least I can help you build up your discipline, do so more effectively."

"You would do that?"

"Beleren, to have potential such as yours on my side, I would do far more."

"Just make sure you do better than his last teacher," Baltrice snickered.

The sharp crack of ceramic sounded across the table as the mug shattered in Jace's grip. His entire body so rigid he could have been having a seizure, he glared at the woman through abruptly glowing eyes, and if wishes could kill, it would have been her neck breaking within his fist.

"What do you—How . . .?" He could scarcely choke the words past the bile in his throat.

"Come on, Beleren," Baltrice smirked at him. "Everything else we know about, you didn't think we'd learn about Alhammarret? I understand you're still a wanted man in every town within a hundred miles of Silmot's Crossing."

His vision veiled in a film of red rage, Jace found himself standing, his chair lying on the floor behind him. "You will never utter that name again."

His voice was surprisingly steady, not even raised in a shout, but it slashed across the table, an invisible blade. Baltrice recognized the danger sign for what it was, but backing down before this upstart never entered her mind. She, too, rose to her feet. The air above the table grew heavy with tension and gathering magic. Tezzeret said nothing, perhaps curious to see if one would relent.

And Jace turned away, unwilling to start a fight he wasn't certain he could win. Eyes downcast and cheeks slightly flushed, he straightened his chair and slumped into it. And yet, one corner of his mouth turned up, as though he'd succeeded in making some sort of point.

With an ugly, arrogant grin, Baltrice too returned to her seat.

"Baltrice," Tezzeret announced, "wait for me outside."

The woman's smile died as though shot with a crossbow. "What? Boss, I—"

"I need to speak with Beleren, and I need to do it without the two of you threatening each other every second breath."

Jace's jaw twitched as he suppressed a smirk.

"But, boss, what if he—"

"I am in no danger from Beleren. Go."

With a scowl and a final flash of fire in her eyes, Baltrice left the table, hoping against hope that the little bastard would be stupid enough to refuse Tezzeret's offer. Then, given what he already knew, the boss would have no choice but to let her . . .

So wrapped up was Baltrice, daydreaming about what she'd do to Jace Beleren if she had the opportunity, that it didn't occur to her until later:

For the life of her, she could no longer remember the name of Jace's mentor.

CHAPTER TEN

They sat on the floor, across from one another, in the heart of a cavernous room beneath the Rubblefield complex. Here, though the perimeter of the room was stone, the internal walls were thin metal, divided into slats that folded and slid along runners in the ceiling. With those walls, the huge room could be divided into any number of smaller chambers, of almost any shape. At the moment, the "sub-room" was an almost perfect oval.

"I assume I don't need to tell you," Tezzeret began after several moments of silence, "just how potent a tool telepathy can be to an organization such as mine?"

"No," Jace said with a faint grin. "I think I can figure that much out on my own."

"Excellent. You've passed the 'not a raving imbecile' test. I—"

"What I don't understand," Jace said, "is why you don't already have access to such powers. I know my talents are rare, but they're not *that* rare! Are they?"

"You wouldn't think so," Tezzeret admitted, "but you'd be surprised. In all my years, I've come across only two mind-readers other than yourself. One of them is dead, and the other—well, isn't available for employment."

"But—"

"I've tried building a great many devices," the artificer said, refusing to be interrupted again. "Tools to accomplish what I and my agents cannot. They, too, came up short. I built two crowns of etherium—"

"Etherium?" Jace repeated.

Tezzeret clenched his jaw at yet another interruption and held up his artificial hand. "Etherium. A powerful, magic-rich alloy capable of holding any manner of enchantments. It's also exceedingly rare, since the secret of its creation is all but lost across the entire Multiverse. This hand is probably more valuable than the entirety of this district."

Jace's eyes widened.

"As I was saying, then," the artificer continued, "two crowns of etherium, one of which should have allowed me to read the thoughts of anyone wearing the other. We managed to communicate, speaking as though we were right beside one another across a distance of miles, but I could never read any thought he didn't choose to project. I constructed a sarcophagus of needles and tubes, into which a subject could be placed. I managed to extract the equivalent of two words' worth of thoughts before the machine turned the subject's brain into so much gargoyle guano."

Jace shuddered.

"I even once fashioned a crystalline chamber," Tezzeret reminisced, eyes glazing slightly, "capable of storing the memories and personality of a dying man. But the mechanism that should have allowed communication with the mind within failed to work, and since I'd built it purely for communication, I hadn't included any means of placing him into a new living body. So I've no idea how much of him was actually preserved.

"My point," he concluded sharply, coming back to himself with a sudden blink and glaring at Jace as though somehow he were at fault for the digression, "is that, though it comes so easily to you, and though it's a form of magic wizards have been struggling to develop for ages, it's actually proven to be a very rare, and very elusive, talent.

"And that means that we've got to get you, Beleren, as skilled as we possibly can."

"I can live with that," Jace said with a fierce grin.

"I'm so glad to hear it. Talk to me."

"What?"

"Talk to me." Tezzeret leaned forward, fists on the table. "Not with your mouth. With your mind."

For an instant, Jace stared. Tezzeret wasn't certain if he was concentrating, or had somehow failed to understand the command. Then . . .

Like so? The words formed directly in Tezzeret's mind. Jace's lips, his tongue, his teeth moved not at all.

"Precisely like that," Tezzeret told him. "I see you've done this before."

It's come in useful a time or two.

"How far?"

Jace shrugged. "Never tried it beyond a few yards or so," he said aloud

"We'll have to test that." He pointed a metal finger at the door. "There are several guards in the hallway outside. Can you communicate with them?"

"Hm. I've never tried this outside line of sight, except with people I already know."

"Then now's a good time to start."

A moment more, and Jace's eyes grew wide, his jaw muscles twitching as though he were repressing a shout. And then the door flew open and a trio of guards dashed inside with the clatter of mail, hands reaching for their swords. The room abruptly smelled of oiled steel.

"Boss?" one asked. "Is everything okay? I thought I heard someone shouting for us."

"And you?" Tezzeret demanded of the other two.

Both shook their heads. "Heard nothing, boss."

"It's a start." Tezzeret pointed to the first guard, though he'd turned back toward Jace. "Can you include him and me both?"

"What?"

"Can you talk to both of us like this?"

Jace frowned, felt his fists clenching. *I'm . . . not sure.*

Tezzeret glanced at the guard, who nodded. "I heard him, boss."

"Excellent!"

The young mage was tiring swiftly, in mind if not in muscle. The sensation was like trying to juggle two balls in two different directions.

And then his entire body slumped when Tezzeret pointed to another guard. "All three of us, now."

It took Jace half a dozen tries before the second guard also heard his mental "voice." His entire forehead was drenched in sweat, his mouth had gone dry as a mummified bone, and his vision was starting to blur. Tezzeret and the guards were starting to look as fuzzy as their reflections in the steel walls.

"No!" He shook his head—a bad idea, as the world spun around him—as Tezzeret pointed to yet a third guard. "Tezzeret, I can't. I—"

"You are not giving up already!" Tezzeret shouted, face slowly going red. "I won't allow it!"

"But . . . But I—"

"Do it! Damn you, Beleren, do it now!"

Jace cast out his voice to encompass all four men. His head felt as though it would split open, like someone had stuck a pry bar through his skull and was steadily working it this way and that.

"Pathetic," Tezzeret said, rising to his feet. Yet despite his tone, he reached out and helped Jace to sit back against the wall, rather than leaving him curled on the floor. "I expect better of you, Beleren. I know you're capable of more than this." He turned to the nearest guard even as he rose. "Once he's recovered, he's not

ARI MARMELL

to leave until he's proven to you that he can at least still reach three of you. I want to know—and I want him to know—that pain and prior failures aren't going to hold him back or undo what we've accomplished."

"You got it, boss."

And then the artificer was gone, leaving the guards to stare at Jace, shuddering not merely with pain but with the shame of his first failure.

✳ ✳ ✳ ✳ ✳

Jace lay upon the thick down mattress, arms crossed behind his head, and stared up at the ceiling—just as he had for many hours, across the span of many days. And he wondered, not for the first time, if Tezzeret's notion of an exciting life was perhaps different from his own. Oh, he had his training sessions to look forward to. They weren't anyone's definition of "fun," and he might have thought seriously about leaving after that first one—except that they worked! Damned if, in mere days, he hadn't felt his mind expanding, comprehending spells he'd never used before, honing even familiar incantations like a razor's edge.

But those sessions were sporadic, occurring when Tezzeret had the time to devote from his many other concerns on many other worlds. And Jace was getting more than a little bored.

The Consortium's Ravnica compound was, or so Tezzeret had claimed, one of the nicest on all the various worlds. Jace had passed through marble-walled and lushly carpeted halls, kitchens capable of producing foods that nearly qualified as magic in their own right, libraries boasting any book one could ask for, on any topic one might imagine. His own domicile was a suite of chambers, complete with self-lighting chandeliers that glowed without heat; a fireplace that never ceased burning and produced either warmth or cold depending on Jace's command; even a few mechanical servants that were, if not as efficient or unobtrusive as Emmara's animate dolls, still more than capable of accomplishing whatever menial task Jace might assign them.

For the first few days, it was a paradise, and Jace luxuriated in an opulence he'd never known.

After *two months* of dwelling here with nothing to do but peruse said libraries or wander about the streets of Ravnica (something he'd been quite capable of doing before the Consortium, thank you very much), he was ready for a change of pace. But neither Tezzeret himself nor the Ravnica cell's own leader seemed ready to actually let him do anything.

That local lieutenant was an enormously corpulent, sausage-fingered fellow with untamed hair and beard of darkest black, so short and squat that Jace briefly wondered if he might be one of the mythical dwarves he'd heard of on other worlds. Paldor was his name—"Almost like platter," he would say at every opportunity, hands clutching at one roll of fat or another, "so really, could my parents have expected anything else?" It was a joke nobody found funny, but that never stopped him from repeating it.

He seemed a friendly enough sort, willing to show Jace around and introduce him to other members of the cell, but Jace wondered more than once just how black a dark side the man must possess to have worked his way so high in Tezzeret's ranks. But of course, Paldor's duties prevented him from spending more than a few moments on that project, and again Jace found himself left to his own devices. He couldn't really even go out to make new acquaintances on his own, for he didn't know how many members of the Ravnica cell knew about the Consortium's other-worldly nature—and he wasn't about to spill Tezzeret's secrets to the uninitiated.

And so he lay on his back, and stared, and brooded, and fell into that state of half-sleep that comes so often when one lies abed with nothing important to do. And it took him several moments of trying to rouse himself to realize that someone was pounding upon his door.

Jace took a moment to tug the worst of the wrinkles from his tunic, flung open the door, and found himself staring, or so it appeared, into a slightly warped mirror.

"You'd be Jace," the man suggested.

Jace blinked eloquently in response.

"I'm Kallist. Kallist Rhoka. And you need to either learn to sleep more lightly, or get yourself a doorbell. Preferably one taken from a church steeple."

"Um," Jace added.

"We've been summoned. We're supposed to be in Paldor's office in, oh, five minutes ago. So unless your magic can either take us back in time, or summon up a really potent excuse, I suggest we get moving."

Still not entirely certain what was happening, Jace got moving.

Although he'd long since mastered the ins and outs of the complex, he allowed the other man to lead, and took the time to study his guide. Now that he was a bit more awake and a lot more alert, Jace realized that they did not look quite so similar as his drowsy senses had at first suggested. Kallist was clad in black leather armor over deep blue padding; a match to Jace's own wardrobe in color, perhaps, but certainly not in style. The various blades that Kallist wore about his person also indicated a wide gulf between their skill sets. Still, they could certainly pass as relatives, a fact that Jace refused utterly to dismiss as coincidence.

Kallist clearly knew the winding halls at least as well as Jace, since he hesitated not at all in his path to Paldor's office, on the uppermost floor of the highest building. Jace was vaguely irritated, as he panted for breath at the top of the stairs, to note that Kallist wasn't even winded.

The office, which Kallist entered after giving a perfunctory knock, was massive but largely empty. A mahogany desk, quite broad but abnormally short to accommodate Paldor's stature, occupied the far end of the room. Several chairs stood scattered before it, arranged in a vague semicircle. On the wall above hung a large clock of brass gears and heavy pendulums. The rightmost wall was one large window, staring out over the slowly recovering expanse of Rubblefield, while the leftmost . . .

On the leftmost wall was a peculiar contraption, smaller but far more complex than the clock itself. Tubes of glass twined over and about each other; some seemed almost to be tied in knots, bending at impossible angles. Through those pipes flowed long wisps of . . . It wasn't smoke, exactly, for no smoke had ever been so unnatural a color. It took Jace long moments to recognized the æther of the Blind Eternities, for never had he seen so much as a puff of that stuff in the physical world. He couldn't begin to imagine what purpose the device might serve.

But that was it, the entirety of the office. A great deal of space, with little purpose except, perhaps, to show visitors that Paldor could afford to waste a great deal of space.

Paldor looked up from the desk, scowled briefly at the clock above his head, and then took several steps away from the desk. Today he wore what Jace would politely have called a robe, and more honestly thought of as a tent. It was wine-purple and made Paldor look like a giant, bearded grape. "Welcome to your first assignment, Beleren," he said.

No response. It required a not-so-subtle "Ahem!" from Paldor to draw his attention from the peculiar contraption on the wall.

"Ah, yes," Jace said. "Sorry."

Paldor scowled, then shook his head. "You've heard the name Ronia Hesset?"

"I've come across it. Who is she?"

"The head of a merchant family who used to have connections with the Orzhov and with whom the

Consortium has had a great many dealings since the guilds went away. She's even dealt with Tezzeret himself, a time or two. She doesn't know our true nature—or the existence of other worlds at all, for that matter—but beyond that, she knows as much of the Infinite Consortium as any outsider.

"Of late, more than a few of our transactions with her House have come up short. For a time, Tezzeret and I were willing to let it go; most mercantile sects have one or two corrupt members, and she's done well enough by us in the past. But now she's claiming to have lost an entire payment, several thousand-weight of gold in value. Since this happened at roughly the same time one of her relatives paid off an outstanding debt to certain criminal interests . . . Well, you can see how this might arouse my suspicions."

"Aroused?" Kallist muttered from behind. "I'd say they were downright seduced."

"Your job," Paldor told Jace, "should be simple enough for a man of your talents. We'd hoped to just have you meet with Hesset, read her that way, but she's refused any meetings for the next few days. 'Too busy,' she says. And frankly, Tezzeret's not willing to wait. You'll accompany Rhoka into Hesset's home. He gets you into her house; you then get into her mind. If she's truly innocent and ignorant of these thefts, you'll return to me, and I'll deal with it. If she's behind them, as I suspect at this point she must be, you tell Kallist and he makes an example of her."

Jace frowned sharply. He'd known that working for the Consortium would require what he preferred to think of as "extra-legal" activities. Hell, that was how he'd lived for years. But murder?

His gut churning, Jace opened his mouth to object, or perhaps simply to inform Paldor that this had all been a mistake, that service to Tezzeret wasn't for him after all.

The words wouldn't come. The fear of losing out on all the opportunities Tezzeret had promised—to say nothing of the far greater fear of what these people would do to him if he backed out now—formed a fist around his vocal cords that he could not shake. And so, feeling a new sickness in his gut that definitely wasn't fear, he nodded.

"Kallist's already studied the layout of Hesset manor," Paldor told them. "You shouldn't have much difficulty."

Jace turned. "And you've chosen Kallist in particular since you have a swordsman who happens to greatly resemble your only mind-reader—or a mind-reader who resembles your best swordsman," he added with a sarcastic smirk at Kallist, "and you might just be interested in seeing how well they work together on a simple assignment, so you know if you can take advantage of their resemblance down the road."

Paldor grinned broadly. "Now you're thinking like a member of the Consortium. Now get moving." Paldor twisted in his seat and lifted an oddly shaped tube-and-funnel contraption from the wall. No magic, here, but a simple speaking device, designed with perfect acoustics to carry his voice to the room beneath. "Captain," he said, grinning at Jace and Kallist, "please have a pair of Hesset Estate servant's uniforms made ready for Rhoka and Beleren . . ."

Jace didn't have to be a mind-reader to tell, from the sound of Kallist's groan, that he wasn't going to like the outfit.

And that was pretty much that. They gave Jace half an hour to change—into a horrible set of livery, with canary yellow leggings and deep red tunic—and to gather what supplies he felt he might need, admonished him to trust his partner when he asked if he could have some time to memorize the layout of the estate, and then they were on their way.

"I feel like a fruit salad," Jace said to Kallist as they made their way out of the Rubblefield.

"Tell me about it. I'm afraid to look down at my feet, for fear of burning my eyes out of my skull."

Silence for a time, as the pair made their way toward the Hesset property. Jace found at least some relief in the fact that much of the district was middle-class, so he and Kallist weren't even the most garish people on the streets.

"This operation," Jace commented as they finally approached the outer wall of the estate, "seems a bit half-assed. Wouldn't it have made more sense to wait for a more social opportunity to have me read Hesset's mind, rather than break into her house?"

"Probably," Kallist admitted. "Tezzeret's got a pouch of jade arriving in two days; surprise shipment, something that another cell just got hold of. Other people, outside the Consortium, have begun spreading rumors about our losses in dealing with Hesset's people. He really wants the matter settled—and blatantly so—before there's any risk of losing the jade to someone who decides those rumors mean we're vulnerable."

"Got it." Then, exercising a sudden suspicion, Jace added, "I've never before met a planeswalker who preferred blades to spells."

"You still haven't. I've worked with enough of your kind, Tezzeret included, to have a pretty good idea of what's really out there. But no, I wouldn't know a spell from a spittoon."

And then they were there, and further conversation would have to wait.

The outer wall of the estate proved no trouble at all. Jace cast his sight out and beyond the wall, watching until neither guard nor dog nor drake was present. Once it was clear, Kallist tossed a rope—enchanted to grab hold without need of a hook—and they were up and over, Jace somewhat less gracefully.

"That's a handy trick," Kallist whispered to him once they stood within the grounds. "Maybe I should learn a spell or two."

Jace's reply wasn't even a whisper; it sounded only within Kallist's mind. *Perhaps you should.*

Kallist started, gave Jace a look the mage couldn't begin to interpret, and led the way forward.

Traversing the grounds gave them no more trouble than had the wall. Between Kallist's trained senses and Jace's supernatural ones, they sensed the approach of any guard or beast, and took appropriate cover behind one of the estate's various hedges or trees. Still, a pair of great hounds, tugging their keeper along by the leather leash, nearly discovered them. The topiary behind which they crouched might block the eyes of the men, but not the noses of the dogs. Even as Kallist reached for his blades, cursing the inevitable racket, he noticed Jace muttering under his breath. And without the slightest pause, the hounds passed them by.

"What did . . .?"

When Jace answered, he spoke aloud once more. "Most people think of illusions only as sight or sound. It's harder to do smells, but if you know what you're doing . . ."

Kallist grinned. "You have got to teach me how to do that. But, uh. . . Try not to do that too often, all right? That mind-speaking-thing is weird."

The front door proved but a momentary obstacle. Kallist fiddled with the lock as Jace kept watch, and while Kallist seemed to be doing more cursing than actual manipulating, the device did eventually pop open with a dull snap. Jace allowed his vision to go unfocused, examined the door and the entryway for magical alarms, but if any were indeed present, they were of a sort he couldn't recognize.

"Should it really be this easy?" Jace asked as they softly closed the door behind them.

The other shrugged. "Well, I don't normally have someone with me who can see through walls or plug up dog snouts at thirty feet," he whispered. "So I'd expect it to be easier."

A few moments passed as they made their way through darkened halls.

"Should it really be *this* easy?" Jace pressed again, after the third hallway that boasted no guards at all.

"No," Kallist whispered with a sigh, "probably not."

The manor was fairly typical, as manors went. Lots of halls with many rooms to each side; nice carpeting and fancy paintings in fancier frames; a collection of chandeliers, fireplaces, sweeping stairs, and dining tables that were all far larger than necessity dictated. The strong scent of rose petals wafted along the corridors, and Jace couldn't tell if it came naturally from the many vases that decorated the various mantles and shelves, or if a touch of magic were involved. The utter lack of dust or dirt, however, was certainly magical, since even the most obsessive maid could not have done so perfect a job.

Once, and once only, Kallist and Jace had to duck into a small alcove as they heard the footsteps of heavy boots approaching. They watched a trio of guards, all armed and armored as though they were truly knights marching to war, pass their shadowed shelter and disappear down the hall. Not a one of them bothered even to glance left or right as they walked their patrol.

Jace and Kallist shared a suspicious look, shrugged in unison, and continued toward the stairs.

Still nobody interfered, and within a matter of moments, they found themselves outside what Kallist swore was the bedchamber of Ronia Hesset herself. Slowly and steadily he reached for the doorknob, only to freeze as Jace's hand latched onto his own.

"What?" Kallist hissed. "Don't you need to see her to get into her mind?"

"Since I don't know her well, yeah," Jace nodded. "But . . . I don't know. Shouldn't we oil the hinges or something? What if the door squeaks?"

Kallist's lips quirked in a larval grin. "Jace, as a thief, you make an excellent wizard."

"What?"

"Tell me what you notice about this door."

"Well, it's heavy wood. Crystal doorknob. Opens inward . . . Oh."

"Yeah. 'Oh.'"

"Why don't we just crack open the door, then?"

"Why don't we?"

Kallist gently turned the knob, and then shoved swiftly to minimize the duration of any noise the door might indeed have made. It opened only a few inches, enough so that he could reach the hinges on the inside—but as it happened, the door didn't squeak at all. Far more slowly, he inched it open farther, until both men could look into the opulent chamber.

Even in the faint moonlight trickling through the window, they could make out a towering wardrobe, a large canopied bed with silken sheets, and a form wrapped in the blankets.

"Ready?" Kallist breathed, barely even a whisper.

Jace nodded. *Please,* he thought to himself, begged the Multiverse at large, *let her be innocent.* Then he and Kallist could leave, and neither Ronia Hesset nor any part of Jace's soul would die tonight . . .

Jace stared at the sleeping form, spent several nerve-wracking moments gathering his focus, and found himself strolling the byways of someone else's mind.

CHAPTER ELEVEN

With a gasp, Jace was back in his own head.

"Well," Kallist asked. "Is she guilty?"

"I can't say for certain, but I'd imagine so," Jace murmured sadly.

Kallist blinked. "What do you mean, you can't say?"

"That's not her beneath those covers. It's one of her guards, wide awake, and there are more on the way. Kallist, they knew we were coming!"

"That would seem to suggest some amount of guilt," Kallist said dryly. "I—"

Afterward, Jace was never sure if he'd sensed a flash of the decoy's intentions through some lingering strand of his telepathic link, or if he'd just seen movement from the corner of his eye. In either case, he yanked Kallist aside with both hands as a crossbow twanged from within the room. The bolt flashed through the tiny crack of the open door, punching with alarming accuracy through the spot formerly occupied by Kallist's skull.

"Kind of you," Kallist offered, reaching out with a foot to hook the door and draw it near enough to slam shut.

"You just remember this on my birthday," Jace found himself saying, more than a little stunned at his own composure.

The other chuckled softly and then drew Jace into a small side corridor, where they'd be at least momentarily hidden from anyone coming up the stairs or from the room. They both half expected the door to come flying open, but apparently the guard within was content to wait for reinforcements. "All right, Jace. Do we start hunting for her? It'll be a lot harder, now they know we're here."

Jace didn't know why Kallist was deferring to him, but he shook his head. "No. I have no idea why we haven't heard the tromp of running guards already, but they could be here any second. Better we get word of what's happened back to Paldor. He can arrange for her to fall off a bridge or something some other day."

And he can get someone else to do it!

Though his expression remained too bland for Jace to tell if he agreed or was simply following along, Kallist nodded. "All right. Then let's get the hell out of here."

They stepped from the corridor, and the swordsman took a moment to draw his largest blade—a nasty broadsword, serrated along the length of one edge—and drive the pommel hard into the bedroom's doorknob. The crystal shattered, and Jace heard the crunch of the mechanism within.

In response to Jace's questioning look, Kallist shrugged. "One guard stuck in the bedroom is a guard not standing between us and the door."

They were off, moving along the hall, down the stairs, hugging the walls and shadows in what both recognized as a feeble attempt to remain unseen. Jace felt that every step they took, every breath, every heartbeat was a gong announcing their presence to all and sundry.

At the bottom of the stairs, Kallist instantly dropped into a crouch, broadsword in one hand, long poniard in the other. Jace froze for a split second, wondering what his companion had heard. And then the guards were on top of them.

There were three of them, appearing from doorways near the base of the stairs: a man and two women, all of whom looked enough alike to suggest they were related. Chain hauberks, short-handled axes, close-cropped black hair, and vicious scowls were identical across all three, and they moved with an expert precision intimating not merely a high degree of skill, but long practice fighting as a unit.

They fanned out, the man and one of the women moving to each side of the stairs; the third came up the middle, axe weaving a hypnotic pattern in the air.

Jace threw a writhing, razor-finned eel in her face.

It wasn't real, but against an untrained mind, its phantasmal nature made no difference; fear was fear, and pain was most assuredly pain.

She screamed and fell back, thrashing at the phantasm and just about braining herself with her own axe in the process.

Her comrades hesitated, torn between rushing to her aid and carving her attacker into stew meat. Kallist hesitated not at all. With a leap he was between them, lashing out with both blades. Jace, who had just drawn breath to cast another spell, found himself frozen in stunned amazement as he watched his companion work.

Kallist seemed constantly in two or three places at once. He lunged to his right, forcing the male guard to raise his axe in a desperate parry. Steel grated on steel and Kallist was facing the other direction, using the momentum of the axe on his sword to aid his spin. In the midst of his turn, his dagger came up to intercept an overhand slash from the woman behind him, and Kallist lashed out with a kick. The guard's leg folded beneath the impact, dropping her into a painful crouch, and Kallist was once again facing the man he'd attacked first, broadsword coming around for a second strike.

Again and again he flickered between them, parrying to one side, attacking on the other. Sword met axe, axe met dagger, fist met armor, foot met flesh. The man moved in on Kallist to pin him in a flank with his comrade. Kallist gave him a dagger through the thigh for his troubles, sending him toppling to the floor even as the woman rose. Hurling herself from the path of Kallist's crushing broadsword, she teetered backward, momentarily off balance long enough for Kallist to turn back around and knee her brother in the face just as he began to rise. Cartilage folded, blood flowed, and this time when he hit the floor, he didn't seem liable to rise any time soon.

The woman dived, rolling beneath the circle of Kallist's whirling steel, and drove the haft of her axe into his groin. Kallist folded like an origami stork, but even through the pain he lashed downward, the blade of his dagger punching through her leather gauntlet and pinning her hand to her weapon. Her mouth opened in a sudden gasp, and Kallist drove the point of his broadsword between her teeth.

Both hit the floor at the same moment. Only Kallist rose. Limping and wincing, he reached out and slashed the throat of the guard still struggling with the phantom eel, and also, for good measure, the unconscious soldier on the floor.

"All right," Jace gasped when he could once again gather his thoughts. "You have got to teach me how to do that."

Kallist grinned, though his face remained pale with pain. "It's a deal."

They swiftly found their way to the foyer, and just as swiftly found that getting there had been the least of their problems.

"That," Kallist said, peeking out a front window from between two curtains, "is a lot of guards."

ARI MARMELL

Jace could only nod. This, then, was why they hadn't faced more opposition inside the house: The bulk of Hesset's warriors were gathered in the yard outside, blocking all possible paths to the outer wall of the estate, and they appeared more than content to wait there until the stars burned out.

It made a certain amount of sense, really, and Kallist cursed himself for not anticipating it. In the house, there were far too many tiny rooms, closets, nooks, and crannies in which to hide. But outside? Somehow, neither of the intruders thought that hiding behind a bush would suffice this time around.

"All right," Kallist said, "since you hate my plan so much, why don't you come up with one?"

Jace blinked. "You haven't suggested any plan."

"I know, but trust me; you'd hate everything I've thought of so far."

Jace snorted, but then his brow furrowed. Kallist grinned. "You've got something?"

"I might." Jace turned to him. "Please tell me that you've met Ronia Hesset personally."

Kallist nodded. "Once or twice, during her dealings with Paldor, but only in passing."

"It'll do. I need you to do two things for me. First, I've been ordered in no uncertain terms not to read the minds of anyone working for the Consortium without permission. So I need your permission."

"Um . . ." Kallist looked sick.

"I promise I'm only looking for one thing."

"And what's that?"

"That's the second thing I need from you. Picture Hesset, as thoroughly as you can. The details of her face, the way she moves, her posture, the sound of her voice . . . Everything."

Kallist smiled broadly in sudden understanding. "Not bad, Jace."

"Tell me that after it works."

Φ

A few moments' concentration, to ensure that Jace had her face and her voice as accurate as Kallist's memories could make them. A few moments more, and the guards outside saw one of the upper windows of the manor come flying open. Ronia Hesset leaned out, blood trickling from the corner of her mouth as though she'd been struck.

"Get up here!" she shrieked, voice tinged with desperation. "Now!"

From inside the coat closet, Jace and Kallist listened as boots pounded past them. It would take only minutes, if even that, for the real Hesset to hear the sounds of her soldiers returning, to meet them and order them to resume their posts outside.

Jace and Kallist darted back into the hall, taking one final look out the window. There in the yard stood a dozen armed men; only half the guards had gone running at their "employer's" call.

"Think we can take them?" Jace asked.

"We'd better, since there's going to be twice as many in a few minutes.

Kallist all but flew through the front door, blades weaving intricate patterns in the air. Jace followed a step behind, casting even as he ran; a trio of small drakes appeared in the air around him, razor-edged claws raised to shred. And like a small but determined tide, the Hesset household guards surged forward to meet them.

✳ ✳ ✳ ✳ ✳

When he and Kallist had limped their way back to the Consortium complex, bleeding from a dozen small wounds, Jace had hoped that would mark the end of his involvement with the Hesset affair.

It hadn't.

He sat now to Paldor's right, behind a long table in a room in which he'd never been. A heavy ledger sat open before him, in which he made constant scribblings with a feather quill that never required ink. It didn't matter

ARI MARMELL

what he was writing, and in fact he'd long since ceased doing anything more than random doodles. He just had to look like a secretary.

For the past hour, various Consortium employees who'd dealt with Hesset's mercantile interests marched past them, one by one. Paldor, with his usual jolly expression, asked them a few questions about how things had gone, what they felt about the cooperation between the two organizations, and so forth. Each gave his or her own answers and was dismissed. Jace kept scribbling.

All he could think, in those moments when he was entirely inside his own mind, rather than partly within someone else's, was *Be innocent, be innocent, be innocent.*

His head throbbed and his eyes blurred with exhaustion. Never before had he attempted to read so many minds in even a single day, let alone an hour, and he truly didn't know how much longer he could keep it up. Even though all he sought was innocence or guilt, honesty or deception, the fact that he'd already managed as many as he had was nothing short of astounding. He credited his few training sessions with Tezzeret for teaching him such fortitude.

Still, Jace was on the verge of asking Paldor if they could continue the hunt tomorrow when he glanced into the mind of a skinny, uptight records-keeper whose name he could not recall, and he found what he sought.

Jace sighed briefly. He'd known it was inevitable. How else could Hesset have known the Consortium was coming after her, let alone exactly when? But still, he'd hoped.

In a predetermined signal, Jace ceased writing, lay the quill down beside the ledger, and firmly closed the book.

Paldor nodded and gestured with a pair of pudgy fingers. Only as a pair of guards clamped his arms in brutal, bone-bruising grips, did the archivist realize he'd been found out—and what must be in store for him at

Consortium hands. He shrieked, screamed, begging and blubbering for mercy until his voice faded away down the distant halls.

Through it all, even as he contemplated many forthcoming hours with the traitor in the complex "discipline chamber," the jovial expression on Paldor's face never faltered.

"Write down anything you learned from his mind that might prove useful," he said to Jace, raising his ponderous bulk from behind the table. "And then go get yourself a drink. You look like you could use it."

Jace, who wasn't sure he could ever stomach food or drink again, nodded dully and once again lifted the quill.

✷ ✷ ✷ ✷ ✷

It turned out that stomaching drinks wasn't as difficult as Jace had predicted. In fact, as the tavern turned fuzzy around him, he found rather that *stopping* might be the more problematic choice.

He could leave the Consortium, but he'd lose out on what might still prove the greatest opportunities he'd ever been offered. And even if he should ask to leave, they'd never let him go. He'd just sent a man to be tortured and probably murdered because of betrayal, and would almost certainly have to do so again. Jace knew they would never show him any mercy should he try to flee.

His thoughts turned around in his head like a serpent consuming its tail. But whatever he might consciously decide, in his soul he knew that he would stay, because he feared what might happen otherwise, or what might not.

And so, if he could not drown the fear, at least he could drown the guilt.

It took him a few moments to realize that someone was sitting next to him—surprising, even in his inebriated state, given the sheer amount of space that someone occupied.

ARI MARMELL

"When I said 'Go get a drink,' " Paldor told him, the chair creaking in panic beneath his bulk, "I sort of meant from the dining room back home. We've got a very nice wine cellar there, you know."

Jace shrugged. "Gonna hafta be clearer 'bout those things, Paldor. What'm I, a mind reader?"

Paldor chuckled. "It's just as well," the corpulent crook replied. "I really do need to get out occasionally. Reminds me why I hate getting out." With a grunt, he drew a small bag out from the folds of—somewhere— and plunked it down onto the table.

"Wha's this?" Jace slurred suspiciously.

"This is the good news, Beleren. A bonus. From Tezzeret, for rooting out the traitor. Tezzeret and I, we don't like traitors."

Paldor locked eyes with Jace, and even through his growing stupor, the mage felt the sudden urge to recoil. "Now here's the bad news. You do not impress me. You're supposed to be this great and powerful mind-reader, and maybe you are, at that. But you're weak. You're squeamish. The Consortium employs the best, and frankly, I'm not sure you remotely qualify. If your powers weren't so bloody rare, I'd already be looking to replace your sorry ass.

"So take a few days off. I'll expect you in my office at the start of next week, and we'll see if we can't find you something a bit less distasteful to work on while you build up your intestinal fortitude. But Beleren—if you don't shape up, you're out, mind-reader or no. And make no mistake that when I say 'out,' I don't mean by the damned door."

Jace never saw Paldor leave, for he was too busy watching the bag as though it were some venomous insect. He didn't want it, not a coin of it. The thought made his gut heave, and threatened to undo a substantial amount of the drunk on which he'd been working so hard. Hell, he didn't even know what to do with it, really.

He was living in the Consortium's lodgings, eating their food, and already saving up his monthly fee. He thought briefly of taking the extra money and just running, but he knew damned well it was a foolish notion; he'd be in Paldor's office next week, just as ordered. Maybe by then, he wouldn't even be bothered by it.

But it would look strange if he didn't do *something* with the money . . .

✳ ✳ ✳ ✳ ✳

Emmara Tandris returned home from one of her infrequent outings, arms wrapped around a bag of old adventure tales written in the original Elvish, to find a large crate waiting outside her door. Curious, she lowered the bulky sack to the ground and knelt beside the box.

A wisp of scent reached her, and she couldn't help but smile. She didn't even need to open the box, now; she could identify, by smell alone, the exotic fruits within. She reached out and removed the note that was stuck between two of the slats.

> Couldn't help but remember our last conversation. Hope these'll keep you until they're back in season. You owe me at least one truly enormous dessert.
>
> —Berrim

He'd joined the Consortium, then. There were precious few other ways he could afford this. Emmara stood, grateful for the generous gift, but a part of her couldn't help but wonder what he'd done to earn that sort of wealth.

She hoped, as the smile fell from her face, that he was all right.

✳ ✳ ✳ ✳ ✳

Jace caught the wooden sword, ignoring the sting as it slapped into his palm. The wood was worn smooth and permeated with old sweat. He glanced across at Kallist and awkwardly adopted a similar stance. He tried, and failed, to ignore the dozen other men and women of the Consortium who had backed away to the room's walls, eager to interrupt their own practice long enough to watch the new guy get his head handed to him.

"Here beginneth the first lesson," Kallist said pompously, a twinkle in his eye. "You ready?"

"More than," Jace hissed through gritted teeth. "You're going down, Kallist."

"Only if I bust a gut laughing at you, Jace."

"That was the plan, actually."

It wasn't quite the first time Jace had handled a sword, and he'd wielded both sticks and knives defending himself in his younger years, so at least he didn't come across as ragingly incompetent. In fact, he managed to parry two of Kallist's attacks, the clack of wood on wood echoing through the chamber, before pain and the beginning stages of a truly magnificent bruise blossomed across his left side.

Several of the observers winced in sympathy as the wood slammed home.

Kallist stepped in and extended a hand to help Jace back to his feet. "So," he began, demonstrating a grip, then reaching out again to correct Jace's attempt at imitation, "here's why you missed that parry . . ."

There passed a few moments of discussion and demonstration (and bored shifting by the gathered audience), followed by another quick exchange of blows, and another ugly bruise for Jace. And again. And again.

And again.

But as the second hour of practice wound to a close, and Jace's lungs burned as badly as his sides, fewer and fewer of Kallist's strikes landed. True, he was using only the simplest techniques, and they were running at roughly half speed, but Jace was, at least, learning something.

Jace stepped in, slashing down with an overhand strike so clumsy it was laughable. Several of the observers snickered, and Kallist raised his practice sword in a contemptuous parry.

He felt nothing in the path of his blade but air, and it was finally his turn to hit the floor, gasping and clutching his aching stomach.

He looked up, just in time to see the illusion of Jace's arm and sword fade away, and the real one—which had slammed rather handily into Kallist's unprotected midsection—shimmer into view.

"Here," Jace said, clutching at his battered ribs with his left hand, "beginneth the first lesson." He dropped the sword, reached out a helping hand.

With a grunt, and a muttered "I'm just waiting until there are no witnesses to kill you slowly," Kallist took it.

"Same time tomorrow?" Jace asked him.

Kallist rubbed his aching stomach and grinned a nasty grin. "You couldn't pay me to miss it."

CHAPTER TWELVE

From a balcony halfway up one of Ravnica's great spires, Jace stared downward, his eyesight enhanced by a touch of clairvoyance. He leaned casually against the railing and watched for a few moments as crowds of people ran screaming from the columns of fire that heralded the arrival of Baltrice's firecat. Their quarry, one of the bald and blue-skinned vedalken—named, uh, Serien? Sevrien? Something like that—rolled across the cobblestones and came swiftly to his feet, a gleaming shield on one arm, a brutally serrated scimitar in the other hand.

"Is this what you do with every potential recruit?" Jace asked disdainfully. "I mean, what, you really couldn't think of anything new?"

Baltrice snarled from beside him, keeping half her focus on the struggle below. "It works, doesn't it?"

"So do chamber pots," Jace told her, cocking his head as the vedalken took a blast of fire on his shield, then riposted with a devastating slash that almost took one of the cat's legs clean off. "Doesn't mean I don't prefer indoor plumbing."

The fire-mage glared at him, and Jace wondered if she wouldn't actually have attacked him had her concentration not been required elsewhere.

He wondered, as he often had, just what it was about him that she hated so much. He didn't worry about it too terribly, since he readily hated her back—but he was curious.

"And what are your plans?" she asked gruffly, wincing in sympathy as her summoned pet took another nasty wound below.

"Not sure yet," Jace admitted. "I know I'm supposed to 'test his abilities,' but . . . I mean, the guy's not even a mage."

"Wow, you noticed that? You're as smart as Tezzeret said you were."

"My point," Jace said, ignoring the jibe, "is that it seems like more of a Kallist thing. Why does Paldor want me testing him?"

"Maybe," Baltrice told him, "figuring that out is another test."

It wasn't, of course. Baltrice had specific instructions for Beleren; she just hadn't bothered to give them to him.

She could always claim she had, of course. He was the only mind-reader, after all, so it wasn't as though Paldor could prove otherwise. And he wouldn't dare ask Tezzeret to subject her to one of the artificer's truth elixirs; not Baltrice.

She grinned after Jace as he shrugged and departed the balcony, ready to invisibly follow Sevrien (Serien?) home and conduct his own test. No, a failure here wouldn't cause much in the way of lasting repercussions. But every little disappointment was a black mark in Tezzeret's eyes.

Her grin faded and the old fear returned to gnawing at her gut as Beleren vanished. Good as she was at her job, there were always plenty of people who could kill, a few even as efficiently as she could.

But only one, so far as she knew, who could read minds.

And despite her many years of service, she wondered deep in her soul which of them, should it ever come down to it, Tezzeret would consider the more expendable.

✳ ✳ ✳ ✳ ✳

". . . know what I was supposed to do," Jace lamented bitterly, flopped in a thickly upholstered chair in his quarters. "But Paldor certainly didn't seem happy with me, even though he decided to let Sevrien join up."

Kallist nodded, leaning against a bookcase on the far wall. "What did you do, exactly?"

Jace shrugged. "Sort of an obstacle course. A bunch of illusions, popping up out of nowhere. Tested reactions, accuracy, that sort of thing."

"Hmm. You know, Jace," Kallist offered thoughtfully, "there are other illusionists in the Consortium. Maybe you were supposed to do something a little more, well, uniquely you? Read his mind?"

"Looking for what?"

"How do I know? Or maybe you were supposed to prod at him. Test his willpower. His pain tolerance. Or see how *quickly* you could read his mind! That sort of information could be useful to know about an operative, right?"

"Oh, please, Kallist," Jace scoffed. "What would be the point of that? Of course he couldn't have stood up to me. He can't even wield magic."

"You know something, Jace?" Kallist said after several long breaths. "If Tezzeret's training you to be a dromad's ass, you're certainly shaping up to be a great student."

"What? What did I—?" But the door was already slamming behind his friend, before Jace could finish the sentence.

✳ ✳ ✳ ✳ ✳

"You're late, Beleren," Tezzeret snapped without preamble as Jace entered the stone-walled room beneath the streets. "I'm sure you have every reason to think that

Φ

my time is yours to do with as you will, but believe it or not, the business of running an inter-planar organization actually requires a little attention."

"Uh . . ." Jace all but fell back before the sudden tirade. "Sorry," he continued. "I lost track of the time."

"Did you now? And what were you doing that was so important?"

"Mostly getting chewed out by Paldor, with a side of irritating my best friend."

"Ah. And will I be hearing about this chewing out from Paldor?"

"Probably."

Tezzeret nodded, motioning Jace to move away from the doorway. "Then we'd best get your practice out of the way before I've any further reason to be angry at you."

Jace moved in, glancing around at the now-familiar steel walls—once more in their oval configuration—and at the table that had been placed in the room's center. It was a great stone slab, easily the size of a small bed.

Or perhaps a coffin.

There were no chairs, and sitting on the floor seemed foolish beside the looming table, so Jace just stood, his posture one of mild confusion.

Tezzeret rapped an etherium knuckle on the steel slats. The entire wall chimed like the inside of a bell, and before the reverberations had faded, one of the steel walls slid aside, allowing fetid wafts of old sweat and human waste into the chamber. A quartet of guards followed after, carrying a filthy, unconscious man. His body was covered with an array of brutal burns and recent scars, his hair was slicked to his head by sweat and oils, and he was clad only in gray trousers. Jace, with a growing nervousness in his gut, only barely recognized him as the records-keeper who'd sold them out to Ronia Hesset.

The man he'd turned over to Paldor's mercies, and whom he'd assumed had been killed those many months ago.

"We kept him alive," Tezzeret answered Jace's unspoken question. "Paldor wanted to be sure we knew everything of value, every secret of ours he'd sold. We thought of having you draw it from his mind, but Paldor seemed to feel you wouldn't take kindly to that. Since he really wanted the chance to punish the man, I let it go; Paldor takes betrayal almost as poorly as I do.

"But from here on out, you don't escape the hard stuff anymore. Today," Tezzeret said as the guards dropped the insensate form on the table. "We're going to talk about the mind. Touch his thoughts, Beleren."

"I . . . You said you'd learned everything. What am I looking for?"

The artificer shook his head. "Nothing yet. Don't worry about reading it. Just make contact."

With an uncertain nod, Jace directed his attentions to the man on the table.

"All right," he said, a moment later, not turning back toward Tezzeret.

"Good. Feel his mind."

"What?"

"His mind, Beleren. You read minds, you can talk to them. And as you showed Alhammarret, you can destroy them.

"The mind is its own presence! It's real, no less so than the mana you and I both drink from the world around us. Feel it! See it!"

And Jace did, though he had to close his eyes to blot out the physical world around him. For the first time, Jace felt the mind of another living being not merely as a source of images to be read or as an engine to be turned off, but as something far more. Something all its own. In his own mind he felt the other, turned it, examined it like a jeweler with an unfamiliar stone, prodded at its contours.

Φ

"Good." He heard Tezzeret's voice, heard the honest pleasure and perhaps even pride within. "You see?"

"I . . . I do." Still he kept his eyes squeezed shut, fearful of losing the ephemeral image, or the feather-light touch of the other mind on his own. "But what . . . What's this for? What am I doing?"

"Whatever you want." There was something ugly in Tezzeret's voice, a viscous toxin dripping from each word. "Isn't that the point? If the mind is an object, you can manipulate it as an object!"

Jace found himself shaking, and he felt the first stirring of bile rising up the back of his throat.

"Don't just read his thoughts!" Tezzeret urged, so close now that Jace could feel the artificer's breath on his neck. "Control them! He lies unconscious, but you hold his mind in yours!"

"No . . ."

"This is what power over the mind truly means, Beleren! Reading thoughts? That's child's play, a feeble game for the man who can *control* thoughts! You can make him move as you wish. You can shape his memories!"

"No!"

Jace staggered away, his eyes flying open, and allowed all contact with the limp form before him to lapse. He spun on Tezzeret, fists clenched.

"No?" Tezzeret asked, his voice deceptively mild.

Could he make Tezzeret understand? Could he possibly explain how revolting a notion it was, the thought of reaching into someone's thoughts and stirring them like a pot of soup? Could he make Tezzeret understand just how horrifying Jace found the idea of losing his will to another? How filthy it made him feel, to the depths of his soul, to contemplate doing it to someone else?

What he said instead was, "What you're asking of me . . . It could go wrong in a dozen different ways. It could kill him."

"You're worried about the life of a traitor to the Consortium?"

Jace quailed but stood his ground. "I am if I have to be inside his mind when it happens," he offered as his excuse.

"I see." Tezzeret nodded, then turned to face the guards. "A pity. I was hoping to have you erase all knowledge of the Consortium from his mind, so we wouldn't have to execute him. He truly is a skilled bookkeeper. We could have hired him for some of our local businesses, those that don't require direct contact with Consortium secrets." The artificer heaved an obviously artificial sigh, and waved one of the guards forward.

"Ah, well. I can understand your reluctance, Beleren." He reached out, drew the sword from the guard's belt and reversed it, holding it hilt-first toward Jace. "So, all right. Just kill him, then."

The steel walls seemed to close on him so tightly that Jace actually took a moment to stare at them, to reassure himself they hadn't somehow slipped their tracks. "Why . . ." He cleared his throat, tried to swallow. "Why me?"

"Because Paldor told me of your 'problems' when you uncovered this man's treason!" Tezzeret hissed at him, his voice as cold as those sliding walls. "Because you cannot become what you could be—what you *should* be!—without overcoming the barriers you've placed on yourself!

"You think I'm asking you to kill this man," he continued, his voice suddenly far more calm. "But I'm not. I'm asking you to save him, Beleren. I cannot trust him to live with what he knows. I'm asking you to give me another, more merciful option."

Jace stared at him, his jaw working.

"Now," he continued, breathing deeply, "take the sword or not, as you choose. But either his memories must go or he must. And if you're to have any place in the Consortium, it will be at your hand."

Jace clenched his fists until his fingers turned white, and then slowly released a breath, uttered the first words of an incantation . . .

"No." Tezzeret reached out and tapped him on the head, just barely hard enough to hurt. "No summoning. What you do, you do."

Choking back vomit, Jace spun back toward the table. Mustering everything he had, throwing his all into the spells so he wouldn't have to think of what he was doing, he once more wrapped his awareness around the record-keeper's mind. Again he stared at the fellow's thoughts, his memories, his dreams. And as the better part of him wept, Jace carelessly peeled those thoughts away.

Then he collapsed to his knees, one hand clenched on the edge of the table above his head.

Tezzeret knelt beside him, placed his hand—his left hand, the hand of flesh—on Jace's shoulder. "Thank you, Beleren. Come." He rose, helping Jace to his feet as well. "Share a drink with me in the dining room, before I have to leave Ravnica. Today has been a triumph for us both."

Surely they must have talked, as they trod the corridors of the complex, as they sat and shared a bottle of Paldor's finest wine. They must have, but Jace could never recall a word of it. He only remembered sitting there, drinking goblet after goblet, long after the artificer had left; drinking until he could no longer remember the slack expression on the archivist's face, the stench of his sweat, or the feel of his slowly vanishing mind.

It wasn't until days later that Jace learned that his powers weren't nearly so precise as he'd believed them to be; that he hadn't erased merely the man's memories of the Consortium, but the memories of his life. That he'd left the man an empty husk, an infant in an adult's body.

But by then, Jace had managed to convince himself that he no longer cared.

* * * * *

For a time, then, Jace's life was routine. His assignments for the Consortium primarily required him to verify information or guard shipments of goods, and while he accompanied Kallist on a great many operations, only a few ended in violence. During the many days between such activities, their lessons continued apace, and if Jace never became more than an adequate swordsman, and Kallist never mastered more than a smattering of spells, still the both of them kept trying.

As Tezzeret had promised, Jace's regular practice honed his spellcasting to a level he might never have achieved alone. His pursuit of Consortium goals took him to new regions of Ravnica, and even twice to other worlds. Here he touched the essence of the land, connected with it, absorbed an ever-increasing flow of mana that empowered his spells further still.

As his power grew, the nature of his assignments became ever more nefarious, ever more brutal. After a few months, he was once again accompanying Kallist on assassinations, though still it was always the swordsman to do the final deed.

And eventually, he no longer needed to drink to stifle the guilt.

CHAPTER THIRTEEN

"What's wrong, Jace?" Paldor asked, leaning back beneath the clock that hung over his desk.

"A great deal, actually. To start with, I'm trying to find a polite, respectfully subordinate way to tell you to drop dead, and I'm not coming up with one."

Paldor chuckled, as did the other figure in the room—a figure who was quite definitely not Kallist.

"Afraid to work with me, Jace?" Baltrice sneered at him.

"If by 'afraid' you mean 'would rather run my genitals through a clockwork engine,' then yes."

Paldor stood and slapped his hands on the desk. "This," he rumbled, and suddenly he wasn't nearly so cheery as he had seemed, "isn't going to go any further. Jace, what's your problem?"

"My problem, Paldor, is that I'd rather work with Kallist. Or Ireena. Or Gemreth, or, um, pretty much anyone else."

"That's nice," Paldor told him. "It's also impossible."

"Paldor . . ."

"It's not as though I've a lot of people I can assign to this. The target's not, you might say, local. And

ARI MARMELL

you planeswalking types aren't precisely ten a copper. Baltrice is the only other Consortium walker available right now, so that means you work with her.

"But more to the point, these orders come straight from Tezzeret. You're welcome to try to contact him and bitch, if you want."

"We can do that?" Jace asked in puzzlement. Baltrice snickered.

Paldor pointed to the peculiar, æther-filled glass contraption. "Every Consortium cell has one, in case we need to get his attention. Break it, and Tezzeret can feel the æther within slip away, knows we need to speak with him.

"Of course, they're only meant for emergencies, and I understand they're monstrously hard to create, but by all means, go ahead. I'm sure he'd consider your misgivings a worthwhile usage."

Jace wilted. "I would love beyond all measure to have Baltrice accompany me on this endeavor," he said hollowly. "It's a dream I have."

"I thought that might be your reaction."

"Same arrangement as with Kallist?" Jace clarified. "I'm backing her up, I'll be her eyes, but she's doing the job, right?"

"Aww . . ." Baltrice taunted. "Does Jace have a weak stomach?"

He ignored her. "Right?" he asked again.

Paldor nodded. Baltrice smirked. Jace sighed.

"All right. What's the objective?"

"Take a seat, both of you." Then, once they'd done so, "You ever hear of a world called Kamigawa?" Paldor asked.

Jace perked up like a wolf spotting a limping dromad. "Absolutely! I've heard all sorts of fascinating things about that world. I've thought about visiting for some time."

"Well, tough. You're going, but I don't think you'll

much care for the company."

"You mean Baltrice?" Jace asked smugly. She glowered at him; Paldor only shook his head.

"No. I mean that you're not going to be dealing with, uh, people. We need you two to exterminate the shogun of a nezumi tribe."

"Nezumi?" Jace asked.

"Ratmen," Baltrice sneered. "Vile little creatures."

"I'm sure they'd be just as disgusted by us." *Or at least you.*

"If you two are done," Paldor warned, leaning over his desk. Then, when he was sure they were listening, "We've got nothing against the tribe, the, uh . . . Damn it, I can't pronounce it without spraining my tongue. I'll give it to you in writing before you go.

"It just so happens," he continued, "that this particular tribe lives in a mana-rich swamp. Tezzeret wants access to it for the Kamigawa cell, but their chieftain won't deal.

"His heir, however, is willing to deal just fine."

Land? The Consortium was killing over land, now? When did that happen? For just an instant, Jace's stomach churned once more. He turned his attention inward and banished his qualms like a flawed summoning. He'd made his choice long ago, and it was far too late to make any other.

"What's the point?" he asked instead. "I mean, I can't imagine the tribe's got eyes over the entire swamp at any given time. It'd be more convenient to have their permission, but it's hardly necessary, is it?"

It was Baltrice, oddly, who answered. "Some regions of Kamigawa aren't exactly what you'd call friendly to foreign mages, Beleren. There are—things living in the land. Spirits, demons . . . The locals call them kami. You piss them off, drawing mana's the least of your worries."

"All right. And?"

"And," Paldor said, "the tribal prince swears to us that his shaman's traditions of spirit-binding are sufficient to keep the kami from interfering with us while we establish our links with the land."

Jace felt his lip curling. "That's awfully convenient."

"It is. That's why you're going along. Baltrice's job is to make sure the shogun goes away; yours is to make sure his son is telling us the truth."

One final objection, then. "So why not have the Kamigawa cell deal with this? Why do we have to go all that way?"

The lieutenant shrugged. "Plausible deniability. The tribe's had official dealings with the Kamigawa Consortium. Whereas the two of you—"

"Won't be recognized if we're captured and chopped into rat food," Jace finished for him.

"Something like that. Go get ready; I'll have details on the village for you when you get back."

＊ ＊ ＊ ＊ ＊

Several hours to plan, a night to sleep, another hour to gather what supplies they needed, and then Jace and Baltrice met in a featureless stone chamber, deep in the bowels of the complex. Jace was clad in loose trousers that felt as though they would fall off at any moment, belted by a blue sash tied about his waist, and a wrap-around tunic hanging partly open at the chest. Over it he wore his favored cloak; that, at least, wouldn't particularly stand out where they were going. Baltrice wore a gown of deep red, which hid her preferred leathers beneath. Both had dyed their hair black, but there was little they could do about their skin, which was notably lighter than the norm for Kamigawa natives. Fortunately, the route they'd mapped out didn't pass through any human communities, so they shouldn't have to bear up under close examination.

"Ready?" she asked him, the usual venom gone from

her voice. She and Jace both knew full well the importance of what was to come.

"I'm ready," he confirmed, "but I've never been there before."

She nodded. "I'll leave you a trail through the æther if I can."

Jace took a deep breath. "Then let's go." She turned without another word and left to find her own solitude, leaving him to his concentrations.

He never knew how it looked to any other walker, how it felt, how it rippled through mind, body, soul, rigid past, uncertain future. He knew only that his own experience was as unique to him as the deepest meanings of his forgotten dreams.

To Jace, it began as a moment of sheer exhaustion, so overwhelming as to make death as welcome as sleep. His vision blacked out, his body trembled, wracked with vertigo as his conscious and subconscious minds merged, losing himself among a parade of personalities. He struggled to channel mana from across the Multiverse, compressing it into a point of singularity beyond perception, a tiny mote of metaphysical tinder.

And then in a single moment of exultation far greater than any physical pleasure, Jace Beleren was once more Jace Beleren; and Jace Beleren was once more a planeswalker. His Spark burned within his soul, and ignited the mana-tinder he had gathered.

The world erupted in an invisible flame, melting away before him until all that remained was a shimmering curtain of glowing smoke. With a single hand, he brushed the curtain aside, took a step, into elsewhere.

Jace Beleren was adrift in the Blind Eternities. The tides of creation washed over him, and he did not fall. He leaned without apprehension into the winds that blew from nothingness, spreading tiny particles of probability in their wake. He trod upon the surface of memory, climbed the slopes of tomorrows that had already passed.

Toxic colors circled hungrily about him, winging their way through clouds of song, but they did not disturb his trek. Before his arrival and after his passing, they knew nothing but hue and hunger, wind and want—but for the endless moments he trod beneath them, they knew fear.

Jace's eyes flickered every which way, so far as "way" had any meaning here. He sensed the shifts in terrain, and stepped across them carefully lest he fall into the roiling chaos that bubbled away beneath reality. Obstacles appeared before him—objects and animals and ideas—and he moved around them or slapped them down before they could warp his body or infiltrate his mind and consume his thoughts.

But always he kept a portion of his attention cast forward and downward. Ahead he saw a flickering road, a ribbon of fire that stretched into the distance. At its end was a burning husk, a dead tree that crackled and flamed but was never consumed, and he knew it was the Spark of the woman he followed. He wondered, briefly, what his own looked like to her, then swiftly gave up conscious thought and simply followed.

For a time he could not possibly measure, he walked in her path. It was a tenuous lifeline he followed, the burning line of footsteps she left behind, footprints that wavered and shifted and—a time or two—even rose and floated away. Tenuous, but it would suffice.

And finally he stood before a curtain of smoke, much as the one through which he'd stepped away from Ravnica, though the glow here tended more toward silver. Stretching forth his hand, Jace parted the curtain, and took one final step.

He collapsed to his hands and knees, gasping, and found himself crouched in several inches of standing water, sinking slightly into the muddy bottom. Around him, greenery stretched as far as he could see, and it took him only a moment to realize that he found himself in the middle of a rice paddy.

Baltrice sat cross-legged some few yards away, having had the better fortune to appear on one of the bulwarks of earth that rose between the paddies. Almost directly behind her rose the first of a range of foothills that ran toward the base of a nearby mountain.

"Welcome to Kamigawa," she told him a bit breathlessly.

"Delighted to be here."

It wasn't entirely sarcasm. From Tezzeret, Jace had heard tales of the shogunate realms of Kamigawa. Fascinated, he'd long wished to see the many-terraced temples and ornate palaces, walk the streets and immerse himself in the musical intonation of the native tongue.

None of which he'd be doing today, since his assignment took him nowhere near any of Kamigawa's great cities.

Jace climbed from the murky water, flopped down on the nearest spot of dry land, and just breathed. There were few magics more tiring than walking. He could have risen immediately if he'd had to, but given the opportunity, he preferred to gather his strength. So he lay still and took a moment to examine his surroundings.

Baltrice, he had to admit, had chosen their arrival point wisely. The mounts and bulwarks of earth weren't islands in the traditional sense; the paddies in which the rice grew not much of a lake. But still, it was enough living, rippling water, and enough mingling of water and earth along the feeble "shore," that he should be able to draw some small measure of mana from the land, to refresh his spirit as well as his body.

And the fact that the paddy stood in the direct shadow of the nearby mountain should more than suffice for her needs, as well—certainly better and more efficiently than the paddies themselves would meet his.

Jace allowed his consciousness to seep into the earth beneath him, to plumb its unfamiliar depths. And there, deep within these foreign lands, he felt the presence of others: Elemental spirits and ancient ghosts, born from or drawn to the soul of Kamigawa's lands, and they claimed much of its mana for their own. These must be the kami; Jace steered clear of them, lest they grow wroth and manifest in the world above.

So Jace allowed the merest dregs of the land's power to seep into his soul, and still felt more than a little run down after an hour's rest. Groaning softly, he forced himself upright, scowled at his cuffs, his sleeves, and the hem of his cloak, all now stiff with the residue of the muddy water in which he'd landed.

Baltrice gave him an exasperated look as he rose. Jace wondered briefly what he'd done to piss her off now and only then realized that it probably wasn't him. Perhaps she, too, had found her precious mountain less generous than she'd hoped.

"Where to from here?" he asked.

She frowned briefly in concentration. "I'll need to pick out a few landmarks before I can be sure," she told him slowly, "but I'm guessing about forty or fifty miles to the village."

"Ah. A nice spring jaunt, then."

"You don't like it? You lead next time."

Jace shrugged. At least it meant he'd have one or two nights' sleep before they reached their destination. He could use the rest—even if travel in Baltrice's company was likely to prove about as "restful" as wrestling a gharial.

They walked. The mud beneath their feet slowly gave way to drier ground, the grass ceased to squelch and began to softly crunch. Jace, knowing full well what sort of terrain loomed in his future, enjoyed the stable footing while it lasted. As they moved away from the mountain, he saw a number of people in the distance—peasants, he presumed, judging by their drab clothes and broad-brimmed straw hats—standing knee-deep in the rice paddies. Though they clearly stared in the travelers' direction, none made any move to approach.

And far beyond even them, barely visible over the horizon, stood one of the multi-tiered and terraced Kamigawa temples.

Jace and Baltrice kept silent, each having little desire to speak to the other. He occupied some of his time going back over the plan, such as it was, but as that filled an alarmingly short span of time, he gave up on it.

Finally, the sun faded in the west, unfamiliar night birds took up a continual chorus (with something on the order of a million crickets singing harmony), and Baltrice stopped to make camp and confirm their location. The Kamigawa night, for whatever reason, smelled of chrysanthemums.

And for lack of anything else to do, Jace finally turned to Baltrice and asked, "So how is it you know your way around Kamigawa, anyway?"

"Been here before," Baltrice explained. She stretched her hand over a small pile of wood and tinder, and tensed her arm as though lifting a heavy weight. Sparks rained from beneath her fingernails, and soon they had a small but cheerful campfire dancing merrily away. "Helped Tezzeret establish the Kamigawa cell, until we found local people to lead it. Spent several months here."

"And the nezumi?"

She snorted. "Never did have to deal with them personally. But I'm given to understand they can't be trusted."

"So Paldor mentioned," Jace acknowledged.

That, however, was tomorrow's concern. Jace chewed a few bites of dried meat and retired to his bedroll without another word to Baltrice. A moment's concentration to lay a field of magic over him, one that would awaken him if anyone drew near, and Jace closed his eyes and slept.

* * * * *

Baltrice sat, her back against a log, and glared across the embers of the dying fire at Jace's slumbering form.

It would be easy. A quick burst of flame, or a sudden, overwhelming summons and Beleren would be dead before he could so much as clamber from his bedroll. No more worries, no more looking over her shoulder, no more wondering how high in the Consortium his ambitions reached.

No more wondering if and when Tezzeret would decide that a mind-reader made a better right hand than a flame-caster.

So easy . . . And nobody would ever know. She could say that the nezumi killed him, that he delved too deep into the Kamigawa mana and earned the wrath of the kami, the local demon-spirits. She could even say that he'd grown lost following her trail through the Eternities and vanished from her sight. It was unlikely, but not impossible, and he'd not be the first planeswalker to set out for an unfamiliar destination, never to appear again.

She felt her breath quicken, her blood grow warm. Tiny sparks of flame leaked from the corners of her eyes, though of course she couldn't see them. Even the embers of the campfire flared briefly into a second life, as the magic flowed around and through her.

So easy . . . Baltrice took a deep breath and allowed her jealous anger to fade. The campfire died once more, the flames vanished from her eyes.

It wasn't mercy that stayed her hand tonight. It was loyalty, she told herself, loyalty to Tezzeret, to the Consortium, to the mission. She couldn't know precisely what was ahead, what she would face when she came up against the nezumi. She might just need Beleren, much as the notion turned her stomach. And she would not face Tezzeret having failed, not when that failure was her own fault.

So Beleren could wait for another night. Perhaps, when the mission was complete, another opportunity would present itself.

Finally Baltrice lay down, wrapped herself in her own bedroll, and let sleep come to her.

⁂ ⁂ ⁂ ⁂ ⁂

"Whose idiotic idea was it to send two humans to infiltrate a ratman warren?" Baltrice snapped.

Jace shrugged, though he was pretty sure she couldn't see the gesture. "Just as soon as you manage to recruit a nezumi planeswalker for the Consortium, you be sure to let me know. Besides," he added after a moment, "we both know exactly whose idea this was. If you'd like, I'll be happy to take your complaints to Tezzeret when we get back. I'm sure he'll be delighted to hear how committed you are to his vision."

Baltrice gave him a look that threatened to set him alight without the benefit of magic, but said nothing.

They lay crouched in a slimy, viscous gunk—fluid enough to seep into everything and thick enough to stick. It sloshed across the skin like the touch of a living disease. The water flowed steadily despite the lack of breeze, suggesting the presence of subsurface currents moving among the reeds and towering cypresses whose greedy wooden fists gathered in all possible sunlight, leaving none for the swamp below.

Jace twitched as an insect that must have been the size of a small drake bit him behind the ear. He swore that this was the last time he'd go anywhere near a swamp if he had any say in the matter.

They lay there for hours, covered in muck and leaves. Lay there, and watched, and thought, and argued, and watched some more, because neither was entirely certain what to do next.

The nezumi village stretched across a broad swath of swamp. Twisted huts carved from the husks of trees and bamboo plants stood at various levels, all raised above the muck of the marsh below. Although primitive, they showed a level of craft and skill that Jace found surprising. The doorways and windows were not rough and random holes, but perfectly shaped ovals and circles; the steps that wound their way around the largest trunks were solid and even, albeit clearly carved for nonhuman feet. Lanterns and an occasional banner hung on bamboo poles that jutted from the sides of the structures, and though most of the swamp around here was shallow enough to wade through, many of the homes had skiffs tied up at their base.

None of which was their problem. No, the fact that the sprawling village hosted several hundred individual nezumi, and that the ratpeople appeared to follow no recognizable schedule, nor to acknowledge the rising or setting of the sun—that had them stumped. "Minimal impediments," indeed! Baltrice had spent their first five minutes here cursing Paldor for his faulty intelligence.

So they waited for nightfall, hoping to make their approach in the dark. They watched as nezumi poled their rafts between buildings, conversing on whatever topics might interest a tribe of humanoid rats. Farmers trudged back and forth, waist-deep in the muck, carrying sacks of harvested rice. Soldiers in boiled leather armor, carrying tae yari spears, wicked daggers, short recurved bows, and even the occasional katana, guarded the borders of the community. Some stood post on tree branches or platforms built high in the bamboo, while others traveled on high-walled skiffs.

The sun fell, the stars once again flickered, and the coy moon showed only a sliver of his face. The farmers retired for the night but the hunters emerged in droves, baiting traps and stalking the nocturnal beasts of the swamp. Lanterns cast an aura of light over the community that was barely enough for Jace and Baltrice, but probably more than sufficient for the rodent's eyes of the nezumi. And still the village refused to sleep.

"That's it," Jace said when it became clear that night was no more an ally to them than the day had been. "This is beyond stupid. We can't do anything without more information. Wait here." Without pausing for acknowledgment, he slithered forward through the muck, crawling on knees and elbows. He gave brief thought to cloaking himself in the image of something that belonged here, but decided that appearing as an alligator or a great constrictor would probably get him perforated by an overzealous hunter, and he wasn't familiar enough with Kamigawa to know what other forms might be equally appropriate but less appetizing. Come to think of it, he didn't even know if Kamigawa had alligators or constrictors. He chose, instead, simply to wrap the shadows around him, making himself invisible even to the senses of the ratmen.

He whispered as he drew near, drawing on the lore of an ancient spell he rarely had opportunity to practice, one that would solve the language problem entirely. Many mages sought such magic, but they came far more easily to planeswalkers; something about the Spark, their connection to the world beyond all worlds, opened their minds more readily to the magic of meaning.

His clumsy, filthy course took him just near enough to the outermost patrol of soldiers to hear their words. At first they were unintelligible, a language he didn't know spoken in voices that were far from human. But the words passed deep into his mind, filtered through his spell, and grew clear. He still heard the Kamigawa tongue, but the meaning of the words sprang to mind half an instant after the sounds reached his ears, as though he remembered definitions he'd never actually learned.

". . . meat," one of the guards was saying as Jace's mind finally tuned in to the language. "It's been a while since I've had any good salamander. The day patrols always take the best cuts."

Jace briefly congratulated himself on his wisdom in not choosing an animal as a disguise, and settled in to listen.

"Not sure I learned much of use, though," he told Baltrice roughly an hour later, "except to confirm what

ARI MARMELL

we were already afraid of. The village pretty much never sleeps. I have no idea how we're supposed to get to the chieftain without being discovered. My illusions are good, but I'm not sure I can fool an entire community."

"He lied to us, Beleren. The filthy little rat-prince lied to us."

Jace nodded. "I'd noticed that, yes."

Baltrice's eyes began to glow a faint red, her lip to curl in angry disdain. "We're being set up, used as some nezumi's pawns. And by someone who's either an idiot or who deeply believes that *we* are. I mean, the 'intelligence' he provided isn't even close to accurate."

Again Jace nodded. "We should go, then. Report back to Tezzeret, let him decide—"

"Oh, I don't think so," she proclaimed, her expression abruptly flipping into a horrid grin. "We both know what Tezzeret thinks of betrayal, don't we, Beleren?"

Covered head to toe in clinging mud and bits of decayed plant matter, a spirit of the swamp rising to vent its wrath, Baltrice stood. Flames danced openly in her eyes, her entire body quivered with a sudden strain.

"Baltrice? Baltrice, what are you doing?"

And then, though she spoke not a word in response, Jace had his answer.

CHAPTER FOURTEEN

The sky above the swamp brightened. Almost unnoticeable at first, through the umbrella of heavy branches and dangling moss, the strange light swiftly grew. A second moon appeared in the heavens, red and crackling and angry; and then it was no moon at all, but an artificial dawn.

Even as the nezumi peered upward from their posts, or emerged blinking from their huts, the ball of fire plummeted from the sky and burst on the village outskirts. Entire houses evaporated at a stroke, and the flames fanned outward, carried over the stagnant waters on the back of burning winds. Cypress, bamboo, and nezumi pelts ignited in a terrible conflagration—but the trees and the stalks didn't scream. Smoke rose between the surviving branches, blotting out the stars and spreading the choking, sickening scent of cooked flesh.

Jace screamed at Baltrice to stop, but his voice was lost in the crackling of the fire and the shrieks of dying nezumi. The smoke burned his eyes, and despite the blazing heat, he found himself shivering with a sudden horror.

One murder. *One.* That he could live with. To that, he had long ago resigned himself. *But this* . . .

Unseen behind Baltrice, who exulted in the release of her most devastating spells, Jace raised his hands as though to wrap them physically around Baltrice's essence. He held her mind in those fists, and for an instant, Jace knew he could kill.

Still she was casting. Even as the carnage from the fireball spread, her muscles tensed once more, her lips parted with something like a screaming grunt. His skin tingled, and he recognized the feel of something forcing its way into the world from outside.

It erupted from the swamp at the heart of the fireball's impact, a volcano of fire and fury, and the shallow water around it vanished in a hiss of steam. Humanoid only by the most generous use of the term, it towered above the bamboo stalks, above even some of the trees. It glared about it with eyes of fire, lashed about with hands of the same, for that was all it was. Fire: raw, primal, elemental.

The crackle of its flames was the cackling of Baltrice as it advanced on the village, an inexorable titan of agony and death. Turning their attentions away from the burning huts, the soldiers of the nezumi clan formed a defensive line before the oncoming terror, but few had any illusions that they could do more than die with honor.

"Baltrice!" The dam blocking the flood of Jace's horror finally burst. "Gods and demons, woman, what are you doing? There's supposed to be a tribe left for us to treat with!"

She seemed past understanding. Her arms were spread as she soaked in the heat of the inferno she had ignited. Her eyes gleamed red with fury and fire.

Even so, she calmly turned her head to face him. "Relax, Beleren. I have a plan."

"Really? How's that working out for you?"

She smiled, and it actually looked to be the expression of a rational human being, rather than the guise of pyromaniacal glee she'd worn a moment before. "Why don't you take a look?"

Jace looked, and he had to admit she might have a point. For all its initial fury, the fireball had obliterated only a handful of huts, and most of the others it had ignited could probably be saved. And the elemental itself, though tearing through the ranks of nezumi soldiers as though they truly were nothing but rats, seemed uninterested in advancing into the village proper.

"This isn't about wiping out the tribe, Beleren. Just making sure the prince understands the price of lying to the Consortium, understands the power of those he's tried to manipulate. He'll be a lot more honest with us from now on, wouldn't you think?"

Jace felt sick. "How many did you burn to death, Baltrice? Three dozen? Four?"

This time, she truly didn't hear him, or chose not to respond. All she said was, "We won't have a better opportunity than this. Come on; assuming anything the little rat told us is true, the chieftain's hut is the one in the center."

Not knowing what else to do—or else unwilling to do it—Jace followed. *At least,* he thought morbidly, staring up at a handful of burning trees that had become little more than the torches of titans, *we won't have any trouble seeing.*

Baltrice darted through the dancing shadows, wading through water up to her thighs. She made at least a cursory attempt at stealth, not that it mattered. Every face in the village was turned toward one mass of flame or the other. Jace was certain that the two of them could have marched on the center of the community with a battalion, a full company of drummers and trumpeters, and possibly a war-elephant, and still had an even chance of going unnoticed. He nevertheless took the time to wrap himself once more in a cloak of shadows, just to be sure.

As they neared the large central hut, Jace found his attention drawn to a smaller structure, rising beside the main house. It stood atop an impossibly narrow trunk, one that appeared utterly incapable of supporting the bulk of the structure. It lacked windows, boasting instead a single door and a chimney that protruded from the roof at a sharp angle. But it wasn't the house itself that drew his notice, but rather the sounds emerging faintly from within. Even over the surrounding cacophony, Jace was certain he heard the rhythm of a tribal drum, accompanied by an inhuman, hissing voice raised in an ongoing chant.

Even as he recognized the cadence as the basis of a potent spell, a heavy rain began to fall. The conflagration that had spread from the fireball's impact sizzled and shrank. The elemental seemed largely unconcerned, though puffs of steam shot from its body in random wounds. But behind it, the water of the swamp began to bulge, to shift, and to rise, as something equally primal struggled to be born.

Jace concentrated briefly as he mounted the first of the steps leading to the chieftain's hut. *We're definitely going to have to watch out for the shaman,* he sent in warning.

Baltrice froze in mid-stride, her feet on two separate levels of the stair. Her shoulders tightened as though she'd been stretched on a rack, and when she twisted about to glare at Jace, he was certain those muscles must snap.

"I don't give a plague-rat's ass what our situation might be," she hissed at him furiously. "You put your thoughts in my head one more time, I swear I'll put my fire in yours!"

Jace shrugged and tried to pretend he hadn't leaped back off the stairs in reaction to her sudden turn. "Just thought you should know," he said aloud.

Baltrice burst through the doorway of the chieftain's

hut, ripping aside the leather curtain that served as his door. She had a bare instant to examine in the room in the flickering firelight from outside. It was unevenly round, a single chamber that filled the entire hut. Numerous bones and skulls hung as trophies upon the walls, as did weapons won in a dozen different battles from a dozen regions of Kamigawa. The entire place reeked, and Baltrice noted a filth-encrusted hole in the floor across the chamber, opening onto the swamp a few dozen feet below—the closest thing the rat-king had to a privy.

As she scanned the space before her, something slammed into the side of her skull, something that felt like a stone wrapped in velvet. Her vision swam and she sank to one knee, struggling to regain her equilibrium.

The projectile that struck her fell to the floor at her side, revealing itself to be the head of a light-furred nezumi, its expression still slack from surprise.

"This is the vile traitor for whom you would slaughter my brothers and sisters?" To Baltrice, the words were gibberish, utterly incomprehensible; but Jace, who had made his way to the open doorway, understood perfectly.

Baltrice rose to attack, and a three-clawed foot whipped across her face as a spinning back-kick sent her sprawling across the open chamber. Blood poured from her nose and lip, and one of her eyes was already swelling shut.

The figure that emerged from the dark was hunched forward, as were most male nezumi, making him appear far shorter than his true height. Black fur streaked with patches of aging grey covered his body, save for the scaly pink tail, the clawed feet and hands, and the very tip of his twitching nose. Thick whiskers hung beneath night-black eyes that reflected the dancing fires. He wore a segmented breastplate of salamander hide and a wide-

ARI MARMELL

brimmed conical hat. The naginata he held was longer than he was tall, with a serrated, cleaving blade.

Baltrice, the world spinning around her as she failed to summon a creature to her aid, found herself desperately wishing she hadn't wasted so much of her strength on her previous spells.

"I am Bonetooth," the ratman continued, advancing slowly across the hut. "Son of Swamp-Eye, the daughter of Moon-Hand the Third. I am leader of the Nezumi-Katsuro gang, as were my fathers and mothers before unto the tenth generation."

He stood above Baltrice's prostrate form, the edge of the naginata pressed against her neck until the skin parted, ever so slightly, and the blood welled up from within. She froze, hoping to forestall his stroke long enough to gather her senses.

"You have conspired against me with my worthless son, whose name I cast out along with his head. He has, perhaps, lied to you, as he has me and so many others, and so, though I know you came to slay me, I was prepared to let you leave.

"And then this!" His twisted, taloned finger quivered with rage as he pointed at the flames that shown through the open doorway. "You came to slay one, yet many have died!

"For such a brutal crime against Nezumi-Katsuro, I can offer no forgiveness."

The naginata rose, a single drop of Baltrice's blood glistening along its edge.

And there it stayed. Heartbeats passed, then long seconds, and Baltrice could only wait, looking up at her would be executioner. What was he waiting for?

Only then did she notice the violent quiver in the rat-king's arms. Turning, she saw Jace in the doorway, one hand raised toward Bonetooth, fingers clenched in a grasp that was not quite a true fist. Sweat beaded his brow, and Baltrice knew it was due to no fire of hers.

Tezzeret had been right. Jace felt the shogun's mind, a presence independent from the physical world. He sensed—he knew—that if he wanted, he could hold it, rearrange it, take it with him, rebuild it or destroy it. He knew that that the power Tezzeret had promised him was indeed within his grasp.

But there was no triumph in that discovery. Jace felt soiled, as though the waters of a thousand rivers could never wash him clean, and he tasted bile in the back of his throat. In his mind, he heard the chieftain screaming and shrieking to be free. He swore that he felt, beneath his fingers, the writhing of the nezumi's brain as it kicked and thrashed to escape his hold.

And more than once it almost did just that, almost escaped the paralysis in which Jace held it—not because the shogun was stronger, but because Jace *wanted* to let him go. Through their mental link he felt every urge, every desire, and every fear, and he yearned for nothing more than to release the ratman's mind.

To say nothing of the fact that Jace felt he could happily watch Baltrice pounded and shredded into a carpet of quivering meat. But somehow, he didn't think Tezzeret would understand.

He could keep his grasp on the shogun's mind, nauseating as it might be, force him to guide them out, hold him as hostage against the nezumi's cooperation. But it took too much concentration, too much attention. He'd be unable to defend them if the rats attacked anyway, or against the shaman's spells, and Baltrice certainly wasn't up to helping. He could let Bonetooth go, but how then to prevent him from killing Baltrice, or from leading the village in pursuit of those who'd attacked them?

Had he taken the time to think about it, to really understand what he was doing, Jace could never have gone through with it. But by the time he consciously acknowledged that he had only one option remaining, he'd already followed through.

ARI MARMELL

Jace adjusted his grip on Bonetooth's mind and commanded the shogun, who had already ceased moving, to cease his breathing as well. The ratman's eyes went briefly wide, his entire body quivered, until finally he dropped dead to the floor of the hut.

Keeping his own mind nearly as empty as the corpse's own, Jace knelt beside Baltrice, who looked at him with a puzzled and, for some reason he wouldn't even try to fathom, vaguely hostile expression. "Can you walk?" he asked her. There was just enough emphasis on the last word to suggest that he wasn't talking about a stroll down the stairs.

"I don't . . ." The pounding in her head had subsided, but only slightly. "I don't think I . . ."

Jace placed a hand on her shoulder and concentrated, muttering sounds under his breath that were not words. For an instant, it felt as though something rose from within his chest, tingled its way through his arm, and vanished. His shoulders slumped; he felt—not weak, but certainly weaker than he had a moment before.

"How about now? And I suggest you say 'yes,' because if not, you're damn well stuck here. I'm not wasting any more mana on you."

"I can walk," she snapped at him.

"Good. Go. I'll watch until you're gone; no sense in us both being helpless at once."

"Feeling chivalrous, Beleren?" she asked as she climbed unsteadily to her feet.

"Not even remotely. It's just that I wouldn't trust you to fight off a senile kobold in your current condition."

Baltrice somehow managed to snarl even further without her jaw falling off. "And I'm trying to decide if I'd rather be dead than owe you for this!" She began to concentrate, and Jace turned away to begin his own spell. Again he poked a hole in the skin of the world, reaching into realms of vicious frost. From the gap poured a flock of razor-beaked raptors, their feathers glistening beneath coats of crackling ice.

Jace dispatched them in groups, to cover the door and every window. Not the most potent minions he might have summoned, they would still be sufficient to slow any nezumi soldiers who might intrude while he prepared for his own walk between the worlds.

Long moments passed, each more nerve-wracking than the next, until Baltrice finally faded from sight. Jace strode to the center of the room, very deliberately not looking at the fur-covered body on the floor, and concentrated once more, struggling to complete his efforts before some new enemy appeared.

For just an instant, as he neared the end of his ritual, he thought he might not make it.

The enemy didn't come through a door or a window. An entire wall of the hut simply vanished, torn from its roots by a strength Jace could scarcely imagine. Standing in the gap was a nezumi, far more bent and twisted than the chieftain had been. His fur was bone-white, covered in scars and festooned with piercings. He carried a staff that appeared to be made of petrified moss, and he wore nothing but a skirt belted at his waist and a headband of snakeskin.

But it was not the shaman who had torn the wall from the hut. Something loomed behind him, bits of steam still streaming from its mouth where it had *eaten* Baltrice's fire elemental. Jace had a brief sense of a body made up of multiple cypress trees, with twisted wooden talons and a great gaping maw from which swamp-water fell in a never-ending rain. The shaman shrieked, revealing rows of teeth engraved with mystic runes, and pointed toward him with a quivering paw. The frost raptors swarmed about the intruders, for all the good they would do.

And then the world melted away, a curtain of smoky light parting before him, and Jace could not remember the last time he was so relieved to find himself in the maddening chaos of the Blind Eternities.

⚹ ⚹ ⚹ ⚹ ⚹

". . . known some blind goblins who could've planned things out better than that. What sort of brain-damaged monkeys are orchestrating our operations these days?"

Jace hunched in a chair the middle of Kallist's quarters, idly fidgeting with the hem of his cloak, while the chamber's true occupant sat across from him, drinking a cup of fruit tea that had long since gone cold. On the table between them stood an unfinished game of guilds, one on which they had wagered a bottle of elven wine. Kallist, eying the territories on the board, couldn't help but notice once again how many more of them were marked in his colors than Jace's, and wished he'd never brought the subject up.

"I know, I know," he said, his voice calming, "but if we could just get back to—"

The edge of Jace's wadded-up cloak fell from his fist, hitting the edge of the board and scattering the pieces across the table. He continued to fidget, utterly oblivious; Kallist could only sigh.

"Look, Jace," he said, straightening in his chair, "it could have gone worse."

"Really? Short of my dying, name one way."

"Well, you could have d—oh. Um, all right, maybe not."

"It's absolutely appalling, Kallist. It—"

"All right. I probably shouldn't be telling you this, but you're not the only one to think so."

"I . . ." Jace blinked. "What?"

"Word in the dining hall—"

"That would be the hall occupied by people who don't know a damn thing about off-world operations, and have never heard of planeswalkers?"

Kallist sighed again. "Fine. Paldor confided in me

after you left; I found him drunk in the hall. Apparently this isn't the first time the Kamigawa cell has failed to confirm information before passing it along to Tezzeret—though this is the first time it was anything of import. If he'd known how big a community you were dealing with, or just how deceptive the prince was being . . ." He shrugged.

Jace nodded slowly. "All right. But I'm surprised he'd put up with a cell leader being that careless."

"My understanding," Kallist said carefully, "is that he's not. When it was just a few minor bungles here and there, that was one thing. But now? Our illustrious leader is not happy with the Kamigawa cell. Or with Baltrice, or with you either, for that matter."

"Fantastic. I can't wait for *that* conversation." A pause, then. "But I guess this should at least make negotiations easier for the Kamigawa cell, since they've only got about half as many nezumi to deal with."

Kallist grinned. "Oh, come on. Half? I understand Baltrice killed a fifth, tops." Then, when Jace's glower suggested that he wasn't finding the situation amusing, the swordsman turned serious.

"Jace, what's really bugging you about this?"

"I—"

"Skip the part where you deny it."

"I—"

"And skip the part where you claim it's guilt over the collateral damage. I know that's bothering you. I also know that's not the whole of it. We've worked together for too long."

"You planning to let me finish this time?"

"Possibly."

Jace slumped even deeper into his chair, so bonelessly that Kallist half expected to find him puddled on the floor. "Have I ever mentioned Alhammarret to you?" Jace asked, his voice distant.

"Only in passing. A teacher of yours, right?"

"More than a teacher." Jace recollected. "I grew up in a village called—well, we called it Silmot's Crossing, but that's what we called every village within ten miles. One big community. The name really only applies to the largest. The rest were just—hamlets.

"Anyway, I grew up in one of the smaller ones. Until one . . ."

Jace shook his head. "You don't need my whole life story. The short version is, my father made me leave when it became pretty damned clear that the towns-folk weren't taking kindly to some of the abilities I was demonstrating. Alhammarret took me in at my father's behest. He taught me how to use the magic that came naturally to me and introduced me to a whole slew of spells that didn't. He also made me feel welcome, which was a pretty nice change of pace after the last few years.

"I was happy for a few years, with Alhammarret. Then, one day I decided to see if I was strong enough to read his thoughts."

Jace smirked, an expression of disdain clearly directed inward. "I'd never done that before—to him, I mean. I'd read plenty of other people's minds and never thought much of what I found. One of the first lessons I'd learned was that he'd sense it if I tried, and I guess I had too much respect for him, or too much fear of his implied threats, to challenge that. But you know how teenagers get.

"So I waited until he was distracted, to make sure I'd have at least a few seconds before he could react, and went in. I didn't mean any harm by it; I wasn't looking for anything in particular. I just wanted to know if I could."

Kallist could see, at least in part, where this was going. "What did you discover?" he asked softly.

"That I was a planeswalker." He nodded at Kallist's shocked look. "My Spark had manifested over a year earlier, but I'd never understood what that meant. I found myself drifting in the Eternities when it happened, but only very briefly, and only the one time. Alhammarret explained it away as some sort of delusion, something to do with my own illusions messing with my mind. And after that, he kept me busy enough learning new magic that it never happened again.

"I remember . . . I remember a sensation in his mind that my father knew, that Alhammarret had talked with him about it. I don't know exactly why they kept it from me; maybe they thought they were doing me a favor somehow.

"But I was angry, so angry that he'd lied to me for so long. I'd been furious before, Kallist, but I'd never felt betrayed."

Jace stood and began to pace, as though the emotion of that moment required an outlet. "I wanted to scream, to throw a tantrum, to lash out . . . Everything you'd expect from a kid of that age. But I didn't. I could've asked him why, but I didn't do that either.

"I just . . . seethed. For days on end, going over and over it all. And then, the next time we were practicing, I just . . . snapped. I got inside his mind, and I unleashed all that rage at once.

"I don't let myself remember his face, Kallist, even to this day. I've used my own magic to keep me from seeing it. Because I know that if I do, I won't see the face of the man who taught me most of what I know. I'll see the face of the man I walked away from: bulging eyes, gaping lips, skin slowly turning purple. The face of a mind so broken he'd forgotten who he was, what he was—even how to breathe."

Ignoring Kallist's faint shudder, Jace leaned on the back of the chair. "I've been in enough fights before and after I joined the Consortium that I've probably killed at least a few folks since then—but it was always in self-defense. I never set out to do it, just to stop them from hurting me, or get them out of my way. I've done a lot of ugly things since Tezzeret hired me, but even then, it was always you or Baltrice or whoever who did the actual killing, and most of our targets arguably deserved it. Maybe I was just fooling myself, but I never saw myself as a murderer. And then on Kamigawa, I did the exact same thing I'd done to Alhammaret. Only I did it deliberately."

Kallist nodded, thought he understood. "You're bothered by how killing the nezumi made you feel."

But Jace only shook his head. "No, Kallist." He turned to his friend, and his gaze was empty. "I'm bothered that killing him didn't bother me at all."

CHAPTER FIFTEEN

A week had passed since Jace's return from Kamigawa; a week during which Jace slept only rarely and fitfully, plagued by nervous, frustrated dreams to which genuine nightmares might almost have been preferable. He fretted over who he was, what he was becoming. He worried over the state of the Consortium, wondering how a mission like this one could've been planned and executed so badly, how and why Tezzeret could've made the decisions he'd made.

But most of all, he worried over the fact that Tezzeret hadn't yet spoken to him, and with each day that passed, he viewed the inevitable confrontation with mounting dread.

When a messenger finally pounded on his door that morning, yanking him from another dream-battered sleep and informing him that Tezzeret awaited—not in the training chamber, but in a ruined stretch of the Rubblefield outside—Jace found himself almost relieved.

He allowed himself five minutes to throw some water on his face, climb into a pair of blue trousers and tunic—forgoing his cloak, since he wasn't actually planning to go anywhere—and all but ran through the

ARI MARMELL

complex and down the nearest side streets.

He found the artificer in something of a natural courtyard between four buildings that still lay in shambles, untouched by the district's slow rebirth. Weeds grew up through the broken cobblestones, and the walls were all but painted in a thick layer of bat, bird, and griffin droppings. Whatever rubble might have lain in the courtyard itself, however, had been cleared away; it was all but empty save for Tezzeret himself, who leaned against a wall over a dozen yards away.

"Summon something," he commanded, his voice carrying clearly across the courtyard.

"What?" Jace, who'd just been opening his mouth to offer some sort of greeting or perhaps an apology, found himself utterly perplexed. "What should I—"

"Summon something! Now!"

Shaken by the fury in the artificer's voice, palpable even from such a distance, Jace asked no more questions. Still uncertain what was happening, he reached into the æther, stretched his will between the worlds. Before him, a pinprick hole opened in the walls of reality, and through it slipped a cloud sprite, riding wisps of vapor that drifted through from the skies of some other realm—one whom Jace had summoned many times before. She smiled briefly at him, nodding her head in greeting, and then turned to survey her surroundings with an ever more puzzled expression.

Tezzeret lurched away from the ruined structure and hurled something concealed in his etherium fist. An uneven disk of iron, lopsided and bedecked with tiny jagged protrusions, it nonetheless flew straight and true, spinning across the intervening distance until it crashed to the broken stones mere feet from Jace.

And even as it landed, it shifted and warped, calling upon the energies of other worlds, just as Jace's own summons had. In less than a second, a field of writhing mechanized tendrils, the underside of some horrible iron jellyfish, thrashed across the earth before him. Where they joined with each other at the ground, tiny spots glowed with the dull heat of a smelting furnace, peering out from between the tendrils like inhuman eyes.

Faster than a crossbow bolt, one of the thinnest tendrils lashed out. Its needle-sharp tip punched through the faerie's wings, pinning her to one of the surrounding buildings by what shredded strands remained. The screech of iron on stone wasn't nearly enough to cloak the cloud sprite's terrified scream as a second tendril rose; this one edged along one side, a whipping, flexing blade that gently lay itself across her thrashing torso. Jace tried desperately to dismiss the summoning, to send her away, but so stunned was he by the sudden assault that he left it too late, waited just those few seconds too long. The scream ended abruptly as the tendril pushed. The two halves of her body dropped from the wall, fading before they struck the ground and leaving behind only a tiny smear of blood to show that she had ever been.

Jace turned a furious gaze on Tezzeret. "Why?" he demanded, overwhelmed by a peculiar guilt he'd never before felt at the death of a summoned minion. "There was no reason! There—"

Metal ground on metal as the iron monstrosity struck again, this time with a squat tentacle lacking any edge at all. At full strength, it would have shattered Jace's ribs, pulped his organs; instead, it struck just hard enough to knock the wind from his lungs. His eyes watered with pain and he staggered back, glancing up as it hit him again, blackening his eye and causing it to instantly swell shut.

"Summon something else," Tezzeret commanded darkly.

"No," Jace growled, picking himself up from the floor. "There's no purpose to it."

"Oh, there's a purpose," Tezzeret all but cooed.

A shadow fell over him, and Jace looked up, just in time to see another brutal tentacle, practically a log of iron, snaking toward him. It lifted him up, agony flashing through his gut. When he landed once more, Jace couldn't keep himself from vomiting up a small puddle of bile. He tried to crawl from its reach, hoping, praying that the thing couldn't actually move from its spot. An impossibly long tendril wrapped about his ankle and dragged him back before he'd gotten even a yard.

"Why are you attacking me?" Jace gasped, struggling to drag himself out of the construct's murderous grip.

"I'm not attacking, Beleren. I'm teaching."

And he understood, then. Understood that while Tezzeret wasn't about to kill or cripple him, while he was holding the golem back, the beating wouldn't stop until Jace *made* it stop.

With a furious cry, Jace called out through the pain and the bitter residue in his mouth—and a fearsome, inhuman screech answered that call. From the sky dropped a great beast, its wings spread wide in the vastness of the courtyard. The bulk of its scales were iridescent blue, its face and horns ivory white, and tendrils of steam rose from its flaring nostrils. For a brief instant it hovered, wings flapping slowly, methodically, as it studied its ferrous foe.

"Better," Tezzeret offered from afar. "Not good enough, though."

As though to prove him wrong, the drake surged ahead, twisting almost on a wingtip to avoid a series of vicious strokes as it flew through the thicket of tendrils. It dug its claws into two of the largest, ripping them up and hurling them back against the wall with a deafening clatter. Shrieking its anger, the drake soared up toward the clouds, curling back around until it faced the construct once more. As it neared, its great maw gaped wide, unleashing a torrent of steam so impossibly hot that even Baltrice's fires might have struggled to match it.

The sharp edges of the iron grew soft and dull, and tiny droplets of liquid metal rained down to the floor around the multitude of tentacles. It reached out once more, but its movements were slow and feeble. Several of the thinner limbs looked ready to give out entirely. The drake circled the yard once more, coming back for another pass that would reduce the construct to slag.

But as its foe turned in its aerial acrobatics, the wobbling golem reached out and slammed a limb into a broken, weatherworn gate, lying before the entrance to one of the buildings. Instantly the iron crumbled into rusted particles—and just as swiftly, the tentacles straightened, whole and hearty once more, with no trace of their injuries save several sporadic scorch marks.

More than a dozen of the tendrils lashed clear across the yard, the force of their attack shaking even the cobblestones, to meet the drake halfway. Bladed limbs flew, claws raked across iron, sparks fell to sputter out upon the ground. And Jace could only cringe as the drake plunged, bleeding, into the center of the mass and slowly faded from view. He felt a sob of frustration and fear begin to well up within and mercilessly crushed it down, allowing himself only a faint gasp of pain in its place.

"Again, Beleren!" Tezzeret shouted over Jace's shout of denial, of despair. "Summon again!"

He had almost nothing left. Leaning against a wall, breathing hard, Jace watched with wide eyes as the wriggling limbs reached toward him once more. He'd never summoned anything more potent than the steam-tongued drake; it had always been his ace in the hole, a creature that none of his foes could best. He was exhausted from a week of sporadic sleep, aching from the blows he'd already taken, almost tapped out by the summons he'd already cast. Burning hell, he hadn't even had breakfast!

But he knew, as well, that he could not take another pummeling. It wasn't that he was concerned about physical pain, not anymore: he refused to admit further weakness to the metal-armed bastard across the way.

Jace sank to the floor, his legs hunched, his back against a wall. In and out he breathed, slowly, ignoring as best he could the metal fiend that drew ever nearer. And he reached, carefully, desperately, for the river that flowed through the heart of Ravnica, past the borders of Dravhoc district. The Rubblefield wasn't built on the banks of that river, but it wasn't all that far. Jace's familiarity with it might just be enough.

He touched her mind and soul, felt her respond to his call. He'd sensed her before, though he'd never known precisely who or what she was, felt her watching him as he sent his senses into the æther, practiced the litanies and exercises that, when put together, would comprise summoning spells more potent than any he'd ever tried to cast. This wasn't how he'd planned to test himself, to try such a powerful summons, but Tezzeret had taken the choice from him.

Channeling mana from the river as though he himself were nothing but a tributary, Jace threw his power and his will and his need into the void.

The stone wall of one of the surrounding structures burst outward, reduced to a snowlike powder as something immensely powerful struck it from behind. An enormous leonine body squeezed through the gap, cracking the stone farther as it appeared. The fur that coated her sleek form was an unnaturally deep blue, but multihued wings spread from her back, and her head and face were those of a beautiful, and very angry, woman. Her eyes flickered briefly over Jace's bloodied form, and then to the metallic limbs that threatened him. She hurled back her head and uttered a roar that wasn't remotely feminine, and took to the air with a leap of her hind legs, a leap so powerful she scarcely had to spread her wings at all before she landed atop her foe.

Her great weight and greater strength brought a dozen tendrils crashing to the earth. They thrashed at her, with razor-edged blades and bone-breaking cudgels. Most of its attacks she swatted aside, a cat enjoying the feeble struggling of a dying lizard. Of those that connected, most rebounded from her toughened hide; only once did the golem's blade cut deep, drawing blood as blue as the sphinx's fur. She roared once more, reared high, and came crashing down with all her weight, front paws flying faster than the eye could see. And when she finally stopped and stepped away, Tezzeret's construct was nothing but a pile of shredded strips, for her claws pierced iron as easily as they would have flesh. The courtyard suddenly reeked of strange oils and base metals.

Jace gave her a smile of deep gratitude, even bowing his head as he dismissed the summons, allowing her to return to her distant home. And then he turned and glared as Tezzeret appeared above him, applauding softly.

"Are you happy now?" Jace spat at him.

"Indeed." Tezzeret knelt until he could meet the younger man's eyes. "You've learned three vital lessons today, Beleren. You've learned that strength unused is strength you do not have, that you should never hold back your full potential. You've learned to call allies far greater than any you've yet commanded."

"And the third?" Jace asked, trying hard neither to scream at Tezzeret nor to roll his eyes at this "lesson."

"You've learned that you already strip free will from other creatures when it suits you. What else are you doing, when you summon up a sprite, or a drake, or a sphinx, to fight and possibly to die for you?"

ARI MARMELL

Jace felt the blood drain from his face, and he wondered why he'd never considered that before.

"Baltrice told me what you did to the ratman," the artificer said. "I know you can do it, and now I've shown you that you are indeed *willing* to do it. So the next time I order you to do so, I expect you to obey. Without hesitation, and without complaint.

"Go take yourself to the healers before any of those freeze up on you."

And with that he was gone, striding from the broken courtyard.

Jace watched the artificer depart, and his eyes narrowed in smoldering resentment. Yes, these were indeed the sorts of insights Tezzeret often tried to impart. Yes, he had indeed mastered potent magic today. And no, Tezzeret had never said one word about the failed Kamigawa excursion.

But Jace, clutching at his ribs and his stomach as he rose, staring at the ruins through his one good eye, damn well knew a punishment when he was dealt one.

⁂ ⁂ ⁂ ⁂ ⁂ ⁂

There was only so much the healers could do, and by late the next afternoon, Jace was still sore all over, and so mottled with bruises he looked like a plague victim. Still, the messenger who came pounding on his door had been drenched in sweat, and the tone in his voice left little doubt that when Paldor had said "Right now," he'd meant *right now*. So Jace swallowed the pain as best he could and sprinted through the halls of the complex, squeezing past servants and soldiers where he could, shoving them out of the way where he could not. Finally, his feet had carried him to the foyer just inside the main entryway. There he skidded to a halt, panting heavily, and allowed himself a moment to take in the scene.

Paldor stood beside the doorway through which Jace

had just barreled. His hands were clasped behind his back—but the young mage couldn't help but notice that those meaty hands held a crossbow, cocked and ready to fire. Half a dozen Consortium soldiers and swordsmen, Kallist included, held naked steel in their hands and stood in a circle around a stranger whose crooked grin suggested that he found the whole affair amusing.

He was human, this newcomer, with blond hair slicked back so tightly it just had to be giving him a headache. He was clad in black suede tunic and pants, topped with an ankle-length cloak of deep burgundy, complete with gold clasp and black lace frills at the collar. He wore a curved dagger at his waist but currently held his hands to the sides, well away from the weapon's hilt.

"What's going on?" Jace gasped to Paldor.

The corpulent lieutenant harrumphed. "Fellow claims to be a messenger from Tezzeret's 'master.' "

For a long moment, Jace just stared. "Master?" he finally repeated.

"Nicol Bolas. Bastard's got a warped sense of humor, apparently."

"Who . . ." Jace's eyes lit up with understanding. "Is that who Tezzeret stole the Consortium from?" he whispered, so as not to be overheard. He gave some thought to the mind-speech, decided it wasn't worth the effort.

"I prefer to think of it as having annexed the organization for the greater good," Paldor replied, his voice equally faint.

"And he knows where to find us? He just, what, knocked on our door?"

"Pretty much," Paldor told him. "Bolas has a network as large as the Consortium. We may be rivals, but we still have to communicate. Ravnica's heavily populated enough that nobody's going to risk open war, so it's sort of neutral territory. Here, if nowhere else, we each know where to find representatives of the other."

ARI MARMELL

"I see," Jace said, though he wasn't certain he really did. "And I'm here to . . .?"

"Read his mind. He claims he's got a written message for Tezzeret's eyes only. I want to make damn sure he's not an assassin or some sort of magical construct before I even consider putting him in touch with the boss."

"Do we know if he's a mage? If he'll sense me?"

Paldor shrugged. "He's welcome to raise a fuss if he wants. Um, but Jace," he added as the mind-reader took a step forward. "Let's not push things. We don't know what sorts of sorcery Bolas himself is capable of. We don't want to offend him unnecessarily, and anyway, he's not likely to send a messenger to us who knows anything compromising. Confirm this man is who he says he is and that his intentions are as stated, but don't dig any deeper."

Jace nodded, and took a moment to gather his concentration. The fellow glanced his way and offered a smile equal parts ingratiating and condescending, but if he had any notion what was happening, if he felt anything when Jace touched his mind, it never showed on his face.

"His name's Mauriel Pellam," Jace told Paldor a minute later. "He is, indeed, a messenger for Bolas—or, more accurately, for people who work for people who work for Bolas. And as far as I can tell, he's just here to deliver a message, no more sinister purpose."

"Excellent," Paldor said. Then, more loudly, "All right, boys, stand down. You and you, kindly escort my guest and me to my office. The rest of you, back to your duties."

Jace watched the four men turn and disappear down the hall. He threw Kallist a questioning glance but the other man could only shrug, equally bewildered. Jace left the foyer far more slowly than he'd arrived, favoring his bruised ribs and wondering what the frying hell that had all been about.

The dining room was among the most opulent and best maintained areas in the Consortium's entire Ravnica complex. Multiple tables, from intimate two-seaters to enormous slabs capable of seating thirty with room to spare, stood about the chamber. The chairs were comfortable, upholstered works of art, allowing their occupants to sit for hours without growing sore or restless. Multiple doors allowed access to the halls of the complex, as well as to the massive kitchen, ensuring a clear path for servers to come and go. On every wall hung tapestries of intricate craftsmanship, most of which had the vaguely enticing smell of old cooking permanently trapped between the threads, and the ceiling boasted rafters of wood that served absolutely no structural purpose, granting the entire room a vaguely artistic, homey feel.

The floor, however, was bare hardwood; Paldor had reluctantly allowed the fancy shag carpets to be torn out after the entire cleaning staff threatened to resign.

Tonight, as he sometimes did when there was forthcoming business to discuss, Paldor invited some of the cell's top agents to a dinner provided by his private chefs. Seven of them now sat around one of the mid-sized tables: Kallist and Jace; Ireena, an elf with surprisingly tan skin and clad in a blood-red gown that nobody but she thought looked good on her; the mage Gemreth, with a peculiar, four-winged imp perched on his shoulder and giggling on occasion at nothing at all; the vedalken Sevrien, now clad in the chain armor of a Consortium soldier; Xalmarias, a centaur who had made room for himself at the table by kicking several chairs across the room, clad only in a rich green vest with gold and silver buttons; and of course, Paldor himself.

The soup course, a thick, cheesy tuber stew, had already come and gone. In the center of the table lay a steaming platter of mild vegetable pastries intended to clear the palate for the mincemeat pies Paldor had specifically requested for the night's repast.

As they waited, Jace kept his gaze fixed largely on the table before him. It all smelled so good, but he'd eaten only a few spoonfuls of the soup and was wondering if he could stomach the pies at all. Over the past four days he had all but recovered from his injuries, but a nagging unpleasantness, not quite pain and not quite nausea, lingered in his gut.

"All right," Paldor said around a prodigious bite of biscuit, "let's get started." So long had he been talking with his mouth full, he was able to do so now without the slightest loss of enunciation. "Ireena, we're having some difficulty with our workhouses in the Nalatras alchemical slums. Some sort of poisoning or plague our healers can't cure that almost seems to move like a living thing. We've hired Vess on to help you with this, in case there's a spirit of some sort involved." Ireena scowled but nodded her acceptance. "So, if the two of you . . ."

Paldor went on, and Jace tuned him out. He knew he probably ought to pay attention to what else was going on around him, keep up with the cell's activities, but today he just didn't have it in him to care. He scarcely noticed when the servants scurried by, sliding a dish of mincemeat and bread in front of his face.

Only when he heard his name did he raise his head to stare dully at Paldor, who had flecks of meat and a tiny stream of juices dribbling down the side of his chin. "Yes?"

"Nothing too difficult for you this week," the lieutenant told him, dabbing at his lips with a napkin. "One of the Rubblefield landowners is being stubborn about the value of a property we want for expanding the complex. You and Kallist will be posing as two brothers representing the 'merchant family' that wants to buy it. Kallist will be handling the actual negotiations. Your job is to take a peek inside the man's head and find something we can use to, ah, persuade him to be more reasonable."

"Uh-huh. And if there's no such thing?"

"There always is. You don't get to be a landowner in Ravnica without stepping on folks. But if not? Then you *make* him sign at our preferred cost. The long-term solution's the better one, but we do what we've gotta do."

Jace nodded, pushing idly at his dinner with a fork. "How many guards, if things go wrong?"

Paldor shrugged. "My sources say he usually travels with four. Should be easy enough for you."

"Is that easy like 'real world' easy, or easy like 'nezumi village' easy?" Jace inquired before he could think better of it. "Because if it's the latter, I might need backup."

Several pieces of silverware clattered to the table and a number of mouths stopped chewing as six pairs of eyes fastened on him in wide astonishment. Jace, however, was too angry to feel self-conscious about it.

"I see." Paldor, too, swallowed his current mouthful and lay his fork and napkin down before him. For a moment, his gaze swept over the entire table. "Is anyone here," he asked calmly, "unfamiliar with the recent unfortunate events to which Jace refers?"

Everyone looked away, perhaps trying to spare Jace the embarrassment. While few of those in the room knew anything about other worlds, they'd all heard a somewhat edited version of Jace's recent "failure."

"And you, Jace," he continued. "You feel you've been treated unfairly?"

At that point, even Jace had come to the conclusion that it might be wiser to shut quite thoroughly up, but he couldn't bring himself to do it. "I feel like I've been punished," he said, idly rubbing his aching gut, "for someone else's mistakes."

"Indeed." Paldor leaned back in his chair, stretching his great bulk until his spine unleashed a trio of audible pops. "It's normally not done to speak ill of the leadership of another cell," he said slowly, "but it hardly matters anymore at this point.

"Yes, Jace. The mistakes were, for the most part, not yours. People got lazy, complacent, and didn't bother to check what they were told. My understanding is that the new cell leader is trying very hard to salvage the nezumi situation, since Tezzeret expressed his displeasure to the previous leader in no uncertain and, ah, final terms."

Several of the diners murmured into their hands or their glasses, but nobody said anything intelligible.

"As for Baltrice . . ." he continued.

Paldor reached into his left sleeve and then slammed his right hand down on the table. "Do you know what this is?" he asked Jace, even as several of the others recoiled.

He didn't, but sure as the Eternities were blind it wasn't a normal dagger. The blade was a strange gray metal that shimmered without the need for external light—it might, Jace realized with a start, even be forged of etherium, or at least an alloy thereof. A faint dark mist wafted from the weapon's edge, as though it were slowly evaporating in a cold night, though the blade itself never diminished.

"It's called a manablade," Paldor said when Jace remained silent. "A rare weapon, acquired by Tezzeret some years ago from the Church of the Incarnate Soul."

"Never heard of them."

"Not surprising, and also not the point. The blade doesn't just draw blood, Jace. Oh, when used against someone like me, it's normal enough. A knife is a knife is a knife, right? But," he continued, leaning forward, "it cuts into a mage's soul. Bleeds his very essence into the æther. Wound a caster with this, and he doesn't just lose blood, he loses his bonds to mana. I'm told it's just about the most excruciating experience imaginable."

Jace couldn't help but shudder. What was this church, that they could forge something like that?

"Tezzeret gifted it to me a while ago," Paldor said, "as a reward for the completion of a particularly important operation. But he still borrows it, on occasion. And he borrowed it last week. My understanding," and now there was nothing jovial at all in that normally cheerful visage, "is that he kept himself to shallow cuts. He just wanted to make a point, after all, not permanently injure his best agent. Baltrice's scars'll probably be healed before you see her again. Or at least, the physical ones will." His eyes gleamed sickly. "I was there—Tezzeret let me watch, since it's my blade—and I think the memories will last her long, long after the scars have faded.

"So don't come in here, Beleren, and whine to me about a little soreness after a failed operation." Paldor flicked his wrist, and the manablade vanished once more up his sleeve. "I promise you, you don't know what punishment is. Keep doing your best for Tezzeret, he'll keep making you rich—and you'll never *need* to know."

Jace looked down at the table once more, and nodded.

"Excellent." Paldor's face broke out in his accustomed grin once more. "So, who's up for dessert while we start talking details?"

CHAPTER SIXTEEN

Jace's face was a stony mask as he pushed through the door into Paldor's office, but those who knew him well could see faint ember of smoldering irritation, even resentment, behind his eyes. It was a look he wore frequently these days.

"What could possibly be so urgent," the mage demanded while leaning both fists on the edge of the desk, his voice low but firm as iron, "that you had to pull me out in the middle of an ongoing assignment?"

Paldor looked meaningfully at the desktop, then at Jace. He was not smiling. "Get your hands off."

Jace straightened, but his expression didn't crack. "You know you left Kallist to finish the job alone? No blades, you said. Make it look like a natural death, you said. How is Kallist supposed to make it look natural without me, Paldor? Did you even think of that?"

His face purpling, Paldor pointed across the room. And only then did Jace realize that a figure stood in the far corner, a figure he'd swept past without even noticing.

"Really, Beleren," Tezzeret chided him. "Have you so little respect for your superiors anymore?"

"Is there any way I can possibly answer that?"

Tezzeret chuckled. "Probably not. I *am* sorry for pulling you away from your assignment, Beleren. I'm sure Kallist will do fine, though. He was doing this long before you showed up."

"So he was."

"But I need you for something more important. I need you to accompany me to a meeting."

Jace's eyebrow rose. "Any chance that means you'll finally be taking me to your sanctum itself?"

"Not at all. We're going someplace far less pleasant."

Paldor snickered at Jace's disappointed expression. "Really, what'd you expect? I don't even know where his illustriousness takes his ease."

"I've asked you not to call me that, Paldor," Tezzeret reminded him.

"And I've asked to be taller," Paldor told him with a grin. Tezzeret scowled but said nothing more.

"The meeting?" Jace prompted.

"Yes." Tezzeret wandered behind the desk and gave Paldor a meaningful look. The lieutenant grumbled but heaved his great bulk out of the way so his employer might sit. The artificer scowled at the height of the chair, which made him look faintly ridiculous behind the equally short desk, but at least he had no doubt it would take his weight.

He turned and gave Paldor a second look, equally significant.

"Oh, you've got to be kidding!" Paldor exclaimed. "Boss, this is my office. I—"

"Should therefore know the fastest route to the door, shouldn't you? I'll let you know when we're done."

Grumbling even more loudly, Paldor stomped his way to the door and slammed it behind him.

"How have you been, Beleren? We've not spoken in a while."

Deader every day. How about you?

"Fine," he said. "Everything's just fine."

"So glad to hear it. You'll be accompanying me to a rather delicate negotiation."

"Oh?"

Tezzeret waved a hand. "Bit of a conflict over mining rights in overlapping territories. Nothing that should particularly interest you."

"That's nice," Jace said, "but actually, I meant who are we meeting with?"

"Nicol Bolas."

"Ah," Jace said, after replaying the answer in his mind to be certain he'd heard correctly. "This would be related to that messenger who came to us a few weeks ago."

"It would."

Jace shook his head and allowed himself to fall back into one of the room's sundry chairs. "I've never entirely understood . . . This Bolas is pretty powerful, obviously. Obviously a planeswalker, or he couldn't have put together something like the Consortium. So why usurp it from him? Couldn't you think of any safer way of building an organization?"

Tezzeret grinned. "Some while ago, Beleren, I found myself in the ranks of a cabal that called themselves the Seekers of Carmot. Sorcerers and alchemists, they claimed a great many fascinating discoveries—but the greatest of all, and one they promised to teach me once I'd proved worthy, was the rediscovery of the ancient arts for creating etherium!" He raised his artificial arm, as though he felt the need to remind Jace of its existence.

"Well, of course I was intrigued," he said as though it was the most obvious thing in the world. "The person, or the faction, that learns how to replenish the Multiverse's dwindling stores of etherium would be powerful enough to trade whole worlds!

"Imagine my disappointment when I discovered that it was all a lie. That the tales of forging etherium were a deception orchestrated by the true master of the Seekers of Carmot as one of his various convoluted schemes. And imagine my anger when, upon realizing that I knew the truth, the Seekers attempted to have me killed! After all my years of service!" Tezzeret shook his head, then smiled once more.

"Care to guess who the Seekers' master actually was?"

Jace gawped at him. "So stealing the Consortium was—what? Revenge?"

"I do not," Tezzeret told him blandly, "take kindly to treachery."

Several moments marched by as Jace allowed that to sink in. "All right," he said finally. "So what *about* revenge? You think Bolas is going to meet with you peacefully, just like that? You aren't afraid he might, oh, I don't know, try to kill you?"

Tezzeret smiled and began idly tapping his fingers on the desk. The wood made a hollow sound beneath the impact of the etherium. "Bolas controls his own network of organizations, Beleren, and he's agreed to meet with me leader to leader. He won't renege on the promise of a safe negotiation, not and risk word getting out to others he might need to bargain with later on."

"And you trust that?"

"Not at all. I only agreed to this meeting if we could each set up wards in advance, ensuring that neither of us can attack the other. And we'll be arriving early, to double-check those wards."

"Well, if you're sure . . ." Jace frowned. "So what am I here for?"

"Ah, that." Tezzeret's grin flipped itself over into a faint scowl. "The truth is, I'm not entirely certain what Bolas is capable of. More specifically, I don't know if he can read minds."

Jace nodded slowly. "Paldor implied something similar. So you want me there to let you know if—"

"No. I'm certain I'd sense it if he did it to me. You're there to *block* him."

Jace blinked.

"It doesn't do me any good to know he's reading my mind," Tezzeret said, "if he gets what he's looking for in the process. And there are certain details that might rather substantially weaken my bargaining position if he were to learn them."

"So why meet him in person? Why not send a proxy?"

"Part of the deal," the artificer groused. "He wouldn't meet with anyone but me, and this mining operation is worth a lot. I have to get this matter settled."

Jace frowned. Something about that didn't ring true at all; he'd swear he almost heard an undercurrent of fear beneath Tezzeret's normally unshakable facade.

He also knew better than to question the man. "You know I've never actually met another reader, as far as I know, right?" he said instead. "I've got a pretty good grasp of the theory behind how to block an attempt, but I've never put it into practice. I have no idea if I can do what you're asking."

Tezzeret nodded. "But you're more likely than anyone else, aren't you?"

That made sense; Jace nodded. "All right. Nicol Bolas. Anything else I should know about him, other than that he's a planeswalker with a serious grudge against you?"

"Not really," Tezzeret said, rising to his feet. "Oh, except that he's a twenty-five thousand-year-old dragon and bigger than an ogre's barn.

"Any more questions?"

"No," Jace said sickly. "I think that'll do."

✳ ✳ ✳ ✳ ✳ ✳

After the third time Tezzeret tried, and failed, to pronounce the name of the world for Jace's edification, the young mage gave up on trying to master it. Frankly, it didn't much matter if he knew the name of the world.

He just knew that it was damned cold.

They stood at the base of an arctic mountain range, in a crevice that offered only mediocre protection from the howling winds. Streaks of snow and sleet whipped through the air, turned sideways by those winds, sifting downward past the various crags and stone arches. Sleet stung the face, flakes melted through clothes to shiver the skin beneath. Jace felt the presence of mana in the ice below, yet it was faint, almost anemic. Someone or something—Bolas himself, perhaps?—had drawn frequently and thirstily upon the magic within, leaving precious little until the region had time to recover.

He huddled in a heavy, fur-lined cloak, wrapped about him and held with arms crossed over his chest. Even through his scarf, he saw tiny puffs of mist with every breath. Yet Tezzeret, who was clad in leather leggings and a heavy vest with multiple pockets and straps, looked quite comfortable. From the forearm of his prosthetic hung a brass globe, attached as though with some sort of magnetism or adhesive. It glowed a warm orange and emitted a low hum that made Jace want to reach into his own head and scratch his eardrums until they stopped itching.

And possibly to punch Tezzeret in the mouth for bringing only one.

"Where is he, anyway?" Jace called out, shouting to be heard over the roaring winds. "I thought we were supposed to meet him half an hour ago!"

Tezzeret shrugged. "'Bolas does not wait for you,'" he quoted. "'You wait for Bolas.'"

"I've never cared for that expression." The voice came from everywhere and nowhere, carried on the wind, echoing throughout the canyon. It was deep, the rumble of the mountain's roots as the earth shifted slowly above; it resounded in their ears, utterly unimpeded by the raging blizzard. "It makes me sound so pompous. I despise other people making me sound pompous."

The canyon before them began to darken, as something unimaginably huge took shape. "I prefer," the voice continued, "to do it myself."

And then he was simply there. The eldest planeswalker. The Forever Serpent.

Nicol Bolas.

He filled the canyon, a living mountain of muscle and scale, fire and fang. His dark hide shown green against the backdrop of blinding white; the smoke that rose from his nostrils was thick and red, and rain fell from the heavens where the heat of his breath melted the falling sleet. Vast wings spread wide, extending hundreds of feet from the chasm on each side—and then, impossibly, he drew them in, tucked them tightly against his body and lowered himself to the canyon's floor. The great head turned, aiming a single eye at the two insignificant humans, and within they saw themselves reflected in a black and bottomless abyss.

Jace found himself unable to speak, scarcely even to breathe. Even Tezzeret blanched; anyone who had spent less time with him than Jace himself would never have seen it, but there it was. No matter how well he hid it, the artificer was terrified, and Jace found that more disturbing than the dragon itself. Then, taking a deep breath, Tezzeret strode forward, "accidentally" shouldering Jace aside in the process. The jolt was enough to get him thinking once more; and Jace cast his mind out in a net, surrounding Tezzeret's own. Still, he could not tear his gaze from the impossible beast before him.

"You do us great honor with your presence," Tezzeret began, only the faintest quiver in his voice. "It is my hope, Nicol Bolas, that together we can come to a mutually beneficial—"

"Shut up." Bolas shifted his head, causing a small avalanche of ice and rock to pour down from the ledge against which he stood. "I hate you, artificer, and I find rare cause to bother hating anyone anymore. The only reason I'm not currently picking your spine out from between my teeth is because you were smart enough to arrange these wards ahead of time.

"More to the point," he continued, "I know full well you feel the same about me, no matter how you choose to doll up your words and trot them out like perfumed trollops." The dragon shifted, dragging a single claw across the ice with an ear-splitting screech. "So perhaps we can save the pleasantries for those who might actually care about them, and simply tell me what you propose?"

"Very well. First, I want you to stop . . ." Tezzeret took a breath, coughed once to hide the fact that his voice had nearly broken. "Stop interfering with my operations in the Kankarras Mountains."

"Your operations?" Bolas rumbled. "I seem to recall staking a very public—and perfectly legal—claim to the mineral rights all the way from the banks of the Ashadris to . . ."

After only a few minutes of mountains and rivers, mines and foundries, treaties and neutral grounds, Jace found his mind wandering. The voices of the dragon and the artificer both faded into background noise, not unlike the blizzard itself.

Tiresome, isn't it, Jace Beleren?

Jace practically leaped out of his clothes, which might well have posed a problem given the ambient temperatures. He recognized the voice, yet the dragon's attention remained fixed on Tezzeret, its massive maw moving as it spoke. It took the mage several heartbeats to recognize telepathic speech when he was on the receiving end, rather than the projecting.

Lord Bolas? he sent questioningly.

ARI MARMELL

Nicol Bolas. You'd be surprised how little titles mean after you've claimed pretty much all of them.

Jace found himself nodding and forced himself to stop. Somehow, he didn't think Tezzeret would be all that pleased to learn this conversation was taking place.

I find myself curious, Bolas continued. *How did one such as you find yourself cleaning up the artificer's messes?*

Again, Jace had to stop himself—this time, from shrugging. *It was the best offer I had coming to me.*

Ah. You may find, Jace Beleren, that being the best doesn't make it good.

A moment passed, and still the dragon continued to argue with Tezzeret, offering up not the slightest sign of any other effort.

How did you lose an entire organization, anyway? Jace would have taken the thought back as soon as he sent it, but of course it was far too late.

Bolas merely chuckled, a strange sound to hear inside one's own mind. *And here I'd taken you for a coward.*

Well, I—

In short, Jace Beleren, I grew careless. I have many such factions and cabals that answer to me, and I cannot keep as close a watch on them as I might wish. Not anymore, he added bitterly.

Jace wanted to ask him what that meant but decided he'd pushed things far enough.

The artificer simply worked his way up through the organization until he was near the top—and then he and his minions slew everyone of higher rank. More important, they slew everyone, save those they implicitly trusted, who knew that the Consortium secretly answered to me. Without my own people to counter his commands, he simply stepped into the power vacuum and continued operating as though nothing had changed.

I have, on occasion, attempted to slip agents back into the ranks, but he always seems to detect them. Though the dragon's head did not turn, Jace had the sudden sensation that he was being glared at. *It's almost as though he has a mind-reader in his employ, isn't it?*

Jace, who had more than once been asked to check a new recruit for loyalty and had pointed out those who were harboring secrets, smiled wanly and glanced around for any place to run.

But when Bolas "spoke" again, he sounded wistful rather than angry. *We were gods once, Beleren. Did you know that?*

I—what?

No, I suppose you wouldn't. Not at your age. The dragon heaved what Jace could only call a mental sigh. *The Spark burned so much brighter then. We willed our desires upon the worlds, and the worlds obeyed. And then, the catastrophe on Dominaria and we . . .*

We are less, Beleren. Less than we were. . . The dragon's mind threatened to burn Jace's soul with its sudden heat. *And less than we will be!*

Jace felt his world spinning, overwhelmed at the intensity of Bolas's fervor. *Why . . . Why are you telling me this?*

Why, Jace Beleren? I thought that you would care to know. That, and it made for a magnificent diversion, don't you think?

Even as Jace froze, a lightning bolt of panic flashing through him, he felt the dragon's mind sweep past, arrowing for gaps in the "net" of thoughts and notions with which he had surrounded Tezzeret's mind.

His body rigid, as though he'd long since succumbed to the blizzard's touch, Jace hurled the entire force of his will into a mental lunge. His mind screamed into the ice, and nobody heard. Like a closing fist, he snapped shut the grid of thought, trying to block Bolas before he—

Oh, dear Heaven!

Jace's mind quailed before the greatest power he had ever felt. The innermost depths of Alhammarret's psyche, the very core of the wizard's being, had been nothing, a gentle springtime gust to the roaring hurricane that was this single tendril of the dragon's mind.

That tendril became a spear, stabbing at Tezzeret's mind. The web-work of Jace's magic closed around it, trapping it between ideas. Bolas pushed, Jace squeezed, and for just an instant—precious little time, yet a far more impressive feat than Jace would ever realize—the young mage held fast.

Sweat poured from his brow and froze, forming a tiny hedge of his hair. His eyes watered, threatening to do the same, and Jace blinked them clear before the forming icicles could blind him. His head pounded, and the sky and the snow turned gray before his fading vision. In seconds, what little mana waited to be tapped underground was gone. He strained to reach farther out, hoping for more, and found almost none to be had. Bolas, or whatever wizards dwelt on this inhospitable world, had truly sucked the region dry.

His breathing came in short and ragged gasps, the frigid air burning his lungs. His stomach knotted, his fists clenched inside their gloves. He felt a capillary burst in his left eye, heard something pop deep in his sinuses. He felt a liquid warmth running from his nose, a warmth that didn't last long before it, too, began to freeze.

Still the pressure grew, the mind-tendril shifting in his grasp, and Jace knew, without knowing how he knew, that the dragon had not yet begun to struggle. Maybe—*maybe*—if Jace had remained focused, if he'd caught the attack before it had already penetrated his scattered defenses, he might have had a chance. He could have altered the phalanx of concentration and deliberation that protected Tezzeret, closed the gaps before Bolas exploited them, and just perhaps repulsed the dragon long enough to get Tezzeret some sort of warning.

But now? Every instinct Jace had, every part of his

soul, shrieked at him to retreat, to draw back into his mind and get as far away as possible. With a defeated gasp, he tumbled to the ground. His body shook, and the ice and snow around him turned pink with blood.

Tezzeret saw none of this. The artificer, still in mid-sentence, staggered as the weight of Nicol Bolas's mind touched his own. Only then, jaw slack with shock and a growing alarm, did he glance behind long enough to notice Jace crawling across the ice.

"Really, Tezzeret," Nicol Bolas said, his tone unchanged. "I'm disappointed. Of course, I've already killed him; I've known he was being paid off for some time. But he didn't seem to know who was receiving the ore he skimmed from my shipments. Smart move, using a third party.

"Coming to see me afterward, somewhat less so."

"You can't touch me, Bolas!" Tezzeret insisted, drawing himself back to his full height even as his body began to shake for reasons that had nothing to do with the cold. His left hand was behind him, hovering over a pouch of implements and tools, while his prosthetic was raised high, ready to cast a battery of potent spells. "Whatever you're accusing me of doing outside this place, the wards bind you while you're here!"

The dragon's laughter thundered through the canyons and set the snow atop the nearest mountains to quivering. "Little artificer, you are absolutely correct. I am bound by the same wards you are, and you would be long gone by the time I could break them."

Tezzeret felt at least a bit of tension drain from his shoulders—only to return twice over as an arrow thudded into the ground at his feet, sending shards of ice slicing into the leather of his boot.

"Of course," Bolas continued, as a veritable mob of humanoid silhouettes appeared atop the chasm's walls, "as you've already so generously established when bribing my servants, third parties don't count."

The crunch of his steps drowned out by the sounds of running men, twanging bowstrings, and the hideous rumble of Bolas's laughter, Tezzeret fled.

CHAPTER SEVENTEEN

The snow gave only slightly beneath the artificer's feet, scarcely slowing him, as though he were partly held aloft by some invisible platform. Swiftly he drew even with Jace, and for a moment he appeared disinclined to stop. Only when he saw the younger mage already struggling to rise did he reach out a metallic hand and haul him to his feet.

"Can you run?" Tezzeret demanded of him.

"I—"

"Run or die."

Jace ran.

Arrows fell around them, thick as sleet, and Jace stumbled frequently in the deep snows, slowing their progress. One of the razor-edged missiles sliced through the flesh of Tezzeret's left arm, sending a spray of blood to solidify swiftly on the freezing earth. The artificer grunted, scooped a fistful of snow in his etherium hand and clamped it over the shallow wound to stanch the blood, but otherwise seemed scarcely to notice.

Yet the sleet was their ally, as was the howling wind, for they caused most of the native hunters' bows to aim wide, protecting the fugitives until Tezzeret gathered his wits sufficiently to cast an illusion of shifting white above them, blending, at least from a distance, with the fallen snow.

He dashed around a sharp bend in the canyon wall, bodily yanking a panting Jace after him. From his pouch he yanked a crystal sphere, the same he'd used to spy on Jace during Baltrice's test. Holding it to his eye, sharpening his vision far beyond what might qualify as human, he peered back around the corner.

Distance meant nothing; the falling snow ceased to blur his sight. He saw several dozen men scaling the chasm walls like spiders, some not even bothering with ropes to aid their descent. Each sported a heavy beard of red or brown or blond, and each was clad in leathers and furs belonging to no animal Tezzeret had ever seen alive. Axes and scramaseaxes hung from their waists, short but powerful bows across their backs. Barbarians, then, no doubt hired or pressed into service from native tribes. Of Bolas, he could detect no sign, save for a trace of laughter still hovering upon the frigid winds.

But what worried him most were not the barbarians themselves, though their numbers were daunting indeed. Rather, it was a pair of men already at the base of the cliff, each of whom wore a heavy cloak of red-dyed fur atop his armor. How they got there, Tezzeret didn't know, but they pulled a two-wheeled wagon made of old, cracked wood. Atop it stood a box, perhaps five feet on a side, sculpted entirely of black iron and covered with simple runes that steamed in the icy air.

Even as Tezzeret found himself wondering what might lurk in that cage of steel and spell, one of the bearers leaned in toward the metal, ran a hand over the carven symbols. Starting from that rune, the metal warped, bending and peeling away, a grotesque flower of blackened iron. And the thing within emerged.

A single limb struck the ice and snow, like the front paw of a stalking hound, yet this was no paw but a humanoid hand. Long fingers splayed out as the palm touched the ice, followed instantly by a second hand.

It was humanoid, this thing, and indeed roughly human size, yet it crept on all fours as a hunting beast. Tezzeret could clearly see its eyes flickering this way and that, its crooked teeth behind a scraggly bearded jaw. It was built like a man, it moved like an animal—and it was made entirely of mists, individual wisps woven together, the final steaming breaths of a hundred frozen corpses.

And though it could not possibly have seen Tezzeret through sheets of sleet and a blanket of illusion, nonetheless it raised its head to the skies in a silent howl and began to lope in their direction, the barbarians following.

Again they ran, Jace panting and wheezing beside the artificer, who seemed utterly tireless. More than once Jace stumbled, tripped up by snow drifts over which Tezzeret smoothly ran; and after his third tumble, Tezzeret stopped reaching down a hand to haul him up. Jace felt a sudden chill that had nothing whatsoever to do with the blizzard around them, and redoubled his efforts.

Once and once only, Tezzeret—far more comfortable in the role of hunter than hunted—stopped and turned to fight. Mouthing a complex spell, he hurled a tiny shard of scrap metal. It flew far, and against the wind, to strike the iron box in which the barbarian's ghostly hound had lurked—and that iron began to bend. It toppled slowly off the wagon, accompanied by the sound of rending metal. And then it rose, a mere box no longer, but a construct of enormous size, humanoid but twice as tall as a human, inhabited by whatever spirit Tezzeret had called from the outer void. It stepped forward with a series of clicks and whirrs, ready to engage the barbarians in battle.

And from above, a shadow spread over the ice-veiled sun. Nicol Bolas circled once, wings outspread as though to clutch the world entire, and melted Tezzeret's forged ally to slag with a single fiery exhalation, filling the chasm with choking fumes.

The flames never came near the artificer or the mage, of course, for Bolas was indeed still bound by the ward. And again his laughter echoed through the canyon as Jace and Tezzeret ran once more, the barbarians close on their heels. Jace looked briefly back, and noticed with some puzzlement that the frozen apparition leading those barbarians stopped for a moment to stare at the swiftly cooling scrap; an idea began to work its way through the haze of exhaustion that smothered his mind.

The chasm grew jagged. Spurs of rock reached into their path, grabbing at cloak and limb; narrow bridges arched overhead, from which extra bits of snow sifted down as savages ran from one side to the other seeking a better vantage. Beneath the snow and the ice, the stone grew precarious, until even Tezzeret had to slow his pace lest an ankle turn beneath him or he find himself planted face-first on the ground.

And always the barbarians were there, led by their unerring hound. They lurked above, sending arrows deep into the chasm at the slightest sign of motion. They ran only a few hundred yards behind, following the directions of the ghostly guide from the box. Time and again Jace and Tezzeret took cover and heard only the winds, hoped that they might have lost their pursuers long enough to walk from this world, only to hear the echoes of nearing boots as they began their concentrations.

Eventually even the seemingly indefatigable Tezzeret was wheezing, and Jace had to keep one hand constantly on the wall to prevent himself from toppling over.

Turning on his heel, the artificer dragged Jace into still another tiny crevice, one that would provide no shelter at all once their pursuers spotted them. But this time, Tezzeret cried out, calling upon every iota of mana he could spare without stranding him on this forsaken rock of a world. To each side of the fissure, the clinging ice melted into running rivulets, the stone grew red hot. Slowly—too slowly, Jace feared—it poured across the front of the crevice, sealing it away from the main chasm. Tezzeret continued to stand, chanting, face sweating despite the cold, and as swiftly as it had melted, the rock began to cool. In a matter of instants, a featureless wall of stone separated prey from hunters.

Jace staggered, all but falling against the wall. His head still pounded, and he could hardly speak for the frozen crust of sweat and blood that caked the side of his face. He knew that casting much of anything was unwise, that he had to save his physical strength to get out of this world.

"That'll hold the savages out," Tezzeret grunted, "but I don't think it's going to stop that other—thing. How does it keep finding us?"

Struggling to stay alert, Jace whispered hoarsely, "I think it senses our warmth, Tezzeret." Again he tried to dig deep into the surrounding ice, hoping, pleading for a source of mana into which he could tap. And again he found nothing but dregs.

But what he found instead was inspiration.

"Tezzeret!" he hissed into the shadows. "That gadget of yours? The one keeping you warm!"

"What about it?" Tezzeret asked suspiciously.

"Can you make it generate cold instead?"

"Beleren, what good could that possibly—you're not serious!"

"No, of course not. It's a joke I've been saving for just the right bloody occasion."

"Do you have any idea how cold the air would have to be to block our own body heat? If we take even half a minute too long, we'll freeze to death!"

Jace scowled. "And you're arguing with me, wasting

what time we have, because you have a better idea."

Tezzeret scowled back and began to fidget with the device on his arm.

Outside, the beast of the frost had placed a single hand upon the newly formed wall separating the crevice from the outside world, when it abruptly stopped. Uttering a canine whimper, it lifted its head and sniffed heavily at the air. Puzzled, it tried again, and yet again.

Nothing. No heat at all, save its masters and their packmates behind it.

For many long moments it stood, confused as it had never been before. But the tattered soul that empowered the spectral thing was not that of any hound, however much it behaved as one. It had once been a man, and though all traces of that man were gone and forgotten, the beast could reason still. Thus, when it could not reacquire any trace of its prey, it made straight for the point it had scented them last.

But those few minutes of confusion made all the difference. When it finally seeped into the crevice, its misty form passing between the rocks and snow where even a beetle could not have creeped, it found the hollow empty.

✳ ✳ ✳ ✳ ✳

"How are you doing, Jace?" Kallist asked, leaning against the wall beside the doorway.

Jace looked up from beneath a veritable mountain of blankets. "I'll be fine," he said, "though that may be the last remnants of the kalyola brandy talking."

The other man grinned. "Feeling no pain, are you?"

"Kallist," Jace said, and chuckled, "I'm not sure I can even feel my *head.*" His face quickly turned serious, however. "What about your assignment?" he asked. "Were you still able to make it look natural?"

"Barely. It required a whole lot of fire. You really

don't want to know any more about it." He smirked knowingly. "And don't think you can change the topic that easily, either."

"Honestly, Kallist, I'm fine. It was just a toe; I've got nine more. The healers say I shouldn't even be limping after a few more days."

Kallist nodded. "You think Tezzeret had to have anything amputated?"

"I have no idea, but you be sure to let me know when you plan on asking him. I'd like to be elsewhere."

"Well, it won't be today," Kallist said, his own expression turning serious as well. "Today he wants to talk to you."

"Oh, for the love of . . . ! He can't give me a few days to—"

"He sort of wants to see you *now*, Jace. He's waiting in Paldor's chamber."

"Fine." Jace tossed the blankets off to one side of the bed and turned so he sat upon the edge. From the nightstand he took a length of bandage from a bath of herbs and potions, and began the arduous task of wrapping his mutilated foot. Kallist did his best to ignore the wincing and the occasional hiss of pain.

"The next time someone tells you that freezing to death is a 'pleasant way to go,'" Jace muttered, his face grown pallid, "you tell them to come talk to me about frostbite." His foot properly wrapped, he rose and threw on his heavy cloak, not bothering to change out of his bedclothes.

"If Tezzeret wants to see me before I'm done convalescing," he explained, "then he can damn well live without the formalities."

By the time they'd reached the office door, however, and Jace heard the muffled sound of Tezzeret ranting at Paldor within, he began to wish he had taken the time to clean up and change, if only to put this off a little longer.

And maybe to deflect at least a tiny portion of Tezzeret's fury.

Jace hadn't taken more than three steps through the door when Tezzeret was before him. Two hands, one of flesh and one of metal, grabbed his shoulders and dragged him forward, until his face was inches from Tezzeret's own.

"You idiot!" Tezzeret hissed. Even through the lingering pain, Jace could feel the artificer's hot breath against his cheek. "Do you have any idea the money you've cost me? The operations you've ruined?"

Maybe it was the pain. Maybe it was still the lingering effects of the kalyola brandy. Maybe it was just panic. But whatever it was, Jace said exactly the wrong thing in his defense.

"You don't understand!" he protested weakly. "You have no clue what you were asking of me! I don't think I could have stopped him even he hadn't distracted me—"

He knew the words were a mistake the instant he spoke, but he had no time to regret them. He felt the hands gripping him tense, and had barely drawn breath before they hurled him to the floor.

Tezzeret dropped to one knee beside him, grabbing Jace's hair in an etherium fist. "I should kill you," he whispered, his voice barely more than a gentle breath. "You've opened me up to all manner of problems and reprisals—but so help me, I've put too much effort into you to just throw away. So I'm going to give you one more chance. *One.*

"But I'm also going to make damn sure you learn from this debacle."

Without releasing his grip, Tezzeret reached out with his other hand. "Paldor? Your blade, if you'd be so kind."

Jace looked up, dizzy, his brain refusing to settle on any one detail. He saw Kallist still standing in the doorway, jaw clenched, his hand hovering near his sword. Jace was grateful for the thought, but equally grateful that Kallist hadn't been foolish enough to actually draw steel.

Then he saw Paldor hand over the black, steaming dagger, and blind panic erased all other emotions. He felt the edge of the blade on his back, and knew what was coming, knew that he couldn't do a thing to stop it.

And then he knew only pain as the dagger sliced open his flesh and his soul.

CHAPTER EIGHTEEN

None of the Consortium healers would touch him, not this time. Everyone knew just how he'd been injured, and nobody was willing to interfere with Tezzeret's discipline. For almost two days, Jace tossed and turned in agony, unable to sleep, barely able to move. His sheets and mattress were stained with dried blood. The cuts along his back and his arms were shallow but long. The pain was excruciating, but not nearly so much so as the pain within.

Jace felt as though he'd been burned from the inside out. The very notion of spellcasting made him queasy, and he'd been unable to absorb so much as a sliver of mana, no matter how hard he tried to concentrate.

By the evening of the second day, he knew that he could take no more of it. Staggering out of bed, he pulled on the first tunic he found, wincing with every move, every bend. He slowly made his way out of his chambers and down the hall, heading for the nearest exit.

If nobody in the Consortium would help him, he'd go to someone who would.

He'd made it as far as the first main corridor when someone appeared from the shadows off to the left.

"I was wondering if you were going to try something like this," Kallist said.

"Have to. No choice. Hurts too much."

"Jace," his friend told him, voice ripe with worry, "you can barely stand. How do you plan to get out? I don't think the guards would hurt you, but they're certainly not going to let you leave without permission, not until they're sure your punishment's up. Go back to bed. I'll bring you something, some brandy maybe, to help you sleep."

"No. Kallist, please. You've no idea what it's . . . I need your help."

Kallist frowned, and then sighed deeply. "You owe me," he said softly. "How long do you need to get to the exit?"

Jace took a moment to picture the halls, thought about his current state. "Ten minutes."

"All right. Get close and be ready."

Jace never did find out exactly what Kallist did to trigger the magical alarms that protected the complex from unauthorized entry—but he did so, and clear on the other side of the building. By the time the chaos was sorted out, and the patrols returned to their standard routes, Jace had slipped out the nearest door and onto the streets of Rubblefield.

What should have been a five-minute walk took him fifteen, but he finally found himself in the next district. It took another twenty minutes, given the lateness of the hour, to flag down a coach-for-hire.

"Where to?" asked the centaur who was both driver and hauler.

"Ovitzia," Jace gasped, all but collapsing into the seat.

"Hrm. I don't know, sir. That's an awfully long trip for this late at night. Maybe—"

Jace groaned, reached into a pouch and dropped a handful of gold coins on the shelf before him without even bothering to count.

"Ovitzia," the centaur announced, standing suddenly straight. "Right away, sir."

The jostling of the carriage over the cobblestones, though agonizing, almost managed to lull Jace to sleep with the promise of relief to come.

✳ ✳ ✳ ✳ ✳

"You sure I can't get you anything, Berrim? You really need to keep your strength up."

"Just my shirt," Jace said, shuddering slightly—and not just from the chill—as Emmara's fingers softly, gracefully traced the newly healed scars across his back. "It's pretty cold in here."

"You'll get dressed when I'm satisfied these are healing properly, and not one second before. And Berrim," the elf added, "if you make one snide remark about me touching you like this, I may just heal your mouth shut."

Jace clamped his teeth together, swallowing the comment he was about to utter like a half-chewed dumpling.

They sat together, not at Emmara's dining table downstairs, but at a small desk in her library—"library" being defined as "that bunch of pillars with the bookcases between them." It and the guest quarters were the only areas Jace had seen in the two days he'd been here. He'd slept a great deal as his body recovered from Emmara's magic, and tried to pass the rest of the time perusing those shelves. Unfortunately, the only books that were written in any script he could read were either cloying romances or high adventure fiction for which, thanks to recent events, he was very much not in the mood.

"All right," she said finally, standing up and handing him his wadded tunic. "I think I'm done. It looks like the physical damage is mostly healed. How about . . .?"

Jace hadn't given her much in the way of details,

of course, but he'd had to explain the nature of the manablade to ensure she could heal him properly. He frowned briefly, turning his attention inward, flexing muscles that weren't at all physical.

"I'd feel better if I could get near the water," he said finally, "but I think I shouldn't have any trouble once I do. It feels like everything's working."

"I'm glad."

"Are you sure you won't let me pay you something?" Jace asked. "I really feel like I owe—"

"Berrim, no." A shallow smile, then. "Although, if you find yourself in possession of another shipment of fruit . . ."

For a time, they sat in silence. Then, "I think he's losing it, Emmara," Jace said softly.

"Tezzeret?"

He nodded. "He's always been a hard man, but now he's getting cruel. Or maybe . . . Maybe he always was, and it just wasn't aimed my way." Jace shook his head miserably. "I knew from day one he wanted power. It's part of what drew me to him; I thought I could share in it. But now I think he's honestly going mad with it. He may have just started a war with a competing mercantile interest, for no better reason than he got overconfident in his abilities. His and mine both, actually, but he's only interested in my mistake, not his."

"And was your mistake so very awful?"

Jace shrugged. "My mistake was not realizing from the get-go that I wasn't powerful enough to do what he asked of me. But he should've known that, Emmara, even better than I. It's almost as if he's forgotten there's anything he can't do. So every time something goes wrong, it's somebody else's fault.

"But that's not even the worst of it." Jace knew he should stop, that even without offering details he was revealing more about the Consortium than Tezzeret or Paldor would approve of. But he found that once he'd begun, he couldn't stop. "I think—I think I'm more scared about what he's doing with that power than what he's doing to acquire more. I'm about as far from a saint as you can get, but some of what I've seen, especially lately . . . Some of what he's done to me . . . I'm scared to death of him, of what he might yet do."

"So why do you stay?" she asked softly.

There it was, the question he'd hoped wasn't coming, though he had asked it of himself a thousand times since he'd first felt the manablade on his skin.

"Because he *has* shared his power," he admitted finally. "My magic is stronger now than I ever thought it could be. Because I'm rich, and I don't want to go back to being what I was."

Emmara placed a soft hand on Jace's own, and pretended not to notice his was shaking. "And maybe," she whispered, "because you're afraid of what he'll do if you leave?"

Jace looked down at the table and said nothing at all.

⚹ ⚹ ⚹ ⚹ ⚹

"What am I going to do with you, Beleren?"

The question didn't seem to demand an actual answer, so Jace didn't offer one.

He stood arrow-straight in the lieutenant's chamber, where he'd been ordered to appear in no uncertain terms the instant he returned to the Consortium complex. Paldor paced behind the desk, the room shaking mildly with his tread, and glancing at Jace only occasionally.

"I mean, on the one hand, I think it's pretty clear that Tezzeret intended his punishment to, ah, linger a lot longer. That's why he wouldn't let you see any of our healers."

Jace scowled but still said nothing.

"On the other," Paldor said, suddenly stopping and turning to face the mage directly, "nobody actually *ordered* you to stay put, did they? Everyone just assumed you knew better, but I guess it's never come up for you before. And it's not as though you ran off on an assignment, since nobody figured you'd be up for any sort of duties for at least a few weeks."

The lieutenant drummed the fingers of one hand on the desk. The other was hidden inside his robe, where Jace knew the manablade rested. Jace licked his lips and otherwise tried not to appear half as nervous as he felt.

Finally, Paldor shrugged. "Go back to your quarters. We'll call this whole situation over and done with. But Beleren? Next time the boss punishes you, you do not try to weasel out of it. Consider that a standing order. And I suggest you see about keeping pretty much to yourself until your next assignment comes down."

With a sigh of relief he couldn't quite suppress, Jace turned away. Just as he reached the door, however, Paldor's voice stopped him cold.

"Oh, Beleren? Kallist *did* know better. And he was punished for his little part in your song and dance."

Jace's fist clenched hard on the latch. "Is he . . . Is he hurt?"

"A lash or two, nothing that won't heal a lot faster than you did. Plus a few fines and some menial chores. Just enough to make my point."

"And that is?" Jace couldn't help but ask.

"That is," Paldor said, his gruff voice suddenly very heavy, "that I know what happens in my building. And that when you decide to take a flying leap into a pool of crap, it splatters on the people near you. You get me?"

"I get you," Jace whispered.

"Good. Then get the hell out."

✳ ✳ ✳ ✳ ✳

Some weeks later, in a large but modest chapel built in the shadow of the ancient Ethereal Temple, an old man leaned back in his chair and sighed as he pondered that evening's address. Talqez was his name, and he was the August Questor of the Church of the Incarnate Soul. His skin was the rich brown of an old chestnut, his beard the gray-white of moss. In conjunction with his deep green robes of office, it had inspired his youngest students and parishioners to dub him Grandfather Tree. He'd never admonished them for it; in truth, he rather enjoyed the endearment.

For all his life Talqez had served his faith, first as a simple congregant and apprentice, then mage and Questor, until he finally occupied the highest ecclesiastical seat. And it was, quite frankly, getting almost impossible to give an original address anymore.

The August Questor waved a hand across the paper, watching the last paragraph fade and disappear. He turned aside, took a swig from the half-empty mug of mead (now warm) and a bite of the half-finished plate of venison (now cold) that sat on the desk's far side. Sighing, he returned to the paper and began again. He lifted no quill, used no ink, but simply ran a finger across the page and watched the words appear. A simple magic, yes, but a practice of one of the central tenets of his faith—that a worshipper of the Incarnate Soul never used manual labor, however minor, when he'd mastered a spell to do the job.

So focused on his sermon was he that he scarcely noted when the door to his rectory office opened behind him. "Have a seat, my Sibling," he offered by way of distracted greeting. "I'll be with you in a moment."

Nothing struck him as wrong at all until he heard the double-click of the door not only being shut, but locked.

✳ ✳ ✳ ✳ ✳

Jace had laughed when they first described the Church of the Incarnate Soul to him, for their faith was perhaps the most peculiar he'd ever encountered. The members of the Church believed devoutly that mana was nothing less than divinity made manifest. To learn the arts of magic was to touch the power of gods, and should a mortal ever master all the secrets of mana—beyond the greatest archmage, to truly master it *all*—he would ascend to godhood himself. Indeed, they considered planeswalkers to stand on the verge of divinity, and prayed to them en masse, though they engaged in little if any direct interaction.

Jace had no idea how such a peculiar system of beliefs had arisen (though he suspected planeswalker interference many generations past), nor did he know how Tezzeret had learned of it in the first place. Indeed, the Church might have wound up just another sect to grow, to fade, and eventually to be forgotten by even the most vigilant historians, were it not for the rumors: the same rumors that brought Jace to their world now.

Due to their study of mana, the Church possessed—or at least was rumored to possess—spells and techniques for manipulating magic beyond the ken of other mages. Rumors and whispers maintained that they had items capable of storing enormous amounts of energy, of converting one type of mana to another; that they could draw mana from lands that seemed utterly exhausted, from worlds that had never known the touch of magic; even that they could manipulate how *other people* channeled mana, empowering their allies and rendering their enemies as helpless as any normal mortal.

How much of this might be true and how much pure nonsense, nobody could say with certainty. But they'd shown enough power in public, including the forging of devices like Paldor's manablade, that even those who scoffed at the Church's beliefs did so silently and made every effort not to rile them.

For some time, Tezzeret had contemplated various means of forcing the Church to ally with him, of suborning its leadership. It was, he insisted, a tool he must have, a resource that would allow the Infinite Consortium to stand up to and defeat anything their enemies—be they Bolas or anyone else—could throw at them.

And now he insisted that Jace Beleren acquire it for him. The artificer made no bones about the fact that this was, bar none, the most vital undertaking he'd ever assigned the mind-reader. And though Tezzeret didn't deign to say so, Jace knew he was being trusted with such a mission only because nobody else could do it—and he knew, as well, that it was his one and only chance to atone for his "failure" with the dragon Nicol Bolas.

So he found himself on yet another foreign world, wearing the green robe of an Incarnate Soul acolyte, trying to prepare himself to transform the mind of an elderly priest into something resembling a child's toy. Into something Tezzeret could command.

The office was a small room set above and to one side of the main sanctuary, where half a dozen parishioners had already arrived, clad in their best wool leggings and leather jerkins, for evening ritual. It contained only a small desk, a pair of rickety chairs (one of which was in use by the August Questor himself), a bookshelf that had overflowed into numerous stacks of books and papers, and a strange multihued circle upon the wall that Jace believed was the Church's greatest symbol.

The walls were thin, and the voices below had not yet grown loud. Jace hoped that whatever happened would happen quietly.

He found himself nodding as the old man offered him a seat—*damn, but the man had a soothing voice!*—and stepped inside, turning to lock the door behind him.

The August Questor was no fool, Jace gave him that; he turned instantly, at the sound of the bolt clicking into place.

"I don't believe you're one of my assembly," Talqez said blandly.

"Ah, no," Jace said, suddenly at a loss for exactly how to proceed.

"Then who . . ." The old priest's eyes grew suddenly wide, and to Jace's shock Talqez dropped to the floor, abasing himself at the newcomer's feet.

"Worldwalker!" the man proclaimed, and Jace almost felt sick at the reverence in his voice. "You do me great honor!"

"Get up," Jace snapped, for some reason angrier than he'd been in a long time. "Get up!"

The priest rose, but only to his knees, his eyes brimming with tears. "I never thought to meet one of you in my lifetime," he breathed, reaching out a hand as though to touch Jace, to confirm that he was real. "I never dreamed . . ."

"How did you even know?" Jace asked, real curiosity in his voice. "We can't even always identify each other."

"What sort of priest would I be, if I did not know those who stood in the light of divinity itself? We know you— perhaps better than you know yourselves."

"Damn it, get up!" Jace demanded angrily. "I'm not a god, you old fool! I'm not even close!"

"You need not believe," Talqez said, smiling behind his beard. "It is true, all the same."

Jace felt his fists clench of their own accord. "I'm no god," he said again. "And you wouldn't call me one, if you knew why I was here."

"Oh, I know," the August Questor said calmly. "You would have been welcome, had you come among us openly. For you to feel the need to sneak in, clad as you are—you can only be here for me."

"Then let's get it done." Jace dropped into a crouch and called out, hands clutching at the air as though to yank it open and reach for the mana within. The air turned suddenly humid as a wet wind whipped through the chamber, spinning parchments around their feet.

Bestial forms began to take shape, slowly, faintly, in the accumulating dew. Jace's eyes, even his fingernails, began to glow blinding blue.

He focused his mind into a stabbing blade, ready to cut into the August Questor's mind, to interrupt any spell he might cast before it could manifest. Indeed, Jace was ready for anything . . .

Except for the old man to simply spread his arms wide and close tight his eyes.

Jace knew that he shouldn't question, should take advantage of any opportunity no matter how strange. He swore he could hear Tezzeret shouting over one shoulder, Kallist coaxing over the other.

Seconds passed as Jace stood frozen with indecision, his minuscule soldiers buzzing and hissing around him.

Then, cursing, he raised a hand. The winds died as rapidly as they'd risen as Jace allowed some of the accumulating mana to fade back into the waters of the world. Still scowling, he crouched on the balls of his feet.

"August Questor?"

The old man opened his eyes, and his smile broadened in contentment. "You are a planeswalker," he said simply. "I don't know what good my life will do you, but if that's what you have come for, it is yours to take."

Jace felt his stomach turn and his hands shake. He replied, his voice strangely gentle and even sympathetic, "You misunderstand me, Questor. You're no use to us dead."

Only then did Talqez seem to understand. Only then did his face blanch, did his breath catch, did he seem to consider resistance rather than submission.

But by then he had waited too long, and Jace was already inside his mind.

ⲫ

⨍HAPTER NINETEEN

Jace!" Kallist sat up, surprised, as a familiar figure appeared in the doorway. "I hadn't heard you were back yet."

"Good." Jace's voice was low, practically a monotone. "Then maybe Tezzeret hasn't either."

Kallist stood. "Jace, what—?" He stopped, staring at his friend's bloodshot eyes. "What happened?"

What happened? Jace bit his lip, clenched his fists, anything to keep from falling, weeping, to his knees. Such a simple question . . .

What happened?

Did he have the words even to answer? To explain to anyone but another mind-reader what it was to feel another man's faith? To not merely hear, or to see, but to understand his belief in something larger than he was?

How could he explain what a horrible revelation it was for someone like Jace Beleren to realize that faith was directed at him? That someone could be so deluded—or so devout—as to think *him* holy?

He couldn't explain, even if he could find the words.

Nor had that been his only motivation, the only reason he fled the church, leaving the August Questor, puzzled but unharmed and uncompromised, behind him.

"I saw the Questor's mind, Kallist," Jace explained. "I saw how many of the rumors are false—and how many aren't. The Church . . . There's a lot they can do, with magic, with mana, with those who manipulate magic and mana."

"Yeah?"

"And," Jace's voice hardened, "I don't care for the idea of Tezzeret having access to that power." He trembled faintly, remembering the touch of the manablade dragging across his skin. "Not over other sorcerers and planeswalkers, certainly not over me. It's too dangerous. It's too much. I can't trust him with it, Kallist, not after seeing the sides of him I've seen."

The blood drained from Kallist's face like someone had pulled a plug. "You failed," he whispered.

"Yes."

"On purpose!"

"Yes."

"Gods and demons, Jace! Why did you come back here? They'll kill you once they figure it out!"

Jace smiled shallowly and shrugged, emphasizing the sack he carried slung over one shoulder.

"You can't possibly have come back just for your stuff," Kallist challenged.

"No. I came back so you could come with me."

"I—you what? What are you talking about? You can't."

"I can't walk with you, no. But Ravnica's a big world. Not even the Consortium can search all of it. I have places I can—we can go, where we should be safe."

"Look, Jace," Kallist said slowly. "You're a great friend. I hope you make it; I'll even do what I can from here to make sure you do. But I'm not going to just walk away from my life for you. I'm sorry."

What little smile he had managed fell away. "No, Kallist, I'm sorry. I didn't want you caught up in this. But I'm not asking you to come for my sake. I'm *telling* you for *yours*. We've been friends and partners for almost three years, and Paldor already knows you've helped me out—in violation of policy—before. If you tell Tezzeret, 'No, I don't know where Jace went,' do you think for one minute he'll believe you?"

"He would eventually," Kallist muttered, but his own face had fallen as well.

"And what will have happened to you in the meantime, while he convinced himself? What'll become of your place in the Consortium after, with the shadow of suspicion hanging over you?"

Kallist turned away, then spun back, driving a fist through the uppermost drawer of his dresser. "Damn you, Jace!"

Jace only nodded in agreement. Kallist shook his hand, sending an array of splinters and blood across the furniture, and then moved about the room gathering what he thought he'd need. Jace could only watch, sorry for what he'd done—and yet, deep within, secretly rejoicing that he wouldn't be going alone.

Eventually Kallist stepped up beside Jace, and either his anger had already begun to fade or he was doing a damn fine job of hiding it. "All right. I've got a plan."

"You do?" Jace asked, startled.

"Sure. First, you reveal to me that you're actually the reincarnation of the greatest wizard of the Azorius Senate."

"Umm . . ."

"And then you use that great power to smite our enemies."

"I see." Jace managed a second grin. "And if I find some flaw in this plan?"

"Well, then you'd better have one to replace it, because that's all I've got."

A R I   M A R M E L L

It was only on the last word that Kallist's voice quavered, and Jace knew that his friend was afraid. It was, in its own way, more startling than anything else that had befallen him. In all their years working together, Jace had seen his friend worried a hundred times; but he'd never seen him afraid.

"Actually, I do," Jace said slowly. "But I think you might decide that yours is better."

✶ ✶ ✶ ✶ ✶ ✶

"Jace!" Paldor said standing behind his desk as the door to his office burst open. "You're supposed to be—"

Jace whispered a sound that was not a word. Paldor staggered a single step and fell senseless to the floor by his chair.

"Dead?" Kallist asked softly.

"No. Not even unconscious in the most technical sense. But it'll be hours before he can form a sentient thought again."

"And what would we have done if Tezzeret had been here?"

Jace shrugged once, moving toward the leftmost wall. "Died, I imagine." He took a long moment to examine the æther-filled contraption hanging from the wall. Then, "Lock the door. You get started on the window while I deal with this."

Carefully, examining each tube, every knot-like twist, Jace began to construct an illusory duplicate of the device whose destruction could call Tezzeret to Ravnica. And then, just as carefully, he began to shatter that illusion, while cloaking the real device in an image of blank wall.

He had no idea how long the image might last once he was gone—he'd rarely tried to maintain such an illusion from a distance—but every moment of delay was a moment they could run that much farther. With Paldor down and Tezzeret unreachable, the ensuing confusion might buy the fugitives extra hours, possibly even days.

Kallist worked diligently at the massive window that occupied one wall of the room, attempting to provide them an unguarded exit. He knew well that the magically augmented glass would never shatter, so instead he struggled to pry it loose from its moorings, even going so far as to jam the tip of his broadsword into the top of the frame, wiggling it as a makeshift pry-bar. And if he occasionally envisioned Jace's face when he slammed the blade home into the wood, if the clench of his jaw was as much resentment as it was exertion, well, it didn't distract him from his endeavors.

It took them half an hour—a half-hour they really couldn't spare, but would be worth it if it bought them more time to run—but finally Jace was content with the broken image he'd made of the device, finally the window slid from the wall to strike the carpet with a muffled thud. The warm, sweat- and dirt-flavored air of the slowly recovering Rubblefield wafted into the office, tousling hair and sleeves and Jace's cloak.

"So what now?" Kallist asked gruffly. "You going to fly us out of here?"

"Actually," Jace began, "that's exactly what—"

The door to the office slammed open, the wood splintering as the heavy bolt was torn aside. Baltrice stood framed in the open doorway, fire dancing across her fingertips, something long and scaly writhing through the cloud of smoke that filled the hall behind her.

Jace cursed, even as he spun toward her, hands raised. Damn it all, he hadn't even known she was on Ravnica! What was she doing here now? He could probably take her—almost certainly could, if Kallist was willing to help—but could he do it fast enough? Could he do it before the guards arrived, or with sufficient strength remaining to make his escape?

She took one step forward, a second, and then, with a bitter curse, dropped her hands to her sides.

"Get out of here, Beleren!"

For an instant, Jace couldn't move. He couldn't have been more stunned if she'd announced that she was having his baby. "What?"

"For Kamigawa," she snarled. "We're even now, Beleren, your life for mine. If you're stupid enough to let me catch you after this, *I will* kill you, and I'll enjoy every minute of it!"

Still thunderstruck, Jace nonetheless turned toward the window. He'd have time to be flabbergasted later, damn it! Sporadic flashes of azure light whipped about him, carried by a wind that gusted up from the floor in time to his steps as he moved toward Kallist and the open window. Pure telekinetic force lifted them high, spreading forth from Jace like invisible wings. And then they were gone, speeding off into Ravnica's darkened skies, already beginning to descend beyond the nearest buildings as Jace's strength quickly burned out.

And behind them, in the office now open to the night air, Baltrice grinned broadly. Let him go; they'd find him, sooner or later. But even if they didn't, it hardly mattered now. Jace Beleren was, at least to her, to the position and the power she'd worked so long to achieve, no longer a threat.

She almost found herself whistling as she turned and strode from Paldor's office, not even bothering to check on the fellow who lay, staring at nothing, behind his desk.

✳ ✳ ✳ ✳ ✳

They'd spoken little after that, during the many days of their journey. Kallist had brooded nearly the whole way, his every expression and monosyllabic grunt discouraging all attempts at conversation. They passed through a dozen districts via wide open streets and underground passages so cramped they had to crawl on hands and knees, atop bridges so high that clouds passed beneath them, blocking all view of the ground, and alongside buildings so massive that even their shadows pressed down with the weight of years. And ever so gradually, they felt the first easing of the tension they carried between them like a wounded companion, as the territories of the Infinite Consortium fell ever farther behind them.

Eventually, their route took them to the banks of one of Ravnica's great rivers, and the streets that ran beside its coursing waters. For many days more they followed it downstream, until the breezes turned cooler and the tang of saltwater spread before them, the whispering voice of a sea that was now partly buried beneath the great city's unstoppable sprawl.

And finally, as they neared their destination, Kallist had begun to open up again. "Why Lurias?" he'd asked Jace one morning. "I've never even heard of the district before now."

"That's partly why," Jace had answered. "And because my friend Rulan—did I ever tell you about Rulan? Well, he's . . . Let's say he'd have made a great Orzhov, except that he's not a completely soulless bastard. He's got a lot of contacts with moneylenders and banking guilds. And Lurias is one of the smaller districts where he helped establish one of the accounts I've been feeding with everything the Consortium paid me. We'll have funds enough here—for a good while, if we're careful."

"Sounds positively fantastic," Kallist muttered.

There was more to it, of course, but Kallist—even with the limited magic Jace had managed to teach him—would pick up on that soon enough.

Built on the delta of this nameless river, buildings not nearly as tall or grand as those of Dravhoc lined the lengths of streets not nearly as wide. The arches were modest, the rare spires made of simple stone or brass rather than crystal. It wasn't a poor district by any objective measurement, but it was certainly far less than Kallist or Jace were accustomed to.

Of potentially greater import, however, was the world beneath those humble streets. Most of the delta was soggy, shallow marsh—which was itself responsible for Lurias's poor foundations and irritating insect population. But at the district's far end and along the banks of the river, the waters rushing into the buried sea were clean and clear. Those neighborhoods were built not atop swampy knolls but on tiny islets, and it was there—there amid the saltwater and its rich mana—that Jace hoped to make his home.

The first halfway acceptable option they found was a fourth-story flat, decently sized for the price, albeit in need of a fierce cleaning. It boasted three rooms, a number of tiny windows, and walls a hue so drab that it couldn't even muster up the enthusiasm to qualify as gray. Jace negotiated the landlord down to a rent that wouldn't eat through his reserves too quickly—without using any magic, thank you very much—and then he and Kallist ensconced themselves within like it was a fortress. Jace ventured out only under cover of an illusory disguise, acquiring what supplies they considered absolutely vital. They didn't want to show themselves on the streets until they were certain the Consortium hadn't somehow followed them here.

So Jace gathered foodstuffs; a few bits of cheap furniture to suffice until they could acquire better; and new clothes, since nothing either of them owned was of sufficiently low quality to blend in with the other citizens of Lurias. Jace chose the garish bright hues of the middle classes—mostly in blues, of course—while Kallist instead adopted the drab and colorless garb of the lower.

And then there was nothing to do but wait and talk. For days.

". . . isn't going to work," Kallist was insisting one morning, over a breakfast of cold eggs, warm juice, and cheap meat. "I'm not prepared to live like this, Jace. Not indefinitely."

"You think I am?" the other replied around a mouthful of egg. "It's just for a little while, until it's safe to find someplace a little more . . . more . . ." he floundered, shrugging.

"More like a home, and less like a refuse pit?" Kallist finished bitterly.

"Something like that."

"And how," Kallist continued, getting up from the table, "do we plan to afford said palace?"

Jace could only roll his eyes and pour himself another glass. It was an argument they'd had at least five times over the past two days, and he was already well and truly sick of it.

"I told you," he began, in the tone of a man who doesn't expect to be listened to *this* time, either. "I'm a mage. I'll tote crates or stand at a vendor's stall when my other choice is starving, but not a moment before. My savings—"

"Aren't going to last nearly as long as you think, damn it. Even if you do stay in ratholes like this, which I, for one, have no intention of."

"Oh, so you're making plans for *my* gold now?" Jace challenged.

"Since I seem to have lost the means by which I was making my own, yes, I think so."

For long moments, they glared at one another over the table.

"Jace," Kallist said finally, voice much calmer, "why are you fighting me on this? We both know that you'd have no problem making money—without 'lowering yourself' to menial labor."

"In a district like this? I don't think so."

"Not everyone here is poor. There are more than a few merchants, bankers, and politicians who could spare a few gold coins in exchange for their secrets staying secret."

Jace found himself staring intently at the fruit juice—he didn't even know what kind, he realized, and he'd already drunk a glass and a half—in his hand. "That's, uh, not exactly the best way to lie low, you know," he hedged.

"You're an illusionist," Kallist deadpanned. "I'm sure if you try *really* hard, you can think of some way to keep your identity secret."

"Any major use of magic like that risks drawing attention, Kallist." But the twitch in Jace's voice told the both of them it wasn't his only concern.

Silence again, for a couple of minutes. Jace actually squirmed in his seat, knowing how well his answer was going to go over. "I can't," he said finally, slowly, raising his gaze to meet Kallist's own. "Kallist, I . . . I can't go back to being what I was before the Consortium. If I do, everything I went through with Tezzeret was meaningless, and I can't accept that. I can't. I'm sorry."

Kallist's mouth moved, but no sound emerged. Jace, who had more than once seen his friend's expression just before driving his broadsword into someone's torso, felt a sudden urge to back away from the table.

And then he lunged, not at Jace, but at the old used overcoat they'd purchased for him, hanging on an equally old, equally used coat rack. Without so much as a word, he was at the door.

"Have you decided it's safe to be out and about on the streets?" Jace asked him.

"A lot safer for you than if I stayed here," Kallist barked. The slam of the door cut off any retort Jace might have chosen to make.

✳ ✳ ✳ ✳ ✳

At the terminus of a long hallway that led literally nowhere, a sheet of fire appeared from the æther. Though blindingly bright it emitted no heat, for it didn't exist entirely within the bounds of any particular plane. It parted in the center, a curtain drawn back on the stage of reality, and Baltrice stepped through from the Blind Eternities. She was striding down the long passage before the flames had fully faded, her boots echoing on the floor.

Every surface here was metallic and cold, every angle severe. Through windows of mesh, she saw humanoid servants and clockwork golems tending to cables as thick as oaks, pulleys strong enough to heft an elephant, creaking brass platforms the size of cottages. The halls echoed with the constant sounds of movement, the hum of machinery, the crackle of magic, the tromping feet of guards. Doors rotated in and out of existence; entire rooms rose and fell, giant elevators that provided access to a number of levels.

There were no signs, no hints of how one might find one's way around. Here, in the cold mechanical heart of the Infinite Consortium, those who belonged knew where they were going—and those who did not had far greater worries than becoming lost.

Baltrice knew where she was going. This hall, that staircase, this catwalk above a seemingly bottomless pit of machinery, that elevator that shuddered slightly as it moved not merely up but sideways, rotating as it went . . . And there she was, staring down a long hallway at a deceptively mundane door.

Standing before it was a figure clad entirely in armor of brass plates, covered with ornate etchings and fluting. Even Baltrice, arguably the master's closest associate, had never learned if this were some humanoid garbed in plate, a mystic construct in vaguely human form, or—just possibly—a simple decorative sculpture. She knew only that it stood outside Tezzeret's door, day and night, leaning slightly on an impossibly broad-bladed sword that no normal man could have lifted, let alone wielded.

The door slid open at her approach, rising into the ceiling with a series of clicks and clanks, and she stood at last within Tezzeret's inner sanctum.

The room was perfectly circular, its center occupied by a metallic ring-shaped desk. Its surface sprouted a vast array of glass rods and imbedded stones, all pulsing with mana, all controlling who-knew-what. A thick metal pylon rose from the hollow at the heart of the metal ring. This, she knew, was the support for Tezzeret's chair. She looked up, past four separate levels of additional controls and pipes and iron frames, to the chair's uppermost height. There, she could just make out a dark form seated in the ugly contraption, inhaling the mana-infused steam that flowed from the highest tubes. Even from here, she could see his entire body shudder in ecstasy at the touch of the vapors—all except the etherium hand clenched on the arm of the chair, which somehow remained still even as the shoulder and torso above it quivered like an angry serpent.

Patiently, though patience was not normally among her virtues, Baltrice waited. Eventually the flow of steam subsided, a single hiss fading from the symphony of sounds that permeated the chamber. A second, louder susurrus swiftly took its place, as the pylon began to rotate, the chair to descend—and in mere moments, Tezzeret sat before her, ensconced in his mechanical throne, a god who had deigned to descend from his clockwork heaven. His hair lay plastered to his forehead and cheeks by the lingering condensation.

"Welcome back," he told her, slicking back his hair with his left hand. "I believe the Infinity Globes are almost perfected. Just a few more tweaks, and I should never again have to worry about being trapped like Bolas's barbarians almost . . ." He stopped cold at her expression. "You bring bad news." It was not a question.

Baltrice nodded once. "Of Jace Beleren."

Tezzeret frowned. "Did Beleren fail at his assigned task?"

Trying hard to keep all traces of gloating out of her voice, Baltrice said, "It's a bit worse than that, boss."

Tezzeret sat, utterly still; even his breathing seemed to have ceased. And then Baltrice heard the sound of rending metal, saw one of the desk's levers snap off in the grip of the artificer's etherium hand.

"What," Tezzeret whispered softly, "has he done to me now?"

❊ ❊ ❊ ❊ ❊

It had been a nice break from the ongoing dispute, but a break was all it was.

". . . know it's a good amount of gold," Kallist was saying as they left the flat behind them the following afternoon. "I just don't think we should rely on it."

Jace shrugged. "Maybe not," he said, only somewhat paying attention. "But," he added, looking meaningfully at the streets and buildings around them, "what we have should go an awfully long way."

"Emphasis," Kallist said, glaring at the squat, unimpressive buildings and thinking back to his luxurious quarters in the complex, "on the *awfully*."

They moved through the crowds, struggling to fit into a community where they clearly did not. The volume was jarring, but no worse than Dravhoc's marketplace; Jace easily tuned it out. But he found the middle-class styles garish and the drab garb of the poorer folk depressing. It wasn't that he particularly felt superior to them (he told himself); it was just that he didn't belong.

They had no destination in mind, only a faint desire to get to know this place that might be their home for a good long while. So when Jace, growing ever more disdainful of his surroundings and ever more irritated at Kallist's talk of work, saw what looked to be a tavern and restaurant across the street, he made a beeline for it without so much as a word, or even taking the time to read the sign above the door. Startled, Kallist followed.

The din of the crowd faded away, replaced by—well, by a different din of a different crowd. The floorboards were painted a hideous yellow-brown, jarring until Jace realized it managed to camouflage most of the dirt customers might track inside. It boasted a bar, like any good tavern, but this one was a perfect circle in the center of the room, rather than built along one wall. A spiral staircase ran up and down from within, presumably allowing access to a wine cellar below and who-knew-what above. The common room was filled with small booths, formed by freestanding **C**-shaped walls cradling small tables. A hideously inefficient use of space, perhaps, but it certainly inspired a feeling of privacy. A raised stage that currently lacked any sort of performer rose along one wall, and a door beside it constantly flapped open as servers emerged with dishes from the kitchen.

Jace decided he liked the place and grabbed one of the empty tables. He and Kallist listened attentively as a barmaid recited the day's options, ordered, and then studied each other.

"Look," Kallist began, "I'm not saying you'd need to work in a place like this or anything, but—"

"Oh, for the love of . . . Kallist, give it a rest!"

"I don't think so, Jace. It may be *your* gold, but it's *our* lives, damn it! This isn't only about you. We need—"

"What we need, Kallist," Jace said seriously, "is to make a few more urgent decisions."

Kallist opened his mouth, closed it as the barmaid brought their drinks, and then began again. "Such as?"

"Such as who we are."

"I don't—Oh."

"Yeah."

Kallist frowned. "Well, I've never been on the run from anyone like this before. Are pseudonyms necessary?"

Jace pondered, taking a large sip of wine. "I've used them a lot," he said, working it through his mind as he spoke. "In fact, I've already got a name set up here, with my various accounts. Darrim."

Kallist blinked. "Weren't you Berrim back in Dravhoc?"

"Yeah. I find it easier to remember them all if they're not too dissimilar."

He continued to deliberate; Kallist continued to let him.

"Yeah," Jace said finally. "It's a good idea, at that. It's probably unnecessary—I don't think anyone from the Consortium is likely to happen to pass through, and happen to overhear someone speaking our names. And anyone who knows enough to be actively looking for us here in Lurias is someone who's not going to be fooled by fake names anyway. But still—"

"You," said a voice from just beyond the booth's wall, "would be Jace Beleren and Kallist Rhoka, right?"

For a split second, the two of them gawped at each other, and all Jace could think to say was, "See?"

Both turned, prepared to lunge from the booth. Kallist's hand had dropped to the hilt of his broadsword, Jace's lips were already moving in the first stages of a spell.

"Oh, stop it. If I wanted to fight, I'd have set your booth on fire from behind." The woman who stepped into sight was taller than average, slender, with midnight-black hair and eyes deeper than the Blind Eternities. She wore a burgundy vest and a pearl-hued gown, and her hands were ever so slightly raised, perhaps to show that they were empty.

"How the hell do you know who—" Jace began, only to snap his lips shut as Kallist rose, shoulders clearly tensed to draw his blade.

"I know you," he snapped at her. She raised an eyebrow.

"That makes one of us," Jace muttered irritably.

"I'm sorry." The woman turned, seemingly unconcerned with the jumpy swordsman at her side. "My name is Liliana."

"Jace," Jace said reflexively. Then, a bit embarrassed, "But, uh, you already knew that."

"That would be Liliana Vess, Jace," Kallist hissed at him.

The young mage's jaw clenched.

Liliana rolled her eyes, flopped down in the booth next to him, and polished off the wine remaining in his goblet.

Jace looked at Kallist, who seemed as much at a loss as he was.

"How did you find us so quickly?" Kallist demanded.

"It wasn't hard. There are only so many tables in here, so I just checked each one."

"Don't play games! I—"

"You," Liliana interrupted, "are assuming, because I've done a few odd jobs for the Consortium here and there, that I must be working for them now and looking for you."

"It'd be a remarkable coincidence if you weren't," Jace told her.

"It might be," she admitted, "if you hadn't come to Lurias."

"Huh?" Jace and Kallist asked at once.

Liliana sighed and waved over one of the barmaids. "I'm going to need more wine. I'm here for the same reason you are, Jace Beleren. Because it's as far as I could reasonably get from the Consortium without abandoning Ravnica entirely."

"You're hiding?"

Liliana looked at Kallist. "He's a quick one, isn't he?"

Jace scowled. "Then how did you know we weren't here after you?"

The newcomer threw her head back and laughed, a musical sound that somehow put Jace at ease even though he knew he was being mocked. "I still have my sources, Jace. I think everyone who works for, freelances for, or has even heard of the Infinite Consortium knows that Tezzeret's offering a sack of gold the size of a kraken for your head. Hell, I could probably get back in good with them by turning you over.

"Not," she added at the sudden glint in their eyes, "that I'd do that." Appearing slightly nervous for the first time, she downed a generous gulp of wine.

"I don't buy it, Jace," Kallist said, oblivious that his hovering around the booth with a hand on his hilt was beginning to draw stares. "It's far too convenient. Ravnica's a big world, and this isn't exactly the only district to hide in."

Liliana leaned in close to Jace. "It's true, I could have chosen other neighborhoods, some more comfortable. But have you tasted the mana here? There are other districts built on marshland, but frankly they're even uglier than this one."

Jace nodded slowly. Just as he'd sought out the freshwaters of the coastline, she could easily be here for the swamps beneath the rest of Lurias. But still . . . "It's not that small a district," he protested. "It still seems pretty unlikely."

"It is," she admitted. "Look, I didn't come to Lurias looking for you; I was already here. But I did seek you out when I learned you were here, too. Oh!" she added, as the pair of them went pale, "don't worry. The dead told me; they sensed your power. But there's not another necromancer in the Consortium with the power to command ghosts that strong. Not on Ravnica, anyway. You're safe."

"Until you turn us over," Kallist hissed.

Liliana sighed. "I sought you out because we have a common problem, and I thought we'd be safer watching each others' backs. That's all."

"If you know me," Jace said carefully, deliberately, "then you know there's an easy way to prove what you say."

"Jace . . ." Kallist began, but an upraised hand silenced him.

Liliana blanched but nodded. "I've no interest in fighting you. Too much attention. It doesn't hurt, does it?"

"Not as far as I know."

"All right. Do it."

A moment of intense concentration, and Jace was inside the mind of Liliana Vess. For a moment, he felt the urge to turn away from the intensity. This was a powerful mind, one of the most potent he'd been in since Alhammarret's own, and a confusing one. A love of life but a fascination with death, contentment mixed with ambition; a passion easily ignited, for good or ill.

Stranger still, though, was what lay beyond—the foundation of Liliana's mind. It had . . . No words existed to match precisely—a texture? A flavor? A contour? Something about the feel of her mind was different, unlike any Jace had touched before.

But then, Jace had never delved so deeply into the mind of another planeswalker. And whatever the case, Jace sensed no deception in Liliana's mind—not about the topic at hand, at any rate—nor any hostility toward him or Kallist. He considered delving further, to learn why she was hiding from the Consortium or to unearth some secret that he might use if necessary, but he refrained. He feared she might sense if he took too long in her mind, and the last thing they needed was another enemy.

Slowly, Jace opened his eyes. Liliana blinked once, then shook her head.

"Was it good for you?" she asked with a grin. Then, as Jace fumbled for an answer, she rose. "Well, I'm glad you're here. It'll be nice to talk to someone about something other than fishing and how far the swamp's expanded this year. I'm quite certain I'll be seeing you both around."

And just like that, she vanished into the crowd, with two separate stares—one flummoxed, one suspicious still—trailing in her wake.

CHAPTER TWENTY

Good morning, Kallist. Or have you decided on a new name yet?"

Kallist spun, hand dropping to his sword, before he recognized the form behind him as Liliana's. The sun was still low in the east, casting a cobweb of shadows over the breadth of Lurias, and the air smelled more of dew than of the baked cobblestones and packed throngs that would come later. The streets were largely clear, so soon after dawn, but filling swiftly as humans, elves, viashino, and others set about their daily labors—or perhaps to grab a plate of breakfast prior to said labors.

"Morning," he said gruffly as she fell into step beside him. Then, reluctantly, "Ah, Jace told me that we should trust you."

"But you don't." It wasn't a question.

Kallist shrugged. "Well, I'm not about to stab you on principle anymore. But Jace—Jace is a weird one. He uses people he should trust, trusts people he should avoid, and avoids people he could use. So no. No, I don't trust you yet."

Liliana smiled softly. "You're wiser than he is." The expression faded. "I've heard a lot about you two.

Less in recent days, obviously, but . . . He's dangerous, isn't he?"

"Very," Kallist nodded. "And not just to his enemies," he added with more than a touch of bitterness.

With surprising gentleness, she placed a hand on Kallist's forearm. "It was kind of you to take him under your wing the way you did. I don't think a lot of people would have."

Kallist shrugged once more.

"You two weren't . . . ?" She let the question dangle.

"Lovers?" Kallist laughed. "Uh, no. We were friends, partners, maybe even brothers. Nothing more."

"Were?" she asked with a raised eyebrow.

"Are. I said 'are.'"

"You said 'were.'"

"I meant 'are.'"

"Of course," she said with an enigmatic smile. "Try the marketplace if you're looking for work. A lot of the merchants are hiring private guards. Best of luck!"

Kallist watched her as she turned and walked away, wondering what he should be thinking. His arm continued to tingle where she'd touched it.

≫ ≫ ≫ ≫ ≫

When they ran into each other again that evening—or when she sought him out, he wasn't certain which—Liliana had suggested they stop for a bite to eat. Kallist, frustrated by his day, agreed. They sat in an open-air cafe that was little more than a few round tables with parasols, and a shack from which you could order anything at all, as long as it was some variety of bread and either fish or reptile.

But then, they weren't here for the food. Nobody was. Located near one of the few stretches of coastline not already built over, the patio faced squarely west. From here, each evening, a few dozen of the district's citizens gathered to watch the gold-and-azure gleaming of the setting sun glinting off the waters and shooting like arrows between the taller structures nearby.

Kallist tried to appreciate it, thank Liliana for showing it to him, but his heart wasn't in it. The third time she caught him stirring his fishy stew and grumbling under his breath, Liliana actually stamped her foot.

"Spit it out," she insisted, "before you choke on it. This wretched stew's hard enough to swallow on its own."

"I'm not supposed to be here," he told her.

"And we are? You think I like living here? You think *he* does?"

"It's all very well for the two of you," Kallist snapped. "You can walk between whole bloody worlds! You don't like your life? Hey, go find another one."

"If you truly think it's that simple," she breathed, and suddenly her voice could have frozen the nearby sea itself, "you're the biggest fool I've met on any world."

"All right, maybe," he replied, moderating his own tone somewhat. "But my point is you're used to being uprooted, to seeing everything you know fall behind you. I was supposed to be with the Consortium for the rest of my life! I liked it there! And then Jace . . ." He shook his head. "He drags me into a mess deep enough to drown in and he won't even take responsibility for helping me make the best of it. He owes me, Liliana. He owes me a life! But try getting him to see it!"

"It was my understanding," she said, turning so that the reflected lights flickered like a lover's touch over her face and hair, "that he brought you along because he was trying to do the right thing."

"The right thing." Kallist scoffed. "We were assassins, Liliana. Since when did that matter? But yeah, Jace has gotten really big on doing the right thing—for Jace. If he stopped to give two seconds' thought as to whether it was the right thing for anyone else, well, that'd be two seconds more than he's ever done before."

Smiling, Liliana put a hand on his. Kallist couldn't begin to decide if it was just a friendly gesture or something more. "This place isn't that bad, Kallist," she told him seriously. "If you give it some time, I think you'll find—"

She stopped, her gaze suddenly rising over Kallist's shoulder and out into the street. "Ja—ah, Darrim!" she called to the newcomer, who had been making his way toward the same patio, then slowed his pace as he saw who was waiting there. "Come join us!"

"Liliana," he greeted her with a smile, sliding between the neighboring tables. "I was just looking for you. It's a fantastic view, isn't it? I'm sorry I missed most of it." He pulled up a chair and glanced to his right, his smile fading like the last of the daylight. "Hello, Kallist," he said more quietly, to be certain he wasn't overheard.

"Jace. Or Darrim, if you'd like. We were just talking about you."

"I'm sure you were."

Despite Liliana's best efforts, the conversation ended soon after.

※ ※ ※ ※ ※

Jace pushed open the door of the restaurant where he and Kallist had first encountered Liliana, and to which he'd returned—usually alone—a dozen times since.

He'd learned more about it, in the weeks since their arrival, so that it was no longer just "that building with the faded sign." The tavern was owned by one Eshton, a man of some local celebrity, and boasted the astoundingly imaginative name of "Eshton's Tavern." Thankfully, Eshton brewed beers, ground sausages, and baked dumplings with far greater skill than he named businesses, and the place was well known and well loved as an establishment where one could get a meal and a drink in relative privacy, for only a very slightly unreasonable fee.

This time, once he'd allowed his eyes to adjust to the dim light within, Jace saw an opportunity to turn the tables. He swept across the room, waving to one or two of the other regulars, and dropped suddenly into the booth where Liliana was halfheartedly picking at something that could have been pâté. Her yelp as he suddenly appeared beside her was almost cute.

"Turnabout," he said to her, taking a scoop of the pâté and then wrinkling his nose at the taste, "is fair play."

"Oh, Jace, Jace, Jace," she cooed at him. "You have no idea how many games I know."

Jace winced. "I really wish you'd call me Darrim when we're in public."

"And you're being silly. Nobody's listening to us. What are you doing here?"

"Looking for you," he told her. "We haven't really had a lot of time to talk."

"Haven't we?" she asked archly.

"Well . . . Not alone," he amended.

"I'll tell you what," she told him with a mischievous smile. "Right now, this so-called 'food' is enough to horn in on any conversation. Word to the wise? The sausage, the steaks, and the dumplings here are excellent. You should probably avoid anything else."

"Got it."

"You go get me something that's actually, say, edible, and I'll be happy to sit and talk with you."

"Yes, m'lady," he told her.

"Don't get sassy. That's my job."

Jace grinned and headed to the bar.

Liliana watched him go, a thoughtful look in her eyes, and stretched languidly back in her chair. For a few moments she listened to the ambient noise of the restaurant, the clink of glasses and platters, the dull hum of a dozen different unimportant conversations. And she glanced up as a shadow fell over the table, surprised that

Jace was back so soon—and couldn't help but roll her eyes heavenward when she saw it wasn't Jace at all.

It was an unfortunate fact of life, one she'd learned long ago, that in any tavern, any restaurant, any party—sometimes even in temple services!—there was always at least one man convinced that any halfway attractive woman couldn't live without his attentions. Lots of people assumed such things occurred only rarely; these people weren't the women in question. Was it something to do with the powers she commanded? Some unconscious death wish, or an attraction deep in the soul to one who had touched the spirits of so many others? Or was she seeking meaning where there was none, and it really was just a combination of poor upbringing and unabashed lust?

In any event, Liliana looked up at the fellow standing over the table, leering down at her, and wanted none of it. Though at least this one kept his red beard decently trimmed, had all his teeth, and was clad in a clean outfit (in the usual garish hues of those who wanted to seem richer than they were)—unlike some of the others who'd sought to abuse her hospitality in the past.

"Now what's a beautiful—" was all he got out before Liliana deliberately yawned in his face and turned away.

"Just a goddamn minute!" the fellow snarled, reaching across the table. "You're at least gonna do me the courtesy of listening to what I've got to . . ." And again he stopped, his hand mere inches from her wrist. Liliana looked back, startled despite herself to see the fellow suddenly straighten up and clear his throat.

"Well, this is awkward," he said, and though his voice was the same, his tone, his inflection, were those of another man entirely. "I mean, here you are trying to enjoy your lunch, and I have to barge over and ruin it for you. I really must apologize."

She stared, utterly bewildered.

"It's got to be particularly awkward for your friend," he continued. "I mean, he doesn't know you very well. Would you want him to stay out of it, trusting you to handle it? Or to leap in and beat the crap out of me, even though I've got about fifty pounds on him? He's got to be frantic, trying to figure out the right choice."

Liliana felt a grin stretching over her face, so wide she was sure it had to reach all the way to her ears. She craned her neck, peering around the newcomer, to see Jace halfway between the table and the bar, his eyes locked on the red-bearded man, his brow furrowed in deep concentration. And she laughed, a throaty, musical sound of pure delight.

"I think," she told the nearby fellow, though her eyes remained on Jace, "that he's done just fine."

Jace and his "spokesman" grinned as one; the latter wandered away, shaking his head in puzzlement, while the former returned to the table, two platters of food in hand.

✳ ✳ ✳ ✳ ✳

He tossed, he turned, he flipped the pillow, he punched the mattress, he even contemplated casting a spell on himself. But no matter what he tried, Jace couldn't find his way to sleep.

Dinner had been a disaster. Before Liliana arrived, Kallist had done nothing but talk about his continual hunt for a job in this miserable district, and about how Jace should be finding one, too, if he wasn't willing to go back to his old methods, about how their stores of gold wouldn't last forever, and blah, blah, blah.

And after she'd arrived? Jace, who really wanted to get to know Liliana better than their conversation at Eshton's had allowed, couldn't have forced his way into the conversation with a battering ram. Everything was about Kallist, Kallist's history with the Consortium, the various dangers and hazards he'd overcome in their service. Sure, those often involved Jace as well, but he hadn't realized, until he'd heard someone else tell them, just how much those events had cast him as the sidekick, aiding Kallist in his endeavors.

When all was said and done, Jace knew no more about Liliana Vess than he had that morning, except that she had a habit of salting damn near everything on the table—and that he really enjoyed watching her eat.

Finally Jace rolled out of bed, bound and determined to wake Kallist and have himself a good long rant. Whether he just wanted to yell, or actually hoped to clear the air, he couldn't say—because when he entered the center room of the three-room flat, he saw the door to Kallist's chamber standing wide open and empty.

Jace went back to bed and lay awake for hours more, fighting sleep when finally it deigned to come, until he heard Kallist's steps upon the stair and was certain his friend was returning alone.

✵ ✵ ✵ ✵ ✵

It was roughly a week later when Kallist returned from one of his forays with something approaching good news.

"Found a job, have you?" Jace inquired.

"Shift commander in a local merchant's private guard."

"A guard? You? You're kidding!" Jace couldn't help but laugh and was gratified to see Kallist smile along with him.

"You'd think so, but no. Seems there's been an increase in crime due to the poor crop growth from the swamp expansion. So the merchants can't rely on the city guard to protect them, and there's some sort of underground merchant war going on over what crops are left . . . Well, it's all very complex and economical, and you couldn't care less."

"Not even remotely," Jace agreed, still grinning. "I take it this 'war' means that you'll be doing a little more than guarding?"

"I might have a few slightly less legal job duties," Kallist admitted, "but hey, they pay better."

"Well, congratulations, Kallist." Jace honestly meant it, and Kallist was honestly glad to hear it.

The newfound peace lasted through all of three minutes of further conversation.

"By all the Eternities!" Jace squelched the urge to hurl something heavy and pointed at his friend. "How many times are we going to go through this?! I've told you more times than there are worlds in the Multiverse, I am not going to risk any hugely ostentatious shows of magic just yet, and I'm certainly not going to lower myself to working some miserable, menial job in a district like Lurias!"

"I see. So that's reserved for lesser souls like myself, then?"

"It seems to be what you're good for!" Jace snapped.

Kallist snarled something incomprehensible and was out the door before Jace could apologize—or even decide if he wanted to.

A few moments of grumbling, and then Jace, too, left the flat, slamming the door behind him. Without a single conscious thought, he found his feet taking him once more to Eshton's Tavern—about the only place in Lurias where just looking around didn't just piss him off.

It was abnormally crowded for so early in the day. Jace briefly wondered why, until he remembered hearing something about a local celebration. Celebrating *what*, he had no idea, and didn't care enough to ask. He shouldered his way through a cluster of people he didn't know, waved halfheartedly at one or two whose names he remembered, and slumped at the nearest empty table like a petulant child. Other than placing his order, he said nothing, looked at nobody, for some minutes. Until, that is, a familiar shape appeared beside the table.

He looked up in shock. "You work here?!"

Liliana gave him the same look the bartender might have given had he asked for an entire bottle of irrimberry wine—on credit. "Do I look like a barmaid to you?"

"Well, that certainly looks like my mincemeat pie you're carrying."

Liliana tossed the platter onto the table and sat down beside him, elbowing him to move over and give her some room. "I saw you coming," she told him. "This gave me the opportunity to see if you ordered anything I wanted to steal off your plate." She grinned at him. "And it's a powerful reminder to be careful how I spend."

"Oh? How's that?"

"It reminds me that if I'm not careful, I might actually have to *work* for a living." She shuddered theatrically. Jace couldn't help but grin, despite the sensitive topic.

"So I was going to ask if you minded me joining you," she told him, taking a forkful of buttered tubers from his plate. "Then I saw your miserable expression, and decided I'd better not ask." She smiled at him.

"There's . . . a lot going on," Jace said vaguely. Then, "Surely someone with your abilities should have no trouble earning coin."

Liliana's smile shrank a bit. "Surely. Assuming I wanted to attract all sorts of attention. Mages may not be the rarest things on Ravnica, but they're not exactly common—at least not those with the sort of power you and I wield. So what should I do? Put on shows, conjure spirits for people's amusement? I could work for a merchant family, maybe, but that's not the best way to avoid Consortium attention. Or maybe kill a few hundred peasants until the people pay me off? I don't think I care much for that option either. I could walk somewhere else—thought about it, more than once—but I don't really know anywhere I'd have many more options than Ravnica.

"I'm a little surprised you haven't thought through the same thing, actually."

"I have," Jace said with a frown. "I was just hoping you'd come up with something I hadn't."

She chuckled. "Look at us, 'Darrim.' We're quite possibly two of the most powerful people on this world, and here we are discussing jobs and living expenses. Too bad we can't just turn fungi into gold, right?"

"We were gods, once . . ." Jace quoted under his breath, then merely shook his head at her questioning glance.

"I can't imagine it's a problem for you," he said, trying to cheer the conversation a bit. "That is, I can't imagine you'd have trouble finding any number of people to put you up for a while."

He realized precisely what he'd said at about the same time she did, and blushed outrageously. But even as he opened his mouth to stammer an apology, Liliana burst out laughing.

"You haven't known many women, have you?" she teased him.

Jace raised an eyebrow. "No, but I've always been a quick study," he replied mockingly.

She turned demurely away, which was just as well; Jace would have been embarrassed for her to see the grin that nearly split his face.

In fact, there had been a few women, albeit *only* a few, during his earlier years—and with most of those, he'd simply pulled their desires and preferences from their minds—and none at all since he'd come to Ravnica. When it came to doing things "the old fashioned way," he was almost as awkward as a pubescent boy.

Somehow, though, he didn't think he was comfortable admitting that to her.

For a while longer they talked, Liliana telling Jace a few sparse details of her life. He couldn't help but sympathize, as she spoke of having to leave her home, lest the fears of those she'd once called friends cause her harm.

"Still," she told him softly, "I think maybe I've had it a little easier than you."

"Oh?" He glanced over, puzzled, his grin fading. "Why would you say that?"

"Because I can't do what you can. I'm accustomed to assuming that people won't trust me, or would be frightened of me, once they learn the sort of magic I wield. But you—you have the power to *know* they are. You can see their mistrust and their fear, or you can lessen yourself to be sure that you don't. I can't think of anything lonelier."

It was all nonsense, Jace was certain. He'd never felt that way. Never! But he couldn't seem to bury the doubt that began to cloud his thoughts.

Before he could decide what to say, he heard a familiar voice at the door of Eshton's Tavern, greeting a few of the gathered customers. Jace rose and saw Kallist glancing around as though looking for someone—and that someone, to judge by his eager expression, was not Jace.

"At least," Jace said, his own voice suddenly angry, "not everyone has to be as lonely as I apparently am." And with that he was gone, before Liliana could open her mouth to reply.

✳ ✳ ✳ ✳ ✳

When he returned, after many hours of stomping around the city like an angry giant, he was greeted by a wall of sound: music and laughter, drinking and dancing. The celebration of Whatever the Hell Lurias Had to Celebrate was in full swing, and he gave serious thought to coming back some other time. The last thing he wanted to deal with was a cheerful crowd.

Then he thought about trying to sleep, sighed, and stepped through the door.

The music that had been merely loud outside was a physical presence within, nearly potent enough to leap bodily on the newcomer and demand his coin purse. The stage was full to bursting, and many of the booths had been dragged aside to provide a larger dance floor. Several dozen customers whirled about in a flesh-and-fabric tornado, accompanied by a pair of minstrels in the corner who struggled to keep up.

Elbowing and glaring his way through, Jace stopped at the very edge of the dance and waited until the rhythm brought Liliana to him. He was strangely relieved to discover that she wasn't dancing with anyone in particular.

Their eyes met, and that relief was badly shaken at the ice in her expression. She stepped just far enough outside the ring of celebrants that she wouldn't block their path and glared at him.

"Yes?" she asked, her voice carrying over the music.

"Liliana, I wanted . . ." He trailed off, wondering where Kallist had gone.

"You wanted?" she prodded coldly.

"I wanted to apologize!" he shouted, loudly enough that several nearby customers glanced at him, drew their own conclusions, and snickered. "I shouldn't have . . ." he trailed off and shrugged.

"Shouldn't have been a rude bastard to someone who was trying to be kind to you?" she demanded.

"Uh, yes," Jace said, deflating.

"All right. Apology accepted." Jace saw a brief flash of a grin, a slender arm darting out like a snake, and then he was in the midst of the dancers before he knew what happened.

The next few moments were a blur; Jace had no time to think, let alone to speak, as he struggled with everything he had to keep up. Finally, when he felt that it was a race to see whether his feet would fall off before the sweat washed the nose and lips from his face, Liliana finally guided him away from the throng and into a booth that was miraculously empty of other customers.

"You know, you're a halfway decent dancer."

"I'm a lousy dancer," Jace said panting, tapping a finger to the side of his head. "But that fellow over there, in the black and green? He's an *excellent* dancer."

Liliana's jaw dropped, and then she laughed. "Why, 'Darrim,' are you trying to impress me?"

"Only if it's working." Then, "Liliana, I really am sorry."

"I know," she told him.

Jace grinned weakly. "Will you still believe me when I ask again where Kallist is?"

She frowned, then shrugged. "Kallist left—politely!" she added, poking Jace in the stomach with a finger, "when I made it clear that he'd misinterpreted the nature of our burgeoning relationship."

"Oh?" Jace felt his chest pounding faster than it had during the dance. "And, um . . . What about *our* 'burgeoning relationship'?"

Liliana smiled coyly and ordered another drink. "I don't know. Do we have one?"

"Look, I . . . I know that I showed the manners of a troll with piles earlier. I wanted to make it up to you. I, um, I got you something."

She managed to keep the smile on her face, though inside she groaned. "And what would that be? A bouquet of flowers? A nice piece of jewelry you can't afford? Maybe a doll?"

And then she cocked her head in puzzlement as Jace handed over a thick envelope, sealed with a dollop of melted wax. She slid a finger beneath the flap, ready to break it open, but a soft touch on her hand stopped her.

"Don't open it unless you need it," Jace told her.

"I don't understand. What is it?"

He smiled, almost shyly. "Secrets," he told her. "The personal secrets of half a dozen merchants, bankers, and aristocrats living in Dravhoc District." His smile grew wider at the stunned look that flitted across her face. "I'm not doing that anymore," he said. "But this? This is all old business, for me anyway, so it doesn't count. I wouldn't recommend staying long in Dravhoc at any given time; the Consortium's got sharp eyes there. But I'd imagine you can drop in long enough to collect a few payments.

"If, you know, you're ever desperate enough where the only other choice is waiting tables in a tavern."

Liliana leaned in and brushed her lips across Jace's own, enjoying the sudden startled look before he responded in kind.

≉ ≉ ≉ ≉ ≉

The sun was already slumbering beneath the western horizon when they arrived at the entrance to Jace's flat. He felt light enough that he hadn't even noticed the stairs, and it was with some reluctance that he pushed open the door.

"I guess," he said, taking both her hands in his, "this is where we say good night."

Liliana kissed him once and then turned them about, so that it was she who stood in the doorway, he in the hall.

"This," she said with a smile, "is where we say good morning."

Jace followed her inside and shut the door.

≉ ≉ ≉ ≉ ≉

"I'm leaving, Jace."

He looked up from where he sat on the ragged sofa, a plate of mushrooms and pork sausages on his lap, to see Kallist standing in the doorway. Slowly, uncertainly, Jace placed his breakfast to one side and stood. He'd avoided his friend for several days, now, uncertain what to say. But he certainly hadn't expected those to be the first words they exchanged.

"Kallist," he began slowly, "I don't—"

"It's better for all three of us," Kallist interrupted bitterly.

Jace nodded slowly. "What are you going to do?"

"Get my own flat." Kallist shrugged. "My new position pays more than enough. Maybe not as well as blackmailing the rich and famous, but I'll get by."

"You know I don't do that anymore," Jace insisted.

"No, not until you need to. Or until someone prettier than me asks nicely."

Jace didn't even ask how he knew. "That's different. It's not new information, and it's only in the case of—"

"You're a hypocrite, Jace. It's fine. My own fault, really. I should've known better than to take you at your word, when it came to getting something you wanted— the one thing I might've found to make this damned place a little better!"

"She was never yours!" Jace shot to his feet, fists clenched. "Never!"

"Because you wouldn't give us the chance!" Kallist shot back. "It's not enough that you took away everything I had?"

"Took away . . . Damn it, Kallist, I saved your life!"

"You call this a *life?*"

His jaw opened, to argue, to berate his friend for such an arrogant, narrow view of Lurias, of existence beyond the Infinite Consortium—and then Jace could only think of his own reactions, his own conversations with Liliana about this community in which they found themselves, and the words wouldn't come. He felt his face flush, though he wasn't entirely certain of what he was ashamed.

Perhaps misinterpreting Jace's sudden reticence, Kallist's own expression softened. "Look, Jace, this isn't how I wanted this to go. I know you meant well. Whatever else might've happened, I owe you thanks for that, and I've never said it." It was magnanimous, maybe more so than he really meant, or than Jace really deserved. But then, he was the one leaving, the one with a future, so he could afford to be.

The mage looked up once more, his eyes bright. "You're welcome, Kallist. And . . . I'm sorry it didn't turn out like I'd hoped."

Kallist nodded and was gone from the flat without another word, leaving Jace to stare at the blank and featureless door.

CHAPTER TWENTY-ONE

It took a few more weeks—weeks in which she was never far from Jace's side, weeks that she had to admit were far more pleasant than any she could recall—but everything was finally ready.

She had him fully wrapped around her finger. She knew she could sway him, push him to react exactly as she needed him to react. She knew he trusted her, loved her. It was what she'd been waiting for, working for, and now it was time.

So why did she wait? Why had she stood in the darkened main room of her flat—which she barely saw anymore, so much time was she spending in his—and stared down at her hands, for almost an hour now?

It had to be the risk, she told herself. She couldn't know precisely in what numbers they'd come, but she knew they'd come in force. Maybe she should put it off a little longer? Find a few more ways to test his powers, ensure that he'd come out ahead in the coming conflict? Perhaps—

No. No, that wasn't why she hesitated, and she damn well knew it. And putting it off? That would just make it harder still.

Setting her jaw, she cast her spells, summoned her spectral heralds, sent them out into the darkness of

Ravnica to deliver their messages, repeat their whispers, until they reached the ears of those who needed to hear them.

And then Liliana sat in the dark, wondering when the thought of Jace being hurt had suddenly begun to bother her.

✶ ✶ ✶ ✶ ✶

Ignixnax sped through the winding byways and half-repaired buildings of Rubblefield as swiftly as its four unevenly beating wings could carry it, giggling obscenely as it flew. Rarely did the imp bother to rush for much of anything, save when ordered by the bearded mortal dolt who summoned it—but rarely, then, did it have anything worth rushing for. Today, though, today it had heard whispers from the specters and the hidden demons of Ravnica's shadows, urgent whispers, vital whispers—fun whispers. And it knew those whispers must be shared.

It dived from the heights, flashing through the nearest doorway to the Consortium's complex. As a summoned servant of one of the cell's operatives, its entry was authorized, set off none of the mystical safeguards. Still, many of the guards at the door reacted to what they perceived as a threat, pulling blades, stabbing and swinging at the tiny alien thing that appeared suddenly in their midst. Ignixnax only giggled louder and darted around their swords with contemptuous ease, even taking a second to whip one of them in the face with its barbed tail before proceeding into the halls. And with that it was off into the winding halls, its twitching tail splattering bits of the foolish guard's blood and aqueous humor onto the carpet and the walls, until finally it arrived at its destination. Hovering unevenly, it reached out and scratched deeply at the wood of the door.

The door opened with a series of clicks and the faint hum of a mystic glyph deactivating, and Gemreth stuck his head out into the passage.

"I," the imp tittered at him in profane delight, "know where to find Jace Beleren."

And it was Gemreth's turn to pound through the halls of the complex, sprinting his way toward Paldor's office, Ignixnax perched on his shoulder and chortling all the while.

❊ ❊ ❊ ❊ ❊

Jace was still smiling as he worked his way through the market throng, content enough that he didn't even feel the need to elbow anyone. Here he waved at someone he recognized from Eshton's, there he stopped by a stall to examine a coppersmith's wares before deciding to look a little further. He caught the faint aroma of fresh fish as he watched a pair of stevedores unloading crates of the stuff under the watchful eyes of some private guards. That, in turn, put him briefly in mind of Kallist; he wondered if the man might be somewhere nearby, guarding his employer's shops, or perhaps one of the many warehouses that lined the south and east sides of the marketplace.

And even that thought wasn't enough to ruin Jace's good mood; if anything, he almost hoped he'd run into his old friend, have the chance to talk to him again now that some time had elapsed. He was absolutely ecstatic about feeling *normal*, although he'd never have recognized the sensation and would have denied it if he had. Here he was happy, here he was safe, and if he was still too ambitious and too enamored of his magics for that to satisfy him indefinitely, for a while at least it would be enough.

But Jace Beleren didn't have a while left to him.

❊ ❊ ❊ ❊ ❊

"They come."

Liliana—who mere moments ago left Jace behind in the market, to run his errands as she ran hers—pulled up short, ignoring the curses of the older man who almost ran into her from behind with his armload of loaves of bread. Moving far more carefully, eyes darting every which way, she moved off the main thoroughfare into a darkened doorway.

"You're sure?" she whispered, when she was certain nobody paid her much attention.

"You told us," the voice continued, and now she could barely make out a ghostly, humanoid shape among the other shadows, "keep watch as we spread our tales, keep watch for those who would respond to them. Do you doubt us now?"

"No, of course not."

"Then be warned. They come."

Damn. She'd hoped to have a few more days. They must have really rushed, to get here so quickly!

"Go," she told the lurking specter, "and gather the others. Keep watch over him. Warn or protect him where you can, but do not let yourself be detected."

The specter nodded, vanishing with a faint hiss into the shadows once more. And Liliana herself dived back into the crowd, heading back the way she had come, the words of a spell already skittering like spiders across her lips.

⁂ ⁂ ⁂

Jace felt a faint cold chill running down his spine, a shudder with no apparent cause. His hackles rose, and he spun swiftly to see nothing unusual at all: Just the press of the crowd, the occasional lizard-drawn cart, the various stalls, the buildings rising up beyond the bazaar's borders. He saw nothing alarming, and almost attributed the sudden shiver to an errant breeze, but it had felt so much like the necromantic energies Liliana commanded, the touch of her aura. Was she here, somewhere in the crowd? Was it an attack, something with an effect he hadn't yet sensed? Or . . .

Just then Jace spotted him at the edge of the crowd. He'd never have noticed him had that strange chill not caressed him, causing him to turn; and he'd never have paid much attention even then, for the blue-skinned folk were hardly a rarity in Ravnica's many districts.

But the vedalken stared at him in turn, and Jace needed only to meet his eyes to recognize Sevrien's intense and unblinking stare.

They found us!

Immediately Jace was fighting his way through the crowd, his burning urgency and rising fear at war with his desire to remain hidden, unnoticed. He saw them everywhere he looked, now, men and women who might be wearing the simple garb of laborers rather than their accustomed chain shirts, but who nonetheless moved with the poise of trained Consortium soldiers. He even recognized a few faces, and why not? He'd dwelt in the same building as these folks for quite some time, even if he'd never bothered to learn most of their names.

From all sides they converged, slow but inexorable, gliding or shoving their way through the crowds. Jace glanced back over his shoulder, saw Sevrien turn and shout orders to someone else Jace couldn't detect, pointing not in Jace's direction but off to the side. Was he ordering someone around, to try to intercept him, or . . .

Liliana. Had they found Liliana?

He was all but running now, as much as the press of the throng would allow. Eldritch syllables dripped from his tongue, and with every few steps he was someone else, illusion after illusion flitting across his body. Now he was an old man, shuffling along, wrapped in rags that had once been beautiful finery; now a loxodon, his tusks and trunk and platter-sized ears protruding from above the heads of the crowd; now a goblin, peering this way and that for a merchant who might be willing to deal with her kind. Sometimes the images came from his imagination alone, other times from individuals he saw or bumped into in the crowd; anything to confuse the many watching eyes. Few in the packed bazaar even noticed the sudden changes, so intent were they on their own endeavors, and those who did could only blink and stare, uncertain what they'd just seen.

For a time his misdirection kept his pursuers at bay, confused and uncertain where he'd gone, or even who he was. Still there were so many, and they knew well whom they faced. And slowly, oh so slowly, their noose drew tight, as ever more Consortium swords converged on the market's center.

✷ ✷ ✷ ✷ ✷

"Everything ready?" asked Kallist, standing in the doorway of a great warehouse beside a wagon that creaked beneath a dozen heavy crates. Already a series of administrative and paperwork delays had kept the imported textiles out of the market for hours; half the day was already wasted. The boss was not going to be happy if they lost any more time, but Kallist had his procedures, and procedures would not be rushed.

"Not, uh, not entirely, Commander," reported the guard whose job it was to scout the streets between here and the vendors, to watch for any dangerous activity on the part of their rivals.

"And what does 'not entirely' mean?"

"Well, it doesn't seem to have anything to do with us. But something's going on in the bazaar. A whole lot of people there, Commander, and pretty heavily armed."

Kallist scowled. Was the cold war between the merchant families about to combust? "Could you tell who they work for? Or at least whose shipments they're trying to intercept?"

"That's just it, though. They're not moving in a single block, and they're not focusing on any given family or guild. I've seen manhunts before, Commander, and I'd swear they're looking for a person."

Kallist's heart sank. It could have been someone else they were after—but who? Who in Lurias was that important?

And in that moment, the past months ceased to matter. All that mattered was that the man who'd been his friend and brother, the man who'd saved his life, was threatened.

"The shipment stays here," Kallist barked. "And so do you."

He was off and running, one hand on the pommel of his broadsword, before the guard could even draw breath to question.

✳ ✳ ✳ ✳ ✳

So focused was he on maintaining his illusions, Jace never saw her coming.

A living wisp of smoke, the elf Ireena twirled and flowed through the crowd. She spun around flying elbows, ducked beneath arms that reached for various goods, and none of it touched her. Her eyes stung mercilessly, thanks to the powders she'd sprinkled into them, but she refused to blink them clear. Through the alchemical haze, she studied the crowds, watching, waiting for . . .

There. The powder allowed her to see the faint aura of magic emanating from Jace Beleren as he strove pitifully to hide from them, to follow his movements no matter what pathetic guise he chose. Dancing and spinning like a delighted child, she drew ever nearer to him, and in her hand she cupped another batch of powders, wrapped in a protective leather pouch.

Jace had just worked his way past yet another fish-monger when she appeared, spinning out from behind the stall. With a brilliant white grin that looked somehow hideous in her darkly tanned face, she slapped a handful of bitter particles across his mouth and nose.

But Jace, while stunned by the sudden unexpected attack, was not entirely unprepared. Though he instantly began to cough as the drug worked its way into his lungs, fell choking to the cobblestones and felt the world grow hazy around him, he was able to deflect a portion of the powder with a fierce telekinetic thrust. His eyes watered as his body screamed for air, but he did not fall nearly as helpless as Ireena had intended.

Even as she stepped in to admire her handiwork, Jace rose to his knees and lashed out. His fist, wrapped in the same telekinetic force that had dispersed some of her powder, slammed into her solar plexus with a terrible strength. Ireena fell to lie beside him with an ear-splitting scream, clutching her gut and writhing like a landed fish. She'd live—probably, if it didn't take too long for her to get help—but she was certainly no further danger to him.

Jace tried to rise to his feet and failed, falling back against the fishmonger's stall and then once more to the street as his choking fit continued. His face reddened and he felt himself on the verge of passing out as he struggled desperately to breathe.

The people around him, a few of whom had finally turned his way to see what was wrong, suddenly scattered before the thunder of approaching hoof beats. Jace looked up to see the silhouette of a centaur looming above him. Xalmarias; it had to be Xalmarias, though between the drugs and the angle of the sun he couldn't see enough to be certain.

Paldor really had sent everyone, hadn't he?

The centaur reared, a short spear clutched in his right hand, his iron-shod hooves sharpened almost into blades in their own right, and Jace could only choke, trying to clear his lungs of the powder in time to do something, anything to save his life.

Another figure lunged from the crowd, leaping atop the centaur's back as though he were a wild horse in need of breaking. Xalmarias cried out in indignation as a powerful hand reached out and snagged his spear, trying to yank it from his grip, even as the other buried itself in his hair, wrenching his head back sharply enough to bring tears to his eyes.

ⲫ

"Jace!" Kallist cried out, struggling to keep his seat as the centaur bucked and thrashed, "Go! Run!"

Staggering to his feet, the coughing fit finally beginning to subside, Jace did just that. He hurled himself once more into the crowd, which was now backing fearfully away from the struggle in their midst, trying to lose himself within.

As he pushed and elbowed his way through, Jace carefully cast out with his mind. Remembering every detail of Tezzeret's lessons, he touched first one, then another, spreading himself as wide and as thin as he ever had. He couldn't read a single true thought this way, but then, he didn't need to. Most of the crowd felt little save boredom, maybe casual excitement or—near where Kallist and Xalmarias fought—a growing fear. Jace hoped, prayed, that even his casual touch would alert him to another killer in the crowd, that the sudden bloodlust of a coming attack would warn him before a Consortium blade took him in the back.

And then the emotions around him turned to panic as a dozen people screamed, their eyes turning skyward. Jace immediately dived to the ground in a roll made awkward by his lingering shortness of breath, coming to a stop beneath a cheap vegetable stand. Only then did he look up, and he wondered if it wouldn't have been better to keep rolling.

It flapped through the air above him, awkward but frighteningly swift. It had somehow sprouted wings that it had lacked the last time Jace saw it, that horrible night in his room, but he recognized the old man's cackling face, the scorpion-like stinger that quivered, eager to strike, above its back.

Coming to his feet, he allowed himself to be carried along by the press of the panicking throng. That he could summon something to tear the little horror from the sky, Jace had no doubt, but it did him no good if he couldn't find its summoner—Gemreth, almost certainly, unless Paldor had called in one of the Consortium planeswalkers.

Straining to maintain his mental "net" over the crowd, ever alert for a secondary attack, Jace cast his sight up and out, trusting the press of the throng to keep him moving while his senses hovered elsewhere. From above, he peered about him in all directions, seeking the dark robes and grey-speckled beard . . .

There! Roughly a hundred feet across the market, Jace spotted his foe, crouched atop a merchant's wagon. Allowing his eyesight to return to his head, still moving with a portion of the crowd, he worked his way forward. As he advanced, he glanced over his shoulder, desperate to keep track of the minuscule fiend as well.

He couldn't see it!

A cold rain of fear dripped down Jace's spine. Without eyes on the creature, he was as helpless as anyone else, for he could never detect the little demon's mind as he could a mortal being's. He knew he could wait no longer to call on assistance of his own. It was a tricky thing to do while maintaining his psychic web over the crowd, keeping track not only of the enemy mage but searching for other foes who might lurk nearby, but again—thanks, ironically, to Tezzeret's exercises—he pulled it off.

And the screams of the crowd rose further still as another shape, a larger shape, appeared with a thunderclap in the afternoon sky. Its wingspan wider than many of the vendors' stalls, a steam-tongued drake cast a shadow over the heart of the market. At Jace's silent command it circled, hunting for its smaller but no less deadly prey. Jace himself continued onward, thankful that the flying creatures had distracted the people nearest him so that none had seen him cast his spells.

It was the gleam of triumph in Gemreth's expression as Jace drew near him, more so even than the shriek of the drake, that warned him. Jace spun to see the diminutive demon diving from atop a nearby shop. Even as he dropped once more to the earth, Jace sent a mental shriek for help to his summoned ally.

And the drake replied in the only way it knew how.

A wave of billowing steam washed over the market, a burning spear through the heart of Lurias. In a matter of seconds, Gemreth and his conjured beast were reduced to lumps of seared flesh and sodden bone.

So, too, were a score of the district's panicked citizens. They died in terror; they died in agony.

And Jace felt each and every one of them die.

Through his network of psychic tendrils that scanned the crowd, their dying thoughts flowed into him. They flayed his mind and soul, stripping away humanity and conscious thought, until there was nothing left but pain. *So much pain, so much fear, so many final cries and he'd never again see his husbands or wives or brothers or sisters, would never open the blacksmith shop he'd dreamed of, never watch the seyer-blossoms bloom in the garden. What would the children do without him? Tanarra I loved you, oh gods it hurts it burns please gods make it stop . . .*

Jace curled into a ball, body and soul, screaming in voices that were not his, and all he knew was pain.

※ ※ ※ ※ ※

"Jace!" Kallist had no difficulty finding his fallen friend; the burst of steam and the scent of charred flesh were signal enough. He knelt on the cobblestones, dropping the sword now stained with the blood of the centaur Xalmarias, and cradled Jace's head in his hands. "Jace, are you all right? What happened?"

The mage's eyes refused to focus, and still he screamed.

For an instant, Kallist felt only panic. What had happened? What could he do? Maybe he should wait for Liliana, but where was she? Could he afford to wait that long? Could Jace?

No. No, Kallist didn't think he could.

"Jace!" He held his friend's face close. "Jace, listen to me! It's Kallist; I'm here!"

He took a deep breath; he didn't know what Jace was suffering, but he'd both seen and inflicted enough anguish to recognize it now. A second deep breath, steeling himself against he knew not what.

"Jace, I don't know what to do! Tell me what I can do . . ."

Jace never heard the words, but he felt the thoughts and the emotions behind them. Kallist's mind, which he knew so well, was a beacon in the dark and the pain, a light showing him the way out.

And Jace's screaming ceased. Kallist felt something invade his mind, a touch that squeezed so painfully he thought he must surely die or go mad himself—but it squeezed not with anger, but with fear, a grip of desperation.

Jace felt Kallist's mind in his hands, a rock amid the tearing tides around him. Clinging to it, he hauled himself back, inch by maddening, agonizing inch.

Both men lay, side by side, panting in exhaustion and pain, surrounded by the dead and the dying until Liliana found them moments later. And with Jace leaning on her, Kallist staggering behind, they managed to limp away before Sevrien and his soldiers could find them once more.

✳ ✳ ✳ ✳ ✳

"Fight back? Are you insane?"

Liliana shook her head. "Jace, they found us. They'll *keep* finding us! What choice do we have?"

They were huddled in Kallist's own flat, trying to catch their breath and regroup. The shutters were tightly latched, casting the room in a grim shade, and the door was triple-bolted. Kallist had sworn they'd be safe there, at least for a time, as he hadn't rented the place under his own name. Still, they jumped at every sound, froze at every movement in the stairwell or the street beyond.

Jace sat flopped in a thickly cushioned chair, pale and shaking, though some of his strength seemed to have returned. He refused outright to discuss what had happened, brushing off even Liliana's most concerned inquiries, focusing only on what came next.

"Liliana," he said softly, "we can't. *I* can't."

"What choice?" she demanded again.

"We planeswalk. We go somewhere they'll never find us."

"It means leaving Kallist behind," Liliana reminded him.

"That's fine." Both of them turned to see Kallist in the door to the flat's tiny kitchen, a mug of something or other in his hand. "I'm not prepared to give up my life a second time," he told them. "Besides, let's be honest. They're not really after me. Once they've figured out you two are gone, I doubt they'll spend too much time hunting for me. I'll disappear for a few weeks, and that'll be it."

"Just like that?" Jace asked, and neither Kallist nor Liliana was entirely sure if he doubted Kallist's predictions, or referred to the end of their own relationship.

"I think so," he answered softly. "You do what you need to, Jace. I'll be fine."

For several hours Jace and Liliana talked, discussing possible worlds and destinations, she occasionally trying to talk him into staying and fighting, he always refusing even to consider the notion. And eventually she rose and left, ostensibly to send her ghosts out to see if Jace's flat was safe, so they could recover the rest of his belongings, but mostly because she was sick of arguing.

All right, so he'd need a bit more convincing. She could do that. She had time.

Only when she was well and truly gone did Jace rise and make his way to the next room, to which Kallist had retired, giving the couple the chance to talk. He stood in the doorway, staring at his friend who slumped, dozing, at the table.

He hadn't told Liliana what he'd planned; she'd have tried to talk him out of it. He hadn't told Kallist, for Kallist would most assuredly have refused. And Jace admitted he'd have had good reason to do so.

But Jace couldn't leave him behind, not now. He'd been in Kallist's mind, seen how much his friend still worried for him. And Jace worried for him in turn. He knew Tezzeret—better than Kallist did—and Jace believed, in his heart and soul, that Kallist was wrong. He wasn't safe here, not even if Jace and Liliana were gone for decades.

There was a way. He'd thought it possible for years, ever since Tezzeret had told him of his "mind-storage" device, ever since he'd felt the minds of the traitor and the nezumi shogun and realized they were, indeed, objects that he could manipulate. And now, now that he'd touched Kallist's mind once more, felt its weight, its shape, its essence, Jace was all but certain.

No, a planeswalker couldn't take another person with him through the Blind Eternities. But another mind? That, Jace knew, he could do. He could hold Kallist within himself, just long enough to make the journey and to find another body, a new body, for him to inhabit. It would mean erasing the mind of someone else, to make room for Kallist's own, but Jace was certain he could find someone who deserved it.

Kallist would never forgive him; he knew that before he even started. But he would be alive, and Jace owed him that—even if it wasn't what Kallist thought he wanted.

With a deep sigh, Jace thrust his mind into his friend's. Again he cradled it in his grip, tenderly examining it from all sides. And then he did what he'd never tried before—what nobody, to his knowledge, had ever tried before—and drew it to him.

He was Jace Beleren, mind-reader, planeswalker. And he knew he could do this.

Knew, right up until the moment that Kallist's mind truly entered his own, and everything went wrong.

Jace thought he could keep them separate, that he could keep the him that was Kallist in a tiny corner of the him that was Jace. Two minds sharing a body, yes, but far from equally. As they touched, Jace's protections popped, soap bubbles on the wind, for this was a pressure of a sort he'd never known. It wasn't an attack, it wasn't communication, it wasn't anything he could have imagined—and what Jace could not imagine, he could not weave into his spells.

Already he was experiencing memories not his own, remembering dreams he'd never had. He seemed to be staring at the room from two different angles, staring at two faces, and he couldn't recall which was his. His head began to throb, his concentration to blow away like perfume on the wind.

Desperately he tried to stop the spell, to push Kallist's thoughts back where they belonged—but even if he'd had the power or the focus to do so, Jace had already forgotten how, the knowledge buried beneath the flood of someone else's mind.

Still he pushed, running on instinct now rather than knowledge, struggling to separate the thoughts of his friend from his own, even if he could no longer remember which was which, who was who.

On it went, and on, until finally what had nearly become one was indeed two once more. And Jace, who had been Kallist, and Kallist, who had been Jace, lay unconscious together on the thin rug of the anonymous flat.

CHAPTER TWENTY-TWO

Slowly, so slowly, the rush of returning memories, of a returning life, subsided. Shivering violently despite the night's warmth, Jace Beleren opened his eyes, and found himself once more in the alley—once more *today*—lost no more in the memories of the past. For the first time in months, he was himself, rather than the man whose thoughts and recollections he'd stolen.

His hands and legs were coated in refuse from where he'd fallen, and the stench of the alleyway permeated his clothes. He noticed neither. The sounds of the city, muted but hardly silenced after the setting of the sun, crept into the narrow walkway behind him, and he ignored them as well.

How long he'd lain there, he couldn't say. He felt as though he were awakening from a long sleep, a sleep beset by nightmares of his own device. Jace rocked back on his heels, wiped a sleeve across his face to clear the worst of the tears from his cheeks.

A dozen times he drew breath to speak to his absent friend, a dozen times he faltered.

"How can I?" he whispered finally. "How do you apologize for something like this? 'Oh, I'm so sorry I lost control of the spell. I never meant to steal your mind;

I just meant to commandeer it for a while and stick it somewhere else. Still friends?' "

Jace shook his head, and sniffled once or twice. "You'd know what to say, Kallist. I don't know if I'd want to hear it, but you'd say it. I was so *sure*. So certain I knew what was best for you, so certain I could do it. The great Jace Beleren couldn't fail, could he?"

Jace sank until he sat on the filthy ground.

"You know I came to Favarial to save you?" he said with a bitter laugh. "Well, to save 'Jace.' And it was your strength and your decision that brought me here. You who decided to do the right thing, not me.

"There's so much I wish we could have settled, Kallist. Even if I could never have made up for what I did to you, I could have tried. Maybe even been friends again, now that I understand why Liliana did what she did, why she left 'Jace' for . . ."

And then he was up and running, cursing himself for a thousand kinds of fool. Here he was, moping in alleyways, with who-knew-what still happening to Liliana. He remembered her cry from the stairwell, and a surge of magic passed through him, a spell he could only have wished to cast when he'd still thought himself to be Kallist. He directed his magics sharply down and allowed them to lift him skyward, spreading out in invisible wings of pure telekinetic force that brushed the buildings to each side, the feel of the stone cold against his mind. He took to the air, arcing over the nearest buildings, angling sharply toward the apartment that his mind in Kallist's body had called home.

This was Ravnica. Nobody gave the soaring figure more than a second look.

Before him was an open window, broken and shattered in Semner's attack. Jace swooped inside, the psychic wings fading into nothingness even as his feet touched the floor.

Liliana stared with wide, red-rimmed eyes from the

floor, where she'd slumped exhausted against the fallen table. Shaky as a newborn fawn she rose, and made her way toward him with tentative steps. He feared, at first, that she was injured, but the blood that stained her gown was not hers.

"Jace?" she asked softly, her hand rising, her fingers brushing the side of his face, as light as hummingbird's breath. "Jace?"

He nodded once, trembling at her words, her touch.

"Oh, Jace, I'm sorry!" He almost found himself falling back as she wrapped her arms tight around him, as though afraid he'd simply vanish once more. "I wanted to explain, I wanted to fix it," she sobbed into his chest. "I didn't know how."

"It's all right," he told her through tears of his own. "It's not your fault. I did it to myself, to me and to—to Kallist." His words ended in a soft gasp, and he refused to turn his gaze, to look at the room beyond the woman he held. "I wonder . . . I don't think the right one of us survived, Liliana. I think he deserved it more than me."

"What was it like?" she asked gently, face still pressed against him.

"It . . . It didn't really feel like anything," he replied slowly, thinking back over the past six months. "I mean, I was just him. It didn't feel like anything had changed. Even when . . ." She felt his chest move as he shrugged. "We're not exactly identical twins, but it somehow never occurred to me that my face had changed. If I thought about it, I could have said 'Jace was the one who lost a toe to frostbite,' yet whenever I looked at the stump, it just felt natural. I never even questioned it."

"Your soul," she suggested.

"What?"

"You traded minds, Jace, not souls. Your soul was still you. Maybe that was its way of protecting your mind. Maybe knowing what had happened without being able to fix it would have—damaged you."

"I'm not sure I believe there's any such thing as a soul separate from the mind," he admitted.

"There is." It was scarcely more than a whisper. "Believe me, there is."

Jace nodded, and finally steeled himself for what was to come. Tenderly but firmly, he pulled himself from Liliana's grasp and stepped across the room, ignoring Semner's mutilated corpse as he searched for—

Jace dropped to his knees, felt Liliana's hand on his shoulder and couldn't even turn to meet her gaze. He'd known Kallist was dead, of course, had known since he awoke in the alleyway with his own memories, but to see it . . .

"I couldn't save him," she whispered to him.

"You shouldn't have had to," Jace rasped, rising slowly. "This is my fault."

"Jace—"

"It is. I did this. It's my fault.

"But," he added, turning around, eyes sweeping the room, "it's not my fault *alone.*"

There, lying off to one side, half-propped against the wall, one of Semner's men still breathed. Jace watched him for a long moment, and gathered his concentration as he'd not done in ages. The air around him began to glow, a wintry breezy to waft through the chamber, as he drew on sufficient mana to rip into the man's mind.

There was no finesse, no care, only power and purpose. Jace slashed through thoughts and memories like underbrush, leaving a wake of devastation behind him. The unconscious fellow twitched and shuddered as entire swathes of his life were frayed. He wouldn't die of this. Jace had no taste for killing, not with memories of the Lurias marketplace fresh in his mind. But neither would he leave one of Semner's thugs behind, unpunished for his sins. The result was a drooling imbecile, a man who might be trusted to push carts or carry boxes in exchange for food and shelter. A grim life, but a life nonetheless, and perhaps more than the bastard deserved.

Deeper Jace delved, without sympathy or compunction; he cared about one thing only, held to but one objective. Yet no matter how thoroughly he sifted through the shreds of what had lately been a sentient mind, he couldn't find it. Eventually he had to concede that it was never there.

"He doesn't know," he said to Liliana as he allowed the spell to lapse, ignoring the faint babbling and drooling emerging from what was no longer entirely a man. "He doesn't know who hired Semner. I doubt any of them did except Semner himself."

Liliana gently took his hand in hers. "Is there really any doubt?" she asked him.

"Why would they have sent someone like Semner?" Jace challenged. "They'd have known he wasn't up to the task. If it'd actually been me, instead of Kallist . . ."

"So maybe they didn't send him. Maybe he found where you were—where 'Kallist' was—and decided to try for the bounty they've put on your head. But either way, it's ultimately their fault, isn't it?"

Jace looked away. "It is," he agreed.

"So what," she said, taking his chin and forcing his face around to meet her gaze, "are we going to do about it?"

"We could walk somewhere. Like we meant to do before. Somewhere the Consortium would never find us."

"Is there any such place?" she asked. "Would you really want to live in a strange place, without friends, looking over your shoulder every day?

"Would you really," and her voice grew suddenly hard, "want to let them get away with what they've done to Kallist? To us?"

Again Jace pulled away from her, moving across the room to stare out the window at the flickering lights of Favarial. Fear and anger warred across his face, staking out territories in the depths of his soul.

"You don't know Tezzeret," he whispered finally. "Not like I do. I can't—we can't beat him, Liliana.

"But—"

Jace turned, shaking his head. "We can't," he insisted. "But we don't have to.

"The Consortium will regret what they've done, Liliana. And we can blind them in the process, throw them into enough disarray that they won't be able to come looking for us. Not for a while, at least, not until we're well and truly gone."

It wasn't enough, not nearly. But she dared not push any further, not so soon. And at least it was a start. She nodded, and if Jace noticed the sudden tension in her shoulders, he surely attributed it to the evening's horrors.

Jace returned to the body of his best friend and knelt beside him one last time. Ignoring the blood that was already drying into a thick stain, he lifted the heavy blue cloak that had always been his favorite. He wrapped it around his shoulders and joined Liliana in the doorway. Later, when he'd had the chance to rest, to draw mana from the waters below, he would sprout his wings and take to the sky once more, carrying them as far as he could. For now, they had only their feet on which to rely as they began the long, monotonous journey toward the Rubblefield.

✻ ✻ ✻ ✻ ✻

"Damn it to raging puss-soaked hell!" Paldor ranted at the blinking glow that limned his beard and fleshy features in a blood-red aura. "Why are you doing this to me? Why?"

Oddly enough, the desk didn't answer.

Constructed by Tezzeret, Paldor's desk was attuned to every external door and window in the building through an intricate magical alarm system. Should anyone other than members of the Consortium attempt to enter the complex, the wood glowed, alerting Paldor to the possibility of intrusion.

This was the seventh time the damn thing had gone off in the past three hours.

Paldor practically ripped the speaking tube from the wall and held it to his mouth. "Captain Sevrien! This needs to stop!"

A few moments of silence, and then a breathless voice replied. "Captain's not in the office, sir. We're stretched thin, so he's gone to check on the latest incursion himself."

Paldor muttered something under his breath that threatened to melt the mouthpiece. Then, "Wake the day shift, if you're that shorthanded!"

"Uh, we already have, sir."

More flowery muttering.

It made sense, though. Looking back over the schematic on the desk, it seemed that each false alarm—if indeed they were false—was as far from the previous ones as possible. The guards were running themselves ragged, not merely investigating each new alert, but leaving a pair of men behind to watch the portal in question; *of course* they'd already called in every available blade.

Paldor shook his head as the flashing ceased. Could magic simply malfunction? As long as he'd worked for Tezzeret, he still didn't really understand more than the basics of sorcery. But if it was an attack, or a prelude to attack, where was the enemy? So far, the guards hadn't found a threat, or even an explanation as to how the alarms were triggered.

Not for the first time, Paldor glanced at the glass contraption on the wall. And not for the first time, he rejected the notion before it had fully formed. Tezzeret would not take kindly to an interruption without a tangible threat. Until Paldor knew for certain what was happening, he was better off not troubling him.

"Aarrggh!" In a tempter tantrum worthy of a colicky child, he pounded his fists on the desk when it lit up once more, indicating a window clear on the other side of the building. Grumbling, he rechecked the array of weapons concealed both under the desk and on his person—as he'd done each of the last seven or eight times—and seethed.

But this time, finally, the results were a bit different.

"Got it, Paldor." The voice, the vedalken captain's own this time, emerged clearly from the speaking tube.

"You know what's going on?" Paldor asked hopefully.

"I positioned some men at the windows that hadn't been triggered yet. We got lucky, finally caught 'em in the act."

"And?"

"Faeries," Captain Sevrien reported, disgust in his voice. "We're being pranked by a swarm of bloody, damned faeries. Would've pulled the bug's wings off myself, but it vanished when it saw we were waiting for it."

Paldor nodded, even though Sevrien couldn't see him, but his brow furrowed in consternation. It was certainly possible; some of the smaller and less malevolent of fey-kind were known for such annoyances, and even the great city of Ravnica, lacking the groves and woods of which the creatures were most fond, wasn't completely free of the pests.

But why here? Why in such force? Something knocked faintly on the doors of Paldor's memory but refused, for the moment, to step over the threshold.

"What sort of faerie, Captain?" He hadn't even known he was going to ask the question until it had moved beyond his beard, but suddenly he had to know.

"Come again, sir?"

"What sort of faerie?"

Paldor could all but hear Sevrien shrug. "Beats me, sir. I don't know the first thing about the little bastards. I—"

"Then go to the library or the workroom," Paldor ordered through a vicious snarl, "and find someone who does!" He slammed the speaking tube back into its slot in the wall.

The desk had flashed two more alarms, leaving Paldor gritting his teeth hard enough to have milled a sack of grain, before the captain's voice emerged from the tube once more.

"What have you got, Captain?" Paldor interrupted.

"Well, sir, according to Phanol down in the stacks, based on the description I gave him . . ."

"Yes?"

"He says it was a cloud sprite, sir. Pretty much harmless. Weird thing is, sir, he said they're not known for this sort of mischief, that they . . ."

Paldor wasn't listening any longer, for the memory lurking just outside his conscious mind had finally burst its way in. No, cloud sprites weren't known for this sort of thing. Nor were they particularly common anywhere on Ravnica, and certainly not in the midst of the larger districts.

But most important, he'd finally remembered exactly when he'd last heard tell of the tiny sprites.

"Call your men back, Captain! Set them up guarding the main passageways, and for the heavens' sake, group them into units larger than pairs!"

"Sir, I'm not sure I—"

"We're under attack, Captain!"

Paldor heard Sevrien move the speaking tube from his mouth long enough to bark at his runners to order the guards to regroup. Then, "By whom, sir?"

"Jace damned Beleren!"

Alas, it never occurred to Paldor that, when dealing with a potentially invisible foe, any precautions he might order were already far too late. The faeries weren't a distraction against an incursion to come, but an incursion already committed; and the cell's security had been breeched as early as the third "false" alarm.

"Sir!"

It wasn't the captain speaking, then, but one of his runners, breathless and panting, addressing the captain. But Paldor, growing ever paler, heard it all through the speaking tube. "Sir, I—I . . ."

"Calm down, soldier!" Sevrien barked. "Take a breath!"

"But—but sir, Ireena's team . . . the entire team is down!"

"What do you mean 'down'?" Paldor and the captain spoke at once, Paldor having forgotten that the runner couldn't hear him.

"Oh, gods, sir!" Paldor could have sworn he heard the younger soldier's voice about to break. "Three of the men, sir, I . . . It's as though they were rotting for years, sir! I—I slipped in one of them, they're all over me, they're—"

Paldor heard the sharp retort of a slap, and Sevrien shouting for calm even as a murmur passed through the other men and women in the chamber. Tezzeret's lieutenant found himself sweating.

"—the others?" the captain was demanding. "Or Ireena herself?"

"Just—just sitting there in the midst of it all, sir!" the soldier sobbed. "Staring up at me, like they didn't even know who I was! Didn't even recognize their own names when I called!"

"Good gods," Sevrien whispered. "All right," he said, and Paldor knew from the shift in volume that he'd turned to face another of his seconds. "Where's Lieutenant Calran? I need him to—"

"He's in the hallway, sir," a third voice intoned, so softly Paldor could barely hear through the speaking tube. "He's just . . . sitting there, sir, playing with his sword and giggling like . . . like a schoolboy."

Silence fell, save for the frightened, labored breathing on both ends of the tube.

"Captain?" Paldor couldn't tell, from the tone, which soldier was speaking. "Captain, what do we—?"

Shouts and screams erupted from the tube as something—a door, perhaps?—shattered into a million splinters. Steel sang against leather as swords whirled from their sheathes, and the clatter of iron links of chain echoed through the narrow conduit. A dozen voices rose into a chaotic clamor, Sevrien's own barely audible as he shouted orders that nobody heeded.

Wood cracked, so hard that the floor beneath Paldor's feet trembled. Human voices disappeared beneath a monstrous roar, loud enough that he heard it clearly from the level below without need of the tube at all. The shouts of soldiers were transformed into shrieks of terror, wails of agony that ended in a series of horrible, wet thumps.

And then, once more, all was silent.

"Captain?" Paldor cleared his throat, hoping to still the quaver in his voice. He fumbled at the tube with sweat-slick hands. "Captain? Can you hear me?"

Nothing, nothing at all—and then, a faint childish giggle, accompanied swiftly by a second, a third, and a fourth. And all of them, each and every voice, sounded oh so familiar.

"Captain?" It was a whisper this time, a breath of horrified unbelief. "Captain?"

The speaking tube clattered as someone lifted it from where it hung, abandoned. "I'm afraid the captain can't hear you," a low voice responded. "Or at least he can't understand. He's not really himself anymore."

"Beleren," Paldor exhaled.

"He should have left me alone, Paldor," Jace told him. "Everything that happens now is on his head, and on yours." A squeal of rending metal nearly deafened Paldor as the far end of the tube was yanked from the wall.

He stood, the useless conduit in his hand, sweat beading his face, matting his beard, soaking in the folds of his chins. He cast a frantic eye at the door, contemplating making a run for it, and knew it was hopeless. With Beleren and his summoned monsters stalking the halls, Paldor wouldn't have given even a healthy sprinter fair odds of escape, and sprinting was far from his forte.

Besides, he had a greater responsibility.

With fingers that seemed determined not to work, Paldor yanked a sequence of crossbows and daggers from beneath the desk, cocking the former, unsheathing the latter and hurling them about the room, that he might have a weapon easily to hand from any position. He reached into his sleeve, ensuring the manablade sat securely in its sheath.

Then, and only then, did he turn his attention to the device. He swung the pommel of a dagger, watched the bits of glass scatter across the floor, and though he'd long been an atheist—ever since he learned from Tezzeret of worlds beyond this one—he found himself praying to anything that could hear him, praying that Tezzeret wasn't busy with something else, wouldn't take too long to arrive.

Indeed, the door opened mere seconds later, but it certainly wasn't Tezzeret standing within.

Paldor spun with a dreadful cry. A tiny crossbow fell from his sleeve into his meaty hand, and he fired the weapon. But even as the bolt crossed the room, he simply froze, transformed into a statue of flesh and bone. Only his pupils still moved, widening as he sensed

Beleren digging within his mind. He swore he could feel the touch of fingers upon his thoughts, the weight of eyes upon his memories, the warmth of breath upon his dreams.

"You should have stayed in hiding, you miserable rat!" Paldor raged internally, trying to shout, hoping that Beleren could hear his thoughts. "You want a war? You've got one! I know Tezzeret! He'll see every one of your friends dead. They'll suffer every imaginable agony before it's over, and they'll know it was your fault!"

He never knew if his threats had been heard. Jace closed his grip, and Paldor was gone. Oh, the body lived, and the mind could be taught; the corpulent creature could still be remade and remolded into a new life.

But as a person, as an avaricious and jovially cruel lieutenant of the Infinite Consortium, Paldor was dead.

But still Jace was not through with the man's mind. Into the vast emptiness that had once held a person, he implanted a message, a message that Paldor would speak only when Tezzeret finally appeared.

"That's Ravnica, Tezzeret." Jace spoke aloud even as he implanted the challenge in Paldor's mind, his tone deathly calm. "Perhaps Kamigawa next? Or Aranzhur, or Mercadia. There are so many cells to choose from.

"You should have left me alone. You want me, you decrepit, overrated tinkerer? Come find me!"

CHAPTER TWENTY-THREE

Liliana strode the halls of the Consortium, death dancing in her wake. Wraiths, phantoms, even a swarm of disembodied eyes flitted through the nearby air, darting around corners, to drink the life from anyone foolish enough to stand in her way. Far behind, in the bowels of the complex, plumes of smoke choked the passageways as the Ravnica cell's extensive archives—years worth of magical arcana—were reduced to ash and cinder.

Just as she reached the door to the office, standing out of sight of both Paldor and Jace, Liliana overheard the tail end of the conversation and the threatening tenor of Jace's implanted challenge. Instantly she furrowed her brow in concentration, wisps of black vapor trailing from her hair, her breath turning to steam as the air around her grew cold with darkest mana. Half a dozen smaller phantoms appeared from the surrounding shadows and vanished through the nearest window. One would remain hidden in the skies above this very building; the remainder made haste toward the other Consortium safehouses throughout Ravnica. There they would watch, and hopefully report Tezzeret's or Baltrice's actions, once they finally arrived.

"Bold words," she told him with a faint smile as she stepped into the room, a smile that Jace returned more faintly still. "But I thought you said you weren't willing to take him on?"

Jace shook his head. "No. But if he's . . . if he's on guard, thinks we're coming for him, he . . . uh, should take longer to start looking for . . . for us elsewhere." His breathing had quickened, his face fallen pallid.

"Jace?" Liliana moved swiftly to his side, fear chewing at the base of her spine. "Jace, are you all right?"

"No. No, I . . . I don't think so."

Only then did Jace allow his heavy cloak to fall open. Liliana gasped, hand flying to her lips, at the sight of the fletched bolt protruding from Jace's tunic, and the bloodstain spreading rapidly around it.

"Paldor . . ." Jace said with a sickly grin, "was actually a pretty . . . good shot."

She caught him as he collapsed, barely preventing him from slamming to the floor and perhaps jarring the bolt into a vital organ. She marveled, even as she moved to stanch the bleeding, at the strength and self-control it must have taken to hide his pain long enough to leave his message.

"Jace," she begged, "stay with me." Her hands worked, pressing the hem of her own tunic to the wound. "I don't . . . I don't know how to treat this! I'm not a healer!"

"I know. . . know someone here who is," he gasped between clenched teeth. "But I'm not sure . . . I can manage to get there."

"The sphinx?" Liliana asked. Such a creature soaring over the peaked towers of Ravnica would draw a few eyes, but it wasn't any more unusual than a dozen other sights the citizens would see that day.

"Dismissed her . . . after she dealt with the guards. Brilliant . . . wasn't it?" Jace chuckled, then shuddered as the bolt shifted against his ribs.

Liliana stood. "All right. Whatever you do, don't fight this." Her voice was clear as ever, but her lips quivered of their own accord, as though reciting a litany separate from the words she spoke.

Something rose from the floor by Jace's side, something wispy and insubstantial, a fume on the air that clung only vaguely to a humanoid shape. It reached out, not with a hand, but with its head, on a neck that stretched ever thinner, impossibly thin. A mouth that wasn't brushed against the young man's skin, and his body quivered with a shudder that had nothing to do with the pain of his wound.

"Don't fight it," Liliana had said, yet how could he not? Its touch was unnatural, a blight as it flowed through flesh to caress him from within.

At his strongest, Jace could have resisted easily, kept the phantasmal thing from infecting him. But as the pain flared in his wound, as his blood spilled across the floor, Jace struggled to gather his thoughts, to muster what power he had remaining . . . and failed.

He felt it pour, liquid and cold, through his body, across bones and muscles. His every limb went numb, and the world grew subtly distorted, as though a gossamer veil had somehow unfurled between his mind and his eyes.

"What did you do to me?" Jace demanded. He was startled to find that it hurt less to speak than it had moments ago—but also that a full second had passed after he thought the question before his lips and tongue formed the words.

"You're possessed," Liliana told him in much the same tone of voice she might have used to tell him he had something in his teeth.

"I—what?"

"Relax, Jace. I've told him to obey your thoughts. You're still in control of your own body."

"Why would you . . . ?"

"How do you feel?"

Jace took a moment. The torment had indeed lessened, though he still winced at the feel of the inches of wood currently inside him. "A little . . . better," he admitted.

Liliana nodded. "He'll keep you insulated from the worst of the pain, try to hold your body together so that walking doesn't cause any further damage. You won't be able to go far, but we should be able to get outside, wave down a carriage."

"All right." Slowly, perturbed at the odd delay between intention and movement, he rose to his feet. He felt a faint surge of déjà vu, staggering wounded from the complex. "We'd better get . . . get out of here. Liliana?"

"What?"

"Paldor. Left sleeve."

Liliana took just a moment to kneel beside the catatonic man, and rose clutching the manablade in her fist. "What in Urza's name . . ."

"Manablade. Powerful, could be useful." *And I'll be damned if I'll let Tezzeret have it back!*

She nodded, handing him the dagger, which he fumbled into his belt. She reached down once more to grab Paldor's small crossbow and a handful of bolts. No telling when they'd prove useful, especially with Jace helpless as he was.

"Where are we going?" she asked as they moved toward the door. "Where's this healer of yours?"

"Ovitzia District," he said.

✳ ✳ ✳ ✳ ✳

"Well," Emmara said, craning her neck to look up at the two newcomers on her porch, faintly luminescent in the orange glow of the setting sun and the magic streetlights flickering gradually into illumination. "This is a surprise."

"Emmara!" Jace greeted her, his words growing ever more slurred. "It's great again. You . . . I mean . . ." He blinked once, languidly, reaching out toward her.

"I can't find my hands." His eyes rolled back, their lids fluttering shut, and Jace went limp, dangling upright like a coat on a hanger thanks to the possessing spirit within his unconscious body.

Emmara circled Jace once, as though looking for the wires that held him erect, then knelt to examine the obvious wound. For the entire circuit, Liliana watched with an expression hovering between hopeful and darkly suspicious. A pall of silence hung over them, broken only by the trundling wagons and passersby on the street beneath, the occasional boat passing even farther below, and Jace's labored breathing.

"Can you help him?" Liliana asked, even as Emmara brushed the cloak aside for a closer look at the protruding bolt.

Emmara rose again to her full unimpressive height. "Who am I helping?" she asked blandly. "Berrim? Or Jace?"

Liliana didn't even blink. "Which one gets your help faster?"

The elf narrowed her eyes but nodded. "Bring him inside."

At Liliana's command, the spirit within Jace plucked at tendons and muscles, driving his body into a shamble as awkward as any newly animated zombie. Emmara cast the necromancer a look of profound disgust and found herself reviewing a suite of her own defensive spells—just in case—before following them in and slamming the door shut behind her.

✳ ✳ ✳ ✳ ✳

Darkness gave way to a muddled gray, and then to a fuzzy image of an off-white room.

No, not a room. Rooms had walls. This had pillars, with only a single wall whose window looked out on the street below. He'd made it.

Jace all but gasped in relief, then groaned as agony danced across his ribs with stomping feet and iron shoes.

The world went gray yet again, and when it finally resolved itself once more into Emmara's home, Jace saw a beautiful face and a halo of black hair staring down at him.

"Miss me?" he asked, his voice weak.

"More than Paldor did," she said, sitting beside him—no mean feat, considering how narrow the bed was—and wiping the sweat from his brow. "How do you feel?"

"Like someone—"

"If you say 'like someone shot me with a crossbow,' I may just get the bolt back from your elf friend and stick it back in you."

"Uh . . . I hurt," he concluded lamely.

"I know," she said softly. "And I don't want to see it happen again. But Jace—"

Jace recognized the tone, felt his lips press together in a flat line. *Don't say it. At least give me a few days—a few minutes—to recover first! Don't say it.*

"They'll find us again," she said firmly. "They'll keep finding us, if we don't make them stop."

She said it.

Jace opened his mouth to argue, then froze as the question finally sank home. How *had* Semner found them? The man had no magics, they'd done nothing to give themselves away, or at least nothing he could think of. Nobody of any import traveled through Avaric, so how . . .

He realized Liliana was still talking, and shook off his reverie as best he could.

"Liliana, look at me! This was just one cell, and I've got a hole in me! There's no way we're taking on the entire—"

"Damn it, Jace, listen to me!"

"No."

Liliana leaned forward, staring him in the face. "We can beat him!"

Jace barked out a laugh, then wished he hadn't as the room swam and his chest seemed to catch fire. "Liliana," he insisted through clenched teeth, "you're wrong. You have no idea how powerful Tezzeret is! I—"

"He's not stronger than us. Not both of us together."

"Even if you're right," Jace argued, hoping a new tack would head off yet another repeat of the same argument, "what good would it do? Let's say by some miracle we do get rid of the bastard. What then? Go back on the run while his replacement comes after us for revenge? 'Can't let people think the Consortium is vulnerable,' right? So either way—"

"You're an idiot." Liliana shook her head and rose, pacing to the nearest pillar. "How did I come to care so much for someone so thick?"

Jace watched her, squinting as she passed in front of the open window and the sun laughingly stuck needles in his eyes. "Enlighten me."

"You may know Tezzeret," she told him, "but I've studied the Infinite Consortium itself."

"Tezzeret *is* the Consortium," Jace corrected.

"No, he's not. Think about it. A dozen worlds, each cell with dozens of employees, soldiers, and spies. How many of them even know about worlds beyond their own?"

"Well, right, but—"

"How many of those know who Tezzeret is? And of those who do, how many care? A few of his lieutenants and personal operatives, maybe. Nobody else, Jace. For Urza's sake, why do you think he was able to take over the damn thing to begin with? It's because most of the personnel don't know who's giving the orders. They certainly don't *care,* as long as they get their share of everything!"

Maybe it was the pain, or the lingering disorientation of the wound and Emmara's healing magic, but Jace could not—or would not—comprehend. She couldn't be saying what it sounded like she was saying! Could she?

But she only nodded at his bewildered gaze. "You don't have to hide from the Consortium. We take Tezzeret, and we can run the damned thing!

"No more hiding. No more dashing from home to home, wondering who's watching you, or how to pay for your next meal. You can do what you want. You can make the Infinite Consortium into what you want!"

"Just by getting rid of Tezzeret?" Jace asked skeptically.

"Well, you'll have to kill a few of his closer associates, too, but—"

"Oh, is that all? Kill Tezzeret and a few of his associates?"

"What?" she asked, puzzled at the sudden bitterness in his tone.

"I don't want to kill anyone anymore, Liliana. I certainly don't want either of us to die. And if we try this, we're going to do both. We're going to kill a few people, and then Tezzeret's going to kill us, and none of it will matter."

"Jace . . ."

"No! Even if you're right about everything else, how would we do it? Do you know every world the Consortium touches? The location of every cell, the name of every leader? How to build those æther-tubes so you can feel if someone needs to reach us? We can't rule the Consortium, Liliana!"

"We can once you pull that information out of Tezzeret's mind."

"It's stupid, it's suicide, and it's not happening." Jace lay back in the bed, suddenly desperate for more rest. "I'm going back to sleep," he continued, "until I start feeling better. And then, if you're ready, we can talk about where to hide after we leave Ravnica."

He winced at the sound but otherwise gave no notice as Liliana snarled and vanished into the teleportation pillar. And damn it, he wouldn't feel bad about this! It was a stupid idea. Asinine. The notion that they could somehow take the Consortium from Tezzeret was as ludicrous as taking on the artificer himself. Liliana was fooling herself.

But when the pain finally subsided enough for Jace to return to sleep, his dreams were dreams of power.

✳ ✳ ✳ ✳ ✳

Damn him!

Liliana stormed from the house, ignoring Emmara's questioning glance. For many minutes she walked the streets of Ovitzia, almost hoping someone would accost her, give her an excuse to really cut loose, but of course nobody did. Finally, as her mind began to clear, she found herself before a storefront that had already closed down for the evening.

It would suffice. A swift touch and the wood around the latch rotted away, allowing her to slip inside. She propped the door shut behind her, glancing around at the shelves of rope, hammers, nails, and lumber, smelled the overwhelming aroma of sawdust, and wondered briefly who in Ovitzia built with wood anymore. Then, with a shrug, she stepped away from the windows and began to breathe deliberately, steadily, relaxing for the effort to come.

For many long minutes she stood, unable to calm herself, her body tense. The moment of truth, now—and she had to admit, to herself if nobody else, that she didn't want to go through with it. This would hurt Jace, hurt him terribly, a thought that filled her with genuine remorse. It wasn't a feeling to which she was accustomed, and she found she didn't much care for it. For a few moments, Liliana Vess allowed herself to pretend that she might choose a different path.

But she knew she would not, that she could not, that any thought to the contrary was as immaterial as one of Jace's illusions. And if he wouldn't allow her to talk him into doing what must be done, then the suffering to come was his own fault.

They would both just have to live with it.

Liliana worked her magic and stepped away from the world of Ravnica.

✳ ✳ ✳ ✳ ✳

"Anything?" Tezzeret asked, leaning back in his chair, etherium fingers interlaced with those of flesh and bone. His reflection stared up from the glossy metal panels before him, a warped and twisted view that just might have matched his soul better than the face he actually wore.

"No." Baltrice took a deep breath. "I got nowhere near the complex myself, as we agreed. But I did find a few of Paldor's surviving guards and sent them back to check. The cell's more or less lost, boss. Paldor, Sevrien, and Ireena are all mindwiped, the archives have been burned . . . There's nothing useful left."

Tezzeret screamed, cursing Beleren's name in half a dozen languages, promised a thousand different deaths to the young mage, to any who harbored him, to any who spared him so much as a kind word or a friendly glance. Cracks spiderwebbed the desk as his fist struck it, again and again, allowing a foul-smelling elixir of oils and blood to leak from the eldritch mechanism. Baltrice, who had witnessed more than one such display in her years, took a careful step back and prepared a simple spell to ward off any further projectiles that might indiscriminately come her way.

None did, however, and the storm passed as swiftly as it had arisen, though the redness in his face and the quivering in his neck and jaw were more than sufficient evidence that it roiled still, just beneath the surface. "Damn him . . ." Tezzeret muttered, having exhausted all his more colorful curses. "The Ravnica cell was one of my best. Have you any idea how hard it was to set up?"

"Yes. I've been here through most of it," Baltrice reminded him. He ignored her.

"Why?" he demanded of the Multiverse itself. "Why come out of hiding now?"

Wisely, Baltrice didn't even try to respond.

Tezzeret sighed, the deep, heartfelt lament of the truly put-upon. "I was too kind, that was my problem. Too kind, and too lazy. I should have made a greater effort to find him over the past years, and to put him out of my misery."

As I told you, more than once, Baltrice noted silently.

Another sigh, and the room began to resound with the staccato beat of metal fingers on metal desk. And just as abruptly he froze, a far-off look on his face, a look that Baltrice had seen many times before.

"Who?" she asked him.

"Kamigawa," he muttered after a moment. "Just what I need right now. I swear, if that damn rat-shaman's interfered with another of our shipments . . ."

"Do you want me to deal with it?"

"No," he told her. "I'll handle it. It'll give me time to think, if nothing else."

The room into which Tezzeret eventually walked was highly ornate. Silk curtains in bright hues, chosen to perfectly offset the darker rugs, draped the walls and the open doorways. Paper lanterns illuminated the chamber in a dim yet steady glow, and the scent of heavy incense was almost overwhelming.

Standing before him, bowing low in a show of great respect, was a seemingly young woman clad in a dark kimono, her hair hanging loose around her ears. Only the narrowness of her features and the pale hue of that hair suggested a faint trace of the tsuki-bito moonfolk in her ancestry. The third leader of the Kamigawa cell in as many years, she'd inherited a dangerous post, and Tezzeret honestly didn't think much of her long-term chances. The shaman of the Nezumi-Katsuro had not only never forgiven the attack that claimed the life of his shogun, he'd killed half a dozen Consortium agents, as well as tortured and murdered the cell's prior leader, in an effort to coax Tezzeret into facing him personally. His most recent challenges had been addressed to the "Metal-Armed Emperor," suggesting that he'd learned much from his interrogation of the prior cell lieutenant.

Tezzeret, of course, couldn't be bothered to deal with the rat himself. The cell would handle it eventually, no matter how many leaders it had to go through in the process.

"What is it, Kaori?" he asked gruffly, glancing at the broken shards of tubing on the wall. "You know how hard it is to replace those."

"My sincerest apologies, my lord," she offered, her musical accent almost lost amid the buzzing of the gears. "But there is one here who would speak to you, one whom you have employed in the past, and who swears she bears information that you must hear. She claims she knew of no other way to contact you."

"Is that so?" Tezzeret furrowed his brow, then nodded as one of the curtains on the far wall drifted aside and a newcomer entered from the adjoining hallway.

"Well. Liliana Vess."

"Tezzeret," she greeted curtly.

"And to what do we owe—"

"Forgive me if I don't take the time for pleasantries," she interrupted. "I don't have a lot of time before I'm missed."

"All right. I'm assuming this is important, since you damn well know better than to contact me like this."

"Depends. Do you consider Jace Beleren important?"

Tezzeret leaned forward like a hound straining against his leash. "You know where he is?"

"Not exactly," she lied. "The ghosts from whom I've learned of his recent activities were not so specific. Either they don't know, or they have reason not to tell me. But they've told me much of his activities, past and recent, and I can tell you how to flush him out."

✳ ✳ ✳ ✳ ✳

The sun had set on Gnat Alley—or rather, the sun had set on one end of Gnat Alley, for the longest thoroughfare in all of Ravnica saw neither dusk nor dawn at the same moment on each tip. Here on the ground, beneath the veritable webwork of bridges and suspended streets, the towering spires and floating platforms, the streets were ill maintained, the structures dark and often dilapidated. Squatting in their midst like bloated spiders were numerous brothels, gambling halls, and bars that sold drinks unavailable or illegal topside. Gnat Alley *had* to be as long as it was, for somewhere along its length a brave or foolish stranger could find for sale any goods or services imaginable, and a few inconceivable to any sane mind.

Assuming, of course, that said stranger survived long enough to do so.

In the darkest shadows on the "night side" of Gnat Alley, two human men and a goblin woman sat in a poorly lit booth within one of the many nameless taverns along the street of iniquity. The floor was filthy, the table coated with the remnants of past meals. The ale was so watered down that any customer would certainly drown in it before consuming enough to get drunk, the food had never even been in the same general vicinity as a professional cook, and a fresh dose of vomit on the floor would actually have improved the bouquet.

None of which mattered, since there wasn't a patron in the building who had come here for food or drink.

Tezzeret, who had wisely chosen not even to touch his mug of whatever-it-was, produced a small leather

A R I   M A R M E L L

ɸ

pouch from a compartment on his belt and slid it across the table. The goblin snatched at it, opening it and examining the gold dust within. She blinked once, sniffed once, and then grumbled an affirmative to her companion.

Unlike the goblin, and even Tezzeret, who looked as though they belonged here, the other human was impeccably shaved, his red hair slicked back, his black tunic and wine-hued leggings the height of fashion. Even his nails were manicured.

And since he'd survived more than three minutes in Gnat Alley, dressed in such a fashion, he clearly had just the sort of connections Tezzeret needed.

He smiled a charming, friendly smile at the goblin's report. "Excellent," he told Tezzeret. "I think we're in business, then. Accidents?"

The artificer knew precisely what the apparent non sequitur meant. "Absolutely not." His own grin was wolfish. "Knives, fire, spells. Make a show of it. I want a blind man to be able to tell these people were murdered."

The human and the goblin exchanged startled glances, then shrugged. He was the one paying, after all.

"Then I think all that remains is to discuss names," the dandy said.

Tezzeret reached into another pouch and removed a scrap of parchment, treated to burn instantly to ash the moment it came near an open flame. On it was the list Vess had given him; the artificer couldn't help but smirk at the thought of Jace's face when he found out.

"Rulan Barthaneul, human, a banker in Dravhoc District," Tezzeret read from the list. "Laphiel Kartz, also human, also of Dravhoc. Eshton Navar, human, owns a tavern in Lurias.

"And Emmara Tandris, elf, of Ovitzia."

Liliana glanced up from the table, and the cup of fruit tea she'd barely touched, as her host appeared from within the nearest pillar. "How is he?" she demanded.

Emmara waved a hand and otherwise ignored the question long enough to take a seat—as far down the table as she could without being overtly rude—and requesting a beverage of her own from the tiny construct servants. Only then did she turn again to her guest.

"He's improving," she said simply.

"Delighted to hear it," Liliana said, her tone suggesting nothing of the kind. "Of course, that's what you've said every time I've asked you for the past two days! But you still won't let me see him!"

"That's because when I let you talk to him the first time, you got him so riled up that I think you set him back almost a day," Emmara retorted. "So how about you stop pestering me, and him, and let me do my work?"

For several breaths they glared at one another, the tension finally breaking only when the construct clumped back into the room with the elf's juice. Emmara took a large sip, and then sighed, shaking her head.

"He really is doing a lot better, Liliana, but I don't want you going up there just yet. He still needs to rest a while. I've had a hard enough time convincing him that whatever it is you two need to do, it can wait until he's fully recovered. Would you go dashing into his chamber and undo all that work? Get him excited and running about, so he can tear open an internal wound that hasn't had time to mend?"

Liliana grumbled something unintelligible and slumped back down in the chair. She failed to notice the elf's wince as the slender wood creaked beneath the unexpected impact.

"You care for him a great deal," Emmara said. It was not a question, yet she sounded unsure.

ARI MARMELL

"You sound surprised," the other objected.

"I am," the elf admitted. "I don't tend to think of your sort as being all that compassionate."

"My 'sort?'" Liliana asked dangerously. "Human?"

"Necromancer," Emmara retorted.

"Yes, I am," she said without shame. "Death, undeath, age, and decay. None of which makes me any less human." She placed just the slightest weight on the last, as though daring the elf to make an issue of it. "Jace is . . . important to me."

"To you?" Emmara asked. "Or to what you want?"

"And what of you?" Liliana demanded, suddenly eager to change the subject. "You're a healer, or so Jace tells me. Why is he not up and around after almost two days?"

"I could mend his wounds more swiftly," the elf admitted. "But the bolt struck deep, uncomfortably near several organs that he wouldn't do well without. I've chosen to take the more careful route, to ensure the inner damage is repaired before I seal the outer. The magic is at work, even as we speak. He'll be well enough, soon enough."

"Thank you," Liliana said grudgingly. Both sipped from their respective glasses, examining one another in silence.

"You and Jace . . ." she began finally.

"Berrim. I knew him as Berrim."

"Whatever. You two weren't together?"

"Of course not!" Emmara protested, taking her meaning. She actually shuddered. "He's *human.*"

Liliana couldn't help but grin at the elf's revolted tone.

"We were friends," Emmara continued. "Or I thought we were. Perhaps I'll know for certain when he tells me precisely who was Berrim and who was Jace. And why I only learned of the latter when a number of very unpleasant people started searching for him. The guilds may be gone, but I still have my sources. It didn't take me long to learn the Consortium was looking for someone who went by both names—and several others, besides.

"I've lived long enough to understand change, Liliana, be it cities, governments, names, or people. And from what I've heard of Jace, I can understand why he might have preferred to become Berrim. But he could have trusted me enough to tell me. Now I don't know who my friend actually was. Do you know who it is you actually care for?"

The almost-but-not-quite-hostile conversation continued, but Jace ceased listening. With a moment's effort—made only moderately more difficult by his lingering injury—he allowed his senses to recede, pulling away from the table but not dismissing the spell of clairvoyance entirely.

Sadly, his eyes squeezed tightly shut, he dropped his head into his hands. Much as he felt his use of a pseudonym had been justified, he couldn't blame Emmara for her anger. She'd thought him a friend, he'd *claimed* to be a friend, yet he'd failed to trust her even with his own real name.

Everything he'd ever done, he'd done for what he thought were the best of reasons. How had he managed to screw it all up so dramatically?

And how could he know he wasn't doing just as badly even now?

Yet for all that, she'd taken him in, tended his wounds, even though she owed him nothing, knew that he wasn't who she'd believed him to be. Perhaps unsurprisingly, he found his thoughts of Emmara turning to thoughts of Kallist. Jace Beleren wondered if he'd ever been worthy of a single one of his friends—and he wondered, too, if all of them would have to suffer for him.

He tried to shake off his self-pity before it consumed him, focusing instead on the immediate. Without either opening his eyes or ending his clairvoyance spell, he concentrated on the room around him. He felt the heavy blankets that lay atop his legs as he sat up in bed, felt the itchy, greasy sensations of his hair, which had soaked up the sweat of his pain and was more than overdue for a wash. He prodded at his bare ribs with a finger, felt a faint divot in the flesh and a deep ache in the muscles of his torso, but nothing that approached the earlier agony. He remarked to himself on just how much he owed his elven host, then cut the thought short before it could drive him right back into the arms of the brooding funk he was struggling to evade.

Gradually, he removed his fingers from the wound, letting his hands flop to the mattress beside him, but continued to poke at the injury with his mind. He dwelled on the sense of warmth that had flowed through him at the healer's touch, the "taste" of her mana flooding over his soul, the sensation of his flesh stitching itself together. For just an instant his spirit quivered on the verge of discovery, an understanding of a new and brighter magic than any he had practiced before. The lingering pain in his wound lessened by a featherweight. And a part of Jace exulted, warmed by a spark of joy not in using the power for his own ends, but with the experience of a magic worth casting purely for its own sake.

And then the moment was gone, blown away along with Jace's concentration as someone pounded on Emmara's front door with a brutish, heavy fist. Jace fell back against the pillow with a gasp as the sharp sound not only came to him faintly through the floorboards, but directly into his mind via the spell that kept a portion of his senses hovering in the room below.

Curious and perhaps more than reasonably annoyed at the interruption, he directed the spell to flow outward, moving it past the many pillars that supported Emmara's manor, slipping it through the wood of the heavy portal, allowing him to take a good solid gander at the man outside. He saw nothing of note, just a large, vaguely gorillalike fellow with a crate under one hand. A courier of some sort, obviously.

But Jace's paranoia was in full bloom, and he took a moment to really concentrate, to scan the surface thoughts of the man outside. It was difficult, reading his mind through a lens of clairvoyance, but that just made it a better test of his recovery.

And then Jace was out of bed, stumbling and slipping against the lingering pain, careening off the wall as he lost his balance, reaching desperately for the nearest teleportation pillar.

CHAPTER TWENTY-FOUR

Kerstophe shifted foot to foot, burning with nervous energy, as he waited for a response to his knock. In the crook of his left arm, he adjusted the wooden crate, utterly empty. In his right hand he held a thin stiletto, held backward so the blade was hidden up his voluminous sleeve.

He heard a faint rattling from behind the heavy door, and a small portal—one so expertly blended in with the contours of the wood that he hadn't noticed it was there—slid open, revealing roughly a quarter of a pretty elven face. "Yes? Who is it?"

"Delivery for you, m'lady," he said, voice respectful but as bored as any good courier's.

"What is it?"

"Couldn't say, m'lady. Nothing written on the outside, and it's certainly not my place to open it or to ask."

"All right. A minute, please."

Kerstophe's pulse quickened, and he felt excitement radiating from his chest—to say nothing of places somewhat lower down. It always got him worked up, this moment just before it happened. Especially when his "partner" was a pretty girl.

He heard the thump-and-clatter of a bolt being drawn and a chain being unhooked, and the door swung wide. He smiled down at the elf with an almost excessively friendly grin.

"Emmari Tandars?" he asked, dramatically mangling the pronunciation.

"Close enough," she offered with a smile.

"Fantastic," he said. With a smooth motion born from years of practice, he reversed his grip on the stiletto, stepped in close until their bodies nearly touched, and sank the blade deep into her flesh, directly beneath the sternum, angled upward.

They gasped as one, she in stunned agony, he in pleasure. The elf staggered, and he withdrew the blade and shoved, so that her body tumbled backward and out of the doorway, dead before it hit the floor. Just as casually he knelt to lay the empty crate on the floor beside her, then stood, calmly shut the door, and wandered back down the steps to join the traffic on the street below.

A dozen passersby or more, and nobody had seen a thing.

✳ ✳ ✳ ✳ ✳

Jace, clad only in the leggings he'd worn in bed, dashed out from behind the door and dropped to one knee beside the fallen elf. His hands were already reaching for her, his jaw clenching at the sight of the growing pool of blood, when her eyes snapped open like the jaws of a drake. Jace released a breath he hadn't even realized he was holding.

"Emmara?" he asked, his voice soft.

"That really hurt," she grumbled, slowly sitting up. Already the wound in her gut had started to close, the blood to dry. Jace knew that if she hadn't begun the healing spell in advance, the wound would have been lethal; as it was, the ugly bruising around it didn't fade with the wound itself, and he knew that Emmara was likely to be in more than a little pain for days to come.

ARI MARMELL

"I'm so sorry to put you through that," he told her. "But I didn't have time to set up any sort of illusion—at least not anything he'd believe after sticking a knife into it." He reached a hand out to help the elf rise. "I just—"

Glaring a mixture of anger and pain, Emmara pushed his hand away and rose, albeit shakily, under her own power. Then she turned that heavy gaze directly on him, matched by Liliana's own glare as the necromancer emerged from behind a nearby pillar. Both women stood with arms crossed, scowling darkly, warped and twisted reflections of one another.

"What?" he asked them.

"Would you care to explain, 'Berrim'?" Emmara demanded.

"I figured—" he began.

"Were you afraid I wouldn't be up to defending myself?" she continued unabated.

"And you should *certainly* know better in my case," Liliana added darkly. "Oh, heavens! We're in trouble! Let's wait for the wounded man to come charging in to save us!"

"I—" he tried again.

"You have any idea the sort of damage your lunging around could have caused?" the elf demanded. "And I don't just mean to me! There's a reason I had you resting in bed, you idiot!"

Liliana, Jace thought sourly, *is a bad influence on her.* "I didn't race down here to save you two!" Jace shouted, clutching his ribs as the dull ache returned. "I did it to save him!"

That, at least, was sufficient to draw a confused silence. Jace took the opportunity to move from the door and collapse into the nearest chair—a velvet-upholstered monstrosity that might well have been older than the elf who owned it.

"You," he said, stabbing a finger at Liliana, "would have had one of your specters eat his soul, or maybe rotted his flesh off his bones into a puddle of really smelly goo."

"Of course," she said.

"And you," he continued, turning to Emmara, "well, I've never seen you in danger, but I'm betting that your response to a man trying to stick a knife in your gut would be a lot uglier than your healing spells."

"You'd win that bet," she told him, still puzzled.

"So," Jace said, trying to lean forward in his chair and failing, "then what?"

Liliana and Emmara looked at one another.

"Is there anyone here," Jace asked, "with the slightest doubt that your delivery came courtesy of Tezzeret?"

Emmara frowned. "It would be quite a coincidence for it to be anyone else, under the circumstances. Unlike *some* people, I don't have whole swathes of angry enemies clamoring for my head."

"Exactly!" Jace exclaimed, as though pouncing on a long-sought prize. "Emmara, the only reason Tezzeret could have to come after you is because you're a friend of mine."

"Might be," the elf corrected under her breath.

"So if I hadn't talked you into letting the assassin 'kill' you, then what? What happens when the assassin fails to report back, hmm? Who—or what—does Tezzeret send next?"

Liliana nodded in sudden understanding. "But this way, the assassin goes back and reports the job done, with nobody the wiser."

Jace smiled. "And of course, without the resources of a Ravnica cell, he's got no way of finding out any time soon that his hired killer was duped."

Emmara flushed ever so slightly. "You're right, of course. I'm, um, not accustomed to dealing with the assassin's mindset. My apologies, Jace. Thank you for stepping in."

"You're welcome," he said sincerely. He turned to Liliana, opened his mouth to ask when *her* apology was forthcoming, and then thought better of it.

"Emmara," he said seriously, "you might be able to count on the deception to hold. I doubt Tezzeret's going to expend what few resources he has remaining on Ravnica following up on a report of a successful kill. But I can't promise that. You may want to consider moving."

The elf gazed around her at the dozens of columns and groaned softly.

"In the interim," he said, rising to his feet with a faint groan of his own, "we'll get out of your hair."

Again he found himself pummeled by a pair of stares, this time unbelieving.

"Jace—" Liliana began.

"You're not ready for—" Emmara said at the same time.

But Jace shook his head, raising a hand to forestall them both. "Kallist is dead," he said, his voice soft. "And now someone's tried to kill Emmara." Both women were startled to see Jace fighting back tears. "I've never been much for heroics; you both know that. But until Tezzeret invited me into his damned Consortium, I never set out to hurt anyone. And now that I've started, it seems I can't make it stop.

"I can't undo the trouble I've caused you, Emmara." *At least not yet,* he added mentally, thinking back to Liliana's ambitions. "But I won't put you in any further danger. We're leaving."

In the end, neither Liliana nor Emmara could offer any argument to change his mind, despite the occasional shudder of pain that wracked his body, or the brief moments of dizziness that threatened to knock him off his feet. Thus, fully clad once more and carrying a pouch of medicinal herbs given to them by their host, Jace and Liliana exchanged their farewells with the elf—along with Jace's promise that some day, when the danger had passed, he would find Emmara and tell her the truth about his life, about who and what he was—and moved once more into Ravnica's bustling streets.

They walked arm in arm so Liliana could catch Jace when his sporadic weakness overtook him, lest he fall to the earth amid the marching feet of the thick city crowds. His jaw was clenched in a grimace of constant discomfort, and Liliana felt his arm tremble on more than one occasion.

"When you think about it," she said, hoping to keep his attention focused, "Emmara owes Paldor her life."

Jace blinked. "How do you figure?"

"Had he not shot you, we wouldn't have been at her home. And without us there, without the forewarning that something was amiss, how much attention would she have paid to a courier at her door?"

"You may be right. I'll be sure to thank him the next time he's actually a person."

She chuckled, more so than the comment actually warranted, and Jace found himself smiling. They walked in silence—well, without speaking, as the crowds around them hardly qualified as anything less than deafening—for several more moments.

"How did they find her?" Jace finally asked. "They didn't know to question her when I first disappeared, so why now?"

Liliana could only shake her head. For a long while, Jace said nothing more, concentrating purely on putting one foot in front of the other while his companion searched the streets for a tavern or hostel where they might lay low until his strength returned. Only when they'd firmly ensconced themselves in a small, dusty room did he speak again.

"I . . ." He cleared his throat, trying to keep the worry out of his voice. "Liliana, I need you to do something for me. It may take a few days, even as fast as your specters travel, but I can use the time anyway."

"Of course," she told him. "What do you need?"

✳ ✳ ✳ ✳ ✳

He'd been right; it had taken a while, almost four days. By the time the last of the spectral spies had returned with news, Emmara's magics had completed their work and Jace was feeling almost himself again—despite three nights of sleeping in a bed so fragile it seemed a particularly weighty dream would collapse it entirely.

"How did it go?" he asked, almost afraid of her response.

"You were right," she told him gently. "It wasn't just Emmara."

Jace hung his head, slumped down against the far wall, ignoring the furniture entirely. "Who?"

"Gariel's fine, at least," she told him. Of course, she'd already known he would be; she hadn't given Tezzeret his name.

"Who?" Jace asked again, almost pleading.

"Rulan, Laphiel, and Eshton. They're all gone, Jace."

Jace buried his face in his hands, too exhausted even to weep. "I'm running low on old friends to get killed," he told her.

The look she turned on him was one of pity, yes, but tinged around the edges with a growing disdain. "This won't stop until we make it stop, and you know it. So *cut it out!*"

"You're right," he said after a moment to catch his breath.

"I don't understand," she said more softly. "How could they know?"

Jace jerked his head up, staring at her, but she had turned away, peering through the filthy window at the abstract shapes moving outside. For just a moment, a dark and terrible suspicion crept from the depths of his mind and lodged itself in his thoughts.

But no; no, that couldn't be. Jace shook his head, as though trying to physically shake the notion loose. He knew her intimately; he'd been inside her thoughts. It simply wasn't possible, and no trace of the foul thought remained in his expression by the time she turned back to face him.

"I don't know," he answered. "But it stops now. You were right, Liliana. Obviously, Tezzeret's got sharper eyes than I thought, and now he's turned them on my friends. He doesn't want to let me run? Fine. No more running. No more hiding."

Liliana crossed the room, squeezed his shoulder in reassurance. "We can beat him," she promised. "But we have to find him."

Jace turned to meet her gaze, and his eyes flashed a deep, inhuman blue. "Watch me," was all he said.

Of course, Jace hadn't the first notion of where to find Tezzeret. But it had occurred to him, during his restless nights waiting to learn the fate of his friends, that he just might know how to find someone who did.

✻ ✻ ✻ ✻ ✻

Wearing his accustomed black suede outfit and burgundy coat, and his even more accustomed arrogant smirk, Mauriel Pellam swaggered up the steps to the second-floor gallery. It was always his first stop when he returned to his lavish penthouse after more than a few days away from home. Setting eyes on the various portraits and tapestries, the small gold busts of famous men and the great bronze sculpture of Razia—breasts thrust forward in an awkwardly erotic pose that the angel herself would undoubtedly have found both ludicrous and personally offensive—all this reminded him why he did what he did. Why he worked for such people as he did, delivering goods and messages whose import he scarcely understood. It was all worth it, to afford such luxuries as these.

He had just passed beyond that sculpture when something flashed out from behind it, something that had waltzed past the building's guards and even its eldritch glyphs and alarms without so much as breaking a sweat. Pellam found himself flat on his back, staring up into a pair of unblinking ice-blue eyes.

"Let's talk for a moment," Jace Beleren said to him, "about the messages you carry on behalf of Nicol Bolas . . ."

✳ ✳ ✳ ✳ ✳

The chain was a long one, with nearly a dozen links. Pellam received his instructions from this man, who got them from that vedalken, who in turn received them from that other fellow . . . But each led him one step farther, and none could keep their secrets from him.

Until finally, near dusk some days later, Jace found himself standing at the gate of a vast estate, located just beyond the borders of Dravhoc District. The surrounding iron fence was high, topped with jutting spikes that each boasted a rune of not insubstantial power. At that gate stood a pair of guards; one merely human, the other loxodon, the gray leathery flesh of his arms and his trunk covered with tribal scars, his tusks capped with iron blades and carved with religious runes. Those tree-thick arms hung crossed over his armored chest, and a flail with a head roughly the size of a small continent hung from his waist. Beyond the guards, the path wound its way through a garden of flowers that should not have been in bloom this time of year, to the home of a man Jace knew to be one of Ravnica's greatest sorcerers. That he was also Bolas's chief agent and contact on this world had come as no great surprise.

"I'd like to see the magus," Jace told the guards as he came to a halt before them.

"So would a lot of people," the loxodon told him. "Not going to happen."

Jace, who had spent hours drawing as much mana as he could from the shores of Dravhoc's slope for just this purpose, sighed dramatically. "I just knew you were going to say that . . ."

※ ※ ※ ※ ※

He found Liliana waiting in the corner of the cold and dusty room they'd rented, adjusting the pull on her stolen crossbow and sitting in a rickety chair that was so close to giving up the ghost that she almost felt she could reanimate it. The glare she aimed at Jace as he stepped into the chamber could have flattened a herd of aurochs.

"It worked," he told her, shutting the door behind him.

She continued to glare.

"What's wrong?"

"I don't appreciate," she said icily, "being kept in the dark like this." *And I definitely don't like not knowing what you're up to!* "Especially," she added, taking note of the holes burned into his tunic, the bits of blackened flesh on his arms and chest, "when you're obviously walking into danger. We just got you healed up, damn it! I should've been with you!"

"Wouldn't have been a good idea," he said, grunting with pain as he removed his cloak and the tatters of his tunic. "The point wasn't to kill or even mindwipe anyone. I needed information. I did *not* need to make a new enemy in the process."

"What are you talking . . . ?" She trailed off, stunned first at the extent of his wounds, and then at the sight of the bloodstained manablade that he dropped to the table. "Damn, Jace, what have you been doing?"

"Talking to people. The wizard needed some convincing." Jace had been reluctant—more than reluctant, almost nauseated—to put the knife to the man's flesh. He knew the pain it caused. But he'd had to know, and he wasn't sure he could've won without the weapon to aid him, or broken through the wizard's defenses without weakening the man first.

"All right," she said, not sounding mollified at all. "So could you at least explain why you wouldn't tell me where you were going?"

Jace offered an embarrassed smile. "Because you'd have tried to stop me, and I didn't think we had the time to argue about it or to find another option."

"Why do I not find that reassuring? Jace, what did you do?"

"I knew we couldn't find Tezzeret on our own," he told her. "So I decided to find someone else who could."

"Oh, sure. You bring back an oracle in your pocket?"

Jace couldn't help it. "That's not an oracle," he told her with a leer.

"But no," he continued hastily when her glare very clearly told him that he was not funny, "I was actually talking about Nicol Bolas."

Liliana shot from the chair as though it had grown fangs. The expression she turned on him could not have been more incredulous had he actually puked said dragon into existence on the floor.

"I'm taking you back to Emmara's," she insisted. "Obviously, you're delusional with fever."

"Think about it!" he insisted. "He's got as large a grudge against Tezzeret as we do—well, close, anyway. And with his sort of power . . ."

"Then why wouldn't he have gone after Tezzeret himself?" Liliana challenged.

Jace just shrugged. "Bolas didn't get as old as he is by taking unnecessary chances. And even if he doesn't know where Tezzeret's sanctum is, he can certainly help us find it."

"Assuming he doesn't just eat us first."

"You have a better idea?" Jace asked.

"Yes."

"What?"

"We *don't* go looking for Nicol Bolas. Besides," she added as Jace opened his mouth to argue, "you're just trading one wild phoenix chase for another. You've a better chance of stumbling into Tezzeret on the street by accident than you do of finding Nicol Bolas."

"But that's just it, Liliana!" Jace crowed. "I *did* find him!"

Liliana exhaled sharply, trying to calm her racing heart. It took her a good long moment before she felt steady enough to speak. "And just where is that, exactly?"

"What do you know," Jace asked her, "of a world called Grixis?"

CHAPTER TWENTY-FIVE

Even from the shifting wastes of the Blind Eternities, viewed through a storm of undreamed thoughts and unseen hues, it was clearly a world like no other. It was different. It was wrong.

For Grixis was no world at all, but an echo, a shadow, the phantom limb of a dismembered reality. Once, so very long ago, it had been Alara, a world rich in magics. But Alara was sundered, its corpse devolving into five separate shards, each bereft of vital aspects of mana that allowed both the natural and the supernatural to remain in balance.

Some were places of beauty, having left behind the worst of what they once were. Unnatural, yes, and doomed to eventual dissolution, but beautiful all the same.

Grixis was not one of these.

Within the Blind Eternities, the winds that buffeted Jace's soul without so much as touching his skin grew mighty, howling with a voice far beyond sound itself. They rushed inward as though to fill the void to come, swirling about the fading lands that clawed and tore and orbited one another in their slow spiral of decay. Here, as nowhere else in all the known Multiverse, the curtain of color that demarcated the real from the potential, the finite from the eternal, bulged and writhed—a creature in pain, or a birthing caul from which something unholy sought to rise. It twisted inward as though grasped by great fists, pulled and warped by the unnatural essence of what lay beyond. Nigh inaudible beneath the winds, the distant echoes of Alara's death cry still lingered in the currents of potential, and even the Blind Eternities themselves faintly recoiled from this most aberrant of realities.

Amid the chaos, Jace waited, his shoulders hunched against the storm of forces that would have destroyed lesser beings. Within the curtain the five worlds spun; the colors grew lighter and darker, the thrashings of the border calmed or grew fierce, as the shards rose and fell on eternal tides. Only after three full iterations of the cycle, when the planeswalker was certain he knew which hue and pattern, which ebb and flow, was which—when he knew which of the shards lay most immediately before him—did he press through the walls of the world to find himself on the plains of Grixis.

Where, he swiftly discovered, things were even worse.

❋ ❋ ❋ ❋ ❋

A shriek, tormented beyond the fragile borders of sanity, pierced the cavern's depths. It echoed, high and harsh, from broad passages and flying arches, returning again and again, melding into a symphony of tones.

Few noticed, for it was just another scream.

The cavern was lit only by a flickering of hellish flame, leaving most of its features submerged in darkness—and for that, any sane observer must have been grateful. What walls could be seen were broken bone, and the ceilings wept tears of blood that smelled of putrescence and formed warm and quivering stalactites of foulest, clotted brown. Windows of fingernail, not individually torn from any hand but naturally grown in broad sheets, allowed a blurred observance of chambers more terrible still, where the walls were stone-stiff scabs over gangrenous wounds in the earth, and the floors were teeth gnashing and eager to grind the unwary.

In the cavern's center, a trio of men lay staked to the ground, their hands overlapping to form a starburst of suffering. Their bodies were covered with tiny, infected cuts, and their eyes were wide and staring, unable even to blink. Though their mouths were open in constant wails, they formed no words; like their eyelids, their tongues and teeth had long since been torn free and discarded.

Walking over and among them were a man and a woman, both unclad save for simple leather kilts and pouches hanging at their waists. Each was horribly deformed—he boasting a grotesque hump above the kidney, forcing him always to lean right; she with no left arm, but a fully functional hand jutting from her shoulder—and both were adorned with a sequence of unholy runes, scarred into the flesh of their upper backs. They walked with heads uplifted and eyes rolled back in their sockets, yet never once tripped or broke the rhythm of their slow, deliberate dance. And with each third step they chanted horrid words, and cast strange powders from their pouches that burned and sliced the flesh of the men beneath them.

The three men ceased their screams abruptly, thrashing bodily as one, threatening to tear their hands from the iron stakes. Two of them subsided as swiftly as they began, resuming their incomprehensible shrieks, but the third babbled and moaned what might have been words had he still had a tongue to speak them.

"Master!" the deformed woman shrieked, her eyes reappearing in their sockets. "Master, come quick!" Her cry echoed again and again, carried by magics woven into the array of caverns, reaching beyond these chambers of horror into rooms far more comfortable, far more mundane. With a sigh, the one she called lay down the ancient tome he perused, his great bulk shifting, wings stretching and folding, as he moved to answer.

"I am here, Caladessa." The great voice rumbled down from a ledge above the highest arch, near the cavern's ceiling dozens of feet above her head.

The witch looked up and bowed. "Hold him," she ordered, turning to her male counterpart. He shuffled over to the mumbling man and knelt upon his chest, putting an end to what thrashing and writhing the stakes allowed.

The one called Caladessa knelt beside the pinioned man and stretched out a thumb and forefinger, both tipped with long and jagged nails. She reached in, digging at the corner of his eye, and with a practiced movement stripped away his cornea as easily as she might have peeled a fruit.

She turned away, ignoring her victim as his mumblings turned once again to hollow screams. Her companion stepped away as well, thankful that this was the subject's first divination. He always hated the labor involved in replacing a staked vessel once both orbs were expended.

Caladessa ran the tiny film across her tongue, removing any traces of the man's tears, any dirt that might have flecked his lidless eye; her own vision must be unblemished, lest she draw the master's displeasure. Then, once more staring upward, she squeezed her right eye shut and carefully lay the cornea over the left.

"What see you, soothsayer?" boomed the voice from above.

"Two have come to Grixis, master," she replied, falling into a strange, vaguely disturbing cadence. "World-walkers, mana-drinkers. Vital still, they stand amid the rising dead."

"Two?" The cavern resounded with shifting scales from above. "Two . . . Tell me."

"Mind-breaker, thought-taker, eye-blinder, dream-raker. He walks the intentions of others as easily as he walks between worlds, but knows not his own.

"Death-bringer, corpse-talker, spirit-rider. She teeters on the edge of death, and fears to fall in after those she has sent before her. A blossoming of truth that rots around a seed of endless lies."

"Ah," came the voice from above. "Them."

For long moments, the great dragon pondered. Then, "Summon Malfegor. Tell him to take over observations here until I return."

Not bothering to wait for further acknowledgment, Nicol Bolas unfurled his great wings and vanished into the darkness at the apex of the looming cavern, leaving nothing but scurrying feet and shrieking throats behind.

✳ ✳ ✳ ✳ ✳

From the spiritual winds of the Blind Eternities, Jace stepped through the curtain of reality into the equally fierce physical winds of Grixis's revolting terrain. Physical—but far, far from natural. They leached the warmth from his body, carried a noxious fume of exhaustion and despair. The hem of Jace's cloak grew ragged and worn, the leather of his boots supple and thin, as though each had seen years of use in the span of seconds. His flesh ached, his vision blurred; as he cowered against the winds with an arm raised to protect himself, he saw tufts of the hairs on the back of his hand grow brittle and flake away.

With those winds rose an oily fog, swirling and dancing in a maddened ballet of wretched plague. Thick tendrils of the stuff writhed past his face, coating his lungs with a film of fluid decay. Like murky water, it thickened and thinned, but even at its clearest Jace could see no more than perhaps thirty feet ahead. At its worst, Bolas could have set down from the skies within arm's reach, and Jace would never have seen him.

In the midst of it all came the faint pitter-patter of a light rain—a rain not of water, but of teeth.

"Liliana!" He could all but feel his own words whip past him, carried away by the deadly winds. "Liliana!" He called again and again, between fits of violent coughs, called until his voice grew hoarse, but never heard any response.

Desperately, he pushed out with all his might. This was no formal spell, no focused and molded effect, but a raw and unpolished burst of mana unshaped. He flung the incorporeal veil before him, a shield between himself and the murderous winds. And for a time, at least, it armored him. The chill in his flesh grew less, and though buffeted still by winds nearly strong enough to knock him sideways, he found himself able to breathe cleanly. The pall of exhaustion refused to fade, but at least it grew no heavier.

Leaning into the horrible gale, one arm still shielding his face, Jace began to walk—and it was only then, as he took his first step, that his already overwhelmed senses acknowledged that the earth on which he stood was not ground at all.

Pale as a week-old corpse and just as pliable, an endless plain of flesh sprawled before him, giving way with a grotesque stretching beneath the soles of his boots. Little grew upon that horrid expanse, at least as far as the storm permitted Jace to see: just a flaky lichen that resembled an infection upon the rotting skin. Sporadic hills were great boils rising from the flesh, and tiny hollows where something had punched through that flesh were filled with a pus-like sludge shot through with veins of brackish blood.

Jace felt his stomach heave, his skin crawl as though it were determined to flee even if he were too foolish to run with it. In that moment, nothing else mattered, not Nicol Bolas, not finding Tezzeret, none of it. Had Liliana stood with him, had he not lost her somewhere in that nightmarish storm, Jace would have turned around and bent all his remaining strength to walking from Grixis, never to return.

But lost she was, or perhaps it was he who was lost; in either case, Jace allowed his churning innards a moment to settle and pushed on into the winds. His head ached with the sounds, with the strain of searching for any sign of Liliana while still maintaining the all-but-uncontrolled film of magic that shielded him from the worst of the tempest.

Ten yards, twenty, fifty, and he found himself descending slightly into a bowl-shaped depression, a lesion in the flesh. And there, just as he decided that things couldn't possibly get any worse, Grixis proved him wrong.

Beneath him, the quivering earth split, and the hands of the dead reached out to claim him.

Only three or four initially, but then a dozen, and a dozen more. From graves that had been dug into the flesh and then healed over, from tumorous abscesses where fallen corpses were simply absorbed by the ground, they hauled themselves into the raging storm. Most had once been human, a few were ogres, and many were the twisted remnants of no creature Jace had ever seen. Some were naught but skeletal remnants of the people they once were; others boasted shifting, viscous skin sluicing from rotting muscles and viscera. All clawed and grabbed for him, hauling themselves hand over hand toward this source of the life for which they lusted, which they needed to stoke the smoldering remnants of their own inner embers.

More than a few collapsed the instant they arose, their remaining life stripped away by the entropic, consuming winds to which not even the undead, apparently, were immune. But others held firm, though they lost flecks of hanging skin and muscle and even bone to the tempest, and advanced upon their prey. Driven by an instinct beyond meager hunger, they were eager to consume from him whatever life they could, to prolong their tortured existence that much longer.

Jace retreated before the nightmarish advance, but there was nowhere to go; the dead roiled from the earth in all directions, a sprouting garden of rotted bone. He backed up the incline, his balance more precarious with every step, moving with the wind now, rather than against it. Desperately, he threw spell after spell into the mass of shambling dead, all to woefully meager effect. Driven only by hunger, they lacked any sentience for his mind to command; drawn by the scent of his life itself, they refused to be slowed or hindered by even the most intricate illusions. And Jace could summon nothing so potent that it wouldn't swiftly be slain by the storm, not without dropping his concentration on the mystic shield that protected his own body from those dreadful gusts.

He struck, instead, at the magics animating them, rather than at the undead themselves. Focusing as intently as he dared, he unraveled the chains of mana that bound a fragment of the soul to these lurching bones, that allowed lifeless joints to bend and dead muscle to flex. Stabbing his hand outward as though hurling a spear, Jace dispersed the mana within first one of the crawling zombies, then the next. They slumped, limp and truly dead as they long should have been.

But still they came, and still he retreated, and each time he severed the last remnants of life from one, three others had advanced upon him. Jace was swiftly tiring, for these were no simple necromantic spells he was countering, but the natural order of things in this impossible realm of Grixis. Soon he'd not be able even to slow the undead horde—but then, it wouldn't matter, for the deadly storm would shred his eldritch shield and drain the life from him before the first of the corpses closed their deathless fists around his limbs.

And he wondered, then, if he even had a legitimate death to look forward to, or if he would be as they were, slumbering beneath the skin of the world only to rise in insatiable craving at the passing of any living thing.

The crawling swarm grew too thick to navigate, so close that every step Jace took landed not on the fleshy earth but on a writhing, grasping limb. He stumbled, almost fell, and he felt the first of what must be many hands clasp tightly around his ankle.

But even as it squeezed, bruising him to the very bone, the undead froze. Rigid, they formed a motionless carpet of corpses across the landscape. Only their rotted eyes moved, as they gawped into the fury of the punishing storm.

As a goddess striding from the heavens, Liliana appeared on the raging winds. She stood, arms outstretched and head thrown back in potent ecstasy, held aloft by the crackling black aura that flowed effortlessly from her pale skin. The tattoos burned with dark fire on her back, as though her skin had opened to reveal an endless void beneath. Ignoring the storm, she gently descended until she set foot upon the vile ground; her hair and tunic lay perfectly still, indifferent to the tempest around her.

"Uh . . ." Jace began.

"It's incredible!" Her voice, though a whisper, carried clearly over the howling winds. She turned to him, and Jace would have fallen back were he not held fast by the grip on his leg. Black mists poured from her eyes, which had themselves grown dark as moonless night; from between her lips as she spoke; even from beneath her nails, flowing out to join with the inky aura that had borne her aloft.

"Oh, Jace, you have no idea! The power in this place . . ." Her smile widened further still. "I've never felt a concentration of manas like this, never knew it could exist."

Jace, who felt only a fraction of what Liliana was drinking in and found it terrifying, could only shake his head. "There's no light, Liliana. No life in these magics."

"I can live with that," she told him bluntly, her tone somehow jubilant and cold at once.

"Well," he said, after struggling to clear his throat, "then I guess it's a good thing you didn't know about this place years ago. You might have come here instead of hiding on Ravnica."

Liliana's gaze snapped to him, and the darkness cleared from her eyes. She scowled with a bitterness Jace couldn't interpret, and then raised a hand. The undead cowered back, releasing Jace's ankle in the process.

"They're barely animals," she told him, sounding vaguely irritated, "but some recognize the notion of 'the great winged beast' that terrifies them. They'll lead us to him, or at least to the area where they most frequently sense his presence."

She was moving before he could so much as ask a question, following a coterie of crawling corpses across the wind-blasted plains. Jace, hobbling slightly at the pain in his ankle, could do little but struggle to keep up.

* * * * *

It could have been hours or days; with the strange, sunless sky lurking above, Jace couldn't really tell. The fleshy earth gave way to a more rocky, scab-like substance; the planeswalkers and their undead entourage moved now through a twisting chasm that reminded Jace—in shape if not in hue or in temperature—of the arctic crevice through which he and Tezzeret had fled, so desperate to escape the very creature Jace now sought.

With every mile, an ever greater number of corpses shambled up from the earth. Liliana's eyes grew slightly wild as she dismissed many who already followed, sending them far away so that she could command those who rose nearer, but Jace was far from certain she could keep it up indefinitely. The crackling black aura around her hair, the depths of her eyes, and the dark tattoos were growing painful to look at.

"There are so many," she whispered to him once, even as he'd opened his mouth to ask if she was all right. "I've never felt so many."

Finally, one of the dead indicated that they were nearing the home of the "flying thing," waving a desiccated hand vaguely forward. With a gasp of relief, Liliana cloaked herself and Jace in a faint field of necromantic magics that would blind the undead to their presence, and allowed her command over the corpses to fade. Then, almost at a run, she led Jace away, farther into the winding crevice, until they found themselves in a cul-de-sac. They sank in unison to the foul earth, and for long moments they lay sprawled, gasping for breath.

"That may have been the most horrible thing I've ever seen," said Jace.

Liliana nodded. "I thought . . . It felt for a time as though I would lose myself in them, Jace. It felt like I was trying to bend the will of Grixis itself."

"But you both handled it very well," said Nicol Bolas.

CHAPTER TWENTY-SIX

He hadn't dropped from the sky, hadn't crept from hiding. He was simply *there*, where nothing but dust and foul odors had been before. His wings stretched high between the opposing walls of the crevice, and his bulk was a living avalanche that filled the passage entirely.

Jace and Liliana scrambled to their feet and shrank back against the far wall. Both knew full well that if Nicol Bolas had wanted them dead, they would already be so much ash on the wind or detritus in the back of his throat. But such knowledge was nothing in the face of instinctive fear.

And yet, for all the terror that wracked his body—both at the sight of the predator before him, and the sudden influx of memories from their last meeting—Jace couldn't help but blurt out, "What is it with you and crevices?"

"But then again, they were only the risen dead," the ancient beast said blandly, ignoring Jace's comment. "I imagine you'd have fared somewhat worse had you run into any of Grixis's demons. Why have you come here?"

"Demons? Here?" Liliana asked in a strangely small voice. She recovered swiftly, but in that one instant, she'd sounded more frightened than Jace had ever heard her.

"Of course. Why are you here?"

"What about those undead?" Jace asked. "Is the whole of Grixis like this? I can't imagine that—"

"Keep trying my patience," the dragon rumbled, as twin tendrils of dark smoke snaked from his nostrils and danced their way skyward, "and I'll lay you out among them to find out for yourself. I may have more time on my hands than anyone else in the Multiverse, Jace Beleren, but that doesn't mean I appreciate seeing it wasted. So once more, and *only* once more: Why are you here?"

Apparently unwilling to risk letting the frazzled and frightened Jace irritate the beast any further, Liliana squeezed his arm—tightly—and said, "We seek your help, Nicol Bolas."

"Do you, indeed? And do you recall what I just said about wasting time? Why would I involve myself in your petty affairs?"

"These are affairs that already involve you, great Bolas," Jace told him. "Tezzeret. We seek the location of the Infinite Consortium's inner sanctum."

"Ah. You should have simply said so, Beleren. With that, I am happy to help you.

"Or I would be," he said, as Jace's face began to brighten, "if I had the slightest notion where it was."

The words were a physical blow to Jace's gut. The sounds of Grixis faded, as though he'd shoved cotton in his ears; his shoulders slumped, and he could actually feel the angry "I told you so!" radiating from Liliana. He'd been so *sure*.

But the dragon was not finished. "I can, perhaps, set your feet upon the path to find that information."

That got their attention. "Then, uh, why haven't you acquired it yourself?" Jace couldn't help but ask.

"Because, little planeswalker, I have many potent abilities, but remaining hidden in a closet for weeks on end is not among them."

He nodded at their bewildered faces, as though it was the reaction he'd hoped for.

"You remember, I'm certain, the icy realm in which you and I first met?"

Jace smiled grimly. "I've been thinking of it a lot recently."

"Excellent. Then you'll remember that the artificer and I were discussing mining operations."

"I will. Uh, I mean I do."

"We were not arguing over land, little mind-reader. We were arguing over what waits *within* that land. Many of the ores of that world have long been inundated with all manner of mana; they seem almost to absorb it. Tezzeret believes such ore to be a vital component in the creation of etherium. And although he's never managed to perfect that process, he uses the material for other purposes. I do so as well.

"On a mountainside, quite distant from my own territory on that world, the Infinite Consortium keeps an establishment that serves as both a mine and a foundry. There, they slowly chip from the earth a vein of particularly mana-rich ore. At random intervals ranging from a few days to more than a month, either he or his hellhound Baltrice appear to take possession of the refined ore—never more than a small amount, so they may carry it with them—and return with it to the Consortium's heart, where they move ahead with whatever experiments they're conducting."

Jace and Liliana exchanged distraught glances. "Are you suggesting," Jace asked haltingly, "that the two of us should hide in a damned Consortium foundry for who knows how long, just for the shot at reading Baltrice's or Tezzeret's mind? Which would also, incidentally, warn them we were there."

"Oh, no," the dragon assured them. "It's not remotely that easy."

"Of course it's not," Jace muttered.

ARI MARMELL

"Not even the personnel know when the planes-walker arrives for the processed ore, or see them when they do so. Small crates filled with ingots of the metal, barely light enough for a strong person to lift, are left in a tiny room with thick stone walls and only a single door, constructed of heavy steel. When a shipment is ready to go, they leave it within, and some days later, it's gone. And before you ask, no, the room is not large enough to hide in and remain unnoticed, not even with your potent illusions.

"The foundry is heavily patrolled, with living soldiers and at least two of Tezzeret's clockwork golems. Even the workers are trained in battle and carry alarm whistles enchanted to be heard clearly above the worst roaring of the furnaces. And all this, of course, was the level of protection and security *before* you and the Consortium declared war on each other. It's doubtless increased since then.

"And *that*, sorcerer, is why I've not made efforts at rooting out this information."

Again the two mages stared at one another. Finally, however, Jace turned back to the dragon and forced across his face the widest grin he could muster.

"Piece of cake," he said.

✳ ✳ ✳ ✳ ✳ ✳

"Piece of cake," Liliana taunted as they crouched low on the mountainside, peering over heaps of rock at the enormous installation. "Would that be chocolate or lemon-flavored, oh master baker and tactician?"

Jace ignored her, picking bits of shale from his sleeves, flicking frost from his gloves, and staring at the high smokestacks and fortress-like walls. Or rather, staring past them; he'd sent a small band of faeries and homunculi to flitter invisibly about the complex, then read their minds to gain a solid notion of the layout.

If anything, Nicol Bolas had exaggerated their chances.

Multiple squat structures, some of stone and some of a steel alloy that resisted rusting beneath the frost, clung grimly to the mountainside. The thick fumes that rose from within mixed haphazardly with the clouds above, and even where the mages lay, some quarter-mile up the mountainside, the falling snow was tinged gray.

Some of those buildings, his spies had observed, covered mines dug deep into the stone, traversed by carts propelled by squat animated constructs. Others played home to enormous basins of molten metal, so hot that any precipitation to touch the outer walls instantly melted and ran down the sides.

Inside, an array of catwalks spanned the structures, interwoven and intertwined like the home of some giant iron spider. A veritable forest of chains hung from the ceilings, ready to carry any of the dozens of machines or the enormous buckets used to smelt ore. Guards strode the narrow walkways as workers completed one task and dashed furiously to their next.

And Jace's summoned infiltrators hadn't even managed to *find* the sealed "arrival" room the dragon had described, let alone determine if it boasted any viable flaws or weaknesses they might exploit.

For a very long while Jace and Liliana watched, shivering in the cold, each waiting for the other to come up with a workable plan. But this was not all the young mind-reader contemplated during those dark, cold, and endless hours. His encounter with the dragon had reawakened other suspicions, worries and concerns he'd tried desperately to push from his mind.

Again he wondered how Semner had found him after so much time, without the use of magic far more potent than the thug and would-be mage could ever possess. Again he wondered how the Consortium had found Emmara, Rulan, and the others—how they'd connected them with Jace himself—when they'd never proved able to do so before. Again he noted that circumstances had conspired to force him into a corner, removing options one by one until all that remained was the one option he'd worked so hard to avoid. And though he'd chosen not to bring it up, perhaps afraid she wouldn't answer, perhaps afraid she would, he wondered why the normally fearless necromancer had flinched so strongly at Bolas's mention of demons on Grixis.

It was impossible. He knew it was impossible, for he'd been inside her mind, albeit only once and long ago. And yet the more he thought on it, the more his misgivings thrust themselves to the fore as he drifted on the edge of sleep every night, the more he came to realize, with a sense of sick horror gnawing parasitically at his gut, that no other answer fit nearly so well.

So muddled had his thoughts become that he honestly couldn't recall whether he was considering the foundry or the woman beside him when Liliana finally snapped. "This is useless!" she barked at him. "What can we possibly do here that Nicol Bolas couldn't?"

"Hide in a closet," Jace muttered, remembering the dragon's words.

"Fine. So if we wanted, and if we got really lucky, we could watch helplessly from inside the walls instead of outside. Big hairy deal."

But Jace was slowly smiling as a notion—a long shot, yes, but viable—finally dawned on him. "And there are some," he said smugly, "who can hide where we can't."

"Um, yes. So?"

"So, Liliana, here's what we're going to do . . ."

✳ ✳ ✳ ✳ ✳

A sheet of flame erupted from the æther, split down the middle, and once more Baltrice appeared in the heart of Tezzeret's sanctum. She tried and failed to curse between ragged gasps for breath, for all her efforts were bent toward not dropping the heavy load she carried. Face coated in sweat and as red as the fires she commanded, she strained to lower the crate to the floor. Only when it landed did she release her breath in an explosive gasp and hurl a litany of obscenities so foul they threatened to corrode the metal of the hall around her.

Oh, but she hated this task! Of all the duties asked of her as Tezzeret's right hand, the collection of refined materials from the foundries involved in the Consortium's etherium project was by far the worst. It was time consuming, it was laborious and exhausting, but more than that, it was demeaning! Toting crates back and forth? That was a servant's job!

But until the artificer either found another planeswalker willing to be employed as a menial laborer—unlikely!—or found a means of artificially bridging the worlds—even more unlikely!—she was stuck with it.

At least she was here, though, and she could leave the task of toting the damned box down to the laboratory to someone more suited to it. Still flexing her aching fingers, she wandered around the corner, gone in search of one of Tezzeret's golems.

Behind her, hidden not only within the crate but within the metal itself, the phantom flexed and rolled, a wisp of errant mist. It could never have survived such a slow trek through the Blind Eternities on its own; the entropy and the errant magics would have shredded its essence into so much ghostly confetti. But hidden away within the solid weight of the bars, the journey had merely been one of maddening torment, rather than utter destruction. Now it need only wait for its mistress's summons to draw it back across that realm of roiling chaos; far more swiftly than its journey here, it would flit back, drawn by a call it could not deny, tracing a route between that world and this.

It could not simply describe the journey to them, for what good were mere words or even concepts such as direction and distance in the Blind Eternities? But it had possessed the one called Jace Beleren once before, and with his cooperation it would do so again. With a melding of their minds, a sharing of the senses, the joined man-and-ghost could find their way. Ensconced within his flesh and protected by his Spark, their thoughts linked by magics only Beleren could perform, it would use its own sensory impressions and the planeswalker's powers to retrace its ghostly steps once more.

Liliana Vess and Jace Beleren would have their guide.

CHAPTER TWENTY-SEVEN

For even the most powerful and most attentive planes-walker, arriving at a single, specific spot—such as, for instance, Baltrice's ability to appear in the foundry's sealed room, or the dead-end hall in the Consortium's heart—was a matter, not merely of intent, but of regular practice and intimate familiarity.

Perhaps unsurprisingly, possession by a spirit that had made the journey to the world in question precisely once failed to qualify as either. And thus Jace and Liliana had found themselves in the midst of a seem-ingly endless desert, the sun beating down on them with hammer-heavy blows, and no trace of Tezzeret's sanctum—or any other signpost of civilization—in sight. Even the various summoned scouts they sent soaring high above them found no sign of the artificer; they had, however, spotted a slow-moving dromad-drawn caravan, trudging through the sands some few miles away.

Now, their skin already turning red beneath the blazing heat, the planeswalkers sat on simple wooden stools before an older, leather-skinned fellow named Zarifim. Clad in voluminous, sand-hued robes, he appeared almost a part of the desert itself. The rest of his brethren, similarly dressed, waited politely some yards away while their leader conducted his negotiations.

". . . easily spare the clothes you require, my new friends," he was saying to Jace. "But such things are not easy to make."

"I understand," Jace told him. "How about *four* jugs of water, then?" He begrudged the mana it would take to summon so much water to this parched environment, but they needed the desert garb—and, more important, the directions Zarifim could offer.

To his credit, the old nomad didn't jump on the deal immediately. "Forgive me for doubting your judgment, but you appear so ill-prepared for desert travel. Can you spare such a quantity of water? I would hate for our deal to leave you dying of thirst before you reach your goal."

"I appreciate your concern, friend," Jace told him, ignoring the impatient tapping of Liliana's foot beside him. "But we'll make do, I assure you."

"Very well. Then we have a bargain." The nomad gestured and several of his brethren came forward, carrying robes akin to the one he wore. "Not to keep questioning you, my new friends," he said hesitantly, "but are you certain you wish to approach the Iron Tower? Even we go there only when we have many valuables to trade, and then only reluctantly. It is a bad place."

"I don't doubt that at all," Jace admitted. "But from your description, yes, it is exactly where we must go."

"So be it. I wish you the luck of the heavens. You must start from here, traveling due west for two days. Then . . ."

* * * * *

It was, in fact, four days later when Jace Beleren and Liliana Vess strode from the seemingly endless deserts, their skin chapped and wind-burned despite their protective magics and native garb, to finally arrive at the metallic monstrosity that was Tezzeret's home. Despite the heat, Jace had insisted on wearing his blue cloak, though he did so beneath the nomad's robe. He knew damn well that he was being superstitious, even silly, but he'd owned it so long, survived with it for so long, he felt naked facing Tezzeret without it. Both were tired from the journey, both were worried that the sands had offered them little in the way of mana suited to their magics. They could only hope to discover some viable source within the sanctum itself, or risk finding themselves truly overmatched.

It rose from beneath the sands, a shallow hill that gleamed blindingly in the pounding sun. Perfectly smooth, at least from this distance, it might as well have been shaped from a single slab of alloy; only one solitary tower in the structure's center, stabbing daggerlike at the heavens and boasting numerous spires and protrusions of its own, marred the otherwise pristine surface of the gentle slope. Uneven heaps of sand surrounded it, rising and falling waves constantly reshaped by the desert winds.

The mages studied it, hands held high to shade their eyes from the brilliance. From their current vantage, it was impossible to say precisely how large the structure might be, for the desert here was flat and featureless, their view obscured by sand-speckled breeze and the haze of rising heat.

Finally, Jace turned to Liliana and said simply, "How much magic do you suppose it takes to keep the place cool?"

She snorted, and they trudged their way closer still. As they walked, each summoned a small flock of minions—tiny fey, in Jace's case, with the power to make themselves invisible, while Liliana called up a handful of translucent spirits—and ordered them on ahead.

They learned much as they neared the looming structure. It was not, as they had supposed, perfectly circular;

rather, they had appeared toward the back of what turned out to be a crescent, shallower on the inner curve than the outer, and at the tips than the rear. The tower emerged from the highest point, at the apex of the crescent's bend. And it was not, in fact, constructed of a single sheet of metal, though the individual pieces were so perfectly fitted together that it might as well have been.

But most important and most discouraging, neither the mages nor their unearthly minions could find anything resembling a door. It seemed very much as though the structure had simply been sealed up during its construction and left that way.

Again and again the fey and the phantoms circled the complex; again and again they came up empty. Crouched behind a sand dune, Jace and Liliana grew ever more frustrated.

"Is it possible," Jace finally asked, "that there really isn't a door? Could Tezzeret be relying solely on tele-portation magics?"

Liliana shook her head. "Obviously, there's more to this world than desert. Carrying enough material to build this thing from other worlds would have taken centuries."

"Right. So?"

"So the same is true of supplies, Jace. Tezzeret's got to have people delivering food, building materials, and whatnot. Carrying supplies across a desert means caravans. Dromads or camels, wagons, you name it. You think he's teleporting entire wagon trains through those walls?"

"Ah. Fair point. So where's the damned door?"

"What, I have to answer *everything*?"

Again they lapsed into silence.

Ultimately, it proved to be a far simpler matter than they were making it out to be. Inspired by their successful efforts to track Baltrice, Liliana finally called up the smallest, weakest, and least offensive phantom she could muster—the better to avoid setting off any alarms or safeguards—and sent it through the walls to wander the structure's passageways. It took the ghostly entity only a short while to find a hall, occupied by several guards, that appeared to dead-end against the outer wall, and to report back with its location.

Of course, that still left them without a means of opening said door—but now, at least, Jace was in his element.

"Ask your phantom," he said to Liliana, gathering his own concentration and beginning the first stages of a clairvoyance spell, "to point me in the direction of the guards."

⁂ ⁂ ⁂ ⁂ ⁂

As it turned out, the "door" was a section of the wall itself, enchanted to fade away at the command of the guards inside. Jace's and Liliana's nomad garb wasn't sufficient to get them to open that door; but the illusion of a Consortium guard uniform beneath that robe, which Jace casually pulled aside, did the trick. One of the guards now lay senseless at Jace's feet out in the shifting sands, a second dead in the hallway where Liliana's specter had caught him before he could reach the speaking tube to report their arrival.

The whole affair had taken roughly half a minute.

"You know you might have triggered an alarm sending in that specter!" he snapped at Liliana as he dragged the fallen guard out of sight of the doorway. "There's a reason we sent the weakest spirit we could to do our scouting, remember?"

Liliana shrugged. "As opposed to what would've happened if I'd let that man report us? We're invading Tezzeret's sanctum, Jace! I think we're past the point of mincing about, don't you?"

Jace grumbled, which she took—correctly—as a sign that he knew she was right but didn't want to say so. "What now?" she asked him.

"Well," he said, after taking a moment to calm himself, "nobody's running to attack us yet, so we'll assume the alarm's not capable of detecting phantoms after all."

"Or that there is no alarm," Liliana suggested.

Jace, remembering the setup on Ravnica, didn't believe it for a second. "Have your specter drag the body out here," he ordered.

"Not sure one of them can do it alone, Jace. They're not real comfortable manipulating solid objects."

"Fine." Jace grimaced, and the unconscious guard rose unsteadily to his feet. "He'll help." Even as the mismatched pair set about dragging the other soldier to join his fellow outside, Jace was shoveling aside heaps of sand, preparing a secret, shallow grave. Once the corpse was outside, Jace raised a second illusion—one that, he hoped, would convince anyone inside that the wall was still closed.

"Assuming there *is* an alarm," Liliana said a moment later, "how do we get in?"

The guard stood motionless as Jace rifled through his thoughts. "It's like the alarm on Ravnica," he confirmed. "It's designed to detect the presence of unauthorized entrants."

"All right. So what do we do?"

"We have a polite little conversation," Jace said with a smile, as the soldier strode back into the hallway and lifted the speaking tube from the wall, "with someone who has the power to authorize us."

It proved no harder for Jace to overpower the shift commander, a gold-skinned desert elf named Irivan, than it had been any of the others. Carefully he commanded the unconscious fellow to rise, to move to the alarm controls and authorize the planeswalkers to pass. Liliana nodded at Jace and turned away, watching the elf as he spoke into a strange gemstone inlaid into the wall—and thus she missed the darkening of Jace's gaze as he looked upon her.

For Jace had learned something within Commander Irivan's mind, something that worried him far more than any alarm. Surely the Consortium's ranking officers, if not the average soldier, would have been briefed on the organization's many enemies. And indeed Irivan knew full well who Jace Beleren was. He knew, too, of Kallist Rhoka; of Nicol Bolas; of the fey Oberilia Zant, who had stolen from Tezzeret's minions many a valuable artifact; and of half a dozen others whom Tezzeret had deemed a threat to his empire.

But despite her claims so long ago that she too was hiding from their mutual foe, Jace found no knowledge at all of the sorceress Liliana Vess.

CHAPTER TWENTY-EIGHT

Commander Irivan strode purposefully down the metal corridors. Following several steps behind came a pair of Consortium soldiers, or so it would appear to any passerby. Trying desperately to behave as their illusory guises suggested they should, Jace and Liliana struggled to neither gawk at the iron-and-steel perdition through which they passed, nor to wince at the perpetual thumps and whistles and hums that echoed through those passageways.

Walls and ceilings of gleaming metal were lit by recessed globes that glowed without emitting the slightest trace of heat. Some floors boasted tiny patterns in the steel, providing some amount of traction, while others boasted thin layers of carpeting, and still others were nothing but grates that allowed a distorted view of the levels below. Though pristine in appearance, the halls smelled cloyingly of smoke and burning oils.

Doors that were themselves mere sheets of metal either slid aside or irised open as they moved through, or as other guards and workers passed them by, complete with a faint hissing somewhere inside the walls. Heavy windows allowed occasional glances into chambers full of animated metallic limbs, of precarious platforms that rose and fell of their own accord, of glowing spheres that pulsed in patterns Jace could not begin to comprehend. That there was some method behind the mechanized madness he did not doubt, but he couldn't hope to guess what it might be.

Only slowly did it dawn on Jace and Liliana both that, despite their fear and consternation, they were actually feeling better than they had outside. At first Jace attributed it to being out of the desert heat, but no, it was definitely something more. It almost felt as if . . .

That was it, then. Mana flowed through the walls, the floors, the essence of the Consortium sanctum. And not just any sort of energy but *all* sorts, from the soothing auras of the ocean to the burning soul of the mountains to the deathly magics of the swamplands. Something in the building, some ingrained magic or alchemical-mechanical process, transformed the ambient mana of the world into any form imaginable. It was subtle, it was difficult to access—as though the walls themselves sought to keep the power contained within—but it was there. Jace almost slumped in relief as he devoted a portion of his attentions to tapping into that source, as he felt his strength slowly but surely rise once more. He could only imagine Liliana felt much the same.

And then they passed a great chamber just as the pistons inside began to pump. Any relief Jace had been feeling evaporated into so much mist, and he couldn't suppress a gasp of unmitigated revulsion.

He'd known there must be not only mechanical ingenuity but mana driving these machines, but he hadn't realized what sort. As they passed, he felt the ambient energies in the air turn dark and cold. Just barely, beneath the clatter and the hiss, the rumbling and the rattling, Jace thought he heard faint screams of living essences bound within the machine, providing the pseudo-sentience it needed to follow its master's commands.

Never had he hated Tezzeret more than he did in that moment; never did he understand more clearly the nature of the devil to whom he'd nearly sold his soul.

A low hiss from Liliana snapped his thoughts back to the present. Irivan had stopped in his tracks while Jace's mind drifted, and it took him a moment to center himself and re-establish control, to set the elf marching ahead once more. And just in time, for as they passed by the next door in the corridor, it slid open and Baltrice herself stepped out into the hall.

All three guards stepped to the side, standing against the wall that she might go by unhindered. She did so, with scarcely a nod of acknowledgment. Only once she had passed did she briefly turn back to peer directly at Jace; no recognition shown in her expression, but her eyes narrowed ever so minutely, as though she were bothered by something she couldn't entirely pin down. And then the thought had passed, as had her gaze, and she was gone around the next bend in the hall.

Jace exhaled loudly, and the group moved on.

And so they progressed, protected by Jace's illusions and ignored by workers and guards alike, through the lower levels of the Consortium's mechanical heart. Guided by the memories and knowledge of the sleep-walker before them, Jace and Liliana inched ever nearer their ultimate goal, and not a soul was aware of their presence.

Jace knew better than to note, or even to *think*, that it was going too smoothly; he knew all too well it wouldn't last.

Indeed, it did not. They set foot upon a spiral stair, one that wound its way gradually up to a heavy door made not of steel or iron, but of ancient bronze. An array of multicolored stones, similar to those that had served as the controls for the alarm system, adorned the wall beside the ponderous portal.

Neither mage needed even to ask. They knew this must mark the entrance to the tower itself.

Though it was utterly unnecessary, thanks to his mental hold over the elven commander, Jace gave the squat soldier a curt nod. Irivan stepped forward, waved a hand over the gems, and the door rose into the ceiling with a low rumble and another hiss of steam.

Never mind their guises now; Jace and Liliana simply stared, utterly rooted to the floor.

If what they'd seen so far was mechanized chaos, this was mechanized *madness*. Half a dozen circular platforms of various sizes, held aloft by perfectly smooth cables as thick as tree trunks, rose and fell throughout the tower's hollow center, perhaps providing access to the areas above. At no point did the spire boast anything resembling an actual story; balconies, rooms, and structures that might even have been small buildings, had they stood on their own, protruded from the wall at various heights. Some were linked to others by more catwalks; others by stairs and smaller lifts that ran along the wall; and still others could be reached only by the central platforms. And those chambers and "partial floors" moved in turn, rotating around the tower's circumference, slowly sliding up or down, so that none remained at the same height for more than a few moments at a time. Between and around them, great pulleys and more rapidly pulsing orbs of light orchestrated the endless metal ballet that kept the tower in constant motion, yet somehow prevented so much as a single cable from becoming tangled with any other.

It made no sense, couldn't possibly make sense. Jace could imagine no purpose to it, no reason for someone to construct such a convoluted structure, unless . . .

Unless it wasn't a structure at all.

"It's an artifact," he whispered.

"What?" Liliana asked him, tearing her gaze from

the slow dance above. "What is?"

"This. This place. The cables, the rising levels . . . The whole thing's an eldritch machine, Liliana. An artifact, not a building. It just happens to also have people in it."

She sucked in her breath, looking around her. "An artifact that does what? Surely this whole structure can't just be devoted to converting one type of mana into another."

Jace shrugged. "When we find Tezzeret, I'll be sure to ask him."

Shifting his attention from the apparatus above, Jace took a moment to examine his immediate surroundings. The floor was the same odd metal as the glowing spheres, and indeed it emanated a faint reddish pulse. It was a diabolical illumination, like a flame frozen solid, painting streaks of crimson across a series of round railings—present to keep people from stepping under the platforms and being crushed, Jace assumed. A number of doors, which could only lead to a relatively small array of rooms, surrounded the tower's perimeter. Those, and a perfectly smooth bronze spire standing roughly eight feet tall in the precise center of the tower, were the chamber's only obvious features.

"I, uh . . . I guess we head over and wait for one of the platforms," Jace offered halfheartedly. "Maybe there's a lever to summon one, or something."

Liliana had nothing better to offer, and Irivan had never been summoned into the heights of the tower itself, so that appeared to be their only option. Their footsteps resounded on the glowing floor, and their shadows flickered so rapidly in all directions, lit horribly from below, that it seemed they must detach from their masters and take independent flight.

The nearer they drew to the center of the room, the worse Jace's suspicions about the bronze pillar grew. When the entire device suddenly shuddered and split into ten insectoid legs of spindly bronze, topped by a "head" of clattering jutting, animated needles, Jace couldn't honestly claim to be even remotely surprised.

It skittered toward them, a hideous screech arising with each touch of its legs upon the metal below. As it neared, it no longer appeared to Jace as an insect, but almost as a pair of disembodied hands, joined at the wrists and scuttling on skeletal fingers.

A dozen feet from them it halted, shifting side to side as though eager to pounce. The jagged mass atop the legs clicked and spat, spines protruding in and out, a sewing machine grown mad. A thin iris of bronze amid the gears slid open, revealing a lens of verdigris-tinted glass.

The damn thing was studying them!

Jace sent a frantic command, and Irivan snapped to attention. He and Liliana followed a split second later, and the trio stood ready for inspection.

Maybe it was the wrong response, but Jace didn't think so. He swore the thing looked right at him, lens seeming to bulge in surprise, before it lurched again into motion.

With an indifference possible only in a machine, it hurled Irivan aside as it rushed to engage its true target. Jace dived to his left, hitting the floor in a painful roll and rising once more to his feet, as it thrust its jagged head and pumping spines through the space where he'd previously stood. He flung a spear of telekinetic force from his outstretched hand even as Liliana moved in behind the construct and tried to surround it with the same mass of shadowy fragments that had carried away her attacker's blade back in the Bitter End. But the former hardly even staggered the mechanized beast, and the latter seemed to splatter like water as they closed around one artificial leg.

It kicked back at her, and now it was Liliana's turn to dive away lest she find herself crushed or impaled on the great bronze limb. In the same motion it leaped forward, spinning to land beside Jace once more. A desperate shield of force was all that saved him from bearing the brunt of another kick, and even through his protective spell the impact was enough to send him skidding. He groaned as the friction against the floor ripped cloth from his trousers and skin from his thigh. The blood threatened to glue his cloak to the injury as he staggered once more to his feet.

No illusions; no mind-control; no necromantic enervation; Jace and Liliana were fast running out of options. He had no doubt that either of them could summon something great enough to crush the mechanical monster, but doing so would take more power, more mana, than Jace felt they could afford to spend when they'd not yet even found Tezzeret. He gave ground steadily before the machine's relentless advance, feet threatening to slide out from under him on the perfectly smooth surface, and struggled desperately to come up with some other option.

And then he saw Liliana wave, saw where she stood and the lever at which she pointed, and nodded his understanding.

The construct took to the air once more, and Jace dived under it, rolling to his feet and sprinting as fast as his wounded leg would allow. The entire floor shuddered as the beast landed and took off in pursuit. Swiftly, all too swiftly, the vibrations beneath him grew stronger, and he knew the construct was gaining.

A third dive to the side, but the machine had learned to anticipate the trick. A leg lashed out, pinning the hem of Jace's cloak to the floor. Yanked backward in midair, choking through a bruised throat, he landed hard on his back and lay still as the tower spun dizzyingly above. Only the creak of metal, the image of the construct's bulk heaving into sight above him, spurred him to action once more. Tearing open the cloak's broach he rolled swiftly to his right. One leg, a second, a third pounded the floor mere inches behind him as he rolled—and then a fourth came down in front of him, and only a desperate heave that agonizingly pulled every muscle in his torso kept him from barreling right into it.

Jace started to roll back to his left, but one of the bronze limbs thudded down there as well. He found himself staring upward, pinned by a cage of mechanical legs. Above him, the amalgamation of edges that was the golem's head plunged forward and down, as though along a hidden track, spines reaching thirstily for Jace's blood. Another telekinetic shield halted the assault inches from his flesh, and he could feel the weight, the strength of the monster, pressing on his mind.

He screamed beneath the strain, felt his bastion of force slowly start to give. A single spine, pressed forward by a piston of magic and steam, slowly sliced through his defenses and pressed deep into the muscle and flesh of his shoulder. Blood flowed, raining down between the slats onto the mechanisms below.

"Jace!" He scarcely heard her, over the creaking of the bronze and the pounding in his head. "Jace, now!"

Jace grinned up at the machine that threatened to kill him.

From behind them both, a fearsome roar shook the chamber. Jace all but sobbed in relief as the spike withdrew from his flesh, as the construct whipped its head around to see what new threat had emerged.

Wings spread wide, mouth agape in her deafening cry, the cerulean sphinx Jace had summoned to his aid twice before slammed into the construct, lifting it, thrashing and twitching, into the air.

Hurry! he thought desperately to his feline ally. Jace knew that, given even a moment to recover, the machine could shred her like cobweb. *Hurry!*

Another cry, and the sphinx released her prey. Legs waving helplessly, it sailed across the chamber, slamming into, and through, one of the circular railings near the room's center.

Sparks flew, and the construct finally skidded to a halt on its back. Ten legs twisted, reversing their position; the head of gears slid upward through the body, emerging on what had been the underside; and the mechanized beast was on its feet once more.

Thankfully, fast as it was, it was much too late.

Even as it rose, its head struck the flat surface of the platform descending on top of it, the lift platform Liliana had summoned with the tug of a lever. Designed to haul dozens if not hundreds of tons from the floor of the tower, it was a weight and a pressure not even the construct could withstand. Thrashing wildly, bronze limbs bent and snapped beneath the weight of the lift. A groan, the final crack of rending metal, and the platform settled evenly to the floor, bits of bronze debris splayed out beside it. The sphinx lay sprawled atop the lift, a look of contentment on her face.

Jace and Liliana moved together, standing back to back, braced for another attack, but nothing came. The platforms continued their intricate dance, the cables twisted and turned, but nothing more.

Liliana looked at Jace, who could only shrug. "The walls are thick, and the machines are noisy," he theorized. "Maybe nobody heard?"

"I don't like it," Liliana told him bluntly. "You really think there are no guards inside this entire tower?"

"I think I'll take whatever luck falls my way," Jace told her. Then again, there was no telling how long it would take before some guard *did* wander through. "But, uh, let's get the wreckage out of sight, shall we?"

"Right, because nobody's going to notice the *missing pillar*," Liliana scoffed. Still, she moved to help with the smaller bits, even as the sphinx—her expression one of arrogant disdain—rose, stretched languidly, and began batting the larger ones across the floor.

It never occurred to either of them to wonder who else might have been watching through the construct's eye.

In the end, they found that several of the doors on the tower's perimeter led to supply closets, and chose one as the repository for the random bits of bronze, as well as the corpse of Irivan, who hadn't survived being brushed aside by the charging construct. With a nod of thanks for her help, Jace dismissed the sphinx; useful in battle as she was, she wasn't precisely inconspicuous.

He took a moment, stretching out the kinks in his back and flinging his tattered cloak back over his shoulders. "Stay here," he said then, fading into invisibility as he moved toward the door. "I want to take a quick look around, make absolutely certain that we haven't attracted any attention."

"Wait, what? Jace, hold on—" But he was already gone, the door drifting shut in his wake.

Liliana cursed, roundly and for several minutes. What was he *thinking?* The last thing they needed now was to get separated—and she definitely couldn't afford to lose track of what he was up to. They were so close now, *she* was so close, and yet this could still so easily go completely sideways.

As if to prove the point, the door creaked open, but it was not Jace Beleren standing therein.

"What by all the Eternities are *you* doing here?" Baltrice demanded, flames crackling between the fingers of her left hand.

Already on edge, Liliana felt the first stirrings of real panic. How much did Baltrice know? What had Tezzeret told her of their meeting? "Get out of here! You'll ruin everything!" she hissed desperately. "Damn it, go check with your boss! He'll tell you whose side I'm on!"

"No," Baltrice said, suddenly fading away into nothingness. "You've already done that."

Liliana's head fell, her eyes closing of their own accord. "Jace." She forced herself to look up, just in time to see him shimmer into being before her. "Jace, you don't understand. I—"

The breath rushed from her lungs as Jace wrapped his fists in her tunic and slammed her against the rear wall of the chamber.

"Damn you!" He literally shook her, somehow finding the strength in his slender form to hold her completely off the floor. Worse, she felt his anger not merely in his grip, but in her own mind, waves pounding against her thoughts, disorienting her until she wasn't certain she could even stand were he to let her go. "How could you do this to me?"

"Jace—"

"I trusted you, Liliana! I loved you!" His eyes glowed a cobalt blue to light up the entire chamber, and the necromancer could feel the power gathering within his soul. He'd been so sure, so certain that he was imagining things, that his suspicions were nothing but paranoia. His test, his illusion, they'd been meant to *assuage* his worries before moving on, not . . .

Not this.

"Jace," she tried again, placing one hand atop his own, feeling the muscles and tendons flexing within, "I swear to you, I can explain. But not now, not when we're so close! This isn't the time!"

"Actually," Tezzeret's oily voice oozed from the open doorway, "I think it's the perfect time."

CHAPTER TWENTY-NINE

The tower's great bronze door blew completely off its frame like a cork shooting from a bottle. Rending metal pierced the ears and bits of jagged shrapnel dug furrows into the walls. Helpless as a rag doll, Tezzeret landed on his back in the twisted wreckage, blinking to clear his head, wiping blood and particulates from his face.

A cloud of dust filled the chamber beyond, tinged red by the fires below, billowing and rolling to shame the storm. His tattered cloak undulating behind, his eyes tunnels of endless crackling blue, Jace Beleren strode through the cloud, bearing down on the startled artificer. Above him resounded the thunder of mighty wings as the enormous drake that had hurled Tezzeret through the door circled menacingly, dropping ever lower at its master's call. Its scales gleamed even in the diffuse, abysmal light.

Propping himself up on his etherium hand, Tezzeret scrambled to his feet, initiating a spell of his own. The younger mage never slowed, never broke stride. He merely bowed his head, allowing the plummeting drake just enough room to tuck its wings to its sides and burst through the doorway. Shrieking its primal rage, it slammed into Tezzeret once more, bowling him farther down the hall, claws and teeth raking furiously against a protective barrier the artificer only barely erected in time.

Again Tezzeret found himself flat on his back, struggling to ward off the drake that crouched above him, digging at his shields. Around him, guards came running, swords held aloft, only to be forced back by bone-chilling waves of piercing cold that wafted against them as they approached, freezing solid flesh and blood and bone.

Abandoned and betrayed, face to face with the architect of everything his life had become, Jace Beleren's rage overpowered any sympathy he may have felt for the guards as they fell before his murderous spells. They wanted to serve the artificer? They could die with him.

Tezzeret, caught utterly off guard by the mind-reader's fury, allowed himself the duration of a single indrawn breath to marvel at the power he faced, to grow wroth that the power he had fostered in Jace was now being levied against him.

Looking up, he stared into the maw of the chrome-scaled drake, and thrust both hands outward.

A swarm of tiny projectiles pierced the air, and each was a single tip of a triple-forked bolt of lightning. Scales and flesh blackening beneath the assault, the drake slammed upward to collide with a bone-breaking crunch against the metallic ceiling. Booming thunder rolled down the hall, dispersing the dust and knocking Jace off his feet.

In unison Jace and Tezzeret scrambled upright, each glaring at the other across the twitching drake and frost-coated steel. Even as the beast struggled to rise, the artificer clenched his fist. From both walls an array of cables and pipes burst from their sockets, slamming into the wounded creature's flesh, releasing bursts of steam to boil the scales from its body. The drake shuddered one last time and was gone. But the protrusions from the wall remained, writhing blindly like the tendrils of some obscene jellyfish.

Jace shouted, his words incomprehensible, and gestured. From the floor behind him, the shards of the shattered door rose and spun down the hall, scything blades aimed at Tezzeret's flesh. But telekinesis still was not Jace's strongest suit, and the few projectiles that wove their way through the barrier of metal tentacles were easily repelled by the artificer's personal shield.

He had only just begun to laugh, to mock the feebleness of the assault, when Jace's true attack struck. Pain blossomed through Tezzeret's head, sunk its tendrils deep into his thoughts. His vision blurred, his stomach heaved, and worst of all, his concentration wavered.

For a moment, one ephemeral moment, Jace might have won.

But he was Tezzeret, master of the Infinite Consortium! He had constructed artifacts beyond the grasp of archmages, stood against foes as potent as the great Nicol Bolas and survived! He would not—*he would not*—let an upstart like Jace Beleren lay him low!

Grasping fingers of midnight black and blinding blue seemed to emerge from the air around the artificer, wisps of smoke wafting from them, as he gathered the mana running like blood through his veins. Power, pure and uncontrolled force of will, burst from Tezzeret's soul, snapping the conduit Jace had established with his mind, sending the younger mage staggering with the backlash of his broken spell. The artificer glared across the hall, panting, nearly spent—and then he allowed his glower to warp itself into an ugly grin. Deliberately, allowing Jace to see exactly what he was doing, he thrust forth his artificial hand, holding it near the conduits that ran through the metal walls of his home.

Those conduits began to glow. A vapor that was not steam burst from the junctions, swirling about etherium fingers, absorbed into the metal and into Tezzeret's lungs. And just like that, he found himself restored, his soul burning with raw mana, ready and eager to be shaped.

For the first time since the assault began, Tezzeret saw fear peeking from behind the curtain of rage that was Jace Beleren's face, and he rejoiced.

Yet while Jace was indeed distraught, he was not daunted. Straightening his shoulders, he raised both hands, palms upright. "If your home is your power, Tezzeret," he called out, "I'll just have to take it from you!"

As though he could see it, touch it—and perhaps he could, at that—Jace reached out with his mind into the walls themselves and took hold of the fluids running through the conduits within. Those that were already steam heated and expanded further until the pipes around them burst, the metal that contained them peeling outward like the blossoming of iron flowers. The liquids flowing through other tubes froze solid, backing up into the heart of Tezzeret's machines until filthy water burst from a dozen seams. Throughout the complex, glowing spheres grew suddenly dim, moving platforms ground to a halt, as the pressures that drove them and the mana that fueled them ceased to flow. Mana-infused vapors evaporated uselessly into the aether, and cables all around the hall began to shudder and snap.

Tezzeret felt his own fury rising. He had hoped simply to keep Beleren busy until Baltrice and more of his guards arrived. Clearly, that was no longer an option. Already the damage inflicted by his spells would take days to repair; he couldn't afford to let his enemy tear apart any more of his home.

But that was fine, too. The thought of finishing the fight in person, planeswalker to planeswalker, brought a wolfish grin to the artificer's face.

Tezzeret took three running steps and leaped. The hall's surviving cables reached out, propelling him along or yanking sheets of steel from the wall to shield him from the bursting metal and hissing steam. Tucking into a forward roll as he cleared the length of the hall, he began to cast. The artificer landed in a crouch mere feet before his enemy, his etherium hand already darting out to parry the shrapnel Jace had telekinetically hurled at him as he came. In that metal grip Tezzeret clutched a fistful of sand, glowing visibly with prior enchantments and the power of the spell he pumped into it now.

His fist tightened further, and the particles sifted from between his fingers, pouring into the air and swirling around both combatants, an embryonic dust devil that swiftly grew into a raging whirlwind. Long after the initial fistful was expended, the sand continued to flow, to whip about them, until cloak and hair thrashed wildly and all sight of the surrounding hall was obscured.

Jace felt the temperature rise into a baking heat that lay heavily upon him and brought an instant sweat to his skin. Even as he readied a counterspell intended to shield him from the worst of the pounding heat, he felt the rigidity of the metal beneath him give way to the unstable shifting of the desert floor. The sandstorm faded to reveal an endless expanse of wastes, only the very tip of Tezzeret's tower visible over the distant horizon. Despite the warmth Jace tugged the hood of his cloak over his face, shielding his watering eyes from the brightness of the midday sun.

Fully prepared for the teleportation, Tezzeret was of course far less unsettled by the sudden shift than was his enemy. Even as Jace reeled, blinking away his disorientation, the artificer raised fists of metal and flesh. A wall of molten glass burst from the sands between them, sending Jace tumbling away as it slashed at his flesh and burned away the tips of his hair and the ragged hem of his cloak.

He staggered to his feet, fighting for balance on the shifting dunes, and the desert came alive behind him. A dozen tiny metal orbs rained earthward, bursting as they fell, and from beneath them rose a lumbering giant made of nothing but sand. Its limbs didn't bend so much as constantly reshape themselves to any desired angle as it glided across the desert to smash the artificer's foe.

Jace sank swiftly beneath the sands, plummeting through a tunnel burrowed by telekinetic force akin to the spell he'd used to fly, back on Ravnica, and the sand-golem's fists struck nothing but earth. And then he *was* flying; Jace burst from the desert floor and soared into the azure sky, arms outstretched and crackling with power. Behind him the air rippled and split, a gulf from elsewhere, from which appeared a pair of winter drakes and the familiar sphinx. The drakes instantly dived upon the beast of sand, struggling to immobilize it into a lifeless statue with bursts of frigid breath, while Jace dropped onto the sphinx's back and plummeted in a screaming dive toward Tezzeret himself.

Tezzeret let them come, watching, waiting. He hurled a few projectiles, spinning discs that crackled with necromantic energy and would have sucked the life from the sphinx as swiftly as one of Liliana's spells. The beast avoided them easily, but then he'd expected her to. Only at the last, when her claws were instants from his flesh, when she was rolling back into line after dodging the last of his attacks, did he cast once more.

The sands erupted into jagged blades of glass and stone, teeth sprouted by the earth itself to feed a ravenous hunger. The sphinx shrieked as the barrier tore through fur and flesh, ripping her apart even as it held her fast. Jace tumbled over her head and slammed hard to the ground. He looked up, dazed; and the sphinx stared down, her expression vaguely accusing, before the life drained from her eyes and her body faded slowly away.

Jace tried to rise and failed, toppling over when his arm simply refused to support him. The entire left side of his body was horribly bruised, and he wondered how many bones he might have cracked in the fall. Exhaustion threatened to blind him, and he knew that his reserves were sufficient for only a few more spells.

Beyond the nearest dune, the golem of sand had cracked apart beneath the arctic assault, but one of the drakes had given its life, and even as the other raced to aid its master, it flew an erratic path on torn and battered wings. And stalking across the sands came Tezzeret, arcs of power crackling between his mechanical fingers; tireless, relentless, seeming no weaker now for all his spells than he had been the moment Jace attacked.

And Jace knew, even through his burning rage and down to the core of his soul, that this was no longer a fight he could win.

He could, however, survive. He knew where the bastard's sanctum was, now, and knew as well that he had nobody he could trust on his side. With time to recover, to lick his wounds, to find new weapons, he could come back—he *would* come back.

Jace focused his attentions on the space around the artificer, and a trio of winter drakes dropped from the sky. That they were merely illusory, for he dared not spend the mana necessary to summon them afresh, was irrelevant. Tezzeret couldn't afford to ignore them, for among them was the surviving drake, a very real threat. And indeed he halted his advance, casting spells of protection against the cold he knew was coming.

It bought time, that was all, but that was all Jace needed. Distracted as he was by the drakes, Tezzeret could not see his opponent cast a net of illusion over himself, blending in with the desert sands. Then,

ARI MARMELL

summoning the last of his reserves, Jace had the long moments he needed to draw together the surrounding threads of mana and begin to walk.

Slowly, too slowly, the curtain of haze materialized before him and Jace stumbled through. His last sight was of Tezzeret standing amid a whirling wall of illusory wings, and removing a dark globe from a pouch on his belt, doubtless a weapon he'd never get to use.

As the chaos of the Eternities pummeled him, Jace breathed a sigh of relief. Even if Tezzeret had seen him go, even if he'd slain the drake the moment Jace vanished, it would take him minutes if not hours to follow, and by then Jace would be long—

Tendrils of entropy and probability rippled, coiling upward and in on themselves, and Tezzeret stood before him, a vicious grin on his face and a vile gleam in his eye. No hesitation, no delay—he was simply there. In all the Blind Eternities, nothing had ever shocked Jace more thoroughly. He stared at the artificer's soul, an abomination of blood and metal, of hatred and greed, and he could not move.

It wasn't possible, it wasn't . . .

Tezzeret clutched Jace by the collar and *shoved*, muscles and magic working in tandem to carry them back through the barrier of worlds. They reappeared a dozen feet above the desert floor and crashed painfully to the ground.

Jace, too stunned by the sudden assault even to draw breath, felt the remaining air rush from his lungs, felt fire flash across the back of his head at the impact, and then the blinding light of the desert went mercifully black.

CHAPTER THIRTY

As Jace gradually awoke, an armada of aches and pains laying siege to his body, his first thought was to wonder if he should be surprised that he still lived. He decided it wasn't worth the effort, and cracked open his eyelids.

He lay on a pallet of old straw, its needles poking him unpleasantly. He was naked, save for his trousers, and so badly bruised and beaten that he looked as though he'd been rolling in purple paint. One side of his current quarters was a solid wall of metal; thick bars of a matte-gray alloy formed the other three. Other than the pallet and a cracked clay chamber pot, the cell was featureless. He couldn't even see an obvious door, locked or otherwise.

The place probably smelled, too, but over his own stale sweat, he couldn't tell.

The cell itself stood at one end of a large metal chamber, equally featureless, with a single heavy door on the far wall. Jace was pretty certain he was somewhere within Tezzeret's sanctum, but beyond that, he couldn't be sure of a damn thing.

Staggering to his feet with a series of pained grunts, Jace wobbled over and tapped a knuckle on a bar. Solid,

ARI MARMELL

very solid, but not as cold as he'd have expected. It wasn't etherium, but neither was it typical iron or steel.

But of course, Tezzeret wouldn't have been even remotely so stupid as to try to keep a planeswalker in a normal cell, would he?

Just to be sure, and because he felt as though he should at least make the effort, Jace summoned his will, to walk, to cast a spell, to do *something*.

Nothing. He might as well have harbored no Spark at all, might as well never have heard of magic or mana.

"Ah, excellent. You're awake!"

The door had slid open without a whisper, and Baltrice stood framed within. She sauntered to the cell, wearing perhaps the cruelest grin Jace could ever recall seeing.

"Fascinating, don't you think?" she said, tapping on the bars with Jace's manablade before replacing the weapon at her own waist. "Another little secret we, um, borrowed from the Church of the Incarnate Soul. The bars are enchanted to absorb mana, Beleren. Inside, for all practical purposes, magic doesn't exist."

He sneered at her, crossing his arms over his bare chest. She chuckled and aimed a finger toward the wall at his left. The metal shimmered, flickered, and Tezzeret's face appeared.

"Why am I alive?" Jace asked bluntly, refusing to give the bastard a moment to gloat.

Tezzeret merely lapsed into a thoughtful expression. "I believe I've explained to you on past occasions how poorly I take betrayal, have I not?"

Jace rolled his eyes.

"You are alive," the artificer said, "partly because I want to give you some time to truly comprehend the depths of my disappointment—but mostly because I require a few months to complete my arrangements for you. You see, Beleren, since I've actually managed to take you alive, I've decided your talents are too valuable to waste. Mind-reading is a precious commodity indeed.

"So if I cannot trust an agent to perform such tasks for me, I'll simply have to construct a device to do so. An artifact that will preserve and manipulate the portions of your brain that allow for such wonders."

Despite himself, Jace felt the urge to fall back from the image on the wall.

"I should think," the artificer said with an oily grin, "that if I build the device just right, I can retain enough of your persona that you'll remain conscious and aware of what's happened to you, without the slightest ability to do anything about it."

Baltrice leaned in toward the bars, enjoying her captive's fear, no matter how hard he sought to mask it.

"You'll try to escape, of course," Tezzeret said matter-of-factly, as though it were a foregone conclusion. "And you'll fail. Even if you somehow find a way past the bars, I've poisoned you while you were unconscious. It's an eldritch toxin, dormant for now, thanks to the lack of magic in that cell. Step beyond the bars, though, and you'll be so sick as to be nearly dead in a matter of minutes." The image shrugged. "It'll metabolize out of your system in a few months, but I imagine I'll have your new accommodations ready by then."

He nodded to Baltrice, and the image faded from the wall. She grinned in anticipation, overjoyed as Jace began to tremble openly. "In the meantime," she exulted, "the boss has told me that until he's ready to cut you apart, as long as I cause no permanent damage—you're mine!"

Flames erupted on the three open sides of the cell, inches beyond the enchanted bars, and if magic couldn't penetrate the claustrophobic prison, the heat and the smoke could. Jace fell back, arms thrown up to protect his face. His skin blistered, his lungs cried out for air, but he swore, he swore, that he would not scream.

It was an oath he succeeded in keeping for almost a minute.

✲ ✲ ✲ ✲ ✲

He lost track of time, there in that manmade purgatory. How long at a stretch was he left alone, filthy and starving, wondering if the next time that door opened would be the last? How many times did he flinch when the door *did* open, before he knew if it was some servant come with gruel and water, or Baltrice eager for another of their "sessions"?

The lights in the chamber neither dimmed nor brightened. The consistency of the food never changed. Jace slept fitfully, never knowing how long, never knowing if he'd wake up again, or even if he wanted to. His hair was brittle and uneven where the edges had burned away, his skin charred in spots and patches, some of which might never fully heal.

And Jace endured, for what else could he do?

It might have been days, then, or possibly weeks, when the door to the outside world opened once more, and it was neither Baltrice nor a food-toting servant who stood within.

"Hello, Jace."

"Get out of here," Jace demanded, his voice made hoarse by smoke and screams.

Liliana allowed the door to slide shut behind her. Tentatively, as though each step pained her, she moved through the room until she stood barely more than an arm's reach from the bars.

"I'm sorry I didn't come sooner," she told him, her voice quiet. "I told Tezzeret that I was trying to deliver you to him, but it took him some time to even start to trust me, even after his damned truth elixirs. As it is, he's 'letting me stay' while we discuss my future place in the Consortium mostly so he can keep an eye on me."

"Either go away," the prisoner growled, flexing his fingers, "or take a step closer."

"Damn it, Jace! They're going to kill you!"

"So I'm told. You came to watch?"

"I came to get you out, you idiot!"

For the first time in who knew how long, Jace laughed, laughed until his battered lungs could take no more and he collapsed against the bars in a fit of choking.

"Of course," he gasped, when he could finally speak once more. "Because you've helped me so much to this point."

"I have!" she insisted, her face distraught. "How many times have we saved each other's lives, Jace? How many times would you be dead now, if not for me?"

"For all the good it's done me," he muttered, but he couldn't deny the point. "You really want to help me escape?"

"Yes!"

"Why?"

"Because I don't want to see you go through what they're planning to do to you."

Jace shook his head. "No. No, Liliana, you don't get to play that card any more."

"Even if it's true?"

"No. I want the truth. All of it. I want to know why—not just why you want to help me escape, but why all of it." Jace crossed his arms and stepped back from the bars. "Otherwise, I see no reason to depart this delightful establishment."

Liliana's jaw dropped. "You're joking!"

"No, I'm not." His tone left no doubt, no doubt at all, that he meant it. "This hell I'm in, Liliana? It's nothing compared to the one you put me through. So if you expect me to trust you even so far as getting me out, to believe that this isn't another trick, you're going to have to convince me." He glanced meaningfully at the door behind her, then at the wall where Tezzeret's image had appeared. "And I'm guessing," he continued, "that you don't have indefinite time."

ARI MARMELL

She sighed. "No, but I have some. Tezzeret and Baltrice are off-world, and the guards outside the door are possessed. Once I release them, they won't remember me being here at all."

"All right, Jace." She lowered herself to the floor, sitting cross-legged before the cell. After a moment, Jace did the same, waiting expectantly.

"I never did anything," she started softly, staring down at the floor, "that I didn't have to do."

Again Jace found himself laughing, and laughing harder still at the hurt expression that flashed across her face. "Where do betrayal and murder fall on the list of necessities, Liliana?" he asked her.

"What do *you* know?" she snapped at him, her whole body tensing. "It's all come so easily to you, Jace! When did you work for anything? Your mind-reading? You just discovered you could do that. Your money? You blackmailed rich idiots until Tezzeret dropped an opportunity in your lap! Some of us have had to struggle a very long time for what we've gained."

"Oh, please," Jace scoffed. "You're, what, maybe a year or two older than me? You haven't *had* a very long time to struggle."

"You're off," Liliana whispered, "by about a hundred years."

Jace opened his mouth to deny the possibility, and then froze at the expression on her face. "How?" he demanded in a hoarse whisper. "Even archmages age, and you're no archmage!"

"Someone made me a better offer." Her lips twisted in a faint, self-mocking grin.

And with that, Jace knew. "You made a deal with something," Jace breathed, shaken to the core of being. "Damn, Liliana, I've done some stupid things in my life, but you . . . !" He shook his head. "A demon?" he asked, remembering her reaction on Grixis.

"Four of them," she told him. "Four demons, four deals. Jace, you can't imagine what they offered in . . ." She consciously unclenched her fists, which had risen of their own accord as she spoke. "It doesn't matter," she said. "Who they were, why I did it. The point is, I was young, I was stupid, and I did it."

"And let me guess," Jace said, mind racing. "Payment's due."

"Not quite yet. Soon, though." She shuddered. "You have no idea the terrible things they'll demand of me, in order to keep my magics—and my soul."

"Terrible things?" Jace scoffed. "Worse than, oh, say, betraying the man you claim to love, and then conspiring to slaughter his friends?"

"Yes," she told him without hesitation.

Jace stood and paced the cell, the singed straw crunching and crumbling beneath his bare feet. She watched him in silence.

"What's this got to do with me?" he finally demanded. "What did it *ever* have to do with me?"

"The Consortium," she said simply. "I need a way out, and the Consortium's got the resources to help me find it—if I'm in control. Or if I have enough influence over the one who is."

Jace's mouth twitched. No, he didn't buy it. Her plans were too complex, her need too immediate, to gamble everything on an organization that *might* help her find an answer.

But at the moment, he chose not to press. There were other answers he wanted—needed—first.

"All right," he said thoughtfully, replaying it all in his mind. "You heard about me, about my leaving the Consortium. And you decided I could do what you needed done."

She nodded. "Even if I thought I was strong enough to take on Tezzeret, I couldn't take him and Baltrice and his guards all alone. And there was no way for me to find him, anyway, or to take the knowledge necessary to run the Consortium from his mind. But you . . ."

"Right. But me, and my wonderful gift of mind-reading that's done nothing but get me reamed over and over for the past half a decade." The bitterness in his voice could have curdled the contents of the chamber pot behind him.

"So you sought me out, found me in Lurias—within days of my getting there, I might add. I don't suppose you care to tell me how? Somehow, I don't think it was really as simple as your specters picking me out of the crowd."

"No." Did she actually sound nervous?

"Fine. So you pretended to fall in love with me—"

"I didn't pretend!" she protested, but Jace plowed on, ignoring her.

"What I did to Kallist must have presented you some problems." Jace frowned. "Did he have to die, Liliana?"

"I'd hoped not," she said, and Jace found he actually believed her. "But when the spell didn't reverse itself, I didn't see any other option."

"Just like you *had* to do everything else," he spat. "But fine. Everything else was about making sure I had no choice but to confront Tezzeret, wasn't it? The first time, you tipped Paldor off that I was living in Lurias District. That's when he sent Gemreth and the others. So why not just tip them off again, the second time? Why go through Semner?"

"Because—"

"Ah, right. Because you needed me to be me, and you couldn't risk the Consortium sending someone who could actually kill me before that happened. You needed me to try to 'save Jace,' so I could be me again."

Liliana nodded sadly. "When Kallist was 'you,' he had many of your magics, but not all of them. And even if he had, he wouldn't have your Spark. It had to be the real you."

"So Tezzeret thinks I'm after him, I think he's after me. Every time he lost track of me, you pointed him in the right direction, didn't you? Every time I tried to walk away from the fight, you argued me out of it. And every time he came close to killing me, you fought to make sure it didn't happen."

"That wasn't the only reason," she said with another sigh. "But yes."

"And," he added, with sudden revelation, "now that it's all gone straight to hell, you get to foist all the suspicion off on me, and stay in his good graces. So what story did you tell him, exactly?"

"That the spirit you used to trace him here was yours, not mine, and that I decided it was safest to come with you and try to deliver you to him rather than to risk confronting you on my own." She smiled wanly. "Not the most waterproof story, but since his truth elixir didn't force me to change it . . ."

"And that would be why? No, wait. Same reason I couldn't read any of this in your mind when we met. You want to explain how that's possible?"

"No. That, you don't get."

"I know you couldn't have done it yourself, Liliana. You're powerful, but you're not a mind-mage. Who helped you?"

"No."

Jace glowered but let it go. "So if you've managed to keep pristine through all this, why help me escape now?"

"Because I don't want to see you suffer what they're going to do to you." Then, at his expression, she actually slammed a palm against the floor. "I mean it, Jace. I really do care for you. I won't pretend it'll stop me from doing what I need to do, but it's true all the same."

"Say I believe that," Jace said, and he was shocked to realize that he *wanted* to believe it. "What's the other reason?"

"Because I've gotten too close to give up!" Liliana leaned in, her eyes suddenly bright. "We can still win!"

Jace shook his head. "You're insane."

"No, think about it! He won't be expecting a second attack, not from you!"

"I can't beat him, damn it!" He found himself clutching the bars, unsure of when he'd actually grabbed for them.

"Not alone," she whispered.

"You? So who handles Baltrice and the guards?"

"No, I didn't mean me. We get help, Jace."

"Who could . . . You're not serious!"

"You have a better idea? All we have to do is get Tezzeret to Grixis."

"Oh, is that all?"

"Much as he hates you? If he thinks you're escaping, he'll follow you just about anywhere. And if he realizes you're going to Grixis, he'll be that much more desperate to stop you! He knows as well as we do that he can't stand up to you and Bolas."

Jace could only stare. "Even if it proves that easy, you really think Nicol Bolas would interfere?"

"He helped us before. We might have to make a deal, but I think it'd be worth it, don't you?"

That was it, then. Jace could all but hear the last piece of the puzzle click into place in his mind.

Of course. The Consortium wasn't her prize, could not free her from her debt; it was *payment*, payment to the only one who *could.*

And now he knew what he had to do.

"If we're actually going to try this," he told her thoughtfully, "there are a few things I need you to find out first."

CHAPTER THIRTY-ONE

It was some few days later, as best Jace could tell, when Liliana returned. He'd suffered through only a single "session" with Baltrice in the interim; she must be busy.

"We've less time than I'd hoped," Liliana said to him as the door once more slid shut behind her. "The dreadful duo are conducting some sort of experiment, but I don't know how long that'll keep them occupied."

Jace forced himself to stand, ignoring the pains of his most recent burns, and shuffled across the cell. "I thought we were waiting until they were off-world again."

Liliana shook her head and placed a large bundle on the floor near the bars. "I don't think we can, Jace. I think they're close to finishing."

He didn't need her to complete the thought, felt himself trembling again at Tezzeret's plans. "Then I guess we'd better hurry," he said, voice quavering.

Despite his frayed nerves, however, he couldn't help but smile as Liliana began to unwrap the bundle, and he recognized the equally frayed blue cloak that served as the bag. She glanced up at his expression and smiled in turn; for just a moment, it was almost enough to make him forget that more than bars now stood between them.

Her movements swift but precise, she laid out an array of odd devices, near the cell but not directly beside it.

"The guards won't miss those?" Jace asked.

Her grin turned nasty. "The guards have bigger problems right now." On cue, the door slid open, and a quartet of Tezzeret's soldiers shambled into the room. Jace barely had to glance their way to see that they were already dead.

"Infinity Globes," she said, not allowing time for further questions. She lifted a pair of small dark orbs. "It's what he used to follow you when you tried your 'tactical withdrawal.' I understand he started work on them after the two of you had trouble escaping from Bolas's berserkers a few years ago."

Jace nodded, remembering how near they'd both come to dying that day.

"As I understand it," she continued, "They're made of an etherium filigree, so tightly packed it's almost fused. It provides a lot of the power you'd normally have to focus from the world around you, so you don't need to spend more than a few seconds in concentration. It's easier for Tezzeret, thanks to his etherium arm, but they should work for us as well."

"Handy."

She nodded, then pushed them aside. Frankly, she still wasn't certain he'd live long enough to need them. She lifted her other prize, a bizarre contraption of tubes and pipes, and set it beside the cell.

"That's it?" he asked. "It looks like an Izzet water pipe."

Liliana chuckled. "Maybe. But yes, that's it. There's enough mana stored in here to help you recover if . . ." She sighed. "Jace, are you sure this is a good idea?

There's a reason I don't summon these things, you know. They're notoriously hard to control."

"I'm sure it's a *lousy* idea," he told her. "But unless you found something in that arsenal that looks like an antidote to Tezzeret's Stay Where You're Put poison . . . ?"

She shook her head.

"Then it's the only idea I've got," he concluded.

"All right," she whispered. "Then let's get it over with."

At her silent command, the four zombies advanced, one producing a heavy chain they had picked up elsewhere in the complex. Because the undead could not place so much as a finger between the bars without falling inert, Liliana passed the end of the chain to Jace, who ran it around two of the bars and fed it back out. The zombies lifted both ends, stepped away, and began to twist.

Jace stepped as far back as the walls of the cell allowed, crouching in a corner and lifting his arms to protect his face from any flying debris. Liliana moved behind the zombies, muttering under her breath, exhorting them to ever greater efforts.

A high-pitched squeal echoed throughout the chamber, and flakes of metal sifted earthward where the chain rubbed against the bars. Tireless and impossibly strong, the zombies continued to twist.

"Are we sure there's no alarm?" Jace asked, shouting over the rising screech.

"Would it matter?" Liliana called back.

I guess not, Jace thought. He could only hope, with Tezzeret and Baltrice occupied in the laboratory and the guards beyond the cell now deceased, that nobody would be in a position to hear it if there was.

A second, equally deafening tone joined the first, as filings sifted from the sockets in which the bars were housed. The bars began, every so faintly, to quiver.

And then the zombies fell back as one of the links in the chain snapped open. Jace and Liliana took just a moment to reposition one of the shorter lengths, and the undead efforts continued.

It took only a few moments more. With a final, ear-piercing rend, the two bars bent inward and tore loose from their sockets. Jace was free.

Sort of.

Pale and perspiring—not from the toxin, for he'd not yet left the cell, but at the notion of what had to happen next—Jace forced himself to stand beside the gap without quite passing through. Carefully he lowered himself into a crouch and stuck his left arm out.

The zombies shuffled to his side, as near as they could get, ready to drag him out.

"Do it," he breathed.

Liliana began to chant, a litany not quite so deep, but somehow far more sinister, than those she used to call her spectral minions. The air beside her clouded over, filled with a faintly luminescent mist, and once again the runic tattoos sprouted across her back and neck. The chamber's still air grew humid and uncomfortably chill.

Between one blink and the next, the mist was gone, and in its place stood a tall man. Dark-haired and clean-shaven, he was clad in formal tunic, vest, and leggings that might have been the height of fashion on Ravnica a century gone by. He turned his piercing stare on Liliana. For a moment they stood locked in what Jace could only assume was a battle of wills, until finally he bowed, mouth twisted in a scornful moue.

The necromancer turned back to Jace, and he recognized the unspoken message. Last chance to back out.

"Do it," he said again, voice steadier.

Liliana nodded, once to him, once to the newcomer. He smiled broadly, showing a mouthful of fangs that lengthened even as she watched.

Jace shuddered violently as the vampire pressed its mouth to his arm and began to drink gluttonously of his contaminated blood.

✳ ✳ ✳ ✳ ✳

"Jace?"

He felt himself afloat, swaddled in the softest darkness, far from the pains and the fears of the light. He drifted on the border, not between waking and sleeping, but on the edge of something greater, something deeper than slumber. It sang to him in the voice of a thousand sirens, a call far easier to heed than to resist.

"Damn it, Jace! Stay with me!"

He tried not to hear the words, not to know the voice. But it nagged at him, even over the restful urgings of the dark.

That's right; there was something he was supposed to do.

Jace opened his eyes, and even that was a monumental victory. His entire body was a leaden weight, his thoughts mired in painful lethargy, and even his heartbeat felt slowed. He no longer sensed the horrible creature's lips and teeth on his arm, but when he forced himself to look and make certain, all he could see was the corpse-white pallor of his own skin.

Which made sense, really, given that he was currently rather blood-deficient. For no good reason, Jace found the notion hysterical, but all he could muster was a single giggle.

Liliana frowned, though she couldn't quite mask her relief that he hadn't just died on her. Moving swiftly, she pressed the largest tube of the artifact to his face. Jace coughed once as a strange vapor that wasn't quite steam wafted over him, permeating his lungs. He felt a strength growing within him, a potency he hadn't consciously realized he was missing.

But it was a vigor of the spirit only, not the body. Though the mana infused his soul, the languor in his limbs refused to fade. He was able, barely, to turn his head—and he noticed, for the first time, that the zombies had dragged him from the cell while he was out—but nothing more.

"Oh, yeah, this was a great idea," Liliana grumbled. "As long as Tezzeret accidentally trips and falls on something sharp, we've got him where we want him!"

"I'm so glad . . . I don't have the strength . . . to pretend to laugh." Jace closed his eyes.

"Are you sure you—"

"No. Be quiet."

Liliana glared at him—or at least he assumed so, though he didn't open his eyes to check. He let the darkness and the silence roll over him once more, not to fall into it as he had nearly done, but to blot out the distractions, the lingering pain, the sound of his own labored breaths.

Carefully, as though afraid his thoughts might topple if he didn't stack them just so, he cast his mind back to Emmara's home on Ravnica. As he'd done then, he pushed himself to remember the feel of her magics, the warmth that suffused his body at the elf's healing touch, the seemingly endless plains that ran beneath Ovitzia where he'd recently spent so much time. He turned it over in his mind, examining the sensation, delving into it, forcing it to become real, more real than the cold floor beneath him, than the burns that had transformed his body into a map of suffering, than the weakness the vampire had left in place of his stolen blood.

The one and only time Jace had done this before, he'd barely felt a tremor in his wounds before his concentration lapsed. This time, he had to literally haul himself from death's door; to regenerate a loss of blood that should, by all rights, have already killed him.

And *then* he was going to take on Tezzeret again.

Jace allowed himself to break focus just long enough to wonder if he could cure himself of his obvious insanity while he was at it—and then he bent every last bit of will to a task that he knew he shouldn't be able to perform, but at which he could not afford to fail.

CHAPTER THIRTY-TWO

The laboratory was neither a room nor a complex of rooms, but a multilevel network of pipes and tubes that, at various points throughout, formed floors and hollows in which people might work. Smoke and arcs of raw mana, in a variety of peculiar colors and pungent scents, wafted between pillars and spheres that emitted strange, multihued auras. The entire chamber smelled strongly of ozone, and when entering one of its many doors, or climbing up from level to level, one had to be careful where one put one's hands, lest one find them violently shocked.

Tezzeret himself, of course, simply willed the various protrusions to lift and carry him wherever he needed to go. Now he stood within one of those hollow "workrooms," Baltrice at his side, as he turned his creation over and over in his hands, inspecting it for impurities.

"There, if you would," he said, indicating a rough seam. She nodded, tensed in brief concentration, and sparks flew as the metal welded itself together.

"Enough. I think that's as done as it's getting."

Baltrice frowned at the pronouncement. "Really?" She reached out and tapped the many thin protrusions, then the glass reservoir filled with a viscous green fluid. "It doesn't look all that sturdy to me, boss."

"I wouldn't take it into battle," he agreed, "but it'll do until I can devise a more portable version. We'll need a brain to test it on first, of course, but barring any unforeseen flaws, I think Beleren's about to find himself moving to slightly smaller quarters."

Baltrice snickered, a sound that transformed abruptly to a shout of pain as the reservoir bulb shattered, spraying glass shards and its caustic contents across her skin. She struggled to clear her eyes with a sleeve as Tezzeret, utterly bewildered, gawped at the ruins of his creation.

And his gaze grew wider still, jaw dropping in slack amazement, as the manablade detached itself from Baltrice's belt. Carried aloft by a rat-sized drake, it soared upward between the preponderance of tubes. He watched the creature rise, watched until it dropped the weapon gently into the hands of a man who *could not* be there!

"I believe this is mine," Jace called from the level above. Clad in boots and leathers stolen from one of Tezzeret's guards, and his own tattered blue cloak, he loomed over them like a vengeful ghost—and for long seconds, the artificer could only assume that's indeed what he was. *He couldn't possibly have escaped that cell alive! He couldn't!*

But no, he saw the lingering burns on Beleren's neck, on the arm that had reached to snatch the dagger from the air; saw the mind-reader wince as he moved. Tezzeret's disbelief burned away beneath the heat of a terrible, volcanic anger. His entire body shook, and he felt as though he couldn't even draw a breath.

And then the little bastard *waved* at him and produced a damned Infinity Globe from somewhere up his sleeve. It pulsed once, twice, attuning itself to the beating of its wielder's heart. Then Beleren was simply gone, nothing but a few wisps of mana-vapor to show that he'd been present at all.

Tezzeret's cry of rage was bestial, unintelligible. He shoved Baltrice aside, slamming her into the nearest wall as he lunged across the room for his belt of pouches, which he had removed during the course of his work. "Follow when you can!" he snarled at her, yanking another globe from a pouch, almost crushing it in his prosthetic fist.

Baltrice cursed foully as he vanished, struggling to her feet and blinking away the last of the gunk. It would take her longer to reach the arsenal and grab one of the last Globes than it would just to walk under her own power; hopefully, she'd still be able to follow by the time she reached the Eternities.

She had barely begun her concentrations, however, when something black emerged from the wall and passed through her body. Its touch rotted flesh, shriveled away the edges of her soul. Baltrice dropped to one knee, screaming until she thought her throat would bleed.

"Just where do you think you're going?" Liliana asked from above, standing where Jace had disappeared.

Baltrice gaped at her, fire leaking from her eyes and between the fingers of her clenched fist. "You traitor!"

"You have no idea," the necromancer whispered.

Baltrice launched herself upward, carried aloft on wings and jets of flame. Surrounded in an aura of blackest magics, propelled by the touch of a dozen phantoms, Liliana rose to meet her.

✳ ✳ ✳ ✳ ✳

Tezzeret appeared in the Blind Eternities, colors and probabilities eddying around his feet, mixing to form liquid dreams. He knelt in the unreal substance, glowing with restrained power, as he searched for his quarry's trail. Beleren couldn't have gotten far, not even allowing for the strange stuttering and skipping of time here in the void; the trail of his Spark should be visible still, if he could find its end.

And there it was, a wake of aether slowly dissolving into the surrounding essence, a flickering ribbon of liquid fire.

Tezzeret blinked. It didn't lead off into the vastness of the Eternities, as he'd expected, but rather curved, almost as if . . .

His scream unheard in the pounding of the Eternal winds, Jace Beleren slammed into Tezzeret from behind, his entire body alight with magics. Instantly they left behind them the sheet of light that marked the edge of the world, propelled by Jace's will alone through vast impossibilities where even direction and gravity were matters of mere desire. They hammered at one another, with bursts of unfocused power that might, within the bounds of conventional reality, have taken the form of spells but here were little more than primordial energies burning flesh and mind and soul. They hammered at one another with sheer malevolent intent, their very notions warping the streams of chance around them into stabbing blades and poisonous thorns. And they hammered at one another with fists and knees and elbows, a pair of brawlers rolling among the planes.

Where blood and eldritch essence spilled from their wounds, impossible forms of life arose, creatures that did not and could not exist in any sane world, and died as swiftly, torn apart by the currents of the Blind Eternities.

And in time that was not time, they were there. Colors flashed past as they plunged through the outer boundaries of another world, appearing high in the air over a thick copse of trees. Still pounding away with fists and what minor spells they could focus enough to throw, the struggling pair plummeted earthward, crashing through a dozen feet of moss and branches. They finally slammed to a bruising halt in the shallow marsh beneath the boughs, hurled apart by the impact.

Both men scrambled to their feet, struggling to catch their breaths, spitting the stagnant water from their mouths, dripping it from their limbs. Jace was covered with cuts and tears, his stolen garb tattered; Tezzeret's tougher leathers had protected him somewhat better, though much of his hair was burned away, and the flesh of his left arm had been seared a deep red by the kiss of Jace's magics.

Jace glanced side to side, trying to determine precisely where they'd landed. Farther away than he'd planned, but thought—he hoped—close enough. His eyes narrowed in concentration and Tezzeret threw up his hands, crossed at the wrists, to repel whatever attack he was conjuring—but nothing happened, save for a faint glow in those eyes that faded as swiftly as it had flared.

The artificer grinned at his foe's obvious weakness. Both were hideously battered by their rough passage through the void, and yes, Jace had landed the first attack, but even a man as blind as the Eternities could have seen that Tezzeret remained the stronger. Jace's flesh was still pale, his eyes sunken and ringed in exhausted circles, the burns on his skin still livid and bright. What mana he hadn't expended in his escape from the cell had been largely drained by his assault on his foe. Clearly he had little resilience left to him, and even less in the way of magic.

"How did you do that, Beleren?" Tezzeret asked him, his voice ripe with curiosity. "You shouldn't have been able to touch me in the Eternities."

Panting, Jace held up the Infinity Globe, now a tarnished lump of slag. "I knew you'd use one to follow me, you bastard. I attuned myself to it as soon as I stepped from the world—and therefore to you."

Tezzeret's grin grew wider still, lips curling like a

beast bearing its fangs. Mockingly, he shook his head. "Brilliant, Beleren, absolutely brilliant. It's a shame you're going to make me——"

He never did get to tell Jace what he was making him do, for at that moment the younger mage hit the artificer square in the face—not with a spell, not with a hidden weapon, but with a clod of heavy muck he'd scooped from beneath the water as he stood.

Grunting, struggling to wipe the sludge from his face and spitting it from between his teeth, Tezzeret staggered. He sensed the attack coming, heard Jace's splashing footsteps, and blinked his vision clear just in time to parry the deadly thrust. Etherium grated on etherium, mechanical hand on razor-edged manablade. Each glared at the other as metal screeched and bright sparks flashed, showering to the earth around them.

✻ ✻ ✻ ✻ ✻

One entire wall of the laboratory was gone, melted into slag by a blast of heat far greater than it was ever meant to endure. Bits of rod and pipe protruded into the yawning hole, bones around a gaping wound, and the air was choked with acrid smoke.

In the hall beyond, on a meshwork floor that bent and warped beneath their weight, a great serpent of living flame struggled to crush the life from a black-winged angel, curling over and around its foe, searing where it touched. Though unable to fly, the angel battled furiously, sinking the prongs of a jagged trident again and again into the serpent's hide. Each wound was a burst of fire that burned her further still. At the base of the writhing tail, a trio of specters darted about, trying to drive their deadly hands through the flame that singed even their dead and blackened souls with its touch.

Halfway down the hall, on a broad stair that reached high into the levels above, Liliana crouched upon the steps, peering upward through a haze of smoke. Soot and ash coated her face, the vest that had once covered her tunic was nothing but cinders, and she held her burned right arm close to her chest. Black energy flowed and crackled around her, the lingering remnants of what had been a potent necromantic aura. Above, Baltrice sneered down from behind a shield of crystal-line, rock-hard fire.

Liliana was quite certain her power exceeded Baltrice's, yet the fight was going poorly. Though she lacked Tezzeret's ability to command and control the machines that made up the great artifact, Baltrice knew its ins and outs well enough. At her whim, pipes over-heated, sending bursts of steam or flying shrapnel to tear the flesh from her foe. Worse still, she knew which conduits carried the mana-infused gasses that Tezzeret used to replenish his own powers, knew how to tap into them with a simple spell. Liliana, who could only struggle to leach the ambient energies directly through the walls, found herself growing steadily weaker, while her enemy, though wounded deeply by the touch of dead and deathless things, remained strong.

But neither was Liliana finished. As she peered through the smoke, watching Baltrice's fire-shield crack and split in preparation for blasting another lance of flame her way, she whispered a litany of names, twisted her fingers in impossible patterns. She thought back to what she had seen of the mechanical monstrosity that Baltrice and Tezzeret called home.

With a final cry and a burst of unimaginably dark mana, Liliana slammed her arm down on a twisted hole in the metal wall, gashing her flesh horribly and spilling a torrent of blood upon the steps. And speaking through that blood as it coated the gleaming metal, she called upon the ghosts of every man and woman whose essence had been bound to empower the Consortium sanctum, and set them loose upon her foe.

※ ※ ※ ※ ※

Kallist would have been proud.

Channeling the last of his magics into keeping his exhaustion at bay, manablade clutched in a competent if not expert knife-fighter's grip, Jace pummeled the artificer with a sequence of lightning-swift strikes. Tezzeret retreated before him, parrying frantically with his mechanical hand, lacking even the split second he needed to cast his spells or draw upon a more effective weapon.

The blade darted in and out, a striking viper of etherium and enchantment. A slash at the face, a stab at the chest, cross-step to keep pace with Tezzeret's retreat; slash again, feint with the left fist, kick to the gut, another step; a twist and sudden spin, a backhand strike against the artificer's temple, an underhand stab at the ribs, cross-step. For these few moments, Jace drew on everything Kallist had taught him, everything he could recall from several months of *being* Kallist, and allowed all his anger and all his guilt to flow through him. For those moments, he was a mage no longer, but a dervish of deadly edges and pummeling limbs, forcing Tezzeret ever farther back until the trees thinned and they found themselves slowed by the deepening swamp.

It was a punishing pace, however, one he couldn't possibly maintain, and both combatants knew it. His face and tunic were soaked with sweat, and his breathing came in labored rasps. Tezzeret's desperate parries grew smoother and more certain, his retreat more controlled, as it dawned on the artificer that all he had to do was hold Beleren off a bit longer, let him wear himself down, and he'd have the little bastard utterly at his mercy.

And indeed, mere heartbeats later, Jace's attacks faltered. His arm swung wide, a strike took just an instant too long. With a primal cry, Tezzeret slammed an open palm into Jace's chest, his own strength augmented by the magics and the mechanisms of his hand. A pair of ribs cracked as the blow lifted Jace from his feet and sent him hurtling backward to land with a splash in the marsh. The manablade flew from nerveless fingers; even had Jace possessed the breath to stand, he'd have had to scramble to reach it.

"Pathetic, Beleren." Tezzeret strode casually toward him, content now to take his time.

"I thought it was . . . pretty impressive, myself," Jace gasped between coughs of pain.

"Oh, your blade-work was surprising, I'll give you that." Tezzeret crouched to meet Jace's gaze and raised his hand to show the marring and scoring along the metal. "It'll take me a good long while to repair the damage. But really, to what end? You should have known the moment your psychic attack failed even to materialize that it was over for you, that you were just delaying the inevitable."

And Jace—Jace smiled through the pain, an eager gleam in his eye. "I wasn't attacking, Tezzeret. I was *negotiating.*"

With a shaking, unsteady finger, he pointed over Tezzeret's shoulder. A sudden chill running down his spine, the artificer couldn't help but turn his head to look.

Barely visible in the shadowed depths of the cypress trees, the treehouses of the nezumi ratmen rose like grasping fingers from the marsh.

"They're *really* not happy with you just now, Tezzeret," Jace taunted.

The artificer screamed, shooting swiftly to his feet. His entire body tensed in indecision as he struggled to choose between ending his enemy's life while he had the chance, and fleeing before he was overwhelmed.

He had time for neither.

Beneath his feet, black roots and dead vines erupted from the shallow waters. From the many trees of the swamp they stretched through the muddy earth, only to rise and wrap tight about Tezzeret's legs. They held him fast, squeezing until the flesh tingled and the blood ceased to flow. Poisons fell from passing clouds and sprayed upward from writhing fungi, drenching him in toxic effluvia that burned the skin and seared the lungs. Any spell he might have cast was stolen from his throat as he coughed up tiny gobbets of flesh and blood, his whole body spasming in agony.

Ignoring his cracked ribs as best he could, Jace rolled to his feet, stooping to dig for his fallen weapon. The artificer watched with rage-filled eyes, struggling even now to break loose of his blood-soaked bonds. Jace held that gaze for two long breaths, then slammed the point of the manablade into Tezzeret's arm, severing flesh and tendon, cracking bone. Tezzeret screamed as Jace worked the blade back and forth, pressing on it like a prybar. A loud crack, a flash of broken magics, and Tezzeret's etherium limb fell to the earth, an inch of bloody bone protruding obscenely from the metal. Wincing in pain, Jace leaned down to retrieve his trophy, leaving Tezzeret to howl wordlessly in his bonds.

The shaman of the Nezumi-Katsuro emerged from the trees, hunched more sharply and scarred more ornately than the last time Jace had seen him. Fanned out behind came a quartet of lesser spirit-talkers and a dozen nezumi warriors, naked blades glittering in their hands, their tiny eyes glinting in the midday sun. As they passed, the branches curled from their path and the fungi bowed in reverence. The shaman gestured, spoke in the voice of leaves rustling in the wind, and Tezzeret could only scream again as half a dozen branches shot from the trees, stretching impossibly long, to puncture the flesh of his arm and shoulders.

"Greetings, Metal-Armed Emperor of the Infinite Consortium," the ratman hissed as he neared. Only Jace's spell of translation—which he'd cast even as he made mental contact with the shaman—allowed him to comprehend. "I have waited long to meet you in person."

Tezzeret might not have understood the words, but there was no mistaking either the tone or the intent. "Go to hell, ratman!" The artificer ripped his remaining arm free, leaving chunks of flesh behind, and hurled a handful of metal shavings to the earth. Instantly they rose into a towering golem of steel skin and iron gears—and just as swiftly an elemental of swamp-water and cypress trees like the one that had eaten Baltrice's soldier of fire so long ago appeared once more, bursting from the thickest copse. It fell furiously upon Tezzeret's construct, crushing it like a cheap toy before it could take a second step.

Watching every moment of Tezzeret's struggles, Jace staggered to the shaman's side, clutching his ribs as he walked. "Thanks," he wheezed.

The nezumi bared his dirty, jagged fangs. "We do not do this for you, mind-reader," he said with a distasteful glance at the artificial limb in the mage's hands. "You have delivered our true enemy unto us, and for that we excuse you your own part in what was done to us. But we do not forget it. This is justice for the Nezumi-Katsuro, not for you."

"Works for me, either way," Jace told him.

"Go then, mind-reader. None of us will stop you. Should you disturb us again, though . . ."

"Yeah, yeah. Get in line, shaman."

Jace cocked his head, turning his attention as the artificer was lifted bodily off the ground by the wooden shafts. They ground against Tezzeret's bones and began to drag him back toward whatever final fate awaited him at the hands of the nezumi.

"Beleren!" Tezzeret screamed through the pain, each word bringing another bubble of crimson-flecked foam to his lips. "I swear to you, I'll survive this! I'll find you, and when I do—"

"You'll do nothing." Jace allowed the lingering mana in the etherium arm to flow through him, and thrust his mind into Tezzeret's own. Exhausted, wounded almost unto death, and without the stores of magic in his artificial arm, the artificer might, just might, be vulnerable to . . .

Yes!

For long moments, Jace found himself in the agonized, infuriated hell that was Tezzeret's mind. He winced at the images that assailed him, recoiled from sensations he never wanted to know, as he sifted through the artificer's thoughts. And there it was, finally, the knowledge he would need, the knowledge that would allow Jace Beleren to rule the Infinite Consortium as thoroughly as Tezzeret ever had. Names, locations, artifacts, all of it.

And Jace . . . Jace sighed once and let it go, leaving that knowledge to fade with the man that held it. Taking an unwholesome glee in every mental scream, allowing Tezzeret a full awareness of what he was doing, Jace reached out and crushed the artificer's mind.

Jace felt a great weight lift from his soul—not his only burden, nor even his heaviest, but a palpable respite all the same. He sighed in relief, drawing a puzzled glower from the shaman.

Jace ignored it. He turned and strode into the trees, leaving the beady-eyed ratmen and the drooling, babbling artificer behind him.

(CHAPTER THIRTY-THREE

At the top of the stairs, Liliana stood in what could only be called the beating heart of Tezzeret's home. A few surviving specters flitted about her waist, ready to drink the life from any who dared approach. Scattered across the floor lay a handful of arrows, each of which matched the single shaft that currently protruded from a bloody wound in her thigh. Splayed out beside them were the corpses of a dozen Consortium guards, partial remnants of the first wave that had attacked once Baltrice had finally fallen at her feet.

None could reach her now. She had sealed the door to the inner sanctum, a door of solid steel that would hold them at bay for many days. All she had to do now was wait.

With a grunt she jerked the projectile from her flesh, hissing in pain as it tore free. A few moments to tie a makeshift bandage around the wound, and then she was limping across the chamber, eyes skittering over her—well, her and Jace's—new prize.

Wiping a handful of sweat-and-ash paste from her forehead, she examined the gleaming metal ring, the glowing gems and aether-filled tubes, the switches and runes, and of course the great throne that sat in its center. From here, the leader of the Consortium could rule an empire of worlds.

If he knew what those worlds were. If he knew who served him. If he knew how to answer the calls of his lieutenants, and how to construct the devices Tezzeret had given them.

But that was fine, because they *would* know. The plan would work; it had to. Any moment now, Jace would return with the information they needed—and already indebted to Nicol Bolas, to boot. She hoped he would be amenable to her needs, that they could rule the Consortium together in the dragon's name.

And if not? Well, Liliana cared for Jace Beleren, but she had done ugly things to those she cared about before. She would, as always, do what she had to do.

For now, all she had to do was wait.

※ ※ ※ ※ ※

Completely invisible within his cloak of illusions, Jace lurked in the hallway behind the guards as they milled about outside the inner sanctum's door, wondering what to do next, how to get at the necromancer within—and whether or not they even wanted to.

Liliana was alive, then. Jace couldn't quite suppress a sigh of relief. She was alive, and she was waiting for him.

She would be waiting a long, long time.

Jace spun and strode down the stairs, slipping past the occasional guard, heading for the lower levels where he might find a few moments of complete privacy. He didn't know if she would ever forgive him for this, anymore than he knew if he could ever forgive her. And ultimately, it didn't matter.

The Consortium was gone. No prize for Liliana, no prize for Bolas, no prize even for Jace himself. Oh, some individual cells might survive, even thrive, but without Tezzeret, without the knowledge that Jace had chosen to let die with the artificer's mind, the Consortium itself was dead.

And that was as it had to be. He wouldn't live his life in fear, not anymore, and fear was all the Consortium had to offer him. Fear that Liliana cared only for it and never for him. Fear of what Bolas would do to him if he refused to bow to the dragon, and of what the dragon would make him do if he did.

But most of all, fear of himself. Jace's soul had all but died, day by day, from the instant he joined the artificer's foul cabal. Jace had allowed the Consortium to turn him into someone he didn't know, but by all the power in the Multiverse, he would not allow it to turn him into another Tezzeret.

All he could do was walk away, and let the whole of it crumble into dust and ruin behind him. And if that meant he had no idea what to do with his life—if he found himself drifting, as aimless as the day Baltrice's fire rained down from the sky above the open air café— then at least that life was his once more.

And then, as he stepped into the same supply room at the base of the tower where he'd briefly worn Baltrice's face, he knew where to start. In the midst of all the looming questions, he realized abruptly what he had to do next. Because he knew, no matter whether he could ever forgive her, or she him, that he and Liliana would meet again; knew it as surely as he knew that a thousand suns wound rise tomorrow, across a thousand worlds.

When that happened, he would have her answer. He swore to himself that he would free Liliana from her bargain, no matter how long it took, no matter how many worlds he had to scour. He would learn who she was beneath the fear and the desperation and the lies.

And then, if he could love whom he found, perhaps they could begin again.

Jace Beleren stepped from the depths of Tezzeret's tower and vanished into the farthest reaches of the Blind Eternities.

EPILOGUE

Now that she knew where he made his lair, they held their final meeting deep in the caves of Grixis, rather than on the featureless plains of that dead and nameless sphere. Here, separated by many long halls from the divination chambers of the coven, the screams of agony were almost inaudible.

Almost.

Over half the walls in this great circular cavern were covered with faint images, not so much engraved as somehow burned into the stone. Some were dragons, some humanoids of various species, some of races unseen in any civilized corner of the Multiverse for thousands upon thousands of years. They stared out over the chamber, their eyes wide, their mouths agape in silent screams, and who they were none but the Forever Serpent could say.

In the center of it all stood a great stone column, wrapped from top to bottom in velvet-lined cushions. Coiled around it so that the bulk of his body was off the ground, Nicol Bolas studied, with unblinking eyes and a faintly bored scowl, the tiny human standing stiff and furious before him.

". . . to discuss," the dragon was saying, his attention

already drifting on to other matters.

"Nothing more to discuss?" Liliana seethed, her voice rising. "Nothing more than my magic, and quite possibly my soul!"

The cushions rippled up and down the pillar as Bolas shrugged. "You chose to make the deal, Liliana Vess."

"And you made one with me, Bolas!"

"Indeed. A very simple and straightforward one, on which you failed to deliver."

"Tezzeret and the Consortium are out of your way!"

"True." Bolas shifted around the pillar, perusing the images as though searching for one particular face. "But there was the matter, necromancer, of you returning the Consortium to me while I kept my focus on other matters. The plan, unless I rather woefully misunderstood, was to place someone in charge you could influence on my behalf, if not for you to rule it yourself. Unless I've grown extremely nearsighted in my old age, the final results of all your scheming don't much seem to resemble the outcome you promised."

"How could I possibly know that Jace wouldn't—"

The dragon's head whipped around the pillar, his tongue flickering out to stop mere inches from Liliana's flesh. She froze, paralyzed beneath his infinite gaze.

"Do you really believe that making excuses now is your best option?"

"Great and mighty Bolas," she said, trying hard to modulate her voice, "please. I came to you because you're the only one I know with the power to break this pact, strong enough to bend even a cabal of demons to your will. If you could just—"

"If I am, indeed, the only one so gifted," Bolas interrupted, "then I suggest you come up with some other way to make yourself useful. Offer me something else worth the trouble you bring me—and make no mistake, a quartet of demons is trouble even for 'great and mighty' me—and I will make you the same bargain.

"Alternatively," he added, his tone suddenly thoughtful, "you might swear allegiance to me. A planeswalker and necromancer of your power might prove useful indeed, and I would, of course, seek to protect my investment . . ."

Liliana's face went red, her eyes jet black. "You'd have me trade one master for another?"

"Why yes, I suppose I would."

"Go find your own personal hell, dragon!"

"I've got a rather nice one here on Grixis, I should say. When you come up with a better trade, be certain to let me know. You're always welcome here, my dear Vess."

Liliana stared, mouth working as though to voice some new argument she'd not yet considered, and Bolas had at least to give the mage credit. In his youth, had he been in her position, he might well have attacked, even knowing he could not prevail. But with the realization that there was nothing left to say, Liliana turned on her heel and strode from the chamber, and if her shoulders were slumped and even shaking, still she held her head high until she vanished from the dragon's sight.

Bolas flickered his tongue over the stone faces, as though tasting the flesh of those they represented, then uncoiled himself from around the pillar and crept through the tunnels until he reached his workroom. It, like many of his private chambers, utterly lacked a door; he breathed a few syllables of magic, scarcely an effort to one such as he, and caused the wall itself to open for him. Between racks of alchemical equipment and half-built artifacts, through spaces where his great bulk should never have fit, the dragon wound his way to a marble worktable in the cavern's center. Atop the great slab, dwarfed by the scale of the table and indeed the entire room, lay the object of his current endeavors.

No, Liliana's efforts had not restored to him the Infinite Consortium. But they had given him instead an opportunity even he had not foreseen. He'd needed to act fast, before the nezumi could ruin it beyond use. It had cost him greatly to acquire it and would require much labor on his part to make it functional once more, both inside and out. With the right repairs, though— and the right *adjustments*—it just might prove a greater tool than even the Consortium itself.

Nicol Bolas bent low over the mangled and mindless body of Tezzeret. "Now, little artificer . . . What shall we do with you?"

MAGIC
The Gathering®

Confrontation leads
to conflagration
in this hot new
planeswalker
adventure.

THE
PURIFYING
FIRE

By award-winning author

LAURA
RESNICK

On Alaroon, among an encalve
of like-minded pyromancers,
Chandra draws the attention of
an ancient faith that sees her as
a herald of an apocalypse. Will
she control her own destiny,
or suffer the will of others?

KEITH BAKER'S
THORN OF BRELAND

As a child, Nyrielle Tam dreamed of being a soldier. Instead, she became a spy, a saboteur, and when necessary, an assassin.

She became Thorn, Dark Lantern of Breland.

THE QUEEN OF STONE
Available Now

THE SON OF KHYBER
November 2009

THE FADING DREAM
October 2010

Richard Lee Byers

The Haunted Lands

Epic magic • Unholy alliances • Armies of undead
The battle for Thay has begun.

Book I	Book II	Book III
Unclean	**Undead**	**Unholy**

Anthology

Realms of the Dead

Edited by Susan J. Morris

January 2010

"This is Thay as it's never been shown before ... Dark,
sinister, foreboding and downright disturbing!"
—Alaundo, Candlekeep.com on *Unclean*